THE MESSIAH OF
SMYRNA

— a novel —

Sam Goldenberg

Suite 300 - 990 Fort St
Victoria, BC, Canada, V8V 3K2
www.friesenpress.com

Copyright © 2015 by Sam Goldenberg
First Edition — 2015

All rights reserved.

No part of this publication may be reproduced in any form, or by any means, electronic or mechanical, including photocopying, recording, or any information browsing, storage, or retrieval system, without permission in writing from the publisher.

ISBN
978-1-4602-6638-0 (Hardcover)
978-1-4602-6639-7 (Paperback)
978-1-4602-6640-3 (eBook)

1. Fiction, Jewish

Distributed to the trade by The Ingram Book Company

Table of Contents

HISTORICAL NOTE VII

CHAPTER 1
- DULCIGNO, 1673 - EXILE 1

CHAPTER 2
- TORONTO, 2006 - SHABTAI ZVI KABBALAH SOCIETY 19

CHAPTER 3
- SMYRNA, 1665 - THE MESSIAH OF SMYRNA 37

CHAPTER 4
- TORONTO, 2006 - DONALD AND SARAI 61

CHAPTER 5
- ADRIANOPLE, 1666 - SHABTAI IN CRISIS 81

CHAPTER 6
- 1666 - ADRIANOPLE - CONVERSION OF SARAH 95

CHAPTER 7
- TORONTO, 2006 - LILY THEGN 103

CHAPTER 8
- KENYA, 2005 - SISTER SARAI STONE 123

CHAPTER 9
- DULCIGNO, 1673-1674 - DEATH OF SARAH ZVI 151

CHAPTER 10
- SIOUX LOOKOUT, ONTARIO - 2008 - SARAI AND DONALD 177

CHAPTER 11
- DULCIGNO, 1674 - MULLAH ALI 181

CHAPTER 12
- DULCIGNO -1676 - DEATH OF SHABTAI ZVI 225

EPILOGUE
- LOOSE THREADS 247

    DULCIGNO, 1676 – MULLAH ALI AND AMILAH

    TORONTO, 2007 – DONALD AND ROBERTA

    OUTSIDE THE WALLS OF VIENNA, SEPTEMBER, 1683 – TEPEL AND SARAH

ACKNOWLEDGEMENTS 253

FURTHER READING 255

Dedicated to my most loyal fans, my family
Rosemarie, Klaus, Khanh Linh, Toby, Trudy

HISTORICAL NOTE

Shabtai Zvi was born in 1626 in the city of Smyrna (now called Izmir) on the eastern shore of the Aegean Sea in Turkey, then part of the Ottoman Empire. A rabbi and renowned Kabbalist, he believed and proclaimed himself to be the Messiah. His fame spread throughout the Ottoman Empire and Europe. Most Jews and many Christians accepted his claim.

The Ottoman authorities, rattled by Shabtai's extreme statements and the unrest of the Jewish population, arrested him in 1666, forced him to convert to Islam, and in 1673 banished him to Dulcigno (now called Ulcinj) a city on the Adriatic Sea.

Shabtai's wife Sarah, whom he had married in 1664, died in 1674. Shabtai Zvi died in 1676.

CHAPTER 1

- Dulcigno, 1673 -

EXILE

In the early dawn, the sky still dingy grey, the lookout in the crow's nest halfway up the main mast heard someone or something singing. The sound rose and fell, at times melodious, at times pleading piteously, at times quavering softly above the rhythmic plashing of the water against the ship's bow.

The lookout, a boy barely in his teens and conscripted from a Greek mountain village, trembled. But it wasn't the cold January day. He had heard legends of beautiful women — sirens, they were called — who sang so irresistibly that captains and even admirals were drawn to the disastrous rocks on which they sat. He looked fearfully about but the low thick fog blanketing the sea hid the source of the singing.

"Steersman," he called out. "Beware! There are sirens close by."

"Fool!" shouted the steersman. "It is the Jew standing in the bow."

The boy peered toward the bow but could see only the fog flowing beneath his feet. The singing did indeed come from below him and was a man's voice. His anxiety eased. He had never heard of men sirens.

The Ottoman warship moved slowly through the fog as it navigated up the Adriatic Sea, its oars withdrawn, propelled by one sail billowing out from the foremast.

"Remember," the officer of the watch had cautioned him. "Be alert at all times. The Sultan rules these waters but the Sultan has many enemies."

The boy looked in all directions but could see no masts poking above the fog.

Then the fog began to lift, gradually revealing details of the deck and the sea around the ship. The man in the bow appeared, first as a dark smudge within the thinning vapours, and then magically lit by the sun just peeping over the Albanian mountains.

The man held his arms out to his sides and turned toward the mountains. He faces east, the boy thought. The steersman had called him a Jew, yet the man wore the turban of a Muslim. He was tall and brawny, with broad shoulders, a curly, greying beard dominating the even features of his face. He must be rich, the boy noted. His dark mantle had a brilliant sheen and the collar and lapels were covered with black fur. His shirt was white and the caftan striped with indigo. Clearly fine clothing.

The man's voice rose higher in pitch in a language the boy could not understand. He lifted his arms, his fingers pointing toward the heavens. The boy, even from his perch, could see the look of ecstatic happiness on his face.

The singing stopped abruptly. The man fell to his knees and cradled his head on the gunwale of the ship. He howled and wailed and lifted his head from time to time to scream at the sky.

"Steersman," the boy cried out. "The Jew is sick."

"The Jew is crazy," came the reply. "Stop watching the Jew and watch for other ships."

The fog had dissipated completely. The sun hovered above the mountains in a cloudless sky. Here and there, a sail broke the blue expanse of the Adriatic Sea, but there were no galleons or war galleys to be seen. A cold winter wind blew the ship northward. A clatter below deck signalled the oars were out and the ship picked up speed.

Suddenly, the hatch on the main deck was thrown open. A Janissary officer stepped off the companionway, followed by a woman. The officer helped the woman up the short ladder to the foredeck.

She approached the man in the bow. "Husband," she said, gently, consolingly. "Put aside your melancholy. You must be strong for all of us, for your loving Sarah, and for your loyal followers. Come, Shabtai, your dolour pains me. I would not see you like this."

Her words seemed to calm him. He stopped wailing but didn't move, his head still on the gunwale, his arms hanging over the side.

"Madam, he is quiet now. Please ask him whether I may help him up," the officer suggested.

As he and the woman leaned over Shabtai, they came close, their faces inches apart. The officer was momentarily transfixed by the loosely veiled, incredibly beautiful face with its large brown eyes, pale white skin, thin upturned nose and sensual lips. The loose folds of mantle and caftan did not entirely mask the shapely outline of her body.

She smiled her appreciation. "As always, Captain Tepel, you are most helpful."

He had doted on her from the moment she and her husband stepped on board at Constantinople, acting more like a servant than the officer in charge of getting the two prisoners safely to Dulcigno.

"We meet once again, Corporal Tepel," she had said, her eyes alight with approval, when he arrived to present his orders.

He bowed. "Captain, madam," he corrected her. "The Sultan has seen fit to promote me."

"Most deserved, I am sure. Isn't that so, husband?" she said turning to the man beside her but Shabtai's mind was elsewhere.

The captain of the ship noticed Tepel's devotion and took him aside after a few days at sea.

"My friend, I am a man too and I understand and even share your feelings when I see that woman. But in this crowded ship, there is no room to pursue your desires. Even the ordinary seamen laugh and gossip about you."

Tepel reddened slightly, stroked his moustache, and nodded.

"You are quite right, Captain. But this is not our first meeting. You will, of course, remember the Smyrna riots just before the war with Crete. I was a corporal then, charged with dispersing the mobs and keeping order. She bewitched me then. I met her again when I escorted her to Adrianople after her husband had converted to Islam. Her husband is a madman, but she remains loyal to him. Yet she seems to encourage me. When she catches me looking at her, she smiles."

"My friend, her smiles are not reserved for you alone. She smiles at every man who comes near her, even the sea boys."

The Janissary nodded again. "I know that, Captain. But she is not only beautiful. She has a charm and an elegance that is worthy of a noble lady."

The ship's captain agreed: "In a way, she is a noble lady. Rumour has it that she was orphaned at ten years old during the massacres of the Jews in Poland. She was found and brought up by a Polish nobleman. Whatever his intentions, she was well educated but left him after ten years. So she would have many of the attributes of a lady well born."

The Janissary sighed. "Captain, ten years with her would make me very happy. I am enchanted by her. Also, she speaks many languages. She speaks Turkish with you and me and other members of the crew, Hebrew with her husband, Italian with the Italian mercenary on board, and some words in Greek with your sea boy, Demetrius. I note she also reads and writes. An astounding woman."

The two men were silent for a moment.

"Nevertheless, Captain, I shall take your advice and try to cool my ardour."

Shabtai responded to their urging and stood up, swaying dizzily. Sarah held him fast.

"Come, my Shabtai, you must eat and drink a little. Two days have you stood here, praying and scourging yourself with hunger and thirst. Even the Messiah requires sustenance before the Time of Redemption."

"Am I the Messiah, Sarah? Would the true Messiah be ignobly banished by an earthly king? Is my final resting place to be Dulcigno? Is this what the God of Israel destined for me? I have failed or I would not be sent into exile, hidden away from my people and my followers like a leper."

"Not so, my Shabtai. You must not despair. You are the true Messiah. Did not the prophet Nathan of Gaza predict this, long before he met you? Was it not revealed to him and to others in visions? The teachings of Nathan prove that the soul of the Messiah exists from before the world was born and this soul must endure many lives of triumph and tragedy before the final Redemption. Therefore, be of good cheer. Our exile is just another step in your journey."

Once again, her words calmed him. Still despondent, his head bowed, he allowed the Janissary to help him down the companionway and along the narrow corridor to their curtained enclosure. The Janissary bowed to Sarah as she entered the enclosure and was rewarded with a gracious smile and a whispered, "Thank you, sir."

Captain Tepel returned to the deck, flushed with the rapture of that smile. I will have no difficulty living up to the Grand Vizier's instructions, he thought, unless loving her is not treating her with respect.

"Your prisoners will be treated with great respect and will not be chained on the voyage," the Grand Vizier had told him. "That is the Sultan's wish. Furthermore, the prisoner is not to be called by his Jewish name but by his Muslim name Aziz Mehmed Effendi."

"Grand Vizier Kuprulu, may I enquire as to the nature of his crimes? I have only recently returned from the war with Crete and its occupation and am not yet conversant with local events."

At this, the Grand Vizier smiled, stood up and embraced the Janissary. "Captain Tepel, we are well aware of the role you played in our triumph over the Cretans and your courage and resourcefulness in battle. We often fought side by side.

"You will no doubt remember because of your role in quelling the Smyrna riots that Aziz Mehmed was once known as Shabtai Zvi, a man highly respected by his people. He proclaimed himself the messiah of the Jews and caused great excitement among his people throughout the Empire and in Europe."

Tepel nodded. "Yes, Grand Vizier, I remember that time in Smyrna all too well. The Jews of the city, normally well behaved, became unruly and required forceful restraint."

Kuprulu continued, "The Sultan was uneasy but took no action until this man announced that the day of Redemption was at hand, that the Sultan would relinquish his crown and become Shabtai's servant. He was arrested, brought before the Divan, and chose conversion to Islam over death. The Sultan even made him an officer of the court and provided him with a stipend. But instead of gratefully accepting the leniency and generosity of the Sultan, he engaged in duplicitous behaviour. He continued to believe he was the messiah. He was Jewish with the Jews and Muslim with the Muslims which disturbed many Muslims and even his own people who no longer accepted his claims. He cannot be trusted. The Sultan, fearing his execution would cause riotous incidents, decided to banish him to a remote corner of the Empire. We are entrusting you with the task of bringing him and his wife to Dulcigno, safely and without harm. Present this sealed scroll to the Governor — it contains instructions for their accommodation and treatment."

A shout from the crow's nest brought Tepel's thoughts back to the present.

"A city is in sight!"

The ship's captain strode to the foredeck and stationed himself at the bow. Minutes dragged by as he looked through a long tube at the slowly evolving coastline far ahead. Finally: "We approach Dulcigno. Steersman, north by northeast."

He shouted a command to the oarsmen. The drumbeat setting the stroke increased sharply and the ship lurched forward. Another command and seamen furled the lone sail and readied the anchor.

A mehter sounded the call to assemble, its buglelike tone accompanied by a drummer. Captain Tepel's guard of five Janissary soldiers struggled out of their cramped quarters under the foredeck, tidied their uniforms, strapped on their cutlasses, and holding their muskets moved quickly to the companionway and mustered on deck, the mehter bugler and drummer just behind them. Captain Tepel inspected them and told them to stand easy.

He returned to the curtained enclosure of his prisoners. "Aziz Mehmed Effendi and Madam, Dulcigno is close. Please prepare for disembarking."

Sarah emerged first, wearing a fur mantle. Captain Tepel helped her up the companionway. Shabtai came behind them, calm but seemingly oblivious to what was going on.

Dulcigno loomed ahead. A heavily fortified walled city, it stood on a high rocky promontory with steep, unassailable cliffs. The sun lit up the grey stone walls and fortress and glinted off the red roofs of the scores of buildings sheltered within its ramparts. The gate to the city faced them as they rounded the promontory and headed into the bay on the north side. People spilled out of the gate but stood respectfully aside as several officials appeared.

"Ship oars," shouted the captain. Then as the ship slowed, "Cast anchor."

The forward crew paid out the anchor rope twisted around a capstan. The ship strained against the rope as the anchor flukes took hold, and then slowly swung to face in to the wind.

From the far end of the bay, two lighters swept toward them pulled briskly by oarsmen. The first to arrive was grappled to the ship. Sarah went first, lowered to the lighter in a bosun's chair, the procedure supervised by both the ship's captain and Captain Tepel. They offered Shabtai the same conveyance, but he preferred to climb down the boarding ladder that hung from the ship's gunwale.

Captain Tepel bowed to the ship's captain and the two men embraced.

"My orders require me to stay here for some time," Captain Tepel said. "I thank you for an excellent passage. Hopefully, we will meet again."

Tepel climbed down the boarding ladder, followed by his five men, the drummer and the mehter.

The lighter pulled away and headed directly toward the cliff face below the gates of the city. It rounded a pillar of rock and edged against a wooden jetty that extended out from wide stone steps carved out of the solid granite.

At the top, they were met by the Governor and the Qadi of the city, as well as scores of Dulcigno residents who had come out to see the new arrivals. Captain Tepel saluted the Governor and handed him a sealed scroll.

The Governor was an imposing figure, tall and fleshy, and looked even taller with the red pointed cap crowning the large white turban, decorated with a spray of peacock feathers, that covered his head. A dark woollen mantle, open at the front, revealed a silk white knee length shirt and a caftan that fell to his ankles. His feet were encased in brown leather slippers with pointed toes. A ceremonial cutlass in a leather sheath was strapped to his waist by a sash embroidered with gold thread and dotted with precious stones.

In contrast, the Qadi was short and stout, and indifferently dressed in a grimy white turban, mantle and caftan. A straight white beard was surmounted by a bulbous nose and squinting eyes. He carried a gold embossed Qur'an.

The Governor smiled as he read through the scroll, and then handed it to the Qadi, laughing, "Honoured Qadi, your judicial responsibilities are increased by two converts to Islam. Behold! The Messiah of Smyrna and his wife. The Sultan has indeed blessed us."

The last statement bordered on sarcasm, but Captain Tepel decided to ignore it and gently ushered his captives forward.

The Governor cleared his throat loudly, looked sternly at Shabtai, and began in a very authoritative voice, "Aziz Mehmed Effendi, your fame — or should I say your infamy — has preceded you. Your claim that you are the messiah of Israel blasphemes the Prophet. As a Muslim, you are forbidden to utter or to even to think such heresy."

Shabtai, still in a mood of complete dejection, lowered his eyes and nodded.

"Aziz Mehmed Effendi, do you not have a voice and the courtesy to use it?" demanded the Governor, angrily shaking his fist at Shabtai.

Sarah stepped forward and fell to her knees. "Excellency, I beseech you. My husband is not well. I assure you he will do as the Governor wishes."

As she looked up at him, the veil covering her face below her eyes came loose. The Governor was struck by her beauty and the soft plaintive voice of her appeal. For a moment, he stared fixedly at her, as she crouched at his feet, her large brown eyes filling with tears. Captain Tepel smiled inwardly as he guessed the reason for the Governor's hesitation and startled look.

"M-m-madam," the Governor stammered, "I — we — acknowledge — that is, we accept — your petition on behalf of your husband. That is, at this time. But we must be assured that Aziz Mehmed Effendi understands the terms upon which he enjoys our mercy and the salutary conditions of his banishment and exile. However, we will wait until we are informed that he is well enough to learn his responsibilities and obligations as our guest. For the first days, while a permanent residence will be readied for you, you will occupy a set of rooms in the fortress."

"Excellency, I thank you. I am grateful to you. My husband will be soon well."

Captain Tepel helped her up, her veil still hanging loosely from her face.

"Madam, attach your veil properly," grunted the Qadi.

"Captain Tepel, our servants will lead you and your charges to their rooms. You will be lodged in the officer's quarters and your men in the barracks. Please come see us as soon as you can." With that the Governor turned sharply and walked back into the city, followed by the Qadi and most of the curious onlookers.

As Captain Tepel prepared to move into the city, a group of six slovenly dressed, rough looking men, laughing and jeering at Shabtai, blocked the entrance to the city.

"Get out of our way," ordered the captain.

One of them, a swarthy man wearing only a caftan and sandals despite the winter cold, spat at Shabtai, "Captain, we just want to welcome the Messiah and his whore."

A solid smash to the jaw sent the man sprawling. Before the others could come to his aid, Captain Tepel drew his cutlass, stood in front of his charges and shouted, "Muskets."

Mehter and drummer sounded and the five Janissaries advanced on the men with guns levelled.

The Governor, hearing the commotion, ran back.

"Captain Tepel, what is happening?"

"Governor Effendi, these scum have blocked our path and insulted my charges. A Janissary brooks no interference in carrying out the Sultan's orders."

The men, five deadly muskets pointing directly at them and an angry Janissary captain with raised cutlass, had quickly lost their bravado and pleaded with the captain and the Governor for mercy.

"The Governor repeats that it is the Sultan's command that Aziz Mehmed Effendi and his wife be treated with respect. Their conversion was carried out in the presence of the Sultan. Therefore, they are Muslims like us and will be respected as such. Anyone who goes against this goes against the Sultan and is guilty of treason." He raised his voice. "Is there anyone here who does not know what happens to those guilty of treason?"

The men, completely cowed, simply hung their heads.

"Very well then, you may go about your business."

The ruffians dispersed, leaving behind their fallen comrade.

The Governor pointed to two of his aides. "Carry him to the cells. Awakening in a dungeon will teach him a lesson. We will not allow riotous behaviour in our city."

Captain Tepel sheathed his cutlass, stood at attention and saluted the Governor. The soldiers and their captives proceeded to the fortress.

The captain gave his charges a couple of hours to get settled and then called on them. A servant, an olive-skinned girl clothed in headdress and caftan, led him through a small antechamber into a large drawing room. The room was dimly lit by a narrow window that looked out on the fortress wall. With a taper, she lit the candles on their wall sconces. Rugs covered the floor and raised cushions were set around a low table in the centre of the room. A fire burning in a small grate in the chimney corner warmed the room and rid it of its damp winter smell. The stone walls were bare of decoration and glistened with condensed moisture. The servant pointed to a raised cushion and he sat down cross-legged.

There was a loud banging at the entrance door. Captain Tepel stood up as the Governor entered. The girl scurried off to an inner room.

The two men exchanged polite greetings and sat down. The captain expressed his satisfaction with his quarters and those of his men. He offered a musical entertainment of the drummer and mehter when the Governor wished and the Governor readily accepted. Their courtesy to each other masked the strain that frequently existed between administrators and Janissary officers. Technically, the Governor was of superior rank to Captain Tepel but was careful not to insist on it because the Janissaries answered only to the sultanate and as a result held much influence and power.

The Governor felt humiliated. Here he was calling on the two exiles, instead of ignoring them altogether or summoning them to his audience chamber. It is that damn woman, he thought. She warps my judgement. I had to see her again without palace aides and scribes in attendance, without the Qadi, and definitely without this accursed Janissary. Such beauty aligned with a madman.

The captain had similar thoughts. He knew it had been Aziz Mehmed's wife that had attracted the Governor to break normal protocol. That meant he had a rival, and a personal reason to protect his charges from harm. Why she would marry a wretch who believed himself superior to the Sultan was beyond him.

But both men were astonished when Shabtai Zvi walked in and greeted them warmly and affably. His despondency was gone. He stood tall and straight before them, geniality beaming out of his welcoming face. His charismatic presence drew them to stand up respectfully.

"Young woman," he called out to the servant. "Bring in the infusion that I prepared. Gentlemen, please be seated."

The servant brought in three goblets of steaming liquid.

"Gentlemen, please try this restorative mixture of herbs and spices. Ideal to banish the winter cold. I drink this potion after the sleepless days and nights when I fast and pray and try to ascend through the divine emanations of God."

The two men looked at him in wonder as they sipped their tea. For Tepel, the change from the abject melancholic he had encountered on the ship, singing rapturously into the cold air or screaming to the heavens to this strong, elegant, self-confident, loquacious man was indeed miraculous. The Governor, too, compared the rejuvenated Aziz Mehmed with the halting silent man who required the energetic support of his wife. Perhaps Allah had somehow intervened.

"This tea does have a wondrous effect," observed the Governor. "Whence comes it?"

"I am pleased that you like it," Shabtai acknowledged. "The mixture is prepared in Smyrna by a merchant on Synagogue Street. He claims the ingredients come from all over the Empire, as well as beyond its borders. I first discovered it as a young man. Still to this day, with the help of my family, he sends it to me. Should you have occasion to be in Smyrna, just visit his shop — it is the only spice shop on the street — and ask for the potion of Shabtai Zvi."

"Aziz Mehmed Effendi, may we remind you that is no longer your name," the Governor said sternly. The change in Aziz Mehmed was frustrating to him. How could he hope to wrest the woman from such a man?

"Quite so, Governor Effendi, but if you ask for the potion of Aziz Mehmed, the merchant may not know it. Then you must add 'who was once known as Shabtai Zvi.'"

Captain Tepel smiled at Shabtai's effrontery because it was delivered not rebelliously but with seeming sincerity. However the Governor was not so inclined.

"Perhaps we should send your merchant to the same prison you occupied in Gallipoli. There, he would learn your proper name."

"No need," came the unabashed reply. "The merchant is well past his three score and ten. No doubt, he will soon have to defend himself before Allah. Besides, his sons have followed me into Islam."

"Did they convert willingly or, like you had to choose between Islam or execution for sedition?" There was no mistaking the sarcasm and enmity in the Governor's voice.

"Nay, Governor Effendi, I did not choose. It was God who chose for me. He directed me to avoid death because my work for Him was not yet finished in this world and to accept Islam where my work could continue."

The Governor leaned forward and looked at Shabtai intently. "And what work was that?"

The captain began to fear for Shabtai. The Governor was hoping these questions would reveal him as a heretic which would then provide an excuse to excommunicate him, perhaps to isolate him from his wife.

"It is the work that all pious and good men perform daily. Let me explain. When God decided to create the world, He did so through divine emanations which, like shells, held the divine attributes. Below the shells lay the created world. To illuminate and make sacred His creation, God directed His divine light down through the shells. The top six shells received the light and passed it on. The bottom four shells were too weak to hold the light and they shattered. Sparks and shards of divine light were scattered throughout creation. Through piety and prayer and observance of God's commandments, the Holy Sparks can be retrieved and returned to the Almighty. Some of these Holy Sparks fell as well into the Muslim world. I was given the opportunity to help my fellow Muslims capture these Sparks."

All three were silent for a moment and drank their tea. Shabtai, having delivered his homily, sat back on his cushions, a benign and satisfied look on his face.

A fanciful tale, Tepel thought, surely the Governor will see it as such. But the Governor was frowning as he swallowed the last of the tea and put the goblet down carefully on the low table.

"Aziz Mehmed Effendi, we are not an Imam and therefore we cannot judge whether what you have told us is acceptable theology. It does not sound right to our untutored ears. You refer to God — which God do you mean?"

"Be at ease, Governor Effendi," Shabtai said. "Both Israel and Islam — and even the Christians — declare that God created the world. What I have described is the underlying process by which He created the world. As for which God I refer to, there is only one God. Whether He is called Jehovah by Israel or Allah by we in Islam, He is the one true God, the only God, there is no other God, blessed be His Name" — and Shabtai added almost as an afterthought — "and Mohammed is His Prophet."

The Governor was not entirely convinced but indicated his approval and turned to the real reason for his visit. "Your wife — how fares your wife?"

For the first time since he entered the room, Shabtai's smile gave way to a troubled look.

"Gentlemen, my wife is completely exhausted after the long sea voyage. In addition, she suffers from a recurring malady, a catarrh of the nose and throat. When it comes upon her, she breathes with difficulty. She has ingested some of this tea and has inhaled the fumes of steamed chamomile. Both measures seem to have brought her some relief. At the moment, she is resting comfortably. I pray to Allah that He cares for her."

"Nevertheless," the Governor insisted, "the Sultan has commanded us to guard your welfare. We will summon a woman who, in addition to mid-wifery, has extensive knowledge and experience of medicines and has cured many of the maladies in this region. Bring your wife to our audience chamber in the late morning tomorrow."

Tepel was not happy with the direction the Governor's concern was taking.

"Perhaps, Governor Effendi, if the lady is not well enough to leave her bed, the woman could come here."

The Governor was clearly annoyed at Tepel's intervention and responded with a curt "Of course." The two men took their leave of Shabtai.

Shabtai continued to sit on his raised cushion, long after the room darkened as the candles sputtered out, musing on his situation. The demons that had plagued him since his banishment were gone, along with his melancholy. Yet he was not content, uneasy about his future in this tucked away part of the Empire.

The sea voyage had been especially difficult. Many times as he stood in the bow, praying for long hours, and supplicating God to give him a sign, he was tempted to simply lean over the gunwale and allow himself to fall overboard.

At one point, the urge became too strong. Thick early morning fog was flowing over and around him, hiding him from sight. No one would notice. No one would try to rescue him. He had stepped toward the gunwale.

"Rabbi Zvi! Stop!" a voice shouted from the main deck.

Out of the gloom, an apparition appeared. He saw archangel Metatron, messenger of the Lord, the scribe recording man's deeds, seated at a table, writing on a parchment scroll. Metatron, a brilliant golden figure, taller than a man, hooded and cloaked, his face difficult to see in the sharp light radiating from him, laid down his quill and walked toward Shabtai.

"Messiah of the God of Israel, why dost thou contemplate death?"

Made speechless by the sudden appearance, Shabtai shrank back and tried to bury himself in the rope gear in the bow.

"Come, come, Rabbi Zvi, this is unseemly behaviour for a man chosen by the Almighty to be the Messiah. Be not afraid. Loose thy silvery tongue."

Encouraged by the gentle voice of the apparition, Shabtai stood up and faced Metatron.

"Holy archangel, I fear I have failed. If my soul is released in death, it may migrate to a better man who might succeed."

"A noble thought," Metatron said, returning to the table. "One that I shall record in the book of man's deeds." He unfurled a scroll lying on the table and examined it carefully. "However, I see in the Book of Death no mention of thy name in this year. Therefore, be of strong heart, for the Almighty commands that thy mission must continue. Many Holy Sparks must yet be retrieved if the Redemption is to come. Thou must lead thy many loyal followers as Moses led the Children of Israel, else they may go astray."

Metatron bent over the parchment and wrote in a clear and steady hand, occasionally dipping his quill in the ink. The vision slowly faded away.

Shabtai felt his confidence and his faith in himself as the true Messiah restored. Facing the east, he sang rapturously in his sweet tenor voice prayers praising the Almighty. But the demons that had plagued him had not given up.

Sounds of moaning and sighing caused him to stop singing.

There at his feet, a man and woman, almost shielded from sight by wraiths of fog and mist, lay copulating. Their ecstasy mounted to a climactic writhing and twisting and then collapsed. The woman relaxed and let her arms and legs that had grappled the man fall to the deck. Her body began to lengthen, her arms absorbed into the body, her legs became one. Shabtai stepped back hard against the bow, frozen in horror, as the woman's head swung toward him. He stared into the yellow eyes of a serpent, its tongue flicking out, nearly touching him, its breath foul with the stench of rot and death. The man stood up, clothed in fog, only his swarthy face showing, a carbuncle on his left cheek partly hidden by a mangy, scraggly beard. He had no eyes.

"Shabtai, false Messiah, it is I, Samael, leader of the rebel angels, and this is my Lilith. Fear her not. She will not harm you just as she did not harm Eve but gave her knowledge and wisdom."

"What do you want of me?" Shabtai asked, his voice quavering and almost inaudible.

The serpent poked its head under his caftan. He could feel it slithering up between his legs, its hot tongue licking his penis. Despite his dread, he felt his lust rising.

"Come, Lilith, leave the poor man alone," Samael said chuckling. "My Lilith is so difficult to sate. Twice have I pleasured her this morning, yet she thirsts for more."

The serpent retreated and curled up on the deck.

"What do you want of me?" Shabtai repeated.

"We want nothing of you. Heed not Metatron. You are not the messiah and never were. You have no mission to continue. Your followers are leaving you and are scattered, leaderless. The ones who still believe in you are mad and as blind as I am. Choose death and join us. Freedom and pleasure await you. We are not beholden to your God. He has no power over us."

"But you will be destroyed at the Time of Redemption — you and all your followers."

Samael sneered contemptuously, his twisted lips ugly and menacing.

"Perhaps. Perhaps not. But it matters not. The time of Redemption will be in the millennium following six thousand years after the Creation. We are in the year 5433. Therefore there are many years of pleasure left. Come, join us."

"I don't know. I don't know," Shabtai moaned, throwing himself down on the deck, pummeling it with his fists. Then he pushed to his knees, raised his arms, and screamed at the sky, imploring God to give him a sign. Finally, he let his arms hang over the gunwale, tears flowing down his cheeks into his beard.

It was then that Sarah had calmed him with her velvety voice and reassuring words, but he was still bereft of hope as they landed at Dulcigno.

Abruptly, the melancholy had left him. Perhaps it was the few hours of sleep he'd had, perhaps it was the attack of breathlessness that plagued Sarah that had snapped him out of it, or — as he truly believed — the Almighty had heard his lamentations and had relieved him of the demons.

He perceived that both the Governor and Captain Tepel had designs on Sarah. He smiled at the Governor's all too obvious intent to bring Sarah to a place where he could be alone with her. The medicine woman would leave the room when the Governor appeared. He smiled too at Tepel's attempt to foil the Governor's plan. Shabtai was not worried about Sarah. She was always his faithful wife and did what she deemed necessary to protect his interests and advance his mission.

Most of his needs for accommodation and food would be looked after by donations from his brothers in Smyrna and his many friends and followers in Constantinople, Adrianapole, Salonika, and Jerusalem.

However, there were other more important essentials. The Sultan had decreed no visitors or contact without authorization by the Dulcigno administration. Some of the money sent might persuade the Governor or the Qadi to look the other way at times. But the attractiveness of a beautiful woman might be more compelling than even money. For his Messianic mission to continue, he needed to meet and to exchange letters with those who still believed in him, to persuade others to return to the fold, and to challenge the many rabbinical authorities who continued to rail against him. Sarah would open the gates that needed to be unlocked — of that, he was certain.

CHAPTER 2
- TORONTO, 2006 -
SHABTAI ZVI KABBALAH SOCIETY

The meeting leader stood at the head of the room facing the rows of chairs. On the table beside him, an open laptop controlled a ceiling projector which cast its digital message on the wall screen:

"SHABTAI ZVI KABBALAH SOCIETY
THE DIRECT PATH TO GOD."

He watched the attendees slowly trickle in and take their seats. At first, there were only 12. At $25 a head, the take wouldn't even cover the hotel meeting room and refreshments. He could find cheaper hotels for his meetings, but he preferred the Royal for its location in the heart of Toronto's financial district. The audience he wanted to attract was close by, well paid, with many longing for some intellectual relief from their life style of constant intense work, and the telecom strait jacket tying them to their offices. He had scheduled the series of meetings for 5:30 to 7:00 pm which allowed participants time to attend before heading home.

He heaved a sigh of relief as ten more walked in. At least he would cover the expenses and would profit from the purchases of the text book and other related material stacked on the table at the back of the room.

The number of people joining his meetings was increasing at each session. Word of mouth was drawing them in since he didn't advertise, apart from the initial fliers first distributed in the area.

Just as the meeting was about to begin, his wife entered.

"Hi, Roberta," he called out. She waved and took a seat in the back row.

As always, he admired and was even comforted by her loyalty, but felt guilty and embarrassed. They'd separated a year ago, but she insisted on attending as many meetings as she could and helping him. He didn't support her — a lawyer, she made more money than he did.

They'd married young, he 25, she 18 and pregnant. The marriage wasn't forced on him — he really loved her. He was relieved when the baby miscarried and it became evident there would be no further babies. He was quite happy to go through life untrammelled by children. He sought to placate her by telling her this but it pushed her into a deeper depression. It took months before she recovered and things returned to normalcy. The marriage continued for twenty years.

What ended it for him was the diagnosis of breast cancer and the mastectomy that followed. He was unable to handle the deformity. Besides, at this point he met Lily Thegn — young, pretty, bosomy, narrow waist, trim hips, perfect legs.

She was a student in his Comparative Religion class and frequently stayed after the lecture to pepper him with questions. He was easily attracted to her and it didn't take much manoeuvring to start the affair. He was aware he was not her only lover. In fact, she referred to the men in her life as her entourage and welcomed him into her circle. This bothered him at first but then he reasoned his interest in her was strictly physical with no real love commitment on his part. Surprisingly, she had other ideas about him.

"As long as we're seeing each other, I'm it," she told him after a few love sessions. "I don't tolerate competition. You're mine."

He merely laughed and didn't take her too seriously. Their lovemaking was always at his apartment. She would arrive with an overnight suitcase and stay with him for several days. In fact, he never saw where she lived and sometimes wondered whether she had her own place or simply moved from man to man.

"Ladies and Gentlemen, please help yourselves to coffee and canapés," he instructed the attendees.

Just then, Lily entered and sat at the back a few seats from Roberta. Despite his yearlong affair with Lily, the women didn't know each other.

He dreaded the possibility they might chat and discover his significance in their lives. He remembered the toast from his brief stint in the military: "to our wives and sweethearts, may they never meet."

He turned to the audience.

"Ladies and Gentlemen, welcome to this third meeting of our study of Kabbalah. For the newcomers, my name is Donald May and I'm the head of the Shabtai Zvi Kabbalah Society. You are welcome to join the Society but no one is obliged to do so. You will find a description of the Society and membership application forms at the back of the room.

"I see many familiar faces and I thank you for your continuing interest in these learning sessions. Allow me a few minutes to bring the newcomers into our circle.

"In our first sessions, I related the thousand year written history of the Kabbalah, how it developed and spread, and discussed some of the controversies attending its development even unto the present day. To catch up or to review this history, may I direct you to the textbooks and related material at the back of the room.

"What is Kabbalah? Kabbalah is the mystical attempt to come closer to God by trying to better understand the process of Creation and the nature of the Godhead. It tries to answer a number of questions."

Donald paused, pushed a key on the laptop and a new slide appeared on the screen. "Questions such as..." Donald pointed to the screen. "How and why did God create the Universe? If God is perfect why is their imperfection in His creation? If God is Supreme and Good why is their evil in His creation? These are some of the questions the Kabbalah answers. Now, let me introduce the man who is the father of our brand of Kabbalah."

The slide on the screen changed and showed a portrait of a man sitting at a table, pointing to a book. A woven turban crowned a strong face with neatly trimmed dark beard and moustache. He wore a buttoned caftan underneath a mantle that emphasized his broad shoulders. Sad eyes stared out at the audience. The caption read: "Shabtai Zvi."

Donald waited a moment to allow the audience to regard the picture.

"By coincidence," he continued, "this is a special commemorative day for us at the Shabtai Zvi Kabbalah Society. Today, August 3rd, 2006 we remember the birth 380 years ago of a man in the city of Smyrna, located in Turkey and within the Ottoman Empire. This man, Shabtai Zvi, had an enormous impact on the Jewish world throughout the Ottoman Empire and Europe — in other words, all of the Middle East, the Mediterranean countries and Western Europe. He claimed to be the Messiah, a claim enthusiastically accepted by ordinary Jews and supported by the rabbinic authorities in most of the cities and countries where Jews lived. His influence also attracted thousands of Muslims and Christians as followers. All believed that the Time of Redemption had come and Shabtai Zvi would secure for them the Promised Land and the end of suffering, hardship and oppression. In one of his hyper Messianic moods, he proclaimed that he would soon usurp the Sultan's crown and that the Sultan would become his subject. Poor choice of words. He was arrested and eventually exiled to Dulcigno, a remote corner of the Empire.

"Now, why do I regale you with the story of a Messiah who may be false? Well, whether we accept or deny his Messianic claim, he was a highly respected rabbi, learned in all the scriptures and oral and ritual traditions of Judaism and admired for his ascetic and pious life. He was also an eminent Kabbalist which is, of course, germane to our Society. Much of what we will learn in these sessions was preached and practised, and taught by Shabtai Zvi. Because his name in English is Sabbatai Sevi, those of us who follow his teachings are usually referred to as Sabbatean."

A hand went up in the audience, and before he could acknowledge it, Lily stood up.

"Donald, my name is Lily Thegn. I took your course in Comparative Religion at the U of T. We studied dozens of religions, not only the main ones, but also pagan and even ancient religions. I never heard of yours. Is this something new?"

"Thank you for your question," Donald said.

With Roberta in the room, he decided to show no familiarity with Lily.

" Shabtai's heyday was 1665 and 1666 so his teachings are not new. After his arrest, he converted to Islam which was a terrible blow to his many Jewish followers. Those who still believed in him went underground in order to avoid persecution by either the orthodox rabbinate or the Sultan's authorities. Consequently, the word 'Sabbateanism' if used at all was used in private and secretly. Even today, the name is treated pejoratively. The next slide will make clearer what we are and what we believe in."

He watched her sit down and took a deep breath before going on. Across the room, Roberta was eyeing him, slowly shaking her head. Her ability to detect when a woman interested him was uncanny. What was it? A flexing of the skin around the eyes? A stiffening of the posture? A licking of the lips? Perhaps a change in the sound of his voice.

He hadn't been a very faithful husband. Just under six feet, square-faced, long hair tied in a pony tail, rippling muscles emphasized by tight fitting shirt and trousers, he knew he attracted women. Life as a university professor provided many temptations, not only with students but with younger faculty as well. Often Roberta knew and even told him which woman he was sleeping with. He asked her once, "Why do you stay with me?"

She looked at him, a wistful expression on her face. "I forgive you because I see something great in you. I stay because without me, you'll fuck it up."

Her prophesy was accurate. While she was long weeks in hospital, he strayed even further, with less caution, and ended up fired by the university for sexual harassment. He narrowly escaped a pedophile charge because one of the women who complained was borderline adult and couldn't remember the exact date the incident had taken place.

"Let me make one thing very clear. We are not a religion nor do we exist within a religion. We are not trapped in useless ritual and ancient folkways because they rob us of the ability to focus solely on understanding God and worshipping Him. In this regard, the discipline that we use comes from the Kabbalah, particularly the teachings of Shabtai Zvi. We do not do good in order to achieve personal salvation. We do good to benefit God and to restore His unity."

Lily's hand went up again. He nodded to her. She stood up, smiling at him. He wasn't sure whether she was trying to bait or help him.

"Donald, I find that following the ritual in my religion frees me from my everyday existence and prepares me to think about God and to worship Him. Is that not enough?"

He could not help himself. He feasted on her face and the trim body beneath it. He saw Roberta roll her eyes.

"Yes and no," he responded. "If following a traditional religious ritual separates your mind from worldly matters so that you can enter into a mystical understanding of God, then it's fine. If the ritual is a thing in itself, then by observing it and nothing more, you may think you've earned some air miles for your ultimate journey to heaven, but you've achieved nothing."

Another hand went up, this time from a tall, thin, bespectacled woman, short black hair, a pale face dominated by a pointy nose. She wore a pant suit which emphasized her thinness. Well, Roberta can relax, he thought, this one does not attract me.

"Donald, my name is Sarai Stone. Perhaps I'm jumping ahead, but you mentioned that God's unity must be restored. Why is God not unified? Is your concept of God like the Christian concept of the Trinity?"

Donald shook his head. "In Sabbateanism, the concept of the Godhead does embody components which may be likened to a trinity but is quite different from Christianity. We will be discussing this in later sessions. For the moment, let us consider the next slide."

Titled "The Creation," the slide showed the outline of a cloud labelled 'The Godhead.' Below it was another cloud partitioned by a wavy line into two parts; one labelled 'The Godhead,' the other 'Nothingness' and contained a large black dot.

Pointing to the top cloud, Donald said, "Before creation, there was no space, there was only the Godhead. To provide space for creation, the Godhead retracted into Himself as the second cloud illustrates. The space released was totally void, a nothingness. God concentrated the force of creation into a point in the centre of this void and out of this point spewed all of creation."

Donald paused, letting this thought sink in.

"Donald," Lily asked, "How do Kabbalists come to this view of creation? "

Before he could respond, Sarai stood up. "Donald, is this an attempt to reconcile religion with Big Bang theory?"

Donald was not surprised that Lily was eager to monopolize his attention. From the intensity which Sarai Stone addressed her question and her eagerness in challenging him, Donald began to suspect that she too had an interest in him. He held up his hands in mock protest.

"Ladies, give me a break. One question at a time. First, to answer Lily, the Kabbalah was developed over fifteen hundred years of speculation and debate by the most learned and famous rabbis of their time. Much of their speculation was based upon statements found in the Torah, then as now considered the word of God. Kabbalists believe that God has revealed all in the Torah provided one can ferret out His secrets. Out of this analysis has come everything I share with you today and in coming sessions.

"Now, to Sarai's question. Certainly my description of the point in the void out of which comes everything seems to be in accord with Big Bang theory. However, please note, it was Isaac Luria, a Kabbalist who lived in the 16th century who developed this view. If anything, one can argue that modern science has caught up and confirms this concept. Now, let's get on with my presentation."

He drank thirstily from a bottle of water and pushed on to the next slide. He noticed Roberta had gone and was relieved — he still felt guilty when he intended to show special attention to a woman and Roberta was around.

"When I say creation spewed out from a point I am being simplistic. In reality, through this point, Creation began in the form of emanations, call it divine releases. The first one was Keter or Supreme Crown which, like a corporate head office, directed and controlled the remaining process of Creation. Nine more emanations followed and are shown on the screen — wisdom, intelligence, love, power, etcetera — notice, all are considered attributes of the righteous person. From the last — Kingdom — came the world that we know.

Both Lily and Sarai held up their hands.

"No, please hold your questions. It's important that I finish the process of Creation. Now, as the emanations proceeded, two things happened. The last few emanations found their power diminishing the further outward they got from the Emanator. At the same time, God directed His Divinity in the form of a bolt of divine light down through the emanations to illuminate the world we know and to render it perfect and pure. The light hit the weakened bottom emanations or shells as Kabbalists refer to them and shattered them, sending shards of divine light and Holy Sparks all over our world. Until these shards and sparks of Divine Light are returned, the Godhead will lack unity. Our job as humans is to retrieve the Holy Sparks and, in so doing, restore to God His Unity."

An older man raised his hand. "Donald, my name is Jack Escapa. I presume that because of the shattering of the emanations, that's how evil and imperfection entered our world?"

Donald nodded.

"But that suggests that God was a poor engineer. He didn't take into account the strength of His Divine Light and to make the last emanations stronger."

Donald chuckled. "Good point. Kabbalists believe in general that a technical error occurred. Some, including Shabtai Zvi, saw competing heavenly factions as part of the problem. One heavenly faction was happy with the status quo and resisted creation of the world and Man — the other welcomed change and encouraged creation. As a result of their competition, the creation was marred. Even in the Garden of Eden, a most perfect and pure space, evil occurred. Things got so bad, that a dissatisfied God flooded all creation, saving only Noah and family and many animals. But even after the Flood, evil survived."

Jack started to ask another question, but Lily interrupted him: "This is probably a silly question, but how does restoring God's Unity do anything for the world and us?"

"Besides," Sarai asked, "how do we retrieve these shards and Holy Sparks of Divine Light? Surely, devout religious people will have done their share. Or is more required?"

"Both good questions," Donald said. "And both reveal something about your concept of religiosity. Can anyone explain what that is?"

There was silence. Then Jack put up his hand. "I'll take a chance. In essence, they're both asking, 'what's in it for me?'"

Sarai leapt to her feet, glaring at Jack. "I have been a faithful Catholic all my life. I expect no reward on Earth. I look forward to being welcomed by God at the end of my days or at the time of Christ's return. If pursuing a goal of salvation is an ego trip, then so be it." She sat down with an angry "Hmph."

Donald looked at her admiringly. Anger flushed her face, covering the pallor of her skin, making her almost attractive. He relished the fire in her, her quick reaction and articulation.

Lily was more subtle. "Donald, I see nothing wrong with wondering how I fit in the Kabbalah scheme of things, like what do I or the world get out of it. I'm sure it will be difficult and hard work to retrieve the Holy Sparks or to overcome the factions opposing creation. So there must be a reward — so all I'm asking is 'what is the reward?'"

"OK," Donald replied. "What's in it for me? What's my reward? Good questions, deserving of an answer. The reward may be nothing you've ever envisaged before. So let me paint you a picture of the reward." He paused and glanced around the room to ensure he had everybody's attention. "Imagine the sublime peace and utterly profound serenity when this world of dross matter, chaos and evil is Redeemed and incorporated into the world above. Imagine the bliss of a soul in direct communion with God. Our souls are like the flame atop a piece of coal. Redemption destroys the coal but preserves the flame. The soul in such a state of communion rises above the realm of angels and far beyond the world of demons. It has become pure, incorporeal, and basks in perpetual ecstasy, warmed, irradiated by the vast energy of the Godhead close to it. This is the reward that mysticism and the Kabbalah offers you."

As Donald spoke, his voice rose, his arms lifted up toward the ceiling, his face tilted up, eyes wide open and staring into the distance. His audience listened in rapt attention, mesmerized by the glimpse of what they perceived to be a mystical happening. No one made a sound or even shifted in their seats until Donald slowly relaxed his arms and returned from a faraway place to the meeting room.

Donald stood there a moment, dazed, rubbing his hand over his forehead. He saw Lily looking at him, concern puckering her face. What a sweet face, he thought dreamily.

"The reward is wonderful," said Sarai, her incisive voice clearing away the last mists clogging his mind. "But how do we get there?"

"Yes," Donald replied. "I've described the reward. Now, let's answer Sarai's question. As Sabbatean Kabbalists, we practice what Shabtai Zvi taught and did himself. These are — piety and asceticism, prayer, doing good deeds. In the next sessions we will examine each of these. However, there is one method that he practiced and recommended and which earned him much controversy and, in fact, was the reason he was banished from Smyrna at the age of 25 by the orthodox rabbinate of the city. This method he called Redemption through Sin."

Donald paused, savouring the expressions of incredulity on the faces of his audience.

"By the way, Jack, does your family come from Turkey?"

Jack nodded. "We do. We came to Canada in the late 19th century. Why do you ask?"

"Well, you might be interested in tracing your ancestry. You see, the rabbi who was instrumental in getting Shabtai kicked out of Smyrna was Joseph Escapa."

"I'm impressed," Jack said. "I hope this doesn't earn me demerit points. But what did Shabtai do that was so alarming?"

"He indulged in antinomian practices — behaviour and acts contrary to Jewish religious law and even Ottoman law. Shabtai believed that just like seeds, planted in the ground, must rot before blossoming forth as grain fit for bread so must man delve deeply into sin so as to transform it and release the Holy Sparks entrapped in the sin."

A forest of hands went up. Donald laughed and held up his hands in a stop gesture. "Whoa. Hold on. I know your questions. We've all been taught to avoid sin by our parents, our religious leaders, our teachers. Sin will deliver us to hell. Sin may even land us in jail. So how can indulging in sin be a good thing? Am I right?"

The audience nodded, laughing.

"Well, according to Shabtai, the essence depends on whether you enjoy the sin as self-gratification or experience it selflessly in order to transform it."

"But that's ridiculous," Sarai snapped, standing up, her hands on her hips, face flushed. "Sin is pleasurable, otherwise no one would indulge. How can you sin selflessly?"

"Donald," Jack said sarcastically, shaking his head, "Shabtai may have considered sinning as transformative, but my ancestor Rabbi Escapa — even if he isn't my ancestor — called it for what it was — sinning."

Lily stood up and smiled at both Jack and Sarai. "Perhaps Donald will explain that it has to do with the nature of the sin and" — she turned toward Donald —"with whom it is performed."

Donald looked at her sharply. He didn't mind being propositioned but he preferred a bit more subtlety and less publicly. Most of the audience was smiling, Sarai glared at Lily, and Jack simply raised his eyebrows.

"OK," Donald said. "We're all uncomfortable with the concept but let's hear what Shabtai had to say. The sins he laid out were apostasy — you know, converting to another religion — eating forbidden foods — Jews eating pork, Muslims, non-halal foods — and, of course, sex — that is, not sex between a married couple but sexual practices banned by the scriptures. I think you can guess what some of these are, but would include sex between an unmarried couple, and adultery was definitely out. Now, he did a lot of these things but did not suggest his followers emulate him. He reminded them of the old adage — 'the thought is like the deed.' Therefore, thinking sinful acts accomplishes Redemption through Sin but does it in a way that may make it easier to be selfless."

Jack sat there, an unhappy look on his face. "Donald, why should we pay any attention to a madman and more importantly, why should we follow his dictates?"

"How many feel like Jack does?" Donald asked.

All the hands went up except Lily's. When asked why she thought differently, Lily replied, "Why should we conclude he's a madman? He must have had something going for him. From what you said, Donald, he was extremely learned, and had an enormous influence in the world at his time. I see nothing wrong to at least consider his teachings."

"But he claimed he was the messiah," Jack said. "That makes him a madman and anything he teaches becomes suspect."

Sarai snapped at him. "Does that mean all Christians are stupid because they have faith in a messiah called Jesus?"

The meeting was on the verge of becoming a heated debate.

"Ladies. Gentlemen," Donald intervened. "Hold off your judgement of Shabtai for awhile. Let me defend him. Shabtai believed he was the Messiah but was troubled. From his traditional rabbinic background, he well understood that he should have been preceded by a Messiah who would prepare the way for the final Messiah. Kabbalah tradition holds that the soul of the messiah was present before creation and that it transmigrates throughout the generations from one strong leader to the next. The soul inhabited the body of Abraham, Moses, King David, and so on. We Sabbateans believe that, because of Christ's stature in the Holy Land and his vast following after his death, the soul of the messiah rested in Jesus for awhile. Where did it go after Jesus? Why not Mohammed? And why not Shabtai Zvi? Given the inordinate amount of influence he had both in the Jewish and non-Jewish world — he is even mentioned in Samuel Pepys' famous English diary — I have no difficulty in believing that Shabtai inherited the soul of the messiah and that his teachings came from that soul. We now await its next manifestation."

Donald swept his audience with a quick glance. Many of the faces still had expressions of disbelief. Only Lily smiled at him appreciatively.

Sarai appeared somewhat satisfied, probably because he had affirmed his belief in Jesus as *a* messiah if not *the* messiah.

"As far as Redemption through Sin is concerned, many renowned and respected rabbis and Kabbalists have said the same thing both before and after Shabtai. The only difference is Shabtai actually practiced physically what he preached. Condemn him if you wish but the principle remains firm. And so now, I have an exercise that you can try — only if you wish to participate — in Redemption through Sin." He paused, and then added: "By thought."

His audience relaxed when he mentioned the word 'thought'. Lily looked disappointed, Sarai uneasy, Jack dubious.

"First," Donald continued, "all the married men and men with serious live-in partners line up against the wall on my left."

Eight men did so, including Jack Escapa.

"Guys, select a woman who is not your wife or partner and have her stand in front of you and facing you."

There was nervous laughter and shuffling of chairs as the selected women paired with the men. Lily was with Jack. Sarai sat alone, trying to appear above it all, but clearly showing signs of humiliation.

"Come up here, Sarai," Donald said. "You'll be my partner for the exercise."

Her face took on a sudden glow as she approached him.

"Men and women pairs, hold hands, and women step back until you're at arm's length from your partner. That was the hard part. Now comes the easy part. Put everything out of your head, forget about what happened at the office today, and forget about what's waiting for you at home. For the next twenty minutes concentrate solely on your partner and the royal sex you will have with each other. Get right into it. Think about how the clothes will come off, how you will enjoy your favourite position over and over again, or positions you've always wanted to try, relish the experience of unbridled, uninhibited joining and writhing of your bodies, the endless orgasm that will flow from this. Don't shy away from feeling sexual arousal — moan, groan, sigh, whatever moves you. When the mental experience becomes unbearable, visualize an intensely bright spark of light on your partner's body and immediately begin meditating on God's name, whatever it is in your culture or religion.

"Those of you who aren't part of the pairs, think of committing sins that are normally inimical to you but imagine them as positive, pleasurable, wonderful. Again, at the end, visualize a spark of light and meditate on God's name."

He held Sarai's hands and they backed away from each other. Sarai seemed uneasy and he smiled encouragingly. He concentrated on her body, its thinness, and its bony structure. She blushed as he walked his eyes up and down her body. There was something attractive about her, he decided. Maybe it was the wasp-like waist blossoming out into the hip and thighs, the modest bulge of the breasts, the face with its sharp nose supporting large round glasses, the straight black hair.

How would I make love to her, he wondered. No point in slowly and seductively taking off her clothes — the body revealed would not do much for his libido. He was accustomed to women with a more standard body, even voluptuous women, slimmer than the women in a Reuben's painting, but nicely rounded. Like Lily. The thought of making love to Lily roused him immediately. It must have showed, because he saw Sarai's eyes widen, the blush on her face deepen, and felt the grip on his hands tighten.

They stood there for many minutes. He continued to look slowly and evenly up and down her body. He watched her eyes dart rapidly to his, then away, then back again. He saw the desire creep into her features — her mouth was partly open, her eyes just slits in her face, her breathing heavy, almost gasping.

He concentrated again how he would make love to her. He would embrace her fully clothed, kiss her as he ran his hands up and down her back, then turn her, and still holding her, fondle her breasts and run his hands down to her thighs. Then he would pick her up, carry her to the bed, fondle her for awhile, and when he felt the moment was right, get into her.

His sexual reveries ended abruptly. Sarai freed her hands and, sobbing, returned to her seat. She sat there, head bowed, the occasional tear drop falling on her lap. No one seemed to notice. He watched her carefully for awhile, fearing she might be having a breakdown.

Hers was relatively unusual behaviour. Most people took in stride the Redemption through Sin exercise. They all seemed to enjoy the license granted by the exercise. Every now and then, there was a problem. A man or woman would become enraged that a spouse was showing inordinate pleasure. Or someone — mostly women — whose usual sinning had been trivial, like telling 'white lies,' became unnerved at the direct contemplation of sinful sex and the pleasurable, even ecstatic, reaction they felt, quite contrary to their self image of honest, proper people.

The reactions varied. Some just sat down and looked sad and depressed. Others, like Sarai, wept. Still others became hysterical and had to be calmed. He had no sympathy for these people. He found them tedious and disturbing of his teaching sessions. He refused to believe that people could lead such sheltered and repressed lives that even an exercise in sexual fantasy would crack their ego and sense of self. In extreme cases, he would ask the attendee to leave the course.

He found Sarai's reaction puzzling. She struck him as a tough, self confident person. He liked the way she snapped at Jack and stood up to Lily. She may have been hurt by the fact no man selected her, but she was obviously pleased when Donald paired with her. She definitely felt lust and desire, so what happened?

He noticed Sarai had stopped weeping and was sitting quietly, her face expressionless. Well, whatever it was, he thought, she seems over it.

The exercise went on for a few minutes longer. There was much laughing and joking as the pairs took their seats.

"Anyone like to comment on the experience?" Donald asked.

A man piped up: "I don't know how many sparks I recovered but I sure saw lots of them."

Donald smiled. "I hope you're not implying that your partner held all the sparks. The sin was yours and yours alone. How many felt they had transformed the sin?"

A half dozen hands went up.

"OK. As for the others, don't despair. The exercise takes practice and it must become uninhibited. Otherwise you'll never reach the stage required for meditation."

"Donald," Jack said, "I just don't get it. With a partner like Lily, I had no trouble getting turned on. I tried to visualize a spark but I didn't succeed. I definitely don't feel like I've had a transformative experience."

"Did you feel like you were really sinning? If you're accustomed to infidelity, imagining sex with another woman may not feel like sin."

Jack shrugged. "I've been happily married for almost thirty years. I've never been unfaithful. I accept the concept that the thought is like the deed. So touching another woman and imagining having sex with her strikes me as sinful. Yet I felt nothing magical or inspiring."

Lily disagreed, "I definitely felt something supernatural take place. I can't describe it but it left me feeling uplifted. I would certainly like to repeat the sensation."

A lively discussion ensued among the participants. Most felt like Jack, others echoed Lily's feelings. Sarai was silent, serious-faced, staring off into a distant space.

"How do you feel about the experience, Sarai?" Donald asked.

Sarai looked at him, then turned away. "It was fine."

Something's wrong, Donald thought, the exercise has really affected her. He resolved to tactfully suggest she leave the course. Roberta had warned him that he could be held liable if something happened as a result of his courses. He was less worried about the possibility of liability and more concerned that his reputation would be tainted and affect attendance. His courses and books had grown in popularity over the year, his income was reaching respectable levels, and he would do everything he could to keep up the momentum.

"We'll do the exercise again. This time the women do the selecting. Remember, just let yourself go, indulge the feeling of sin, visualize the spark, and meditate on God's name."

Lily came quickly to pair with Donald. He saw Jack approach Sarai, but she shook her head and remained sitting. Another woman pulled Jack away.

Donald concentrated on Lily. He needed little imagination to envisage how she might look in bed. She writhed her hips, stretched out her body emphasizing her breasts, moaning and sighing softly. The wanton look on her face framed by the light brown hair falling in waves around her shoulders maddened him. She smiled at him, seductively stuck out her tongue and licked her lips, and began to narrow the gap between them. He nearly lost control but regained it by swiftly announcing the exercise was over. Lily returned to her seat but not before she had mouthed "later" to him. Sarai was gone.

He conducted a few more minutes of discussion and then dismissed the class. He talked to several participants who had questions or who wished to purchase reading material.

"I think you should get in touch with Sarai," Jack said to him quietly. "She didn't seem to be all there when she left — kind of faraway." Donald nodded.

Lily was the last person.

"Do you want to come to my apartment?" he asked.

"Not tonight. I have other plans."

"Give me a call when I fit your plans," he said. "Otherwise, see you next week in class."

She smiled seductively, "Oh, no, you'll see me right now. I need you very badly."

"Are you starved for sex? The floor is awfully hard."

"I'm starved for you. The floor will do."

He shut and locked the conference room door and wedged a chair back under the handle.

They came to orgasm together and lay side by side on the carpeted floor, breathing deeply, relaxing in the sudden release of sexual tension.

"You should have had no trouble visualizing holy sparks," Donald said after awhile. "The experience was total."

"Is that why you make love to me, Donald?" Lily asked, raising herself on one elbow and looking at him. "To fulfill your Kabbalah nonsense?"

"I make love to you because your body is as lovely as your face, but I never forget about Redemption. If you feel Kabbalah is nonsense, why do you attend my classes?"

She crawled on top of him. "I went to the first session out of curiosity because Kabbalah was becoming popular and besides I felt you needed my support. Your lecture did nothing for me, but you did. I just need to see more of you." She kissed him on the lips and ran her tongue into his mouth. "Are you going to expel me?" she asked, teasingly.

He really should, he thought. Was it a good idea to have her attend his classes when her only interest was him? While they had lust for each other, she would no doubt support his teachings. When the relationship cooled, particularly if it ended acrimoniously, would she go away quietly, or start a scandal? It was just one disappointed lover who had first raised the storm that destroyed his university career.

He had reinvented himself as a speaker and teacher of mysticism and Kabbalah. Slowly but steadily, he was building up a following. His fame as an erudite Kabbalist and charismatic speaker was spreading. His book *The History of the Kabbalah* was selling well. Some authorities, in their reviews, had even compared him to the late Gershom Sholem, the world's acknowledged scholar and master of Kabbalah. Would dallying with women in his classes jeopardize all this? Why take a chance? Was he truly sinning for Redemption or was he sinning because of beautiful bodies and faces?

Lily seemed to read his thoughts. "You don't have to worry — I won't upset your classes. I will help you just as I did today — pretending that my exercise with Jack Escapa was transformative. I'll act as your cheerleader."

"But why bother?" Donald asked, testily. "If it's an affair you want with me, I readily consented some time ago. We've been at it for nearly a year."

She kissed him again on the mouth and ran her lips over his face. "Maybe I just want to make sure my catch is secure. I noticed other women looking at you, even that strand of spaghetti, Sarai. I can understand why you got into trouble at university. You attract women. They throw themselves at you."

"Like you?"

"Like me. But I don't make a fuss when it's over or when I meet someone else. Even then I won't give you up. You're part of my entourage."

He gently rolled her off him, stood up and began dressing.

"Time to go. The hotel staff will be banging on the door soon."

CHAPTER 3
- SMYRNA, 1665 -
THE MESSIAH OF SMYRNA

The room was dark, lit by a guttering candle on a small table and by a beam of pale wintry light poking through a knothole in the shuttered window. The light glinted off the bearded faces of the three men sitting around the table on wooden stools.

One of the men opened a thickly bound book, turned the pages carefully until he came to a blank sheet. He pulled the candle closer, and dipped a quill into a clay pot of ink.

"Rabbis, let our Rabbinic Court begin its deliberations. I record the date —the 3rd day of Tevet, 5426 (*December 11, 1665*), and those present — Solomon Algazi, Hayyim Benveniste, and myself, Aaron Lapapa. As the rabbinic authority of the Jews of Smyrna, we have an important issue to address, one that is tearing our community apart. Namely, I refer to Rabbi Shabtai Zvi and the claim he makes that he is chosen by God to be the Messiah of Israel.

"I note for the record that we have received correspondence from the Rabbinic Court of Jerusalem concerning Rabbi Zvi's heretical and blasphemous acts there, and that he was excommunicated and expelled from the Holy Land. We have also received a missive from the Rabbinical Court of Aleppo which supports his claim with great enthusiasm. Further correspondence from Aleppo describes the unbridled emotion and excitement of our people there who regard him as the Messiah. Not only the unlettered laity but also rabbis and scholars profess belief in his mission. Even the renowned rabbi and Kabbalist, Moses Galante, has arrived in Smyrna to welcome the Messiah.

"Revered colleagues, we have a dilemma. Do we accept Shabtai Zvi as the Messiah and urge all our community to support and follow him, or do we oppose him, declare his claim as heretical, his actions as blasphemous, and purge him from our community?"

For a moment, the only sound was the scratching of the quill as Lapapa laboriously recorded his opening statement. The silence was interrupted by a series of thumps as rocks smashed against the window shutters followed by the scattering of stones and succeeded by loud shouts and laughter. Benveniste looked cautiously through the knothole.

"It is a group of workers on their way home to prepare for the Sabbath. They remind us that they are with Shabtai and we oppose him." He stepped back instinctively as another rock hit the shutter. The noise of the attackers gradually diminished as they walked off.

Benveniste was a tall, slim man, his greying beard framing bespectacled eyes and an aquiline nose. At the age of 63, he was some 15 years younger than Lapapa. There were frequent altercations between the two men as they disagreed on many points in Judaic law and traditions. They kept their acrimony largely subdued under the rules and protocols of debate that served their interactions. Benveniste felt Lapapa was too old, too inflexible in his attitude to the changing times, too rigid in his judgements concerning the cases that came before the Court for resolution. On the few occasions when he was outvoted by the full Rabbinic Court, Lapapa became furious and would stomp out of the meeting.

Lapapa looked upon Benveniste as too young and inexperienced to fully understand the depth of learning and knowledge required to make proper judgements. Besides, Benveniste was a Kabbalist and therefore susceptible to the disease of heresy that led some Kabbalists astray, like Shabtai Zvi, who were not adequately schooled in the Torah and its interpretation. But what irked him most was the feeling that Benveniste wanted Lapapa's position as Chief Rabbi of Smyrna. As long as I live, thought Aaron Lapapa, that shall not be.

"Revered rabbi," Benveniste began, "I ..."

Lapapa cut him off. "I believe Reb Hayyim that Reb Solomon should speak first in order of age and because of the many books he has written that exemplify his piety and understanding."

Benveniste, still standing at the window, nodded and took his seat at the table. "Of course, Rabbi Lapapa," he said curtly.

Solomon Algazi hesitated. He was annoyed by Lapapa's rudeness. This was not the first time he had encountered tension between his two colleagues and did not want to be embroiled in it. There were more important issues at hand.

"Reb Solomon," Lapapa said, noting his unease. "While you take more time to consider, let me tell you where I stand."

Lapapa looked at both of them, confident that they would support his judgement. "Rabbis," he said, "I am strongly of the view that Shabtai Zvi is an impostor, that he suffers from sickness of the mind or is indeed possessed by demons, that he has committed acts of heresy such as the eating of forbidden foods, that he has denied our holy days of fasting and penance and ordered them to become feast days, and has declared that he need not observe the Torah because he is exempt from its commandments and answers only to God. At his open meeting in the Agora, he uttered that which we must never utter, the ineffable name of God, the four letters which we must never pronounce. Others now follow him including the whore, his wife Sarah. Even with her present, it is reported that he has indulged in lewd acts with young virgins and has slept with women who, hopelessly enthralled by his claims, came willingly to his bed. He urges his followers to do the same. He calls this redemption through sin. By his actions and declarations he defiles our sacred Torah, the word of the one true God, blessed be He, and circumvents all the teachings and traditions that have come down to us through the ages. Therefore, my decision is we excommunicate him, purge him from our community, and demand the Turkish authorities oust him from Smyrna. Now, Reb Solomon, have you made up your mind?"

Solomon Algazi was a short bundle of a man. He eased off the stool and stood up. Despite the winter cold in the room, the stuttering light of the candle picked out droplets of perspiration on his forehead. Standing, he stared directly into the eyes of Lapapa, sitting.

"Revered Rabbi, I concur entirely with your judgement regarding Shabtai Zvi. When he first returned to Smyrna three months ago, he lived quietly with his brother Elijah. He made no messianic claims. Rather, he was respected for his piety and asceticism, his punishing of his body through fasting, and his giving of alms generously. Indeed, his singing of the morning prayers at his brother's synagogue in a very agreeable voice pleased everyone. Despite the disquieting news we received from Jerusalem, Constantinople and Aleppo, we saw no evidence of unquiet behaviour. Suddenly, three weeks ago, the acts you describe erupted. Therefore, like you, I must conclude the man is mad or harbours demons."

Solomon paused and watched Lapapa carefully noting down his comments.

"However, Rabbis, let us closely examine the situation we find ourselves in," Solomon continued. Both Lapapa and Benveniste looked at him in surprise. Solomon usually sided with Lapapa.

"The people strongly support him, believe completely in his monstrous claims, follow him everywhere, dote on his every word and action, and become more rebellious each day, threatening any who oppose him. When would members of our community have thrown rocks against the house of the Chief Rabbi of Smyrna? It has become dangerous to speak against him. Consider what happened to Hayyim Pena, a man of piety and modesty, a man who supports our community with generous alms, a man, while less learned than we are, strives to follow our traditions and God's commandments devotedly. In other words, a blameless man, a worthy man. He argued with Shabtai at the open meeting in the Agora. 'Strike this man from our midst,' shouts Shabtai. Pena fled for his life, leaving his house to be pillaged. Some good neighbours managed to get his wife and children away. Therefore, my advice is to do nothing. Let this madness play out. He has excited the attention of the Turks. Some Muslims follow him, too, but most mock him and appeal to the Qadi. It is rumoured that the Sultan's spies watch him. His maniacal pretensions will soon be exposed and ended. I repeat. We must do nothing — neither agree with him nor oppose him."

Solomon pounded the table as he finished. Again the only sound was the scratching of the quill recording Solomon's argument and decision.

Benveniste cleared his throat. "A moment, Reb Hayyim," Lapapa said. "Reb Solomon, as usual you speak with your customary wisdom and rational judgement. We concur in the view that the man is dangerous and has whipped the masses into a frenzy that threatens the good order of our community. I agree, too, that his madness will in the end destroy him. Therefore it is tempting to do nothing as you suggest. Yet to do nothing is a danger in itself. When Shabtai's stature grows too large, the Turkish authorities will squash him. They will then accuse us of approving of this madman, of knowingly allowing him to disrupt the tranquility of the Empire. They will then strike us down for not exerting our authority and fulfilling our responsibilities. Therefore, Reb Solomon, I cannot agree with your decision."

Lapapa turned to Benveniste. "Where do you stand, Reb Hayyim?"

Benveniste, sitting straight up, was easily a head taller than Lapapa and dwarfed Algazi. Benveniste kept the look on his face grim and stern. He knew what he was about to say would not go down well with his colleagues.

"Revered rabbis, I, too, harbour grave doubts concerning the authenticity of Shabtai's claims. I, too, am horrified by his acts which, on the face of it, run contrary to our sacred Torah and breach the commandments of the Almighty as well as the traditions and values laid down by our sages over the centuries. Shabtai believes he has three states of being. In his illuminated state, such as now when his egregious behaviour occurs, he insists the Almighty is with him, gives him direction, and promises to foil those who oppose him. In the state when he screams, tears his clothing, wails piteously, and seeks solitude, he claims the Almighty has forsaken him and demons have possessed him. In between these two states, he is like you and me, and goes about his daily affairs with probity and dignity. Is this a picture of madness or a manifestation of the Divine Spirit? How can we know for certain? Revered rabbis..."

"Reb Hayyim," Lapapa interrupted him, angrily. "How can we know for certain? Are you sowing the seeds of doubt into our deliberations?"

Benveniste held out his arms in a gesture of supplication. "Please, Rabbi Lapapa, allow me to finish. It is not only the untutored that follow Shabtai. You have said yourself that many renowned scholars and rabbis, equal in learning to us, are convinced he is the true Messiah. Nathan of Gaza, of doubtless sanctity and reputation, prophesied Shabtai Zvi to be the Messiah long before he knew him. Should we not consider carefully our position regarding Shabtai? I was first opposed but now I waver in the face of the growing body of evidence."

Lapapa stood abruptly, knocking the wooden stool over. He glared at Benveniste, his mouth distorted into a contemptuous sneer.

"You waver? You waver?" Lapapa shouted. "Waver in the face of what evidence — a riotous mass of fools who share Shabtai's madness, enthusiastic support by men who should know better? Reb Hayyim, there can be no compromise on this issue. The teachings of the sages are clear. Two messiahs will release us from bondage, redeem us, and restore us to the Land of Israel. The first will be the Messiah of the house of Joseph, the second, the Messiah of the house of David. Shabtai claims to be the Messiah of the house of Jacob. Utter nonsense! There is no such messiah. He insists he is the son of God. What of this? We are all the sons of God. Are we thus all messiahs? We are all familiar with his sacrilegious, blasphemous, heretical, scurrilous acts. We cannot simply stand aside and allow him free license to destroy the very foundations of our Judaic life. I say we oppose him no matter the personal dangers and cast him out of our community."

Benveniste rose slowly and paced up and down the room, at times disappearing into the blackness beyond the candle light. He faced Lapapa and spoke calmly and softly.

"Rabbi, one admires your zeal and learning and leadership of our Rabbinic Court. However, you will agree that our sacred Torah, the very word of God, does not mention two Messiahs. The concept of the two Messiahs came later and is part of our Judaic traditions. The Kabbalah tells us that the soul of the Messiah existed before the Creation and migrates from man to man as God directs to surface in the world at times when the plight of his people becomes desperate. Perhaps that is the situation now. All predict — including the Gentiles — that redemption is at hand. Shabtai Zvi has convinced almost all our people in the Empire and in Europe that he is the Messiah. Until we get a sign that he is not, should we not consider supporting him, or as Reb Solomon proposes, neither support nor oppose him?"

Lapapa pounded the table so hard that the ink pot splattered ink on the table and the book.

"Rabbi Benveniste," he thundered, "I, who once endorsed your rabbinic certificate, now revoke it. You are a renegade! An apostate! Like your master Shabtai, a heretic, a blasphemer! Leave my house immediately. Join your pack of rock throwers. You are no different than they.

You are all equally misguided. Shabtai is a demon, possessed by demons, maddened by demons. Samael rides on his shoulders, Lillith strides by his side. And this is the man you want us to follow? Heresy! Blasphemy!"

Breathing hard, Lapapa paused, tears lit briefly by the candle trickled into his beard. "Woe is all of Israel that hearkens to this devil. The Almighty will not brook this departure from His commandments. He will destroy this false messiah who leads His people astray. I pray to the Almighty that He will show us mercy and not destroy us as well."

Benveniste waited until Lapapa had regained his composure and was breathing normally. "Rabbi Lapapa, it is clear the three of us have differing points of view. Nevertheless, two of us — Reb Solomon and I —concur that we should at least remain neutral. Should this not be the decision of our Court?"

Lapapa looked sadly at both of them. He spoke softly, "Rabbis, our Court has ended. Tomorrow morning, when I deliver the Sabbath homily at the Portuguese synagogue, I will speak out against this monster that desecrates our Torah, mocks our traditions and all that we hold sacred from the time of Abraham, Isaac and Jacob. I will explain carefully to the congregation why Shabtai Zvi is a false messiah. You will see, the congregation will embrace my judgement and the tide will turn against him."

At midnight, a thousand burning torches held aloft by a thousand hands lit up the wide stretch of sandy beach bordering the Bay of Smyrna. A thousand voices greeted the cavalcade of horses and riders as it clattered off the last cobbled streets of Smyrna onto the strand. At the head of the cavalcade, on a white horse, rode Shabtai Zvi, resplendent in a white flowing headdress that fell to the dark cloak enveloping his white mantle and caftan.

Lifting his arms, Shabtai acknowledged the adulation of the crowd. He looked past the dancing light of the torches to the black waters of the bay, ruffled by a cold December wind. A cloudless sky displayed its treasure of myriads of starry points and a large, almost whole moon.

"Children of Israel, we greet you," Shabtai shouted.

"The Messiah is here! The Messiah has come!" the crowd called out. Dancing and singing, it pressed forward. Shabtai's horse reared and whinnied shrilly. Shabtai kept his seat. The other riders urged their horses around him to form a barrier. A rider blew a series of trills on a shofar and the crowd quietened.

"Children of Israel, look to the heavens, to the sign that the Almighty has sent. See the waxing moon. It is gibbous, not fully formed. Tomorrow, the moon will return fulfilled. Tomorrow, the son of God will be blessed with fulfillment."

A roar of approval burst out and reverberated through the near streets of Smyrna. Shabtai raised his arms, the shofar blew, and the crowd fell silent.

"Children of Israel, be calm. We do not wish to wake the Janissaries. It is not yet time to grab the Grand Turk by the beard. Be patient. The time of Redemption is soon upon us. Prepare yourselves. Pray, do penance, give alms to those less fortunate, pay all your debts and absolve those debts owed you, resolve not to sin, make peace with those you strive against. And now make way. We go to the sea to wash the sins from our body and to cleanse ourselves for the glorious day coming."

The crowd parted and followed as the riders moved toward the shore. Shabtai dismounted and removed his clothing. A woman aided him.

"Shabtai, husband," she said affectionately, "I fear for you. The water is so cold now. Do not stay immersed too long."

"You must not be afraid, my Sarah," he replied. "It is God who directs me and will suffer me no harm."

Naked, slowly, without flinching, he walked into the shallow waters of the bay. When the water reached his chin, he ducked below the surface. The torches lit up the spot where he had disappeared. As the moments passed, Sarah and the onlookers grew anxious. Some made to rush into the water to rescue Shabtai but the riders stopped them. At last, his head appeared. A murmur of relief spread rapidly through the crowd. Twice more, Shabtai immersed himself and then walked calmly to the beach. Sarah wrapped him in a large woollen blanket.

Dressed and mounted, Shabtai called out to his followers: "Children of Israel, return to your homes. Disperse quietly. Join us in the morning at our brother Elijah's synagogue. Now, we return to Elijah's house to fast and to pray the night away."

The cavalcade moved carefully through the massed throng, the riders insulating Shabtai from those wanting desperately to touch him. Sarah walked in front of Shabtai, calling out loudly but melodiously, "Make way, make way for the Messiah of Israel."

Elijah's house was ablaze with light, the windows unshuttered and open. The faithful gathered outside and watched rapturously as Shabtai moved continuously from one end of the house to the other singing ecstatically his homage to the one true God.

A Janissary patrol pushed through the crowd and stopped to watch the scene. They had no liking for large groups gathering at night and shooed the onlookers away. The crowd thinned out and the patrol moved on.

Long before the Sabbath morning prayers were to begin, the synagogue was packed. The events some of the congregants had seen the night before were passed on to others, often embellished. Shabtai had stayed submerged longer than any man possibly could. God had appeared to him as a golden fish, a sign of good things. He had floated through his brother's house accompanied by a chorus of angels. Even the Janissaries were afraid to intervene. He was truly a man of miracles. Redemption was at hand, the Messiah was among them.

The congregation brimmed over with excitement and anticipation as the deacon ran in: "Rise! Rise! He comes!"

A roar of jubilation greeted Shabtai. All the men were on their feet, waving their arms wildly. Sarah tore loose the curtain that separated the women from the men. Some of the women screamed hysterically, some fainted, others threw themselves prostrate. The turmoil went on without stop as Shabtai mounted the steps leading to the raised platform at the front. A white peaked cap covered his head; a royal blue cloak flowed from his shoulders to the floor, offsetting his white silk mantle, caftan and pantaloons. Finally, after many minutes, Shabtai pulled a shofar from his belt and blew one long shrill note. The crowd quickly fell silent.

"Children of Israel, we greet you on this historical Sabbath day. In a little while the Almighty will reveal why this day will be enshrined in the annals of the Israelites. First, the Sabbath morning prayers call us."

Shabtai became totally absorbed as he moved slowly and gracefully through the liturgy, his dulcet tenor voice soaring and falling melodiously, enthralling his listeners with its intensity and beauty. The congregation joined in vigorously at the responses and, at the rallying cry of Jewry, shouted with him loudly and joyously: "Hear, O Israel, the Lord is our God, the lord is One."

A man entered a side door of the synagogue, pushed through the knot of worshippers, beckoned to the deacon, and whispered into the deacon's ear. Alarmed, the deacon ran quickly up the steps and spoke to Shabtai. The beatific look on Shabtai's face changed to ugly anger.

"Children of Israel," he called out, "we are apprised that, even at this very moment, Rabbi Lapapa speaks out against us behind locked doors at the Portuguese Synagogue. Who will follow us to stop this heresy against our messianic mission?"

The congregation rose to its feet, its roar of protest palpably deadly.

"Bring an axe, Deacon," Shabtai ordered. "We will break down the doors to this monster's den."

"Revered Rabbi, it is the Sabbath. We may not," the deacon said, hesitantly.

"Foolish Deacon," snapped Shabtai. "It is we who command you — we who answer to God alone."

The Portuguese Synagogue was a short distance away on the cul-de-sac that ended Synagogue Street. Shabtai, followed by his congregation, now a brawling, raucous mob, walked quickly and purposefully. Passersby flattened themselves against walls or fled into other synagogues lining the street.

At a signal from Shabtai, the deacon swung the axe roundly into the thick cedar door. Twice more he struck, widening the fissures that now scarred the door. As he was about to swing again, the door opened.

"What means this?' Solomon Algazi shouted. "It is the Sabbath and this is a house of God."

With a sweep of his arm, Shabtai hurled Algazi aside and marched into the synagogue. The congregation faced the interlopers, some in fear, some in anger, and most crying out "Shabtai! Shabtai! Messiah of Israel."

At the pulpit, Rabbi Lapapa gaped, eyes wide in fear and dread, shaken by the effrontery of the invasion. Shabtai proceeded to the raised platform where Lapapa stood, faced the congregants as well as the surging horde of his followers, raised his arms, and above the tumult, shouted: "Silence!" The noise quickly abated.

He confronted Lapapa. "Rabbi, you sin when you speak against us, we whose messianic mission comes directly from the Mouth of the Almighty. Therefore, you blaspheme the Almighty. You shame us. You shame the Children of Israel. Be gone from here, or do you wish the Deacon's axe do its damage on your neck."

Lapapa's face was as white as his beard, but he stood his ground. His voice shook as he answered shrilly, "Nay, false impostor. It is you who blaspheme our God, blessed be He. You are not the Messiah. You desecrate the Sabbath. You incite your followers to ignore the Almighty's commandments. You utter the unutterable name of God. You perform indecent acts with women. You trample on our traditional ways and mock the values vouchsafed us by the one true God. Nay, Reb Zvi, it is you who must be excommunicated and flung from our midst. Leave our synagogue immediately or I will call for the Janissaries."

There was a roar of outraged protest from the mob as it pressed forward to the platform steps. Lapapa shrank back hard against the curtained Torah Cabinet as though seeking protection from the scrolls hidden inside.

Shabtai, face flushed, screamed wildly: "Stand back, Children of Israel. You, Rabbi Lapapa, you call me blasphemous? You are a piece of carrion. You are like the unclean beasts our sacred Torah speaks against. Leave our presence. Return to your stable. You are no longer a member of our community, you..."

"Blessed Messiah, I beg you, hear me out," Benveniste interrupted, coming forward. "All Rabbi Lapapa asks is that you offer some proof. Then he will eagerly embrace you."

"Proof?" Shabtai, a contemptuous sneer twisting his lips, leapt down the platform steps, and faced Benveniste. Both men were the same height, but Shabtai seemed to tower over Benveniste.

"Proof? Is that what you want? What sort of proof shall we offer? Shall we split the Aegean Sea so that you may walk across to Athens to indulge in its brothels? Shall we stop the sun as it wheels downward in the west so that you may keep your shops open a little longer and sell the last of your unclean wares? Or, given your profound inability to understand the word of God or the word of His Messenger, shall we cause manna to fall from the heavens so that, fed, you no longer need to teach your nonsense to your credulous students? Proof? We give you proof."

Shabtai turned to the congregations: "Am I the Messiah of Israel?"

The approval of thousands of voices reverberated to the top of the synagogue's high ceiling and rattled the glass chandeliers hanging there. Benveniste, enthralled, turned to face the mob. Here and there he recognized famous rabbis, like Moses Galante and Daniel Pinto, knowledgeable and serious scholars and sages who could easily discern between a false messiah and a true. They were as enthusiastic in their support of Shabtai as the hundreds of simpler folk surrounding them. Who was he, far less learned than they, to challenge their judgement? In the wind of exhilaration that blew through him, his doubts were swept away. He fell to his knees before Shabtai.

Shabtai held up his arms and the crowd fell silent. He laid a hand on Benveniste's head.

"Rabbi Hayyim Benveniste, we hereby appoint you Chief Rabbi of Smyrna to replace Rabbi Aaron Lapapa who is excommunicated as a heretic and blasphemer for impugning the righteousness of our mission. Rabbi Lapapa, begone from our midst!"

"I will not!" shouted Lapapa. "You have no authority to depose me and to replace me with this spineless imbecile. The Jewry of Smyrna must decide."

"Jewry of Smyrna," said Shabtai laughing, "How vote you?"

The mob surged forward, pushing around both Shabtai and Benveniste, and charged up the platform steps. Lapapa ran to an opening in the back of the altar, raced down some stairs and fled through a back door.

"Wait!" shouted Shabtai. "We will deal with him later. Return to your places. It is time now for the reading of our sacred Torah. Rabbi Benveniste will assist us."

The ornate wooden doors to the Torah cabinet were opened and the curtain concealing the Torah scrolls was pushed aside. Benveniste took out one of the scrolls and showed it to the congregation while all sang the greeting to the Torah. Benveniste held the scroll by its bottom handles and the deacon carefully removed the silver crowns adorning the top handles, the silver breastplate with the Ten Commandments, and the flaxen caftan that clothed it. Benveniste laid the scroll carefully on the reader's desk and rolled it open to the part for that Sabbath.

Shabtai chanted the blessing preceding the reading in his melodious voice, eliciting ecstatic sighs from the onlookers.

"We call first upon our brother Elijah to join me in reading the first portion."

Elijah came dutifully to the reader's desk and stood beside Shabtai as he read the portion. Before Elijah could slip aside after the reading, Shabtai held him back.

"Our dear and loyal brother, you have been a faithful believer in our mission since long before our return to Smyrna. Therefore, on the day we seize the crown of the Sultan, we hereby appoint you King of Mesopotamia, sole ruler of all its lands and people, and all appertaining thereto, including the ancient home of Abraham. All hail the king of Mesopotamia."

The applause was thunderous as Elijah embraced and kissed his brother. Elijah was hugged, touched and thumped on the back as he returned to his seat. Moses Galante was the next to join Shabtai.

After the reading, Shabtai stopped him from leaving and both faced the congregation.

"Children of Israel, Rabbi Galante is an outstanding scholar, a sage of great repute, who has a profound understanding of the Kabbalah, and recognized early the truthfulness and significance of our messianic mission. He has strongly supported us and will now be rewarded. We hereby appoint you, Rabbi Moses Galante, King of all the provinces and states that make up the land of the Italians. Hail the King of Italy."

During the next hour, family, friends and supporters found themselves raised to the stature of kings and princes as Shabtai divided the world into a manageable empire he would control as the Messiah.

When the readings ended, the Torah scroll was reclothed with its covering and ornaments. Shabtai lifted the scroll, showed it to the congregation, and then cradled it in his arms. Instead of returning the scroll to its cabinet as tradition required, he danced with it, swaying his hips seductively, and swirling round and round the reader's desk. Occasionally he lifted the Torah scroll to his lips and kissed it, humming in a high pitched keening voice. Still dancing, he gave full throat to a Spanish song of love, in praise of the beautiful Meliselda, a royal princess.

This night my cavaliers
Bed I a maiden sweet
Whose peer never did I meet
Throughout my many lusty years

Meliselda is this beauty's name
Meliselda who set my heart aflame

By the stream where the banks cling
To the hill that reaches to the sky
Lovely Meliselda met I
Fair daughter of the royal king

Meliselda is this beauty's name
Meliselda who set my heart aflame

I come to bathe, said she
In the cool waters of the stream
Pure maiden that I seem
Yet my lover you must be

Meliselda is this beauty's name
Meliselda who set my heart aflame

Her body — I do not lie
White as the falling snow
Her cheeks like rubies glow
Sunset on a silken sky

Meliselda is this beauty's name
Meliselda who set my heart aflame

Her hair all russet curls
Lined with threads of gold
Her nose uplifted bold
Her teeth like tiny pearls

Meliselda is this beauty's name
Meliselda who set my heart aflame

Her breasts erect and proud
The nipples eager for a kiss
Her thighs a promise of bliss
Delicate feet, soft as a cloud

Meliselda is this beauty's name
Meliselda who set my heart aflame

At the end of the first verse, Shabtai pointed to the congregation and sang the refrain. He began the refrain again, urging the audience to sing along. At first the response was ragged, but at the next refrain, the singing was loud, raucous, off key, but enthusiastic. At the end, the congregation was on its feet and sang the refrain over and over.

As the crowd grew quiet, Benveniste called out: "Blessed Messiah, to some the song may appear profane in the presence of the Torah and on the Sabbath. Surely you will explain its meaning."

For a moment, anger flushed Shabtai's face but quickly gave way to a smile.

"Of course, Chief Rabbi of Smyrna, the song needs clarification. I forget you are not well schooled in the Kabbalah."

He turned to the congregation. "Children of Israel, we decree that this song must hereafter be included in the Sabbath prayers. Let us explain its import. When the Almighty created our world, He placed among us the Shechina, His Divine presence in its female form. The Shechina is the expression of God's love for His chosen people. What is Meliselda — pure, cleansed, and fairest of the fair in face and body— but the symbolic embodiment of the Shechina? Meliselda is the daughter of the royal king. Who is the Royal King?"

The response was immediate. "God Almighty, blessed be He," shouted the congregation.

"And the narrator who sings of Meliselda," Shabtai continued, "who is this narrator? It is you, Children of Israel. Embrace the Shechina for when the Shechina is loved, you are returning the love of God. Only then will redemption occur."

A murmur of approval and expressions of awe and admiration swept through the congregation. Shabtai returned the Torah scroll to its Cabinet and turned once more to the congregation.

"Children of Israel, an important moment has been reached in the sacred history of our people. We call the King of Mesopotamia."

Shabtai sat on a stool. Elijah approached him, carrying a small bottle. He removed Shabtai's headdress. "Blessed Messiah and brother, with this oil, I anoint you." He poured the contents of the bottle over Shabtai's head, worked in the oil with his fingers, and replaced the headdress.

Shabtai stood and raised his arms. The entire congregation rose to its feet.

"Hear, O Israel, the Lord is our God, the Lord is One. Children of Israel, attend our words carefully."

Shabtai paused and looked around. A deathly silence prevailed, no sound of breathing, no shuffling of feet, no sniffling.

"On this 4th day of Tevet in the year 5426, in accordance with the will of the Almighty, spoken to us directly and through the revelations and prophesies of Nathan of Gaza, and in the presence of our loyal congregation, the Kings and Princes appointed here today, and the many rabbis and scholars faithful in their dedication to our mission, we hereby proclaim ourselves the anointed Son of God, the Messiah of Jacob and Israel."

A thunderous avalanche of acclamation, punctuated by hysterical screams, poured through the building. The double doors blew open, window panes rattled and the chandeliers rained down shards of glass. The people in the front pews circled Shabtai and danced wildly and ecstatically around him. The news spread quickly. The other synagogues on the street disgorged their congregations. A seething mass of humanity pressed toward the Portuguese Synagogue, screaming its adulation. Men, women danced together, hugging and kissing unashamedly, some cried unrestrainedly as joy and exuberance overcame them, some fell into sudden fits and shouted out their visions and revelations. The din reached outside Synagogue Street and drew in more of the community who joined the growing mob.

Shabtai appeared, royal cloak streaming out behind him, carried on a chair held aloft by four brawny men. Nodding to his followers, he waved majestically. Sarah preceded him, calling out loudly, "Make way for the Messiah of Israel," and the mob parted like waves before the prow of a ship.

The entire Synagogue Street was now packed with a shouting, screaming mass of seemingly demented people, dancing, jumping up and down, crying, "Shabtai! Shabtai! Our Messiah has come!" or, more dangerously, "Redemption is come! The Sultan beware!" The cries were picked up and became a massive chant.

A clearing in the crowd opened around Shabtai. Men and women, holding hands, danced in a large circle around him, while the four men holding the chair rotated him slowly.

Sarah stood before him. "My husband. My Messiah. I dance for you."

Slowly at first, then more and more rapidly, she leaned and twisted, swayed her hips provocatively, flailed her arms, stamped her feet in tune to some melody only she could hear. She pulled off her headdress and veil and flung it aside. She slipped off her mantle and let it fall to the ground. With complete abandon, she threw herself against the circle of dancers, turning as she went, kissing the men, hugging the women. A man reached out, grasped the bottom of her knee-length caftan, and pulled it up and off her, revealing the tight fitting shirt and the contours of the well endowed bosom that strained against it. Sarah laughed, leapt onto the man, grasping his waist with her pantalooned legs, and thrust her breasts into his face. She freed herself and joined a group of women who had also disposed of headdress, mantles and caftans.

So intent were they on the dance and the celebration, those closest to Shabtai did not hear the warning sounds of the mehters and drums. Sarah woke abruptly from her state of intense frenzy and found herself staring into the open mouthed face of a Janissary officer. Behind him stood a platoon of red mantled soldiers, muskets at the ready. Into the sea of humanity packing Synagogue Street came streams of red mantles, breaking up the mob into pockets, pushing the pockets out of the street, clubbing the reluctant with their musket stocks.

The Janissary officer looked hard at Sarah's face and swept his eyes up and down her body. "Madam, this is unseemly. Dress yourself immediately."

Sarah saw the look of lust and admiration on his face. "Perhaps, noble officer, you could help me."

She realized she had gone too far when the officer angrily whipped out his cutlass, and raised it to behead her. She put a look of contrite entreaty on her face and saw the officer relent. She turned away to find her clothing.

The officer called out to Shabtai. "Sir, what means this madness? Are you responsible for this riot?"

"This is not a riot," Shabtai replied haughtily. "This is a joyful religious celebration of a great event. You will not harm my people. It is time for them to disperse."

He blew long single notes on his shofar until the crowd quietened. The Janissaries backed away, the mehters and drums stopped. There was dead silence on the street.

"Return to your homes," Shabtai shouted. "These soldiers will not bother you. We await the Almighty's direction. The time for penance and prayer has come. We are the Messiah of Jacob and Israel. Hallelujah."

The crowd sang "Hallelujah" as it moved out of the street. Shabtai, now standing on the street, remained with a small knot of followers. Sarah was dressed with her veil firmly in place.

"Sir, you must leave too," the officer demanded.

"We return to our synagogue. It is our right. It is the Sabbath."

Ignoring the officer, Shabtai turned and walked away, beckoning the few remaining people to follow him. Sarah did not move, ready to forestall the officer's anger. A Janissary stepped forward, musket aimed at Shabtai's retreating back.

"Noble officer," she said softly, "I beg you to spare my husband."

The officer signalled for the soldier to step back. Through the translucent veil, the officer could see the white teeth and the eyes above the veil smiling the woman's gratitude.

"What is your husband's name, madam?" the officer asked, gruffly, trying to hide the emotion welling up in him.

"Noble officer, his name is Shabtai Zvi. He has just become the leader of our community in Smyrna. We are overjoyed at his ascendancy. Perhaps you will forgive us for celebrating so zealously? To whom may I address my prayers of gratitude?"

This woman is a devil, thought the officer; I am nothing but potter's clay in her hands.

"I am Corporal Tepel. Address your prayers to the Sultan. Advise your husband to be more respectful in future."

What was required was an abrupt turn away, but still he lingered, unable to withdraw from this woman who beguiled him. He is handsome,

Sarah decided; shorter than Shabtai, but I like his strong tanned face, so clean shaven, and that pointy moustache — how I would like to tweak it.

"Corporal Tepel, I shall do as you wish. I am forever in your debt." She bowed her head and watched with some regret as the corporal marched off with his platoon.

Throughout the next week, the festivities continued unabated. Exhausted revellers collapsed and lay on the street or were carried away by friends and family. Large crowds gathered in the ancient Agora and listened rapturously to Shabtai's sermons. Then they sang and danced wildly for hours afterwards.

Shabtai was everywhere, walking the streets of the Jewish Quarter, receiving the enthusiastic greetings and adulation of his followers, and threatening those who were not immediately forthcoming with words of support.

The Janissaries and local police intervened to break up the largest gatherings. Tension mounted as Shabtai followers became more rebellious and frequently refused to move off. The police responded with increasing violence and inflicted casualties and some deaths among the faithful. The ecstatic crowds took no notice. The Messiah had come. Redemption was at hand. Jerusalem would soon be theirs. What did a broken head matter or even death when the Resurrection was so close?

Shabtai and Elijah were absent when a Janissary patrol led by Corporal Tepel pounded on the entry to their home. The servant who opened the door fled fearfully into the interior of the house as Tepel, accompanied by three soldiers, pushed his way into the entrance hall. It was a Friday morning, cold, with white whispers of snow falling.

The commotion brought Sarah down the winding staircase that led up to the second floor. She was still hastily adjusting her headdress and fixing her veil. In the few seconds before the veil was firmly in place, Tepel caught a glimpse of the features that so aroused him. He felt his resolve to be firm floundering.

"Sir, what means this intrusion?" Sarah demanded angrily.

Tepel, his authority compromised by his feelings, could say only mildly, "Madam, I seek your husband, Shabtai Zvi, on a matter of utmost importance."

Sarah recognized Tepel and felt again his strong physical attractiveness. She stifled her anger and said softly, "My husband is away until early afternoon. Then he must prepare for the Sabbath and can see no one. May I tell him you will return tomorrow night after sundown?"

Tepel realized she was toying with him and should be punished or at least reprimanded. But he saw the sparkle in her eyes and felt she was more inviting than audacious.

"Madam, the matter is too serious to be left until tomorrow night. I need to speak with your husband as soon as possible," he said as firmly as he could.

Sarah wanted to prolong the conversation. In addition to her feelings for him, she had to know what had brought him to their house.

"Corporal Tepel, perhaps you could impart the matter to me and I will bring it to my husband's attention as soon as he returns."

Tepel knew he should not relate important matters to a woman without her husband present or at least a male relative. Yet the use of his name, and her soft, sultry voice were in danger of undermining him.

Sarah recognized and relished the struggle he was going through. She read the wanting of her in his eyes and smiled her encouragement.

"May I offer you and your men a bowl of hot chicken broth to take away the winter cold?" she asked.

The soldiers with Tepel showed immediate interest. They were fed only once a day and extra rations were always welcome.

"That is very kind of you, madam," Tepel said. "We accept your hospitality."

The soldiers followed a servant to the back of the house. Sarah led Tepel into a small room lit by a large window, just off the entrance hall. They settled on stuffed pillows. A servant placed steaming bowls of soup and a plate of cakes on the table between them.

"Now, Corporal Tepel," Sarah said, after they had taken tentative sips from the scalding hot liquid, "may I know this serious matter that brings you to our house?"

"Madam, your husband seems to be at the centre of continuing troublesome activities and riotous gatherings in your community. The authorities have reached the conclusion that your husband incites rebellion. Some days ago a delegation was sent to the Sultan to urge that your husband be arrested and incarcerated or executed. Your husband must insist, and take the necessary steps required, that your community return to its peaceful ways and good order for which the Jews of Smyrna are noted. He must leave Smyrna as quickly as possible. Then, when a warrant for his arrest arrives, I can justly report that all is quiet and the perpetrator gone."

Sarah leaned forward. Her loose veil fell, revealing much of her face. Tepel could see the lines of concern on her forehead, her eyes looking fearfully out at him, and her lips pressed together. There was a long moment of silence.

"Why do you warn us, Corporal Tepel?"

"Madam, I am a soldier, not a civic guardsman. I fight armies, not unruly people who should know better. If your husband continues, the suppression of him will affect all your people, particularly those closest to him." He hesitated, felt his face reddening, and blurted out, "I fear for you."

It was Sarah's turn to blush. Before she could respond, the front door was thrown open and a wave of cold winter air flowed through the entrance hall and into their meeting room.

Shabtai, accompanied by six young students and Rabbi Benveniste, stormed into the hall and shouted, "We are informed that Janissaries have invaded our home." He caught sight of Tepel emerging from the side room. "Sir, what do you here?"

Sarah pushed her way past Tepel. "Husband, they did not invade. I invited them in for some hot broth." In Hebrew, she said to Shabtai quietly, "Husband, please listen to Corporal Tepel. He has an urgent matter to discuss with you. In the meantime, I will look to the needs of our other guests."

The six students followed Sarah. Tepel noted the looks of adoration that spread over their faces. I am not the only one smitten, he thought.

Benveniste stayed with Shabtai and watched him bristle and become angrier as Tepel laid out the danger they were in.

"We fear not the authorities of Smyrna," Shabtai protested. "We are the anointed of God, the Messiah of Israel. The Lord protects us. We will go personally to the Governor to object."

A startled Tepel held up a restraining hand. "Sir, I have come here to warn you on my own initiative. The Governor of Smyrna will question my loyalty if he discovers that I have made you aware of the plans against you. I urge you not to take any action other than what I have recommended. Quieten your people and leave Smyrna."

Benveniste could see the calamity that was about to descend on the Jews of Smyrna. Surely, this was not the time to adopt a belligerent attitude.

"Holy Messiah," he said in Hebrew, "the Almighty *is* protecting you. It is completely unheard of that a Janissary would intercede on your behalf. The Almighty directs you through this messenger."

His placating remarks had the desired effect. Shabtai's anger subsided. "Rabbi, you are right. How could we not see this? We must do penance." He turned to Corporal Tepel. "Sir, we thank you for your advice and the risk you are taking on our behalf. In my sermon tomorrow morning I will request that our people temper their celebrations and as soon as the Sabbath ends tomorrow night, we will prepare for departure. We have duties and obligations elsewhere."

As the soldiers left the house, Sarah had a brief moment alone with Tepel. She thanked him profusely for his help. "Hopefully, we will meet again, Corporal Tepel."

"It is not likely, madam. I, too, leave Smyrna shortly. I am bound for Adrianople."

They stared at each other. Sarah had let her veil loose and smiled wilfully at him. She enjoyed the longing in his eyes.

"Madam, I take the gift of your face with me. May Allah protect you and keep you from harm," Tepel said, bowing and turning away.

"May the Lord protect you as well, Corporal Tepel," she called after him. He nodded but didn't look back and didn't see the tears welling in her eyes.

It was early March before the news reached Smyrna of Shabtai Zvi's arrest. In disbelief, Benveniste read and reread the letter brought him by Rabbi Lapapa.

"So much for your Messiah who would grab the Grand Turk by the beard. The Grand Turk struck first," said Lapapa triumphantly. "Perhaps now you will disclaim to all your belief in the heretic."

The two were sitting in Benveniste's study in his modest home on a narrow lane leading away from Synagogue Street. The only window in the room was still shuttered in the early morning. A candlestick lit up the table between the two men and the book lined wall behind Benveniste.

"The letter is from Solomon Algazi. Neither of you is a friend of the Messiah. How can I be certain it is true?" Benveniste asked.

Lapapa shrugged. "Soon others will hear as well. There can be no doubt. Your Messiah was intercepted on the Sea of Marmara on his way to Constantinople. The Almighty made no attempt to rescue him. No sudden wind blew the Turkish vessel away. The sea did not split and engulf the Turks. Solomon witnessed him brought ashore and in chains. Shabtai lies in prison."

Benveniste ran his fingers reflectively through his beard. "Rabbi Lapapa, your gloating is premature. According to Solomon's letter, the Messiah was brought before the Grand Vizier who sentenced him to prison. Execution is the usual Turkish punishment. Why was he not executed? Does this not indicate that the Messiah of Israel is indeed protected by the Almighty? For whatever reason, the One has consigned the Messiah to prison for awhile, perhaps to wait the moment of Redemption, to restore his strength for the arduous battle that awaits us. No, the fact that he is permitted to live confirms my belief in him. This I will communicate to the Jews of Smyrna."

Lapapa lowered his head and groaned. "What will it take to convince you the man is a false messiah? I came out of hiding believing I would now be safe. I can see that others will believe as you do, that reason will not prevail."

Benveniste reached across the table and put a comforting hand on Lapapa's shoulder. "Rabbi, have no fear of me. I mean you no harm. Stay here until dark when you can return safely to your abode."

Lapapa nodded. "Thank you, Rabbi. I will remember your kindness when the tide turns. And turn it will. The current situation cannot go on much longer. The excitement in our community, in the Empire and in Europe has become feverish. Reports reach me daily that our commerce has stopped, that the rich are selling their homes and treasure to prepare for the move to the Promised Land, and that even the poor have ceased to work and await deliverance. All this has been stoked by that madman you call the Messiah. Our only hope is that prison will shut him up. But if it does not, if he continues to spout his nonsense from his dungeon, then our people will behave even more exuberantly. Then the Empire will do what it always does when it suspects sedition and rebellion. It will stifle him. I pray to God, the Empire will spare the rest of us. All this chaos that Shabtai has wrought will come to an end."

Chapter 4
- Toronto, 2006 -
Donald and Sarai

The Shabtai Zvi Kabbalah Society was located in a shabby strip mall on Dundas Street in the west end of Toronto, not far from Highway 427, the north-south route connecting two main arteries that bounded the city. On some days, even from the confines of his office, Donald could hear the muted roar of the highway. As the Society grew, he would eventually relocate to a more prestigious setting. Right now, this was all he could afford and the rent was reasonable, given the 5000 sq. ft. he occupied.

The Society was above a restaurant and was reached by a narrow stairway that led into a small reception area. A coat rack hid in the corner where the door opened. Four reception chairs, their backs against the windowed wall fronting the building, faced a wide desk where the receptionist sat. The wide desk protected a corridor that led toward the back of the building. Donald's office was immediately off this corridor, toilet facilities and a conference room on the other side. Behind the enclosed space was a large open room for meditation, Society meetings, and classes.

It was the morning after the seminar at the Royal. Donald was busy working on the monthly newsletter for the Society's 150 members. In addition to relating Society events, the newsletter included an essay written by Donald on aspects of Kabbalah, as well as scholarly, academic pieces that had received good reviews. He was also working on a detailed analysis of Shabtai Zvi's teachings and their relationship to contemporary religions. In addition, daily, he answered scores of emails he received concerning points of doctrine and questions of faith.

He was so immersed in his work that he failed to hear the muffled sound of voices coming from the reception area.

A woman burst through the door at the top of the stairs, anxiously interlacing her fingers, and demanded of the startled receptionist, "Donald May, where is he? I need to see him right away."

"Mr. May is occupied at the moment. Do you have an appointment?" she asked, keeping her voice solicitous as she recognized she had a distraught woman on her hands.

"No. I attended his class last night and I need to talk to him. Tell him it's Sarai Stone."

"Perhaps I can help you. My name is Amanda Cadman. I'm an officer of the Society and one of its founding members. Mr. May and I often collaborate on his lectures and presentations."

"No! No!" she said loudly, gesticulating with her arms. "It's personal. I need to see him and him only."

Amanda looked at her appraisingly. She knew Donald was promiscuous and generous with his sexual favours. But this woman didn't look like the type he was attracted to. She was too thin, plain faced, dressed severely in black skirt and white blouse. Amanda was about to turn her away when Donald appeared in the reception room on his way to lunch.

"Donald, I need to see you," Sarai pleaded, and grabbed his arm.

I knew she should leave the course, Donald thought, kicking himself for not following up earlier. "Sarai, what a pleasant surprise! What brings you here?"

"I need to see you!"

He took her hands in his. "Of course, Sarai. I'll always make time for you. I'm just on my way to a Turkish restaurant close by. Why don't you join me?"

He had tried to sound comforting but her anxiety increased.

"No! No! I need to see you here, now, in private." She tried to hold the sobs back but her whole body was shaking.

Amanda looked at him enquiringly. Donald put an arm around Sarai and dragged her toward the corridor. "Amanda, why don't you go to lunch and lock up? I'm not expecting anyone until 2 pm. Sarai, let's go to my office where we can talk privately."

Amanda frowned but nodded. There was no one coming at 2 pm. Donald was signalling that he needed two hours.

In his office, he held her tight and let her cry. She buried her face in his short-sleeved summer shirt, and occasionally hammered his chest with her fists. After awhile, the sobs subsided. He felt her go limp, sat her down in a chair and pulled one up beside her.

He watched her, slumped in the chair, her head back, tears still trickling down her cheeks, mouth twitching, eyes staring at the ceiling. For the first time, he actually felt concern for her. He dabbed his handkerchief over her face.

"Please tell me, Sarai. What is troubling you?"

She didn't respond but straightened up in the chair, took his handkerchief and continued to dab her eyes.

"Does it have anything to do with the Redemption through Sin exercise?"

She nodded but kept silent.

"Sarai, if you find the exercise offensive, please remember, you're not committing physical sin. But if it bothers you, why not excuse yourself from further attendance?"

She looked at him in alarm. "No! No! I want to continue. I just found the exercise... difficult ... upsetting."

I'm not a psychologist, he thought. She must be neurotic. A psychologist would understand why a thought experiment in sexual fantasy could have such a reaction.

"Why was the exercise so difficult for you?" he asked, keeping his voice sympathetic.

There was a long pause. Donald wondered whether she was going to answer. Finally she muttered, "Because I liked it."

"I don't understand," Donald said, beginning to understand. "Is it because you're not supposed to look on sex as something to be enjoyed or even thought of? Is it a religious thing?"

She turned in her seat, facing away from Donald.

"Partly," she said. Then, after a space of silence: "But not the biggest part."

"Sarai," he said, "I know my next question will be 'what's the biggest part?', but I don't really want to conduct an interrogation or make you unhappy. If it's painful to talk about, then don't. But consider where I stand. Given your reaction to yesterday's session, the responsible action for me is to ask you not to attend any further classes. If a sincere and open discussion could allay my fears, then I might reconsider."

She began sobbing again, leaning over, her head in her hands, her elbows propped on her knees. "Don't throw me away," she pleaded. "I couldn't bear it."

She turned to him. A tear rolled down the bony ridge of her nose and hung at its tip. He felt sorry for her, leaned forward and kissed the tear away. She threw herself at him, knocking him hard against the chair back. The chair tilted backwards and they fell crashing to the floor. Stunned, Donald laid there, Sarai on top of him, kissing him, her tears wetting his face. He wrestled her away, stood up, and sat her on his desk, holding her against him until she quietened.

"Did I hurt you?" she asked.

"I'm ok," he said ruefully, rubbing the spot on the back of his head that had collided with the linoleum flooring.

He put her back on her chair, restored his, and faced her.

"Sarai, let's stop beating about the bush. You want me? Is that what this is all about?"

She looked away, blushing. "Yes and no."

Donald rolled his eyes and held up his arms as though pleading to the heavens.

"Metatron, Raphael, Michael, Gabriel, someone help her or help me. Sarai, Kabbalah is a slam dunk compared to understanding you. Let's get really personal. Are you a virgin?"

She blushed again, her eyes intently on the floor. She shook her head.

"Neither am I. I lost mine when I met my wife. When did you lose yours?"

"At 18. First Year University."

"My wife-to-be and I were also at university. Did you ever marry?"

There was a pause. She looked directly at him. "Yes. I married Jesus."

It was his turn to pause. I should have at least suspected it, he thought. She had displayed in yesterday's class her clear devotion to Jesus. Her dress was anything but stylish. In hindsight, all signs are obvious.

"You're a nun?"

"Was a nun. I left the Order a few months ago. I'm beginning to think I should have stayed. I was a nun for 20 years — joined when I turned 19."

A long silence ensued while they gazed at each other thoughtfully.

"Did your joining have anything to do with your first sex?"

She nodded. "It was the proverbial last straw — a dreadful experience. In the four or five years before I joined the Order, my life in general had not been very satisfactory. I know I'm not attractive. Before high school, it didn't seem to matter. As a teenager, I was so skinny, everyone thought I had an eating disorder. I was also terribly shy. I had a couple of girlfriends, also classed as ugly and shunned by our classmates. No boys were interested in me. I sat home Saturday nights, never asked out on a date, never went to the prom or school dances."

"Was university better?" Donald asked, knowing the answer.

She shook her head, tears in her eyes, mouth grim. "Hell would've been better. At least in Hell, there's a community of sufferers. No, if anything, university was worse. Not only did I not have any friends, but I was constantly ridiculed by the boys in my classes. A favourite taunt, especially by one obnoxious bas — sorry, boy — was 'there's the broomstick, where's the witch?'"

"Terrible," said Donald. "You don't have to apologize. He is a bastard. Go on."

She smiled appreciatively. "As humans, we are to remember that all creatures are God's creations and should be loved no matter how ill their behaviour. However, we may hate their deeds."

Donald shrugged. "Kabbalists believe that there is a world of demons. Your antagonist was probably possessed by one. Hopefully, he was able to mature and banish it."

Sarai stood up and began pacing up and down the office. "I don't think he ever did. Let me tell you the rest. It was during this awful time that I began to think about becoming a nun. My family were strong Catholics and I was interested in the Church and Catholic theology. The nuns I came across always seemed happy and did good works. I believed I faced a life of chastity anyway. So what did I have to lose?"

She returned to her chair. "I was close to making the decision and even talked about it with my parents. Then something happened. Charlie

Wingate — the one who made my life most miserable — approached me one day, and instead of the usual insult, apologized. He said he had behaved like a boor, had told the others to lay off and grow up and wanted to be friends. I looked at him in disbelief but he insisted that he was sincere and meant it. Charlie was very good looking — tall, bronzed, muscular body, strong face, and blond crew cut hair. I couldn't believe my luck."

Her voice trailed off as she looked out the window shaking her head ruefully at the memory. " We met frequently in the cafeteria, had coffee or lunch together. He took me to movies, bars, night clubs. I was totally in love with him, happy beyond all my dreams. Of course, we began to make out, mostly groping and French kissing. He invited me to come to his apartment after school one day. His roommates were away and we had the place to ourselves. We made love, beautiful love, several times. When I left, he was fast asleep. I walked home, blissfully unaware of the drizzle, unaware even that my feet were touching the pavement. I sat up most of the night, rapturously thanking God for my wonderful fortune."

She stopped. Put a hand to her head, stood up and again paced up and down the office. "Then I joined as a novice and soon took my vows."

"Just a minute," Donald said, reaching out an arm as she passed him, and pulling her back to her chair. "There's a dot called 'wonderful fortune' and another dot called 'took my vows.' Kindly connect the dots."

She looked away, shaking her head. "The dot between the dots is too painful. I can hardly think about it, let alone talk about it."

"Did you ever confess it?"

"Yes, when I first joined. A public confession — that is, to the assembled nuns. I lay prostrate on the chapel floor. I didn't have to look at anybody. I lay there a long time, humiliated. Too ashamed to look up. Then Mother Superior picked me up, hugged me. Over her shoulder, I could see the nuns — some were weeping openly, some with heads bowed were praying, no one was laughing. I was home, among family, among friends, no judging, just open sympathy, concern. Mother Superior said some words of comfort, I don't know what they were, but suddenly I felt cleansed, free, my life open before me."

An overwhelming desire to embrace her caused him to reach out and pull her on his lap. She didn't resist and buried her face against his chest.

"Tell me the rest. I need to know. You can talk into my shirt. You don't have to look at me."

"All right, I'll really try." Her voice was somewhat muffled but he could hear her well enough. "I slept in the next morning but arrived at the cafeteria at the usual time. Charlie was nowhere to be seen, so I sat down at a table to wait for him. I could tell something wasn't right. My class mates, particularly the boys, were all looking at me, smiling, mocking me. One of Charlie's friends put a recording device near me and pushed the playback button. The groans and sighs and words of love I had uttered played loudly and clearly, greeted by the jeers and applause from all the tables around. It was a setup, a so-called harmless prank. Get me seduced, record the occasion for posterity. My feeling of devastation was complete. Not just the humiliation but the realization that for the man I loved, I was nothing but a joke."

Her breath caught. He could feel the wetness of her tears seeping through his shirt. He reached up and stroked her hair. "What happened then? Did you appeal to the university?"

"No. I picked up the recording and smashed it to the floor. Left and never came back. The convent offered a place where there were no men, no sex, and where it didn't matter what you looked like. That afternoon, I informed my parents I would become a nun."

Sarai dissolved into tears again, low, hacking sobs. Rocked gently by Donald, she got control; of herself, let out a long sigh, and rested her head on his shoulder.

"That's a terrible story, Sarai. I feel for you. Life is far from fair and just. Did the convent at least give you what you were looking for?"

She sat up straight and nodded. "Yes, I think so. I decided to push that evil memory out of my mind and to concentrate on the here and now. It took me a couple of years to really reach that state where I felt I could face the world.

"The Sisters had Missions in developing parts of the world. I elected to become a nurse along with several others and we took our training at McMaster University in Hamilton. I'm not supposed to express pride but I was a good student and graduated with honours. I was dispatched to those Missions which operated hospitals in third world countries and became a top surgery nurse. You probably won't believe this after what you witnessed today, but I was considered remarkable in my ability to handle stress no matter how dreadful the circumstances.

"Like the time we were operating on a young child and a war broke out around the Mission. The gunfire was intense — a bullet pierced the wall, narrowly missing us. The doctor stepped away, but I stood firm and pulled him back to the table."

She stopped, her mind way back, recalling the fear and trembling that she had had to stifle. "We saved our patient, which was the important thing."

She left his lap, face still wet with tears, but a serene smile on her face, and walked to the window, staring out at the broken urban landscape of gas stations, warehouses, fast food restaurants, and empty lots.

"It was a time when I was truly happy," she continued. "I was sent to assist doctors in disaster areas all over the world. I felt I had purpose, that I had discovered why God had put me through the ordeal of my growing up. He had tested me and I had won His confidence. Yes, it was a great time. All those different countries, cultures, people. Hard work. Constant challenge. Resources never sufficient. Making do with poorly equipped hospitals, clinics, hastily erected tents. Fifteen years of absolute bliss. I treasure every moment."

"Sarai, you are truly something special," Donald said. "What you're telling me deserves to be written down. A memoir. You have to write a memoir. You've achieved a Kabbalist goal — ascent toward the Godhead. You've delved into the worst of the imperfections and evils of Creation and transformed them around you. But something puzzles me. Your experience as a nun was obviously very pleasing to you. Why did you leave?"

She shook her head. "I cannot tell you. I don't want to talk about it. For good reasons, I felt I had to leave the Order. And I ask you not to push me."

In the long silence that followed, he could hear the monotonous drone of the highway and the staccato traffic noise from the street outside.

"Ok. We won't talk about it. Your life seems punctuated by crises. What's happened since you left the Order?"

She resumed pacing up and down the office. "At first it was tough. For 20 years my regime had been all encompassing. Every minute of my day was accounted for, whether I was working in the field or recovering at a retreat. Even in travel, there were reports to write, prayer times, meditation. Suddenly I was free. I still carried on my prayer schedule but I didn't know what to do the rest of the day. Fortunately, I was able to find work as a nurse, so that's made a big difference."

"What brought you to Kabbalah?"

"Curiosity, mostly. One of your fliers ended up on the nurse's bulletin board. I had come to wonder about God — you know the question you raised — if God is perfect, why is their evil in the world? If God is perfect, why did he create tectonic plates that crash together and kill 200,000 people? I felt there was merit to the Kabbalah explanation you presented."

She stopped pacing and sat down in the chair opposite him. "The first shock was the concept of Redemption through Sin. Remember, my whole life had been based on a crusade against sin. We had to avoid sin, reject it, pray for the sinner, and hope to persuade him or her to give it up. Now, I'm told, yes, sin is evil, therefore, embrace it, fully, deeply and retrieve the Holy Sparks you find there. Everybody in the class was uncomfortable, except maybe Lily." The last was said bitingly. "Then you and I paired up and went through the motion of having sex. At least, you went through the motion, I didn't know how."

"Oh, come on, Sarai," Donald said impatiently.

"That's right, Donald, I didn't know how. My last memory of sex was as an eighteen-year old and Charlie did all the work. That was the only time I saw a naked man apart from the hurt and broken men I nursed. Anyway, I went through the motions as best I could. When I noticed you were..." She paused, blushing.

"Go on, Sarai, I won't be embarrassed."

"When I saw you were going erect, I was shattered. Sex? A man wanted to have sex with me? It hit me like a flood — I wanted it too! I couldn't handle it. I had to sit down. It brought back my Charlie experience. A moment of rapture, followed by humiliation and discard. I couldn't believe I wanted that all over again."

"Sarai," Donald said placatingly, "love, sex. These are normal and commonplace happenings. You're no longer a teenager. You're a mature, tough woman. You can still have children. What you're telling me, you were ok until you took my class."

She started to get up but he pulled her back. "Don't start pacing again. You've got to face this head on."

She looked him squarely in the eyes. "Donald, understand. For 20 years I had suppressed all thoughts of sex. I scrunched it out of my mind. I never relieved myself like some of the Sisters occasionally did. Even when I was free, I never thought of sex, never entertained the idea of having feelings for men, and never felt that I was missing something. In one moment, without much warning, all that changed."

OK, thought Donald. So I understand. She's clearly unstable. So what am I supposed to do now? Make love to her? Teach her sex is pleasurable as long as you don't take it too seriously? Is she just looking for sex or love accompanied by sex? Dammit, there is something appealing about her. She's a damaged soul filled with Holy Sparks, waiting to be rescued, to be made whole again, to begin her ascent toward unification with the Godhead. It would be an act of piety to possess her, to love her, to relinquish all other sexual claims and desires in favour of hers alone. But, what am I thinking? I sure don't have a history of monogamous love. Even Shabtai didn't limit himself. His legend is replete with strange sexual acts and relationships. Why must I be holier than the founder of our sect? Why must …

"You're deep in thought," Sarai said. "You're trying to decide what to do with me, aren't you? You think I'll go off the edge in one of your classes and make a scene. It's not good publicity to have a class disrupted and someone carried away in a strait jacket. I'm stronger now, Donald, now that I've told you my sad story. You've helped me immensely. But you can help me more. I'm no longer a nun. I want to experience sex again. I want to experience it with you. But I also want you to love me."

He shrugged his shoulders. "Sarai, I'm not a tap. I can't turn love on and off. Besides, love and sex are not necessarily connected. Real love, true love, is as rare as sex is frequent. And it's not a good idea for the class leader to have a relationship with a course participant."

"Unless her name is Lily," Sarai snapped angrily. "Donald, you're a contemptuous liar and hypocrite. I went back to talk to you last night and I saw you and Lily leaving the meeting room. No doubt, she had stayed late to discuss the finer points of Kabbalah."

Donald started to protest, and then shrugged his shoulders again. "OK, I broke my own rule. Should I go on breaking it? What if we have an affair which eventually comes apart? Can you handle that or am I another Charlie?"

In reply, she sat on his lap and cuddled up against him. He tried at first to fend her off but quickly gave up and put his arms around her.

"You're not another Charlie," she said dreamily. "I can tell you like me, that you have feelings for me. You won't seduce me and then tell all your friends about it and mock me."

"Well, you're right about that and about my having feelings for you," Donald said as he gently rocked her. "Why, I don't know."

They sat there a long time, occasionally kissing, until there was a knock at the door.

"Two o'clock, Donald," Amanda called out. "Time for your next appointment."

"We're just wrapping up," Donald replied. "Be right out."

"Can I invite you for supper tonight?" Sarai whispered. "At six. My shift doesn't start until midnight so we'll have lots of time."

He took her address and promised to be there.

He focussed on his writing and research during the afternoon. At five o'clock, he was preparing to leave the office when Amanda put a call through.

"I'm coming to see you tonight," Lily said. "When will you be home?"

"I'm tied up tonight," he replied. "I'll see you at the next class."

"No, you'll see me tonight," Lily insisted. "It'll be late tonight." She hung up.

He sighed. No doubt she would show up. Redemption through Sin was a great concept, but two women in one night was pushing it, he thought.

Lily, naked, frustrated, slapped Donald hard across his face. He, fully clothed, sat back in his chair and gingerly touched a cheek. She straddled his legs and thrust a breast into his face.

"It's no use, Lily. I'm not interested. Maybe some other time," he said wearily. "Please go home."

They were in Donald's bedroom. She slapped him again and walked over to his bed and lay down.

"I will lie here until you're ready."

"I don't want you tonight. It's after midnight. I need to get some sleep," Donald said. He left the bedroom, walked down the hallway to the living room and sat on the sofa. She followed him, poured a glass of wine from a near empty bottle and sat on the sofa beside him.

"What is it, Donald?" she asked, pretending concern. "Menopause? EDS? It must be a sudden onslaught. Last night you had no trouble." She paused. "It's someone else, isn't it? Where were you tonight? She must be pretty good. She drained you, is that it? She left nothing for me. I hope you recovered lots of Holy Sparks for your God. At least He won't feel let down tonight."

"You're talking stupid now, Lily. Go home," Donald said, staring impassively at the ceiling.

She retrieved her clothes, spread around the living room floor, and dressed.

"OK, I'll go tonight. But you're mine until I tell you differently and I don't share."

He saw her out and watched from the apartment window as she drove away.

He had awakened, as usual, at seven o'clock. Over coffee, he thought of his dinner the night before with Sarai. It wasn't much of a dinner. He knocked on her apartment door in a shabby building on College Street near Spadina Avenue sharp at six o'clock. They fell into each other's arms, tore off their clothes, and made love on the floor in the entrance hallway. Afterward, she led him into the living/dining/kitchen area, poured him a glass of cold chardonnay and made a couple of lettuce and tomato sandwiches topped with sliced cheese. She sat on his lap as they ate the sandwiches and sipped the wine. They barely talked.

They made love several more times. He loved her. It was the first time in a long time that he was having sex because he loved the woman.

"Will you come again tomorrow night?" she asked somewhat fearfully. "I'll show you I can really cook. I wasn't sure you'd show up tonight, so I didn't prepare very much."

"If you promise a real meal, then I'll come," he replied with mock seriousness. "To keep up with you, I need lots of fuel."

At 11 o'clock, he drove her over to the downtown hospital where she worked. They told their love to each other, kissed passionately, and parted.

When he returned to his apartment building around midnight, Lily emerged from her car in the visitors' parking space.

"I hope your evening was more pleasant than mine. I've been waiting here since 10 o'clock."

"I told you I'd be out. Now, why don't you get back in your car and go away."

He opened the lobby door to the apartment building and she pushed in behind him. "You either let me in or I start screaming."

He relented. In the elevator, she embraced him and provocatively rubbed her hips against him.

"Keep at it," he said. "The guy who monitors the security screens tells me all about the interesting things that he sees."

She turned to the surveillance camera in an upper corner of the elevator, lifted a breast and threw a kiss.

"God, you're shameless," Donald said, shaking his head.

"Perhaps," she said as they left the elevator, "but the next time, he'll let me into your apartment. How do you think I make my living?"

He stopped and looked hard at her. "How do you make your living? Shall I take a wild guess?"

They entered his apartment. "No need to guess. I'll tell you. Nasty gossipy women would call it prostitution. I prefer to see myself as a courtesan selling sophisticated upper class pleasure to the right kinds of men.

"That's not how I started. In the beginning, I taught elementary school in a private religious school. I soon discovered the Chairman of the Board of Trustees was more interested in my body than my brain. Some of my colleagues and several of the children's fathers showed the same interest. It became apparent that providing pleasure paid better than providing education. I slept my way through most of my admirers and watched my savings grow. Unfortunately one of the men believed we were in love and told his wife we would marry. She and I both objected strenuously and I found myself out of a job. I worked as a saleslady in a chain clothing store and met the CEO of the company on one of his site visits. I'm his personal secretary, now. I'm well looked after and free to pursue my hobbies when he doesn't need me. You're one of my hobbies."

As she talked, she had slowly and seductively peeled off her clothing, piece by piece. It was when he didn't respond, that she had angrily attacked him.

Later that day, Donald arrived at Sarai's apartment at five o'clock. She was naked except for an apron that went completely around her thin body.

"You're too early. I'm making you a proper dinner."

Despite her laughing protests, he dragged her into the bedroom. Afterwards, he slept while she returned to the kitchen. She awakened him a little later to a sumptuous meal of lamb kebabs on a bed of couscous smothered with fried onions and raisins and a tabbuleh salad.

"I spent time in the Middle East and Morocco," Sarai explained. "For a nun, cooking was often a duty and cooking local foods and styles eased the boredom and was the only sensual pleasure I knew. I confess I sometimes gave way to the sin of gluttony."

He reached over and ran his hands up and down her body, still enveloped in the apron. "Gluttony seems not to have affected you," he said affectionately.

He helped her clean up, removed the apron, and led her back to the bedroom. They didn't make love right away but lay comfortably together, he, on his back, she, alongside him, gently stroking his body.

"Was gluttony the only sin you committed as a nun?" Donald asked. "It seems a rather mild sin."

She paused before answering. "There was only one serious sin I committed during my years as a nun. I will not reveal what it was except to say it was one of the factors that caused me to leave the convent."

What could it be? he wondered. She seemed incapable of anything drastic.

"Let's talk about something else," she said, anticipating his curiosity. "Let's talk about love."

"That's always an agreeable subject," he said, pulling her closer and kissing her.

She laughed. "No, I really mean talk. There's no treatment of love between a man and a woman in Kabbalah, as far as I can make out.

Redemption through Sin is not love but a kind of depraved eroticism. When you make love to me, are you looking for Holy Sparks?"

"I make love to you because I love you," he replied, caressing her bony ribcage and pelvis. "Like I said in class, Kabbalah is not a religion. It's a system of mystical enquiry that can sit atop any of the Abrahamic religions — Judaism, Christianity, Islam. Each religion has its own concept of love. In yours, sexual love is restricted to a husband and wife and is integrated with all the other loves — love of parents, siblings, family, friends — even enemies, according to Christ. Love is seen as the force to bring about the unity and harmony of mankind in order to fulfill God's Creation. So you see, love making has a purpose and is not an end in itself."

"What I do see is that, as far as religion and the Kabbalah are concerned, there's nothing special about the sexual love between two people. Yet when we love, I feel there is something special," she said.

"And so do I," he assured her. "There is something special between us. Yet I cannot put aside my study of the Kabbalah. As a fervent Kabbalist, I believe there is a portion of the Godhead that is feminine in principle and is present in our world. This entity is called the Shechina and symbolizes God's love for the world and humanity. Through love we embrace the Shechina and reciprocate God's love. In time, we will restore the Shechina to the Godhead Who, unified once again, will bring about the Redemption."

Sarai sat up and looked at him. "I'm having trouble with your Kabbalah. It seems when you're having sex, you're either retrieving Holy Sparks or embracing the Shechina. What about me? Am I just a step in your personal progress to God?"

He pulled her down into his arms again. "Sarai, I'm starting to sound like a sermon, but everything we do is either a step toward or a step away from worshipping and integrating with God. Don't let Kabbalah worry you. I love you. With you I am fulfilled. Does it really matter how I justify the feeling?"

"I think it gets in the way," she said. "I want to be loved for my own sake, not as part of some greater purpose."

"But sweetheart, all the religions consider love as part of a greater purpose. Sexual love is for procreation and not for pleasure alone. It's only modern Western secular men and women who find pleasure an end in itself. You and I are not secular. We love, we find joy and ecstasy in our love, but our ultimate goal through our love is the worship of God. Is that not so?"

She was silent for a moment, staring at the ceiling, and absentmindedly fingering the contours of his face.

"Suppose I no longer believe," she said. "Would it affect us and our relationship?"

He moved onto his side and raised himself on an elbow. With his free hand, he grasped her chin and turned her face to his.

"How do you mean you no longer believe?" he asked sharply.

"You've answered my question," she said sadly. "Donald, consider me and my life. I have experienced evil personally and professionally for most of it. Evil done to me by malicious boys and girls raised in loving homes and church goers most of them. As a nurse, I helped those afflicted by natural disasters, disease and wars. My life is a testament to the existence of evil. I have even succumbed to its practice myself. In such a contaminated world, I find it increasingly difficult to believe that a Supreme Being exists and oversees us. In a way, I feel sorry for you. Your entire Kabbalah rests on the sole premise that a God exists. Without a God, the whole edifice of Kabbalah collapses."

He lay back in bed, shaking his head. "But you consider Jesus divine and a figure to be loved and worshipped. You were married to Jesus for umpteen years."

"That's why we're now divorced," she said chuckling ruefully. "As my faith dwindled, I decided to leave the Sisters. I see Jesus now as an icon of love. Follow his teachings and much of the evil in the world would disappear."

Donald held his head in disbelief. "So what you're telling me is everything I hold dear, everything I teach, everything I make my living by, all my research and study — everything — is complete and utter nonsense because there is no God. And you're wondering whether this will get in the way of our relationship?"

She crawled onto him and kissed his eyes, nose and mouth. "All I want from you is love, feeling, affection, an eagerness to be with me. I offer you the same. The last two days have been glorious, joyful, ecstatic. We've accomplished this without referring to our beliefs. Don't let ideology get in our way."

"How can it not get in the way?" he retorted, despite feeling the desire for her rise. "You've just told me I'm a zero."

"Quite the contrary," Sarai said, kissing him passionately. "I've just told you you're one hundred percent. You're all I want and I want to be all you want."

They made love and dozed blissfully for awhile.

Donald left Sarai off at the hospital and returned to her apartment for the night. He didn't want another confrontation with Lily.

As he crawled into Sarai's bed under the covers, he smelled her scent — a fresh, unperfumed soap smell. I shall have to feminize her, he thought. Her bedroom was sparsely furnished: a single bed, a night table with a lamp and an alarm clock, and a dresser. The closet, slightly open, was mostly empty. A few pictures hung on the wall. One was of Sarai, younger, in full nun regalia; another, a colour print of the Last Supper; a third, an older couple smiling cheerfully at the camera, probably her parents.

Still very monastic, he thought, like her description of her usual sleeping quarters as a nun: a narrow room, a hard cot, a small armoire, and a table for reading the bible and writing. Her life had been one of hard work, lots of prayer, meditation and frequent confession. It was probably nursing that made it all worthwhile for her, he suspected: the travel, adventures in deprived and dangerous places, her professional competence, and the satisfaction of helping the most desperate and vulnerable people.

Her last posting had been somewhere in Africa but he couldn't recall the country. She wasn't there long, she had told him, and returned to Toronto where she left the Order. Something had happened, he concluded. No doubt, in time she would tell him.

He fell asleep and was astounded to find the narrow dark room give way to a sun-bright vast expanse of grassy plain. He stood knee deep in the vegetation surrounded by innumerable herds of grazing animals. He recognized zebra, antelope, eland, water buffalo, wildebeest, Oryx, Barbary sheep. In the far distance he watched a line of elephants walking single file, nose to tail. Several giraffes extended their long necks to the topmost foliage in a copse of trees. Behind him, where the jungle began, he could hear the raucous cacophony of monkeys and apes. In front of him, lions, tigers, cheetahs walked among the herds but elicited no interest from the grazing animals. Overhead flew endless flocks of birds, silhouetted against the blue vault of the sky.

He could see only a portion of the plain because ahead of him was a large hill which obscured the view. A lion came over the top of the hill and bounded toward him. In stark terror, he shrank back and tried to hide behind a water buffalo. A figure sat on the lion, brilliant light emanating from it. At first he couldn't see through the brightness but then the radiance faded sufficiently so that he could make out the face of a beautiful young woman, smiling happily. She held up a hand and the lion stopped a short distance from him.

"Do not be afraid," she said gently. "Behold! The creatures all around fear us not. There is only peace and bliss in the Garden of Paradise."

"Paradise?" he asked, weakly, uncomprehendingly.

"Follow me," she said.

He strode after her, often running, as the lion trotted rapidly away and up the large hill. At the top, Donald saw that the plain stretched to the far horizon and was covered, not just by wild animals, but also by large herds of cows, horses, sheep, pigs, goats and by flocks of chickens and turkeys. Walking amongst them were crowds of men, women, and children. Some were in small groups talking excitedly but happily, judging by the laughter; others were in large gatherings listening attentively to the man or woman addressing them; many couples walked arm in arm along a river way; children played; an occasional solitary figure sat under a tree and was deeply engrossed in a massive tome. All were naked.

"You see, Donald," the woman said. "There is no strife here. There is only joy and devotion to the One."

"Why am I here?" he asked.

"I offer you a vision of the future," the woman replied. "I seek the love of all mankind. Once achieved, I shall return to the Godhead Who will be whole once again. What you witness is the result — Redemption and the Paradise that awaits all righteous souls. Do not forget me, Donald."

The lion sprang high in the air and sailed down the hill. "Wait!" Donald shouted and ran after them, tripped and fell hard to the ground. He awoke in a sweat, lying on the bedroom floor.

Back in bed, he wondered: random dream or Kabbalah vision? Everything had seemed so real but that was as true of dreams as of visions. Yet he believed he had met and talked with the Shechina and felt his faith in the Kabbalah bolstered. Did it really matter what others believed?

That morning, when he arrived at his office a few minutes after nine, he found an unwelcome visitor. Amanda Cadman tried to warn him as he stepped through the door at the top of the stairwell.

"Donald, you have a person waiting to see you. No appointment. Do you have time?"

"He has time," Lily said. "I won't be long."

"Lily, what an unpleasant surprise," Donald said.

Amanda arched her eyebrows, intrigued by Donald's antagonistic tone. After all, based on her knowledge of Donald, Lily was exactly his type: well endowed, hour glass figure, creamy skin, beautiful face, legs encased in black tights amply displayed.

"Thanks, Donald," Lily said, sidling up to him and kissing him on the cheek."I knew you'd have time for me. Shall we go to your office for a private chat or shall we have a screaming fit here."

Poor Donald, Amanda thought. He can't seem to have affairs with women who meekly go away. Shabtai Zvi had no such problems but then he was the Messiah.

"I know who my rival is," Lily said triumphantly in Donald's office. "I just can't believe it. You must be some kind of pervert."

"Great, Lily. You've had your say. Now go away."

"Oh, I'm going away — at least for a little while. My CEO needs me for the next three weeks — fashion shows in London, Paris, Milan, and Dusseldorf. But as for my rival, I know it's Sarai Stone. I followed you yesterday and checked the names on the tenant list. Sarai Stone. Who would have ever guessed? You've thrown me over for a piece of string. What the hell's with you? I saw how she behaved in class. She's a mental case. Is that it, Donald? You need women you can nurture, What about me? I need nurturing now that I'm rejected for Sarai Stone. I..."

"Lily, I'm not going to discuss my private life with you," Donald cut in. "Please leave. Enjoy your trip."

She stood up. "I'm leaving, but like the Terminator, 'I'll be back.' I won't give you up and I don't share."

She left the office, slamming the door hard.

She's trouble, Donald thought. Strange. Neither Lily nor Sarai believe in Kabbalah and my teachings and principles. Lily's sole faith is pleasure and sexual pleasure is prime. For Sarai, love is the dominant principle. Sex is important to both of them, but Lily is totally happy as a sex object and Sarai demands to be an unequivocal, monogamous love object. Am I strong enough to accommodate her?

CHAPTER 5

- ADRIANOPLE, 1666

-SHABTAI IN CRISIS

The streets leading to the New Kiosk, the Sultan's palace in Adrianople, were lined with the Jews of the city as well as visitors from Salonika, Smyrna, and Jerusalem. All were in their Sabbath best, laughing, singing, and shouting greetings to those on the other side of the street, while many danced in round packed circles. The mild September air and the sun high over fleecy fair-weather clouds enhanced the excitement and joy pervading the crowds.

The news had spread quickly. The Messiah had been freed from his prison in Gallipoli and invited by the Sultan to the Imperial Palace.

"This can mean only one thing," Rabbi Menachem Behmoiras, one of the two chief rabbis of the city, told his congregation during morning services. "The Sultan, as temporal ruler of the Holy land, will acknowledge our Messiah's just claims and recognize his divine mission. Redemption and our return to Jerusalem will follow."

His counterpart, Rabbi Eliakim Gueron, said much the same thing to the worshippers at his synagogue. Both rabbis stationed themselves as closely to the open gates of the Imperial Palace as the sentries would allow. Forced by the city's governor to share in the administration of the Jewish community, the two rabbis, from two ascendant families vying for dominance, were normally hostile to each other and communicated only when they had to. Today, captured by the spirit of their coming triumph over the Sultan and the Ottoman Empire, they hugged and kissed. Each wore a multicoloured festive mantle over a white cotton caftan with indigo stripes, silk pantaloons and brown boots. Around them some of their students and congregants mixed happily as the two camps came together. Yes, thought each rabbi, this is not a day for rancour and dispute but for celebration and harmony.

A roar of greeting and adulation from the far end of the street announced the arrival of Shabtai. The sound spread right up to the gates of the Palace and became deafening as Shabtai rode into sight, sitting in the back of a wagon pulled by two large horses. In front of him, dressed in the formal black robes and peaked headdress of the synagogue, sat Rabbi Benveniste and Samuel Primo, Shabtai's secretary. The wagon was flanked by Janissary soldiers resplendent in bronze battle plate armour and flowing red robes. Behind them came a small band of drummers and mehters, its martial music drowned out by the roar of the crowd.

Shabtai smiled and waved majestically at the celebrants on either side. The crowd pressed forward to reach him but was pushed back brusquely by the escorting Janissaries. The procession moved into the Palace forecourt and the iron gates clanged shut. The uproar in the street continued for a few minutes and then gradually diminished. The crowd waited quietly in patient anticipation of the Messiah's reappearance.

As they entered the gates, Primo shouted into Benveniste's ear, "Today, I feel completely vindicated that I espoused the Messiah's cause and laboured on his behalf to convince the rest of the world of his God-directed mission. There were times when even the Messiah had doubts but I persuaded him otherwise. Blessed be the Almighty for we are about to achieve release from our oppressors."

Benveniste nodded but he was troubled. True, he told himself, even in prison, the Messiah had enjoyed comparative luxury. He was not confined to a cell but occupied a suite of three rooms. In the largest one, on a bench with stuffed pillows under a canopy, he held court. Scholars, rabbis, rich men from all over the Empire and Europe visited him and listened rapturously to his Kabbalist teachings and sermons on the new Judaism. He was served sumptuous meals and treated with respect by the servants and guards. He was allowed conjugal visits by Sarah. Even the prison governor sought, rather than demanded, audience with his famous "guest." Did not all this indicate that the Messiah was real and protected by the Almighty?

Yet, he reminded himself, the Janissary officer was peremptory in his behaviour when he arrived with his troop of soldiers to conduct the Messiah to Adrianople. The order he read out seemed more like a warrant than an invitation. And the soldiers— were they an escort or a guard against escape? It had taken two days to get to Adrianople. At each stop, the Janissaries had dismounted and surrounded the Messiah and kept everyone away, including the faithful who flocked to see him. Were they shielding him as they would a king or avoiding any interference with their prisoner?

Yet, according to Primo, there were many positive signs. The Messiah was not in chains, rode in an open wagon, and Primo and Benveniste were allowed — indeed, requested — to accompany him. Benveniste noted, as well, that Primo was allowed to send messages ahead by followers eager to spread the word of the Messiah's progress.

"Have no doubt," Primo had insisted. "What other prisoner has ever been treated like this? Normally, a prisoner of rank is bound, caged and hurried to execution. But our Messiah is conducted like royalty."

As the gates closed behind them, Shabtai's ebullience, sparked by the reception of his supporters, suddenly froze. Before him, Samael sat, cross-legged, a broad smile twisting the features of his sightless face.

"False messiah, give up this madness you have embarked upon and join us. Much pleasure awaits you. My Lillith eagerly awaits your body and will adopt any form that pleases you. Let these Turks rid you of your mortal flesh and come to us."

"You are demons, rebellious of God, the dark side of Creation. You cannot tempt me. Begone."

"Did you say something, Messiah?" Primo asked as both men turned anxiously to Shabtai.

For a brief moment, Shabtai saw not the two rabbis in their black dress but vultures waiting for their meal of offal. He had never fully trusted Benveniste. The rabbi had become a dedicated follower in Smyrna, and had been respectful and eager to listen to him during his visits to the prison. Nevertheless, Benveniste seemed to fall short of enthusiastic acceptance. Even now, both men, including his long serving Primo, looked at him sombrely. Was this an omen, a message from the Almighty?

Despondent now, he allowed himself to be helped down from the wagon and led into the large entrance hall of the Palace. Benveniste and Primo were asked to remain in the hall. Shabtai, accompanied by two soldiers, followed a Janissary officer down a long corridor. They stopped at an ornately carved wooden door. The Janissary knocked three times and a voice ordered them to enter. Shabtai stepped into a large room, unadorned except for lattice work on the walls and lit by a series of casement windows near the high ceiling.

The only furniture was a sumptuously decorated canopy over an elegantly padded bench. The man sitting there was youthful, black bearded with a round handsome face. He wore a richly coloured mantle covering a flowing white voluminous caftan and pantaloons. A white turban and peacock feather graced his head.

The buzz of conversation ended abruptly when Shabtai entered. An official came forward.

"We meet again, Rabbi Zvi. I am Mustapha Pasha. You remember me, no doubt, from our disputations on the occasion I visited you in Gallipoli."

Shabtai nodded. "I am honoured, sir, that you are here to receive me. Our discussions did not end as you would have wished. I believe you were quite angry when you left."

Mustapha Pasha chuckled. "You must understand, Rabbi Zvi, that Islam is so dear to me that I cannot control my impatience when the invitation to join our faith is summarily dismissed. However, let me introduce you."

He turned to the man under the canopy.

"Grand Vizier Kuprulu Ahmed Pasha, this is Shabtai Zvi, a rabbi of Smyrna and pretender to the kingship of Israel."

Shabtai bowed deeply. "Grand Vizier, I am but a rabbi. I pretend to nothing."

There was a sharp laugh. Samael sat on the canopy. "Quite right, Shabtai, What you pretended to was indeed nothing. Press on. Get this over with quickly so you may be with us soon."

Shabtai was startled by the apparition but the Grand Vizier seemed not to notice.

"Rabbi Zvi, you are summoned here to face serious charges," he said in a soft, even toned voice. "Your stated belief that you are sent by God to lead your people to Jerusalem is treasonous. The Empire holds sovereignty over Jerusalem and does not recognize other claims. Your people, incited to believe you, have become troublesome in many of our cities. We had hoped through imprisonment that you would realize you had been mistaken and so inform your followers. This has not happened. In all cases of treason and rebellion, we have no alternative but to execute the perpetrators as a signal lesson to all who would foment strife in the Empire."

Kuprulu paused to let his last statement sink in. Samael leapt up and down on the canopy in apparent glee, "Ah, Shabtai. How wonderful! Soon you will be among us. Remember, run not to God but to us. Death is but the last moment of life but we endure forever."

"Nevertheless, Rabbi Zvi," Kuprulu continued, "we are prepared to offer you an alternative — an honourable way in which to escape death. You have only to accept conversion to Islam."

Shabtai had paled at Kuprulu's statement but nevertheless stepped back and shook his head vehemently.

"Nay," Kuprulu said, "Be not so quick to express disdain. Consider the one true God we both worship. Instead of calling him Jehovah, you will pray to Allah. Consider the remarkable history of your people. Islam accepts your holy scriptures as prelude to the Qur'an and the teachings of the Prophet Mohammad, blessed be his name. Jews and Muslims alike shun unclean food. We could give you many more examples where our beliefs and yours correspond. Therefore, it is but a small step for you to adopt the turban."

Shabtai bowed his head. "Grand Vizier, I cannot. If I must die a martyr, so be it."

A shriek of laughter caused him to look up. Samael somersaulted across the ceiling, "Excellent answer! They must now kill you. Look! Lillith awaits you as a young virgin. You like virgins, do you not?"

Lillith appeared overhead, looking down on him. He saw the lithe form, the developing breasts, a light sheen of hair on the Venus mount. He stared wildly about, shouting, "Lord, rid me of these demons!"

Startled, the Grand Vizier spoke reassuringly, "We are not demons and calling to your God will not help. We have made you a generous offer — a new life in our faith or no life in yours."

Shabtai hung his head and said nothing.

The Grand Vizier beckoned to an official standing back from the others. He came forward, bowed to Kuprulu and faced Shabtai.

"Rabbi Zvi," Kuprulu said. "Jerrah Kasim Pasha is skilled in medical science and is Governor of Buda. He will conduct your interrogation concerning the charges against you. Hopefully, he can persuade you to see the wisdom of conversion."

Kasim was short, so slim his mantle and caftan hung loosely. His gaunt face with hawkish nose and deep-set black eyes and a scar on one cheek that carved its way through a scraggly beard gave him a sinister look. Surely a demon, thought Shabtai, dreading what was to come.

Kasim spoke in a low, gravelly unpleasant voice: "Rabbi Zvi, are you aware of the gravity of your crimes?"

"Governor, I am not," Shabtai replied. "I have pursued my religious responsibilities with zeal but have no temporal ambitions. I have enjoined my people to pray, to do penance, and to be charitable. These are all divine commandments as written in our Holy Torah."

"Yes, yes, Rabbi Zvi, these are very important duties," Kasim said sarcastically, "and permitted by our wise and tolerant glorious sovereign, Sultan Mehmed IV. However, as to your temporal designs, do you not claim to be the king or messiah of Israel and that you will soon lead your people to the Holy Land and Jerusalem?"

"Sir, it is the one true God who has promised the Holy Land to us. It will come during the time of Redemption, at the end of days. Many of us believe the time is close. But I have never claimed to be the chosen one. It is entirely up to the Almighty to determine the moment and who shall lead our people."

"Liar! Liar! Liar!" screamed Samael. "You cannot escape. Confess and get it over with."

"Come, come, Rabbi," Kasim said, his lips twisting into a sneer. "Think you we are fools that know not what is happening in your gatherings? Our spies and informants report that last winter in Smyrna you proclaimed yourself Messiah, that you would grab the Sultan by his beard, and soon march to Jerusalem. Need I remind you that such statements are treasonous?"

Shabtai did not flinch, "Sir, I fail to remember making such statements. Your informants are either mistaken or lie. It would be blasphemous for me to claim to be the Messiah."

A sweet, velvety voice descended from the ceiling. "Oh, Shabtai, why waste time fighting. Your Lillith wants you, desires you, an eternity of pleasure awaits you locked in my arms and the arms of my daughters."

Shabtai looked up fearfully. A brilliantly lit Queen of Sheba, partly dishevelled, a breast clearly visible, stretched out her arms toward him.

"Look not to the heavens, Rabbi Zvi," Kasim admonished, his voice menacing. "There are those in your community who accuse you of blasphemy and heresy. Very learned and respected rabbis from different parts of the Empire have come forward to denounce you. Your preposterous behaviour has incited riotous assemblies and gatherings. In every case, our investigations lead back to you and your commanding role in these events. You are clearly guilty and must pay a heavy price."

Shabtai, despondency now dragging him down, nevertheless mustered his remaining courage and spoke firmly. "Sir, I am innocent. I am a Jew and allowed to practise my religion according to the tolerant principles of the Empire, for which I am grateful. I preach nothing but penitence, prayer, charity, and devotion to the One above. I do not preach against the Empire or the Sultan, and I have not provoked my people to seditious behaviour. True, my people have become imbued to the point of exuberance in response to my teachings and in their dedication to the Almighty, but I cannot be blamed for that."

Kasim Pasha snickered and turned to Kuprulu: "Grand Vizier, if Rabbi Zvi is innocent then his followers are guilty. They have independently taken upon themselves riotous and troublesome acts and made treasonable statements. Therefore, I recommend, Grand Vizier, that we request of the Sultan the authority to systematically slaughter all the Jews in the Empire, beginning with the two rabbis waiting in the hall and all the people in the streets outside."

There was dead silence in the court. Shabtai fell to his knees, tears in his eyes.

"I beg you, Kasim Pasha," he implored, "spare my people. If you must have a victim, I accept martyrdom."

A round of applause proceeded from the ceiling. "Remarkable courage, Shabtai. You will be a legend," Samael called out.

Kasim kicked Shabtai hard in the thigh and sent him sprawling. The other officials shrank back but Kuprulu remained impassive.

"Fool!" Kasim said, his voice harsh and contemptuous. "Think you we want martyrs? The cause for which a martyr dies never dies. We offer you the opportunity to become a Muslim, to join the faith that superseded yours. The Sultan is generous in his appreciation of those who convert. He will shower you with honours, a court position, a pension, and a special status among us."

He helped Shabtai to his feet. "What say you, Rabbi Zvi? Come, lift up your head and face me like a man."

A sob shook Shabtai's voice. "Sir, I will do anything you ask but I cannot become a Muslim."

Kasim Pasha stepped back, arms akimbo. "Very well then. Guards! Attach the chains."

Two men in bronze battle plate and helmets came from behind Shabtai, noisily dragging the chains along the tiled floor. They shackled Shabtai's wrists and ankles. He stood there, head bowed, his arms held down to his sides by the heavy weight of the chains.

Kasim came close, put a hand under Shabtai's chin and lifted up his head so they were staring into each other's eyes. Shabtai saw the malice and cruelty on Kasim's face and began to regret his decision.

"Rabbi, before we take you away, let me describe your execution. You may believe your death will be a swift cutlass blow, relieving your body of the burden of your head. Certainly, such a death occurs quickly and probably without pain. We do not know for certain since no one has come back to report." Kasim chuckled at his joke.

"Or you may believe we will take you to the public square and stone you. Such an execution would be slower but, nevertheless, quick enough to limit the pain. Sometimes the victim is lucky enough to be hit in the head with the first rock.

"The Christians believe their prophet suffered a terrible death. Crucified by the Romans and hanging from his nailed hands and feet, no doubt he suffered great pain. But for how long? Two days? Three days?"

Still holding up Shabtai's head, Kasim paused. There was dead silence in the court, not even the sound of breathing except the hoarse gasps that came from Shabtai.

"Rabbi, if you insist on a martyr's death, we have a much longer, more painful procedure in mind. First, of course, there will be the traditional flogging which will be carried out in the public square so that all your followers can watch the flesh torn from your back."

Kasim turned to Kuprulu: "Grand Vizier, since we will want him alive after the flogging, I recommend we limit it to 100 strokes instead of the customary 200."

"It shall be as you wish, Kasim Pasha," the Grand Vizier agreed.

"After the flogging, Rabbi Zvi, we shall address ourselves to those instruments of male procreation that hang between your legs. Since you will no longer need them, they will be removed. Shall I tell you how?"

There was a clang and clatter of chains as Shabtai pushed Kasim away and fell to his knees. "I beg for mercy."

"But Rabbi, I am not yet through. What I have described is only the beginning."

Shabtai, on his knees, raised his arms despite the heavy shackles and chains. "I beg to see the Sultan and plead my case before him. He is a wise and benevolent sovereign and will not allow such torture."

Kasim laughed. "Yes, our Sultan is indeed wise and benevolent. That is why he offers you an honourable escape from torture and death. But, what think you, Rabbi? The Sultan is not aware of our meeting? Even now, unobserved, he observes."

Shabtai noticed now a window high up on the wall, latticed with strips of linen. He could just make out a shadow.

"Then there is no hope," Shabtai cried, jumped to his feet, and made for the door. He flung Kasim off who tried to stop him, knocked down one of the guards, but was caught by the chains by the other guard and brought crashing down to the floor.

"Rabbi," Kasim said, "please have the courtesy to hear the rest of my dissertation on the tortures we have in mind for you. It is rude to run off without being properly dismissed."

The guards dragged Shabtai back and left him prostrate before Kasim.

"Rabbi, obviously, our lengthy discussion bores you. Very well. Let me leap to the final torture: impalement. All subjects of the Empire are informed of this procedure. A sharpened, oiled stake is planted in the ground with only a waist-high portion showing. Naked, you are seated on the stake, the point rising up through your rectum and entrails. Struggle is useless. A slow and very painful death.

"But that is not all. Your family will be brought here shortly. Your wife, I am told by my female informants, is very beautiful. Her naked beauty will be displayed as she is slowly lifted and swung onto the tower of butcher hooks. What a sight that will be! You, impaled on your stake in horrible pain, will watch your wife die, crying and screaming, perhaps even cursing you for allowing this to happen. As for your son, he will not be killed. He will be sold into slavery."

Kasim turned on his heel and walked to a position beside Kuprulu. "Take heed, Rabbi," Kasim said. "Decide quickly."

Huge sobs racked Shabtai's body as he wrestled with the dilemma of his choice: a horrible, physical death for him and Sarah or a spiritual death and the end of his messianic mission. Where was God? Had he not performed well? Had he not carried out all the Almighty's directives? Out loud, he cried in Hebrew, "Almighty Lord, why do you desert me now?"

"The Almighty does not desert you now, Messiah of Israel," a voice spoke softly in Hebrew. "Do you not understand the protection He offers?"

Half expecting an angel or Samael, Shabtai pushed himself to his knees and looked at the speaker. A tall courtly man, dressed in a black mantle, white caftan and pantaloons, stood over him. There was a look of sympathy on his trimly bearded face and a smile crinkled his cheeks. A white turban covered his head.

"Who are you?" Shabtai asked suspiciously.

"I am the court physician, Hayatizade Feyzi Effendi. I was once a Jew but felt the pull of Islam. Yes, I am renegade, an apostate, but if you allow me, I can help you."

Shabtai responded sadly, "How can you help me? Either I die or become a renegade like you? How can you say God protects me?"

Hayatizade helped Shabtai up. "Messiah, it is clear to me that God needs you yet alive and has persuaded the Sultan to offer you an egress.

The Sultan always condemns to death those he believes are seditious and stir up rebellion. The tortures Kasim Pasha described are normal for cases like yours. Yet you, and only you, may be spared. Do you not see a Divine Presence intervening on your behalf?"

Shabtai looked bewildered. "But, Sir, why would the God of Israel want His Messiah to become a Muslim?"

Hayatizade sighed. "Messiah, do you believe adherents of Islam are without sin? Do we not need to expunge the rot from our own souls as well if redemption is to be achieved for all? The shards of light, the holy sparks, you speak of — do they not have to be recovered from our midst too? If you accept God's direction, you not only avoid a horrible death for you and your wife and the enslavement of your child, but advance your mission into the very heart of Islam."

For a long moment, Shabtai was lost in the debate raging within him. Then the glimmer of a smile spread over his face. He grasped Hayatizade by the shoulders.

"You are right," Shabtai said. "How blind I am."

"You are as blind as I am," screamed Samael, dropping with a thud beside Shabtai. "They want you alive, fool. But it matters not. At the end of your life, heaven will reject you and you will join us then. Farewell for now." With a powerful leap, Samael vaulted to the ceiling and disappeared.

Disconcerted, Shabtai stared wildly about.

"There is nothing to fear, Messiah," Hayatizade said reassuringly.

Shabtai lifted his manacled hands high. "Blessed art thou O Lord for sending me a messenger to help me find my way."

He faced Kuprulu: "Grand Vizier, I believe my path to Islam is divinely ordained. Therefore, I accept the Sultan's generous offer."

There was a noticeable sigh of relief among the officials. Kuprulu embraced Shabtai. The shackles were removed. Two officials escorted him to the ritual bath and the naming ceremony. Dressed in white silk caftan and pantaloons, he returned to the court. Kuprulu placed a white mantle on Shabtai's shoulders and a white turban on his head.

Once again, he embraced Shabtai and kissed him on both cheeks. "Aziz Mehmed Effendi, we welcome you to our faith."

The iron gates of the Imperial Palace swung open. A troop of six horsemen led the way as Shabtai, seated in an open carriage festooned with ribbons and bunting, appeared once more before his people. Behind him walked Benveniste and Primo, heads bowed, The lapel on Benveniste's mantle was torn, a sign of bereavement.

The roar of greeting from his followers and supporters stopped abruptly when they saw the white turban on Shabtai's head. As the procession continued down the avenue, successive adulations rose and fell.

"Rabbis, what means this?" several spectators shouted at Benveniste and Primo, but the two walked on without acknowledging the question. Others called out to Shabtai, "Have you become Muslim? Are you still the Messiah?"

Shabtai looked about but appeared dazed and uncomprehending. Confused and frightened, the people shrank back from the road. The news spread faster than the procession, down the main avenue and into the narrow streets beyond. There was silence now as Shabtai rode past. Some like Benveniste, tore their mantle lapels, some wept, and most just stared in disbelief.

Rabbis among the spectators found themselves the centre of growing knots of people desperately trying to understand the turn of events.

"There is a mystery here," a rabbi responded. "A mystery only the Messiah can understand and explain. We must await his word."

His answer was picked up by others and passed through the crowd. This seemed to placate many, but others reacted with disgust and anger or tears of frustration and dejection.

"We have been duped," shouted a woman and this too flew among the people.

The crowd slowly dispersed, its previous ecstatic mood now sombre and dejected. There was no more singing or dancing, only the sound of weeping and of leaden feet shuffling along the cobblestones.

The escort troop stopped at a fine mansion, not far from the Jewish quarter. Shabtai was helped from the wagon and assisted into the building. Primo turned into it as well, but Benveniste kept walking, out of Adrianople, to Gallipoli, where he took ship for Smyrna. The journey was long and arduous but not so difficult as the turmoil within him. Over and over, he berated himself for being a fool and allowing himself to be swept away by the fantasy that had gripped them all.

Rumour that her husband had become Muslim reached Sarah before the escort sent to fetch her to the Imperial Palace arrived. It wasn't clear whether Shabtai had been forced to convert or had done so voluntarily. Benveniste confirmed the rumour as he passed through Gallipoli.

Sarah was shocked by Benveniste's appearance. His normally upright lanky form was slumped even as he walked. His face was gaunt, his eyes blood shot from lack of sleep, his clothing in tatters, torn by the vicissitudes of the road and the agony of his grief. He, too, could offer no explanation.

"Your husband seemed shaken, not quite conscious. There was no sign of torture nor did he appear weak or hurt. He cursed Samael and the demons of the lower world. The people were much confused when they saw him. This is an outcome no one expected."

Sarah shook her head. "Come, Rabbi, surely the simplest explanation is that conversion is part of my husband's mission, as directed by the Almighty."

Benveniste looked at her sadly. "Madam, the simplest explanation is he is not the Messiah and never was."

CHAPTER 6
- 1666 - ADRIANOPLE -
CONVERSION OF SARAH

A familiar figure led the guard of five Janissary soldiers, all mounted and flanking an open carriage. Guided by a liveried coachman and pulled by two horses, the carriage stopped directly in front of Sarah's residence. Passersby on the street looked on in curiosity. Sarah came out of the house, followed by two servants and a child.

Tepel could not hide his pleasure as he bowed before Sarah and she could not hide the flush of excitement that suffused her face and reddened her brows and temple above the face veil.

"Corporal Tepel, we meet once more," she gushed, her tone sincere and engaging. She enjoyed his flustered awkwardness as he attempted to greet her nonchalantly.

"Madam, the Sultan summons you to the Imperial Palace to the gracious hospitality and affection of his mother. It is my duty to ensure your safe and comfortable travel to the Palace. I also bring with me a letter to you from your husband, Aziz Mehmed Effendi."

Sarah looked at him blankly.

Tepel handed her a sealed scroll. "Madam, that is his new name."

"My dear Sarah," the letter read. "The Almighty has chosen a strange path for me, one which I had not foreseen. It is a new stage in my life, one which I embrace with gratitude. It is my wish that you join me in Islam. Therefore, please observe the Sultan's generous invitation not only obediently as all subjects must but also gratefully as a mark of distinction. We are indeed blessed by his wisdom and understanding. Allah willing, we shall soon be together again. Aziz Mehmed."

He does not sign 'Messiah of Israel, Anointed Son of God,' Sarah thought. Perhaps he cannot at this point, she reasoned. The letter was no doubt censored.

They set out early next morning at a fast trot. Sarah had left the child under the care of the servants and a neighbour and travelled alone in the carriage. The autumn air had cooled but was still comfortable. The wind played around her, occasionally tweaking the face veil loose. Tepel waited for the moments when her face was fully visible and revelled in its beauty. She carefully restored the veil each time but seemed to have trouble catching the flapping end. He knew she was teasing him and this too stoked his passion. The other guards, after an admonishing glare from the corporal, kept their eyes averted.

After a stop for refreshment at noon, Tepel tied his horse to the carriage and sat beside Sarah.

"Thank you for joining me, Corporal Tepel. It is lonely sitting here with nothing but the sound of the horses for conversation."

He pointed out some of the sights of the countryside as they travelled along and then described Adrianople. "It is not as grand as Constantinople," he said, "but still a very fine city. The Imperial Palace is majestic at the top of a fine avenue. The house you will live in is of the best and well situated. Your husband has been much honoured and is now an official of the court. If your husband fulfills his promises and responsibilities, you will continue to enjoy the respect of the court and, therefore, good fortune. "

"Why would you think my husband would not honour his promises?" Sarah asked, surprised by the forcefulness of his last statement.

Tepel thought, because he is mad, sweet lady. "I judge solely by my experience with him in Smyrna."

They left the coastal plain and were passing through a thickly forested area with only the occasional clearing and forester's hut. The road became a rutted, narrow track forcing the outriders to form ahead and behind the carriage. The carriage swung from side to side, throwing its passengers frequently against each other. Steadying themselves, their hands touched and did not withdraw.

"Corporal Tepel, since I am to become a Muslim," Sarah said, "tell me about your faith, so that I will not appear totally ignorant in the eyes of the Sultan's mother." She glanced sideways at him. She admired his strong profile with its aquiline nose and firm jaw, his beardless tanned face. She fought the temptation to reach out and pull the one end of his moustache pointing straight at her.

He dared not turn toward her. Just the continued pressure of his hand against hers completely captivated him.

"Madam, I am a poor preacher of our religion. I am born a Muslim and can read the Holy Qur'an. I confess I am not always faithful in its observance. The rules I follow firmly are those of my profession as a Janissary of the Sultan. But you, madam, you seem sanguine about the prospect of conversion. My experience with Jews is they prefer death to conversion."

Sarah pointed to the sky. "Corporal Tepel, you see the heaven above us. We all live under the same heaven. And above that heaven is the Almighty. Do you really believe the one true God cares what name we give Him? To make my way in this difficult world, I have worn many cloaks. Since my husband wishes that I become Muslim, then Muslim will I become."

Would you become Muslim for me? Tepel thought. He lapsed into silence as an image possessed him: he was the proud and happy husband of this ravishing woman who would bear his children and would remain his only wife during their long life together.

Sarah, wanting to keep him talking, said, "I am told that the rules of your military service forbid marriage. Are you then like Christian priests?"

Her question shattered his dream and brought him back to reality. Tepel reddened and answered sharply: "Madam, the details of a Janissary's life must remain with the Janissaries."

"Forgive me, Corporal Tepel," Sarah said hastily. "My question was impertinent. Please do not be angry with me."

They bounced along for awhile, jostling against each other, their hands still pressed tightly together. Soon the forest gave way to open countryside and a wider, better planed road. They came to a small town of tradespeople and farmers and stopped in the market square. Passersby looked curiously at the carriage, the woman in it and the Janissaries guarding her.

Tepel helped Sarah from the carriage and escorted her into an inn on one side of the square.

"We will rest here a little while so that you may refresh yourself," he informed Sarah.

The Jewish innkeeper recognized Sarah and spread the news. A dozen Jewish residents came to the square and stood close together facing the carriage. When Sarah reappeared, they shouted, "Shame! Shame! He has betrayed us!" and moved menacingly toward her.

Tepel and his soldiers whipped out their cutlasses and advanced on the protesters.

"Please, Corporal Tepel, do not harm them," Sarah called out. "They are angry with my husband, not me."

Tepel grunted a command. The Janissaries backed slowly to the carriage but kept their cutlasses at the ready. A white bearded elder, dressed in black with a peaked headdress, stepped forward and asked permission to speak to Sarah.

"Please, Corporal Tepel, let him speak," Sarah pleaded. "The people are very confused and disappointed. They mean me no harm."

The Janissaries lowered their cutlasses but kept an attentive eye on the growing crowd.

The elder inclined his head in greeting. "Wife of the false messiah, I am Rabbi Abraham Escapa, brother to the rabbi who originally admitted your husband to the rabbinate, a move we all now regret. Tell your husband he has destroyed our dreams and hopes for a bright future. We cannot accept a messiah who is apostate. The Almighty would not allow His Messiah to apostatize. Therefore, Shabtai Zvi is false and falsely proclaimed that Redemption was nigh. The gentiles mock us as fools and, truly, fools we are." He gestured to the Janissaries. "Your new friends are impatient. Go with them and may you, your husband, and all those who still follow him be accursed." He spat, turned on his heel, and walked away.

Tepel raised his cutlass high and was about to launch himself at the rabbi when Sarah restrained him by grasping his arm. He turned angrily on her.

"Madam, how dare you interfere with a Janissary in the pursuit of his duty? That man spat at us,"

Sarah shrank back but maintained her composure. "No, Corporal Tepel, he spat at me. No one else need take umbrage and I forgive him."

They glowered at each other for a moment. Then Tepel shouted a command, and helped Sarah into the carriage. He and the other soldiers mounted their horses and they rode off rapidly, forcing the departing crowd of protesters to leap to either side.

The road was smooth and the miles sped past. Sarah bemoaned the change in her relationship with Tepel. He left her alone in the carriage, following at a discreet distance. Perhaps it is for the best, Sarah thought. Much as I like him, nothing can come of this. I am tied to Shabtai, Tepel to his Janissaries and the Sultan. She felt the pull of desire. At times in the past, she had given way to her feelings. More often she had used the lust of men for her when it suited her. Even Shabtai had benefitted from her skill in manipulating men and turned a blind eye when she transgressed her marital vows. But Tepel was different. It was clear he wanted her but she felt it was not merely lust but something deeper — love, perhaps.

Although he tried, Tepel could not take his eyes off her. As usual, her veil kept slipping, and continued to entangle him in the beauty of her face. His anger had long since subsided, replaced by a pool of regret. Soon the journey would be over and her presence would be gone. Yet that might be a good thing. He could not think clearly when he was close to her. He had always considered himself decisive, quick to take action, not only in battle, but also to rectify slights against the Sultan or the Janissaries. His men had suppressed smiles when he held back from killing the greybeard. He had allowed himself to be humiliated by a mere woman. Despite this, he admired her courage, respected her coolness. Truly, an admirable woman.

They stopped for the night in a small village which boasted a fine inn. Tepel insisted the best room be given to Sarah and he took a smaller room, a few doors down the corridor. There were no other guests. The soldiers bivouacked in the dining salon, laying their sleeping blankets on the cold stone floor.

In Sarah's room, a brass bath tub filled with lukewarm water awaited her. After the dust and grime of the road, she luxuriated in the bath tub, allowing the water laced with a silky perfumed oil to wash over her. She wondered whether Tepel ever bathed and envisioned him bent over the tub scrubbing her back. There was no way to make the dream a reality. Fatima, the innkeeper's wife, attended her and scrupulously locked the door.

"Women are not safe with soldiers around," she declared. "Are you not worried you travel alone with them?"

"They dare not harm me," Sarah said, chuckling. "The Sultan has ordered that I be brought safely to his mother. They will obey the Sultan's command. They are good Janissaries."

Fatima humphed. "Even so, I would watch out for the officer in charge. He has an eye for you."

And I an eye for him, thought Sarah. Aloud she said, "Thank you for your concern. I will indeed be watchful."

After a supper of lamb kebabs and groats which she ate in a separate room with Fatima, she approached the table in the dining salon where Tepel and his men sat.

"Corporal Tepel, I wish to stroll briefly in the cool night air. I will not stray from the square. Is it permissible?"

Tepel stood up, startled by her audacity, both in approaching him and suggesting she be alone outside.

"Madam, it is impossible. You cannot go about unattended."

The smile on her face reached her eyes above the veil. "Do I understand, then, Corporal Tepel, that you will accompany me?"

"Madam, please return to your table or go to your room," Tepel said curtly, stifling his desire to be alone with her.

Sarah bowed, turned and walked out the front door of the inn. The sun had set but there was still light. She could easily see her way around the square. Several men stood talking in the middle of the square and gawked at her. She ignored them and continued to walk resolutely as the sky darkened. Tepel emerged with two of his soldiers carrying lanterns and followed at a discreet distance. At the sight of the Janissaries, the men quickly left.

"Thank you for allowing me this brief promenade," she said to Tepel as she returned to the inn. He escorted her up the stairs to the hallway where their rooms were located. At this point, they were out of sight. They stood facing each other in the darkness of the hallway. They leaned against each other, embraced, their faces pressed tightly together. They stayed like that until they heard Fatima mounting the stair.

"I cannot, my Corporal, I cannot. Please understand," she whispered.

He held her a moment longer, nodded, bowed, kissed her hand and walked away.

They left early the next morning, the sky grey, the emerging sun still behind a bank of clouds in the east. Tepel did not join her in the carriage, but led the procession.

Sarah thought back to the night and their embrace. She had hoped he would visit her during the night but knew he wouldn't. His principled character would not allow him to ignore her wishes. A man of integrity, she thought, loyal to his Sultan, loyal to his Janissaries, and now, loyal to her.

Tepel had spent a restless night. At one point, he started down the hallway to Sarah's room, driven by the madness of his desire for her. He realized he could never force himself upon her and wandered down the stairs and out into the square. The soldier on duty raised his lamp and was surprised to see Tepel bareheaded, barefoot, and clad only in a caftan.

The soldier saluted. "Is the Corporal well?"

"The inn is stuffy and warm," Tepel replied.

He walked around the square a number of times until his lust dissipated and returned to his room. He rode in front so as not to see her, not to contemplate a life with her, or sadly, not to contemplate the improbability of a life with her.

In the afternoon, they saw a rider approaching at a gallop. Tepel spurred his horse ahead and he and the rider had a short conversation. Then the rider galloped past them. Tepel joined her in the carriage, his horse led by one of the soldiers.

"I have news that may be difficult for you," he said to Sarah quietly. "That messenger is delivering orders to Gallipoli and Smyrna to have all the rabbis who supported your husband arrested and brought to Adrianople for execution. He says that similar orders are on their way to Constantinople. The orders list the names of all the rabbis."

Sarah burst into tears. "But why? My husband has embraced Islam. Why punish our people?"

Tepel restrained the impulse to grasp her in his arms and to console her. Instead, he continued to speak quietly. "Madam, the Sultan is angered by the failure of your community's leaders to preserve the tranquility of the Jewish population. But hear me, there may be a solution. The messenger reported that some of the Sultan's ministers are entreating him to rescind the order. They argue it will cause more unrest and disturb a productive tribute paying part of his subjects. Tomorrow I deliver you to the Sultan's mother who will personally see to your conversion. Plead the case of your people to her. Be assured, she will respond and is greatly loved and respected by her son. The orders may yet be turned around."

Gratitude showed in her eyes along with the sparkle of love. "I shall do as you say. I am terribly grateful to you. This is the second time you warn and advise me. Why do you do it?"

He looked away, then directly at her. "I do it because I wish to see you untroubled and happy. I love you."

And I love you, she thought. It occurred to her that the reason she had rejected him last night was because she did indeed love him. The tryst would have cemented their love and have made it difficult or even impossible for her to return to Shabtai. Tepel was the first real love of her life, but the ongoing mission of her husband, which she still believed in, was too compelling.

Tepel left the carriage and mounted his horse. The remainder of the journey into Adrianople was uneventful. Tepel led the way to the Imperial Palace and came to a halt in the forecourt. Two of the Palace guard and a number of servants in Imperial livery waited.

"Madam, I leave you here in good hands. I bid you farewell. In a week I leave with the Grand Vizier for the campaign in Crete. I shall treasure your memory to the end of my days. Allah bless you."

"I wish you well," Sarah said, tears flowing from her eyes and wetting the veil across her face. "You have been a true friend."

He bowed, mounted his horse, and with his soldiers, trotted quickly out of the Palace, past the iron gates which closed behind him.

CHAPTER 7
- Toronto, 2006 -
Lily Thegn

To Donald's great relief, Lily did not return at the end of three weeks. Hopefully, he thought, the trip to the fashion capitals of Europe has been extended. Perhaps her sugar daddy was keeping her closer to his purse strings. Perhaps she's turned her attentions elsewhere. Nevertheless, he continued to harbour a spark of doubt, not a Holy Spark, he smiled ruefully, just an ordinary spark. She had been so adamant about her ties to him.

He revelled in the good fortune that was coming his way. Each day through email and the post, he received speaker invitations to university seminars and religious group meetings. The fees were not excessive but served to stimulate sales of his books and attendance at his weekly class.

He and Sarai spent all their leisure hours together either at her apartment or his. Despite her declared lack of conviction, she attended his classes, hung on his every word, and helped with the distribution of his books and pamphlets.

In the first class after Lily left, Donald noted with satisfaction that all 25 chairs were filled and several people sat on the table at the back. For the newcomers he gave a brief summary of the course. Sarai sat right in front of him, attentively taking notes. Jack Escapa sat beside her, his attention directed at the slides projected on the wall.

Donald explained once again the Redemption through Sin concept and put the class through one exercise. Sarai showed no reluctance to pairing off with Jack and going through the motions. Some refused to pair up and sat through the exercise. An older man at the back of the class insisted that if sin brought redemption, then he was well on the way and needed no further temptations.

"OK," said Donald after the exercise was over and individuals had reported their experiences. "That was the easy part. Now the hard work begins. Today, I shall present Shabtai Zvi's concept of God and Creation. Remember, for a Kabbalist, the only way to truly come close to comprehending God is to focus on Creation and God's role in making it happen. A Kabbalist does not deny the Biblical story of Creation but sees it as the end of a process. Before the statement 'Let there be light,' a complex system of events took place."

He paused. Everyone was looking at him with interest, some sceptically.

"Shabtai called his concept of God and Creation 'the Mystery of the Godhead.' To this day, we have no absolutely authentic rendering of his vision because he never wrote it down himself. He whispered the concept to his close disciples and swore them to secrecy. It was years after his death that documents appeared purporting to be accounts of his teachings written by several of his confidants. By comparing these accounts, we have a good idea of what he believed."

Jack's hand shot up. "Donald, since he believed he was the Messiah, why was he concerned with secrecy?"

"Good question, Jack. When you hear what his concept is you'll understand his need for secrecy. Let me explain. Contrary to conventional Jewish, Christian and Muslim theology, Shabtai believed that the God of Creation was not the First Cause but the Second Cause — in other words, the God of Creation was Himself created."

A hubbub of protests and questions erupted.

"Wait! Don't make any judgements yet. Of course this sounds heretical and blasphemous and so it was judged by both Jewish and Muslim authorities when they found out. So intense was their antagonism to anyone acknowledging acceptance of this view that Shabtai's followers eventually retreated underground and pursued their beliefs in secret. Nevertheless, let's take a closer look at what he preached.

"Consider a concept most Kabbalists accept —'the root of all roots' — the First Cause — that is, the Supreme Deity is hidden behind a veil impenetrable by humans or any other being. Kabbalists call this Supreme Deity Ein-Sof. These are Hebrew words and mean literally 'without end'. Ein-Sof is unknowable, impossible to comprehend, so hidden it cannot be described. Ein-Sof exercises neither providence nor any influence in human affairs. Shabtai believed that Ein-Sof had Will and manifested this Will when It decided to create. Now, given that Ein-Sof is impenetrable, how could Shabtai believe It had Will? Because, for whatever reason, Ein-Sof decided to create and without a compulsion to create, we wouldn't be here to talk about it. This simple Will he called the Holy Ancient One. It was the Holy Ancient One — that is, the will of Ein-Sof — which caused the retraction within itself and allowed a space for Creation. As I noted in an earlier lecture, all the Emanations that would lead to Creation spewed out from a point or a cleavage in this space. The God of Israel — the Creator of our world — appears clothed in the Sixth Emanation of Beauty and Compassion. Here Beauty means the ultimate in blessedness of both outer and inner form, Compassion the utmost confluence of empathy and mercifulness. Shabtai preached that the revealed God — the God of Israel — is the only being that can be referred to as God. At the same time, a female entity, the Shechina, was released into Creation to ensure that God's Creation would be a loving Creation and ultimately successful. So, to sum up, in Shabtai's Kabbalah, there is the Ancient Holy One, the God of Israel, and the Shechina."

Donald stopped as the hands shot up. He nodded to Jack.

"No wonder, Shabtai had a hard time. A trinity is quite alien to Jewish thinking and I guess to Islam as well. But was this some kind of allegory?"

"No, Jack, Shabtai as well as Sabbateans take this view literally. This is what actually happened."

"Donald, what's your view?" Sarai asked.

Donald didn't answer immediately. The question irritated him. Why was the woman he loved putting him on the spot? Yet, he realized, she would never do anything to hurt him; therefore, she was trying to help him to declare himself. And why not? The founding document of the Shabtai Zvi Kabbalah Society clearly laid out its belief in Shabtai as a messiah and an acceptance of his principles and teachings. Donald's strategy in designing the course was to present Kabbalah concepts in general and to nudge the class participants toward a sympathetic understanding of Shabtai's ideas.

The class fidgeted as he remained silent, seemingly unable or unwilling to answer. Finally he said:

"I have seen the Shechina."

The class was silent. Some registered surprise or smiled sceptically; others raised eyebrows in doubt.

"I saw the Shechina," Donald repeated. "You will tell me I must have been dreaming and so I was. But I swear the vision I found myself in was tactile in every sense, appeared totally real and the Shechina was as close to me as I am to you. I believe I was offered a glimpse of the Godhead and the Paradise that awaits us after Redemption. In answer to your question, Sarai, since I accept that the Shechina is real, I have no reason to doubt the existence of the Holy Ancient One and the God of Israel."

"You were angry with me, weren't you?" Sarai asked as they walked along King Street after the class toward one of the many restaurants in the Theatre District.

"At first, yes," Donald replied lightly. "I felt you were interfering. You have privileged insider information called 'pillow talk.' But then I realized you were helping me, suggesting I declare myself. After all, I am a Sabbatean. So I forgave you."

She leaned into him and he put an arm around her waist. "By the way, as you predicted, Lily didn't show up tonight. I hope we've seen the last of her, not that I'm jealous, of course."

He squeezed her hard against him. "I hope so too, but if she does, don't worry. I love you and you alone. Lily's out of my picture."

But Donald wasn't out of Lily's picture. As he and Sarai walked along, they failed to notice the man following a short distance behind them. Tall, well groomed, and carrying a briefcase, he looked like many of the businessmen making their way to a late dinner or meeting. He sat at the bar in the restaurant they selected, nursing a drink, absorbed in papers from his briefcase, and followed them afterwards into the subway system to Sarai's place of work. That same night, he reported to Lily that Sarai was a nurse at Sacred Heart Hospital.

He and Lily were sitting side by side on the sofa in her apartment.

"You know, I could charge you $200 plus expenses for my detective work tonight," he said.

"That makes me a cheap lay," Lily huffed.

"All right then, $500."

"That's minimally acceptable," she responded and pushed him flat on the sofa.

"Elliott, I need to talk to you," Lily said when she finally got through to the doctor.

"Lily, I thought everything between us was over."

She detected the anxiety in his voice. "I don't want money, just a favour. There's a nurse, Sarai Stone, works in your hospital. I want to know everything you have on her."

He expostulated that divulging personal details of patients and staff compromised his medical ethics but she reminded him that if his wife found out he had compromised his marital ethics, he would be in worse trouble.

"I need the information very quickly. I'm leaving town in a few days."

'Lily, I haven't seen you since those few seminars I gave at the Comparative Religion Course," Father Patrick said. He did not sound welcoming. "What brings you here?"

"You saw me after the seminars as well," Lily reminded him. "Or have you forgotten?"

"I try to forget periods of sin especially sins I'm too ashamed to confess. How can I help you? That's what your message said, you need help." He pointed to a chair.

Lily remained standing. "I need information regarding a certain Sarai Stone. She is a nurse at Sacred Heart. According to her bio, before she came to the hospital, she was a nun with the Order of the Nursing Sisters here in Toronto. I want to know everything about her and why she left the Order."

Father Patrick shrugged his broad shoulders. "It's not easy for a priest to invade the files of a nunnery. Why do you need the information?"

Lily smiled. "I've become a freelance journalist and I'm working on an article about the religious."

He ran a finger around the inside of his clerical collar to ease the strain against his thick neck. "I know the answer to my next question but I'll ask it anyway. What happens if I don't comply or can't get the information?"

Lily turned and started for the door. "Since you know the answer, I shouldn't waste my breath. I'll either feature you prominently in my article or sue the Church for compensation. After all, you promised you'd leave the Church and marry me and here's poor me, believing you and suffering continuing anguish. Whether I win the lawsuit or not, your career would be finished. I'll call you in a few days."

She met Father Patrick two days later in his office,

"I don't believe Sarai Stone left the Order voluntarily. My guess is it was mutual. Why is not clear. I don't think my informant knows either. In her work, Sister Sarai was considered first class and an outstanding operating nurse. She was with the Order about twenty years and worked all over the developing world. Her last assignment was in Kenya at the Order's Holy Cross Hospital and Refuge. It seems it was a short assignment, maybe two to three months. No reason given as to why. My guess is something happened there."

That same evening, Lily left with her boss for the first of their stops: the fashion and textile show in London. She was busy for several days, viewing the fashion parades, attending dinners, preparing notes after each session. She had a good eye for fashion, colour and design and helped in the selection decisions but the prime responsibility rested with her boss and the two staff members who accompanied them, the Director of Purchasing and the Chief Designer. Lily knew they were aware what her main role was but they were gracious — even obsequiously gracious — in their treatment of her.

On the fourth morning, she was allowed to sleep in while her boss and the two staff went to a meeting at the Textile Design Centre. She arose as soon as she heard the hotel door close, showered, dressed, drank a cup of coffee, sat at the desk with pad and paper, and made a long distance call.

At a little after noon, the telephone rang in the administration office of the Holy Cross Hospital and Refuge at the edge of the Maasai Mara

National reserve in Kenya. To the female voice that answered, Lily introduced herself and added, "I'm a Canadian journalist doing an article on the life of the religious in missionary work, highlighting their sacrifices, challenges, dangers and their good works. Can you direct me to the right person to interview?"

"You'd best talk to Mother Superior but she's not here right now. She and Dr. Gustav and several of the Nursing Sisters are on a medical field tour of the area. They will be back in a week."

"Oh, that's too bad. Would you mind answering a few questions? It would help to frame the interview I would conduct with your Mother Superior when she returns. You don't have an African accent. May I ask your name?"

"Melissa, Melissa Gustav. Dr. Gustav is my husband. I'm Canadian, like you."

"Then you're not a nun?"

Melissa chuckled. "No, I'm not even Catholic. I'm a volunteer. I help run the office and nurse when the case load is overwhelming."

"Good for you," Lily said. "By the way, I was given the name of a nurse at your hospital. I wonder if she's available. Sarai Stone."

There was a long pause. Lily thought she detected a gasp.

"Sister Sarai is no longer here. She returned to Canada some time ago. You can probably contact her through the Order's office in Toronto."

"Oh, what a pity," Lily said, her voice regretful. "I was told if I really want to know what the life of a Nursing Sister is, I should talk to her."

"Yes, she was an outstanding nurse, very dedicated, devoted to her patients, hardworking. I knew her for a short time only but was very impressed by her knowledge and ability. She's a real professional. From the stories told about her, she worked in every war zone and catastrophe in the third world. Tough as our Mission is here, she considered it a respite."

"She sounds wonderful," Lily gushed. "I'm surprised she was allowed to transfer away."

Again there was a long pause. Lily knew she was on to something. How to coax it out.

"Well, I don't pretend to know how these people are allocated," Melissa said finally.

But I bet you do know something about Sarai's departure, Lily thought. Have to keep the conversation going.

"Your husband — is he African?"

"No, he's German. He was a top surgeon in Dusseldorf but gave up the soft life to work here."

"What a wonderful pair you are," Lily said with enthusiasm. "Did you meet at the Hospital?"

Melissa sighed. "Yes, under very tragic circumstances. My first husband was badly mauled by a lion while we were on safari and was brought here for treatment. Despite the best efforts of everyone, Dr. Gustav, Sister Sarai and many others, Charles died of his injuries. Sigmund — Dr. Gustav — helped me through the bad time following Charlie's death. I returned to Toronto. A year later, Sigmund attended a medical convention in New York, got in touch and came to see me. The rest as they say is history."

"I'm sorry to hear of your first husband's death," Lily said sympathetically. "I hope you have found solace with your new husband. I'm amazed, though, that you returned to the scene which must hold some terrible memories for you."

"It was a bit of an emotional struggle. Sigmund and I talked about where we should live. At first, the choices were either Toronto or Dusseldorf but I soon realized that Sigmund was still totally committed to the Mission. I agreed to come back here with him. Sigmund is such a wonderful man, so dedicated, so responsible. Charlie's death was a blow to his pride as a doctor. He feels he somehow has to make it up."

"I know doctors hate to lose patients but your first husband must have been very badly injured. Perhaps there was nothing anyone could have done."

"That's right," Melissa said sharply.

There's definitely something there, Lily thought. "How have you adjusted to life at the Mission?" she asked.

"I'm very happy here. After Charlie's death, my life in Toronto was so empty, so devoid of meaning. It all changed when Sigmund showed up. I get a sense of fulfillment every day now. I'm busy making a real contribution to very needy people. Someday, we'll probably leave but not for awhile, I hope."

"How did you meet your first husband?"

"I was a nurse in the fracture unit of Cedarbrook Hospital and Charlie came in with a broken arm from a skiing accident. We hit it off. He was a business executive and became CEO of CTG Corporation. But I think I've talked long enough about me. Call back in a week and Mother Superior can tell you all about our work here."

"Wait! Don't go," Lily said. "From what you've told me, you would make a fascinating story. Can you not give me more information?"

Again a pause. "No, I would like to discuss it with Sigmund since he would be involved. Call back in a week."

"But consider the story," Lily insisted. "Nurse marries business executive, enjoys easy living in Toronto, husband badly hurt in safari accident, rushed to Mission hospital, despite best efforts of doctors and nurses, succumbs to wounds, doctor marries widow who returns with him to Mission. A wonderful story, better than a story about Sarai Stone who's no longer there." — A sudden intuition hit her.— "Did Sarai Stone leave just after your husband died? Was it because of that?"

"I think we've talked enough," Melissa said and the line went dead.

"I think you've talked enough," Lily said out loud.

Lily placed another call, this time to Toronto. It took several tries before a sleep bedraggled male voice answered.

"Hi, Sebastian," she said. "I've got a job for you."

She smiled, waiting patiently, as the reply, laced with profanities, complained about the early hour.

Unfazed, she said, "I knew you'd be happy to hear from me. Besides, it's not early. Here in London, it's past 10 o'clock. Splash some water on your face and come back with pad and pen."

"Can I pee as well?" he asked.

"Just hurry up."

She waited the few minutes until he returned.

"The CTG Corporation in Toronto — you know it?"

"Know it?" he exclaimed. "I have shares in it."

"The Corporation changed heads about two years ago?"

"That's right. The CEO at that time was a guy by the name of Charles Wingate. He died in a safari accident. Eaten by a lion. Top business guy.

When he died, the shares dropped. That's when I bought in. I've done very well since. You see, Lily, I'm not only a first class private eye but also an astute investor. Why are you interested? Is there something I should know about? Are my shares about to tank?"

"Look, stop worrying about your shares and listen to your client."

"Client? Is this a cash job or 'in kind' again?"

"Sebastian, don't be vulgar. Find out all you can about him, the women in his life, and any details that strike you as odd. His widow married the doctor who treated and lost him. Also, you remember that woman you followed, Sarai Stone, who turned out to be a nurse. She was a nurse at the hospital where he died. My gut tells me there's more to the story, maybe even a love triangle. I'll call you in a few days."

Lily was tied up for a week as she and her boss and his two staff moved on to Paris and the French designers. At the end of the Paris stay, her boss informed her that his wife insisted on joining him in Milan.

"She will fly home from Milan so you meet us in Dusseldorf. I've arranged with the hotel for your earlier arrival."

Lily pouted. "I was so looking forward to Milan."

"Next time," he said. "We'll make a special trip."

"Lily, I have to hand it to you," Sebastian said when Lily finally caught him in. "You sure can ferret out improbable connections. From my contacts at the firm, I was told that Wingate had been attacked by a lion, taken to and treated at a nun's hospital and died there. A Dr. Gustav, the one who treated him, wrote a report, describing Wingate's condition and what he did to try to save him. The doctor apologized profusely in the report and said he did everything he could. Over a year later, he married the widow, Melissa Wingate. I don't believe there was a love triangle in that case but it's possible. You know, the doctor falls in love with the wife and lets the husband die."

Lily interrupted impatiently, "Sebastian, so far you've told me what I already know. Is that it?"

"Hell, no," he replied. "I'm just coming to the juicy parts. Wingate's Executive Assistant, a woman by the name of Sandra Billington, made a big fuss at the time of his death. Claimed she was carrying his baby and demanded a settlement. She was not mentioned in Wingate's will but her lawyer insisted that Wingate was planning to change his will after he returned from the safari. The widow said she knew nothing about this and didn't feel she had any obligation. Eventually, the company hushed the whole thing up and gave her something to keep her quiet."

"So there was a love triangle after all," Lily said triumphantly.

"Wait, it gets better. I contacted Sandra Billington and met with her. I claimed I was doing a follow-up on behalf of CTG. She repeated what her lawyer had said that Wingate planned to change his will but she added he was going to cut his wife out entirely, divorce her, and marry Sandra. Sandra is convinced Melissa killed him, either pushed him into the path of the lion or did something in the hospital. Sandra believes it's too much of a coincidence — just as he's about to get rid of his wife, cut her out of his will, he dies."

"Well, Sebastian, you've done very well. That's why I pay you the big bucks."

He laughed. "Lily, you can relax. This one's a freebee. Thanks to my intense meetings with Sandra, we are now an item, plus the baby — a cute little boy of nine months — already calls me 'da da.'"

"Are you telling me you're settling down?"

"Lily, I intend to give it a real try."

"Fine with me. Sandra will be happy. You're good in bed. Send the report to my apartment. Goodbye."

She started to hang up but heard him shout, "Hold on. Don't go yet." She returned the receiver to her ear.

"I have one more piece of information that'll completely throw you. It's my farewell gift to you. Are you ready?"

"You've just kicked me out of your life. It better be good. It will help me cope with the loss of you." She didn't hide the sarcasm in her voice.

"I'm sure you'll find morale boosters elsewhere. Anyway, there's one more fact I discovered quite by accident. As Sandra and I got to know each other, we began sharing bits of our past. Wingate had given her lots of things, jewellery, clothing. She said she was going to get rid of most of them now. But there was one thing she wanted to keep. There were three volumes of photographs that Wingate had kept in her apartment for safekeeping. The guy was an avid photographer. There were pictures of everything — all kinds of animals, birds, famous places, famous people, and women — all the women he had known and I guess screwed. Many were naked, including his wife. Each picture was carefully captioned with the woman's name and date of the picture. We came to one photo showing a rather scrawny woman lying naked, flat on her back. Sandra explained that Wingate had boasted about seducing this girl as a university prank. Apparently he recorded her groans and sighs and played it back to all his buddies. Now, talk about coincidence. Guess whose name was on the caption."

"Sarai Stone," Lily said.

"My story about you gets more interesting," Lily said to Melissa when she came to the telephone. "I've discovered that your marriage to Charles Wingate was on the rocks and he was going to divorce you and cut you out of his will. Fortunately for you, a lion got in his way but, unfortunately for you, didn't finish the job. In his reports to CTG your Dr. Gustav stated the patient was very ill but was making progress. Then your husband is dead and you marry the doctor. Also, there's Sarai Stone..."

"How dare you!" shrieked Melissa. "You don't know what you're talking about. I've heard enough from you."

The line went dead. Lily dialled again and asked the person who answered the telephone for Melissa or Dr. Gustav. She was told to wait.

"How may I help you?" a calm, even female voice said.

"Who are you?" Lily demanded. "I wish to speak to Melissa or Dr. Gustav."

"Neither one is available at the moment. I am the Mother Superior of the convent and head of our mission here."

"My name is Lily Thegn and I'm a freelance journalist. I'm working on a story that concerns your mission. I am particularly interested in the events surrounding the death of Charles Wingate which appears to have suspicious elements."

Mother Superior's voice remained calm and unperturbed as though they were discussing the refreshing Kenyan spring weather.

"My dear Miss Thegn, how can anyone imagine there was anything suspicious about the death of Mr. Wingate? The poor man was attacked and badly mauled by a lion. This was witnessed by a truckload of safari tourists. He was grievously injured and brought to our hospital where he died of his wounds. As in all safari accidents, the Kenyan authorities investigated, found that the safari operators had followed all the rules and were blameless. They examined Mr. Wingate's body and agreed the wounds were consistent with a lion attack, and that Dr. Gustav and nurses had performed miracles to keep him alive as long as they had. As head of the hospital, I was very much involved in Mr. Wingate's case and agreed with all the decisions regarding his care. Everyone worked long and hard to save him. His death was a tragedy for all of us."

"Mother Superior, I know the official story. I also know that Dr. Gustav believed the patient was making progress and was optimistic about his survival. I also know there were two women there at the time who had no liking for Wingate — his wife Melissa and Sarai Stone. As a result of his death, Melissa avoids a messy divorce and Sarai Stone returns abruptly to Canada. Why shouldn't I be suspicious?"

"Miss Thegn," Mother Superior said, her voice still unruffled but with a harder edge to it, "you are imagining a story based on coincidence and speculation. The facts are simply otherwise. Every procedure undertaken in his care and every medicine given him have been duly recorded in accordance with our policies. The Kenyan authorities examined these records and certified them in order and correct. They could find no questionable acts and agreed that the care had been meticulous and in the best interests of the patient. Dr. Gustav and the nurses, including Sarai Stone, are highly skilled in their professions and have impeccable reputations. Only our Lord could have saved Charles Wingate and He chose not to."

Mother Superior paused and cleared her throat. "Miss Thegn, if you publish your fanciful scenario, you will not only sully the good names of hard working and dedicated medical professionals but harm our mission and the essential health care we provide the people in this region. Please consider carefully what you do and may God bless you. Good day."

And may the devil screw you, Lily thought, these religious are all so righteous.

With the help of a good tip and a grateful smile from Lily, the Concierge at the Park Hotel in Dusseldorf called several of the main hospitals and identified the one where Gustav had worked and was still registered. After some persuasion, he was able to set up an appointment with a doctor who had been a colleague of Gustav.

She dressed carefully in a blouse with the buttons opened just enough to allow an alluring hint of her décolleté, a tight fitting skirt that just touched her knees, and high heeled shoes. Dark glasses rode on top of her head although the sky was overcast. She draped a beige fall coat over her shoulders and carried her handbag, a notebook and a folded umbrella.

The lead driver in the taxi line saw her coming and leapt out of his cab to open the door for her and help her into the car. At her direction of the Universitätsklinik Düsseldorf, Moorenstrasse 5, he realized German wasn't her mother tongue and tried to engage her in the best English he could muster. No, she assured him, she wasn't sick, but was visiting her husband who had fallen ill on a business trip. Looking disappointed, the taxi driver turned his attention to navigating the dense traffic to the southern part of the city where the hospital was located.

She waited over an hour in the doctor's waiting room before he showed up. Hermann Werner, encased in hospital greens, was young, about Lilly's height, uneven stubble clung to his thin cheeks emphasizing the sharp nose and distracting from the deep set blue eyes. As soon as he saw Lily, he pulled off his scrub hat, bowed, and apologized profusely for his tardiness.

"These surgeries sometimes take longer than we expect," he explained.

Lily introduced herself. "I realize you are between operations," she said. "Therefore, I will be quick. I am a freelance journalist doing a story on Dr. Gustav's marvellous work in Kenya. I am Canadian, the Mission which employs Dr. Gustav is Canadian and I believe Canadian audiences will be very interested. I understand you worked under Dr. Gustav when he was here. It would help me immensely if you could tell me as much as you can about him."

She spoke slowly, pronouncing each word. He replied in impeccable English with a British accent.

"Fraulein Thegn, it will please me to assist you. I cannot speak too highly of Dr. Gustav. He is an outstanding surgeon and an excellent teacher. He taught me my profession. I assisted him in many surgeries. He explained everything as he operated. To be very frank, we were astounded when he announced one day that he had accepted to be the doctor in a Kenyan Mission."

"You had no inkling that he was considering such a move?" Lily asked.

"Not at all," Werner answered, shaking his head.

He sat down beside Lily. She turned toward him, leaning slightly forward as she wrote in the notebook perched on her knee. She felt his eyes slip into the valley between her breasts and saw him furtively lick his lips.

"We were not only colleagues but often had a beer together in the Alt Stadt," Werner continued. "After work hours, of course," he hurriedly added. "He never hinted that he was considering such a step. Sometimes he would complain that the pressure was becoming too much but then we all complained."

"Did he ever lose patients?" Lily asked.

Werner frowned. "Fraulein Thegn, it is the sadness of our profession that as conscientious as we are, as well trained, as advanced in technique and facilities and equipment, now and then a patient dies in front of us or soon afterwards. We then have the onerous duty to inform the patient's family and try to comfort them. As a top surgeon, Dr. Gustav tended to have the most difficult cases. Yes, some died but he achieved miracles. Some of his techniques have become standard procedure. His writing on his work has been translated and appeared in Lancet, the British medical journal."

"He certainly seems very competent," Lily said. "Are you in contact with him?"

"Yes, he writes to me either by post or email every month and returns here every three months or so for a few days. We laugh at some of his experiences but also marvel at what he has accomplished. He gives much credit to his medical team at the Mission. His favourite joke was that he is isolated with 18 women and all avowed celibates. Of course, now that he is married, he no more says that."

Lily joined Werner in his chuckle.

"Dr. Werner, is it possible to describe some of Dr. Gustav's work at the Mission without, of course, betraying confidentiality? It would help me round out the picture of him and the Mission and make my story more interesting." She looked at him appealingly.

They were interrupted by the measured tones of a female speaker on the PA system.

"I must go," Dr. Werner said. "I am called to the next surgery. I would like to continue this conversation. May I invite you for dinner tonight? Then there will be enough time to answer all your questions."

It took two nights of dinners, strolling around the Alt Stadt and the Rhineufer Promenade, and two nights of intimacy in Werner's plush apartment before Lily felt confident to broach the all important subject. They were lying blissfully at peace side-by-side in the doctor's bed.

"Hermann, one thing has always puzzled me about my Mission story and the people who work there. It concerns the death of Charles Wingate — you know, the man whose widow Dr. Gustav married. My sources had access to his medical reports. Dr. Gustav fully expected the patient to survive yet he died."

Werner yawned. "Lily, these things happen all the time in medicine."

Lily turned toward him and stroked his chest. "I know, Hermann. My own mother died even as the doctor told me the danger was over. But within Wingate's company, there are some who speculate that Dr. Gustav had fallen in love with Wingate's wife and allowed the husband to die so he could marry her. Do you..."

Werner sat bolt upright. "Absolute nonsense, Lily," he expostulated, angrily interrupting her. "How dare anyone think that! Sigmund would never do such a thing. He was proud of his work, dedicated to medicine and his patients. You may take my word for it. Sigmund did everything he could to keep the patient alive."

"Don't get excited, Hermann," Lilly said soothingly, stroking him gently beneath his waist. "We journalists are very cynical and trained to investigate all ideas and angles. But, based on your description of Dr. Gustav, since he wasn't personally responsible, it must have bothered him that the patient died despite his judgement that things were going well."

There was a long silence. Werner lay back in bed.

"Yes, it did bother him, it bothered him very much," Werner said after awhile. "At his next visit to Dusseldorf that's all he talked about with me.

I will tell you what he told me if you promise never to reveal it, to keep it confidential, and it cannot appear in your story. Do you agree?"

"Of course," Lily said. "It won't be the first time that I keep sensitive information to myself."

Werner hesitated a moment longer. "Very well then. Sigmund could not prove it but he believes there was a criminal act carried out by one of the nurses."

It was Lily's turn to sit up. "That's terrible. Why did he never report it?"

Werner reached up, fondled a breast and pulled her back to him. "Because he couldn't prove it. It was just a suspicion based on some flimsy evidence. The Mother Superior of the Mission held a meeting with Sigmund and the three nurses involved in Wingate's care. According to Sigmund, there was a very heated argument between him and one of the nurses who resigned. Sigmund is convinced she was the one responsible. But without real proof, there was nothing he could do. The whole thing was hushed up."

"Do you think his pride was hurt and he blamed his failure on a nurse?" Lily asked, snuggling up against Werner.

"No, that would not be Sigmund. Something happened that was not right. Of that I am sure."

The room was full and the class had started when Lily walked in to the Thursday evening session.

"Sorry I'm late," she called out. "Please continue, Donald."

The entire class turned to view the new entrant. She reeked sexuality in her black tight fitting dress, the bodice open just enough to reveal an ample bulge of breast, black sheer hose and stiletto black shoes.

A couple of men whistled, some of the women gasped, Jack shook his head and rolled his eyes. Donald saw the sudden tension in Sarai and felt it himself. Trouble has arrived, he thought.

"You're not late at all, Lily," Donald said sarcastically. "In fact, you're just in time. We're discussing the existence of evil in God's Creation. Find a perch on the table at the back."

"She can sit on my lap," a man offered.

"Not now," Donald said. "We'll do Redemption through Sin later."

He ignored her grimace of annoyance when Lily realized there was no chair available. She flounced noisily onto the table, dislodging a stack of books to the floor. Donald smiled reassuringly at Sarai and watched her relax.

"As I've said in previous classes," Donald continued, "the existence of evil is the drive behind all Kabbalistic thinking and teaching. Without evil there would be nothing to speculate about. The world would be perfect, divinely perfect. We would find ourselves in the Garden of Paradise, our souls in communion with the God of Israel and in harmony with the Holy Ancient One. Death, disease, disasters would be unknown to us. This is the utopia blighted by the existence of evil in all its forms. Evil persists because we constantly revive and fortify it through our sinful deeds. It is no wonder that every religion exhorts its followers to refrain from sin, to be penitent, charitable, generous, kind, to do good deeds. This is a necessary precondition for redemption to come."

Donald paused. Most of the class were listening intently, although some looked on with noticeable scepticism. Lily sat, arms akimbo thrusting up her breasts, a cynical smile parting her red lipsticked mouth.

Donald continued, "Most religions concern themselves with sin as the primary aspect of evil because natural disasters and epidemics seem beyond our power to control or even to predict. The Kabbalist believes that Evil manifested itself during the process of Emanations that were a necessary part of the Creation. Specifically, it was the growing separation of the Emanation of Judgement from its customary union with Loving Kindness and Mercy that led to the existence of Evil. In other words, totally rational judgement untempered by any humane restraint is evil, sinful. There are lots of examples — think Hitler, Stalin — men who judged their greed for power required the sacrifice of tens of millions of people. Psychopaths are a perfect example of unrestrained totally rational judgement. So if you want a quick and easy definition of sin it is whenever you make a judgement that takes no one else into account but yourself."

There was stark silence as the class seemed to need time to digest what he had just said.

After a moment, Jack Escapa raised his hand. "Donald, that's a very profound sense of sin. I don't disagree with it but I'm trying to understand how it helps me to know when I'm sinning. Sin seems to be relative anyway. If a Jew or a Christian marries two women at the same time, apart from being illegal, it is considered sin. If a Muslim has four wives or a Mormon fundamentalist — like that guy in Bountiful, BC — has 26, it is not sin. The Christian may consider the Muslim and the Mormon Fundamentalist sinful but who's to say their judgement in having multiple wives was not guided by loving kindness. After all, the husband still has to support his wives and the larger number of children that are likely to result. Besides, the husband believes he's following the dictates of his own religion."

"Jack, what nonsense you're spouting," Lily said. "You know damn well when you're sinning. We all know — we get that feeling of guilt. We all went through the exercise Redemption through Sin. We all picked the sin that made sense to us. But if you want an expert on sin, there's no better person to consult than Sarai Stone. She..."

Donald sensed the growing unease in the class. Lily's tone had been biting and accusatory. She was standing, a triumphant leer on her face, her lips twisted in a sneer of contempt. A snake, Donald thought, a snake stalking its victim, about to strike.

"Lily, this is a class on sin as a concept," he interrupted. "It's got nothing to do with individuals. Would anyone else care to comment?"

Lilt was not to be stopped. "Donald, I'm not singling out Sarai as an individual. She used to be a nun not so long ago. Nun's know all about sin — they have to confess regularly. Sarai can help us understand the concept, can't you Sarai? What would you consider your greatest sin?"

"Hatred," snapped Sarai without turning around.

Lily laughed. "Hatred? Hatred of whom? Me? Don't worry, I won't take you away from your precious Donald."

"Lily, that's enough," Donald said sharply. "This is a Kabbalah class, not a venue for a personal vendetta."

"Not a vendetta at all," Lily said. "Sarai has pointed out that hatred is a sin. I agree with her. But hatred needs an object to make the sin complete. Hatred of whom? Dr. Gustav? Or was it Charles Wingate? You see, Donald, hatred is a sin that may lead to other more important sins, like the sin of murder. We can all agree that murder is a sin, can't we?"

Sarai stood up and faced Lily. "You stupid bitch. You don't know what you're talking about."

"Don't I, Sarai?"

"Lily, get out!" Donald shouted. "This is completely uncalled for. You're disrupting my class." He strode to the door and opened it.

"I'll leave," Lily said. "I'm only doing this to protect you. You should get to know your girlfriends better."

He slammed the door behind her and locked it. He apologized to the class for the interruption. The rest of the session was desultory as he tried to delve deeper into the Kabbalistic concept of Evil and at the same time keep his mind off Lily's accusation.

"I'd like an explanation," Donald said when they were alone in Sarai's College Street apartment. "She's accusing you of murdering Charles Wingate. Is he the guy who tricked you in university?"

"You believe her, don't you?' Sarai said morosely.

"I believe she knows something I don't."

Sarai looked at him intensely, longing for the grim face to relax into its usual show of affection. "I will tell you what she's referring to."

CHAPTER 8
- KENYA, 2005 -
SISTER SARAI STONE

The Maasai Mara National Reserve is located just inside Kenya at the northern end of the Serengeti region. The Order of Nursing Sisters Holy Cross Hospital and Refuge lies nestled in a wooded area close to the Reserve. The white stucco walls and red tile roofs of the buildings in the compound rise above the fence that surrounds it.

The largest building is the hospital with 24 patient beds on two floors, two operating rooms, a clinic on the ground floor, a dispensary, a kitchen, and a refectory with a long table for the nuns and smaller tables and chairs for patients and visitors and other hospital staff. There is a convent to accommodate the eighteen nuns who provide medical and other care services, a small house for the resident doctor, a church for both nuns and laity, and a chapter house with a room for the itinerant priest. Two large shipping containers behind the hospital contain medical supplies, food and everything else that may be needed. A utility building houses the diesel electricity generator and a laundry. Men and women from the village behind the compound assist the Sisters as orderlies and in maintenance and do the cooking.

On a warm spring afternoon in early October, a triage nurse sat at a desk on the veranda of the hospital beside the front entrance. She interviewed each of the patients in the long line and decided how best to treat them and how urgent was treatment required. Occasionally, she would usher a patient into a screened area on the veranda for a quick examination.

The patience of these people is remarkable, she thought. They still smile after long hours in the hot sun. She remembered the Toronto hospital waiting rooms and the sometimes grumpy, angry patients after an equally long wait but in sheltered conditions.

Sister Sarai had arrived at Holy Cross barely four weeks before and had quickly acclimatized herself to the setting and routine. Having worked in other developing countries, she was not overwhelmed by the number of patients or the long working hours. After dark, few patients came on foot but there were still in-patients to look after. In addition, as one of the two trained experienced OR nurses at Holy Cross, she was often called upon at all hours to the operating room.

She did not complain; she relished the busy life, the incessant demand for care, and the reward of success as she set someone back on the road to health.

She rubbed a damp swab across her face, wiped the sweat out of her eyes, and ran her fingers through her short hair under the plastic cap that covered her head. Unlike the other Sisters, she wore scrubs when nursing: a short sleeved green shirt and loose green slacks.

"I prefer not to wear my habit when I'm nursing," she had told Mother Superior.

Mother Superior was very agreeable. "My dear Daughter, just do here what you've done elsewhere, and you can wear whatever you want." There was a pause and then a slight recantation. "Well, perhaps not whatever you want. Scrubs will be fine."

Sarai liked the head nun immediately but recognized in her a steeliness that made her grateful that she would be allowed to work in scrubs. Sarai had met her briefly years before in transit to their assignments. Then she was simply Sister Veronica, a tall gangling woman from Ottawa who had entered the Order after graduating and interning as a nurse. Sarai had admired Veronica's composure and self-confidence and hoped she would see her again.

The afternoon was well along, the sun slanting to the western horizon, when Mother Superior summoned her from just inside the front door.

"Sister Sarai, we've received a radio alert. A safari tourist has been badly mauled by a lion on the Reserve about an hour's drive away. The tourist is still alive and the guide is bringing him and his wife here. They expect to arrive by sunset. We don't know what to expect but Dr. Gustav has asked that an operating room be readied. You will assist him. Sister Maria will take over here."

Dr. Sigmund Gustav, a middle-aged German from Düsseldorf, was a stocky man of medium height, with a pleasant, round goateed face. He blamed his girth on too many visits to the pubs in the Altstadt. He insisted that his present diet, the heat, and the hard work would eventually return him to his university fitness. He would jokingly complain to the occasional European visitor that here he was, locked in with eighteen women and all celibate.

Sarai liked him. He was comfortable to work with, an excellent doctor, a skilled surgeon, and, like everyone else, shouldered the long hours without complaint. He had already performed two minor surgeries that day using local anaesthetics. Now he and the other OR nurse, Sister Constanze, also German, were setting up the equipment for a full anaesthetic.

"Depending upon the condition of the patient," said Dr. Gustav in his gravelly accented voice, "either we stabilize him for the helicopter to Nairobi or do what we can if he needs help immediately. Sister Sarai, you will assist me. Sister Constanze, you will be the anaesthetist."

The sun was poised on the western mountains when the safari vehicle drove through the front gate of the compound and stopped short of the steps at the main entrance. The patient lay on a blanket in the corridor between the two banks of seats. Two of the local men, on duty as orderlies, and the tour guide carefully carried him out and placed him on a stretcher. Despite the fading light, it was evident to the medical staff that the wounds were horrendous.

"Please be careful with my husband," a sobbing woman called out and followed the stretcher into the emergency examination room

Under the full glare of overhead lights, several nurses quickly cut away the man's blood soaked clothing. His face was scratched and bitten and one eye was gone. His left arm was partly severed above the wrist and the hand hung at a strange angle. His torso was covered in scratches with deep cuts in his midriff where the lion had sunk its canines. His legs were also scratched and bitten but less so than the rest of his body.

Dr. Gustav and Sarai moved closer to examine him while the nurses tried to stanch the blood seeping from the wounds. Sarai looked closely at the man's face. She froze, looked wildly about, stifled a gasp, and stepped back.

Mother Superior calmed the wife who was still weeping and quite agitated. "Madam, we need some basic information regarding your husband," she said gently, taking the woman's hand. "Name, age, citizenship, any other medical conditions, blood type, medicines, allergies."

"Yes, of course," his wife said, her voice still catching. "I'm so worried about him. Please do what you can."

"We always strive to do our best and pray that God will reward our efforts," Mother Superior assured her.

"His name is Charles Wingate. I'm his wife, Melissa. He's 40 years old, we're Canadian from Toronto. I don't know his blood type. He has high blood pressure for which he takes ..." She rummaged through her bag and produced a small viol. "...Metoprolol. He has no allergies as far as I know."

"Except he seems to be allergic to taking direction," the tour guide cut in, his tone sarcastic and unsympathetic. "We stopped to watch a lion attacking a wildebeest. I told everyone to stay put. Charlie decides he needs a better camera view so out the back of the truck he goes. He doesn't see the other lion coming in for the kill. By the time I shoot the lion, the damage is done."

Melissa glowered at him. Mother Superior angrily ordered him away. "This is no time to air your grievances. A man is badly hurt. His wife aches for him. Please leave us. You may stay the night. The orderly will show you where."

For a moment, Sarai had hoped she was wrong but the mention of his name removed any doubt. She scanned his naked body which was still being sponged and disinfected. The washboard stomach was gone and the chest muscles had sagged but the penis with its brown birthmark just above the foreskin was unchanged. She had met Charlie once again.

Hate the sin but love the sinner, she reminded herself desperately but the thought did not stop the flood of rage and hatred that threatened to engulf her. I'm a nurse, she screamed to herself. I heal the hurt and sick no matter whom. I'm a nun. I don't wallow in vindictiveness. If a man slaps you on one cheek, offer the other. It's up to God to punish this man and He has already acted in the form of a lion.

Charlie groaned, tried to move, and opened his good eye. "Wha's goin' on? God, pain awful," he moaned.

Melissa ran to him, pushing brusquely aside one of the nursing Sisters. "Charlie, it's Melissa. You're going to be ok. You were attacked by a lion. We're in some kind of hospital. Charlie, just do whatever they tell you."

Charlie's one eye looked about the group. He watched a man test a hypodermic needle and felt the stick pain as it plunged into his arm. He saw women staring at him and then he saw one whom he thought he knew.

"You," he said thickly, spitting up blood. "Wha's name?"

Sarai didn't answer nor was it clear to whom he had spoken.

"Charlie, just relax," Melissa pleaded. "Soon you'll know everybody. Don't get excited. They know what to do."

Charlie tried to reply but more blood welled up. Dr. Gustav ordered him up to the operating room and went ahead of the stretcher. Sarai remained behind, unable to move, striving to push the hatred aside and replace it with, if not love, at least duty.

Mother Superior put an arm around her. "Is something wrong, Sister Sarai?"

Sarai turned to her, lips quivering and eyes distraught.

"Sister Sarai, we can talk later about what is troubling you," Mother Superior said gently. "Right now, your duty calls you to Dr. Gustav's side."

Sarai nodded, walked quickly up the stairs and caught up with Melissa.

"The surgery will be lengthy," Sarai said to her. "You would be better off waiting downstairs in the refectory. The church is always open if you wish to pray."

Melissa, tears filling her eyes, smiled gratefully. "Thank you. I'm not much of a church goer but right now I'll do anything that might help."

She's an attractive woman, quite voluptuous, just the type Charlie would go after, Sarai thought bitterly.

Melissa squeezed Charlie's foot as he was carried into the operating room. "Don't worry, Charlie," she called after him. "You're going to be alright."

Scrubbed, gowned, masked, gloved, Dr. Gustav and Sarai stood on either side of the supine anaesthetized patient. Sarai stared fixedly at his penis, remembering it hugely erect and inflamed and the pain in the days afterwards.

Gustav carefully examined the major wounds, made quick decisions on procedure and communicated these to Sarai. It took him only a few seconds to realize she was not responding.

"Schwester, bitte!" (Sister, please) he admonished her, forgetting he was speaking German. He pulled a sheet over the offending organ. The other assisting nurses looked up sharply, surprised. Sister Sarai was relatively new but surely, with her experience, she had seen naked men before.

"I'm sorry, Doctor, my mind was elsewhere. You have my earnest attention."

They worked long hours on Charlie, patching him up as best they could. The partially severed hand still had an uncut main artery. Gustav managed to reattach the hand although he doubted it would survive. "We'll have to watch that hand. There's a great danger of infection and gangrene. It may yet have to come off."

The sky was greying when the OR team finished. Charlie was trundled off to an empty bed in a six bed ward just off the operating room. Flanked by intravenous pole and oxygen tank, he lay there, covered in bandage, drainage tubes emanating from under the covers and disappearing into bags hanging below the bed. Gustav was satisfied that nothing more could be done and went to his quarters for a few hours sleep. Sarai found Melissa dozing in the refectory and led her to Charlie.

"He survived the operation reasonably well," Sarai told her. "But he's still in a very fragile state. Dr. Gustav says it would be too dangerous to move him at the moment to Nairobi. We'll know more in a few hours."

Melissa nodded and looked around the ward. All were local villagers: an old man snoring audibly, two young men, one with a plastered leg suspended by a pulley traction system, and two incredibly thin women. Melissa caught the word 'AIDS' on the charts at the foot of the women's beds.

"Can we find another room for Charlie?" she asked, frowning.

Sarai said quietly, "May I remind you, Mrs. Wingate, we're in the middle of Africa."

"Oh, no, Sister Sarai," Melissa responded quickly. "I wasn't being racial. Is there a private room? I know Charlie would prefer a private room. And don't worry about payment."

Sarai couldn't help smiling. "Mrs. Wingate, we're a small field hospital. There are no private rooms. Mr. Wingate is close to the OR in case immediate surgery is required. As for payment, please talk to Mother Superior. Our services are free but we welcome donations."

Melissa said solicitously, "You look very tired, Sister Sarai. I suppose you're off to bed now. Will there be other nurses to look after Charlie?"

"Of course, Mrs. Wingate. Here comes the Ward Nurse now. The anaesthetist will be coming by shortly and I'll be back in a few hours."

Sarai was dreadfully tired. She'd been up and on duty over 24 hours. Despite her fatigue, she stopped in at the church before going to bed. She prostrated herself in front of the altar and cast tearful eyes on the painted portrait of Jesus. She was profoundly disturbed by her implacable hatred of Charlie and prayed fervently for Divine help in ridding her of this demon. But what was the demon? Was it the sin of hate that she was asking the Lord to relieve her of or was it Charlie himself. She rose and sat in one of the pews, mulling over her dilemma, and soon fell asleep lying on the hard bench.

She awoke to find Mother Superior sitting beside her in the pew.

"I looked for you in your cell and then came to the church. Something troubles you, my Daughter. Is it the man?"

Sarai pushed herself to a sitting position, rubbed her eyes, breathed deeply, and head lowered, replied. "No, Mother. It is not the man. When he arrived, I was overwhelmed by the extent of his injuries and lost confidence we could help him."

Mother Superior frowned. "We both know you are lying, Sister Sarai," she said gravely. "There is something more."

Sarai shook her head, "There is nothing more, Mother. I got control of myself and I hope you agree that I performed well."

Mother Superior took Sarai's hands in hers. "Yes, my Daughter. According to Dr. Gustav, you performed extremely well, confirming your reputation as an outstanding OR nurse. However, Dr. Gustav reports you were frozen at first. He says you seemed fascinated by the man's reproductive organs, an observation confirmed by your colleagues. I know you must have seen naked men before. Are you familiar with Charles Wingate or was it simply a crisis of lust versus your vow of celibacy?"

Sarai blushed, but, looking directly at Mother Superior, said firmly, "I have no desire for this man, Mother. I feel no lust and my vow is as intact as it has been since I joined the Order. The man has a vague resemblance to my father and the thought of my father so badly hurt filled me with a sorrow that immobilized me. Once I pushed the memory of my father out of my mind, the paralysis left me. I'm over it now."

Mother Superior appeared unconvinced but said resignedly, "Fine. Continue to treat him but wear your full nun's nursing habit unless you're called to the OR."

Sarai returned to her cell and, after freshening up, dressed. She returned to the ward in white coif and wimple, white tunic and scapular, woollen belt holding her rosary and a silver cross hanging from her neck. Melissa was asleep beside her husband's bed, her body bent over, and head resting on the bed. Charlie was still unconscious.

Sarai nudged Melissa awake and said softly, "Mrs. Wingate, I need to examine the patient."

"Of course," Melissa said, yawning, and stepped away from the bed. "Will Sister Sarai soon return?"

"I am Sister Sarai," she said smiling.

Melissa looked sharply at her. "You're in full uniform. I was used to the scrubs. It must be warm and awkward to do medicine in your nun's habit."

"Not really. We get quickly accustomed."

She pulled down Charlie's covering sheet and examined the bandages on midriff and chest. All seemed in order. The drainage bags had been emptied but were filling again with liquid that reminded Sarai of the colour of blood pudding. Charlie's pulse was weak but regular, his blood pressure still low. He had a slight fever.

"He's doing as well as can be expected, Mrs. Wingate. I shall be out front at the triage station. Please get me if something seems amiss or he wakens."

A short time later, Sarai was called. She found Charlie groaning in pain and quickly administered morphine. He opened his one eye and twitched it about uncomprehendingly.

Melissa leaned over him. "Charlie, it's me, Melissa. Can you see me? I'm right beside you."

His wife's face swam into his field of vision.

"Melissa," he said, whispering hoarsely, "you're a bit fuzzy but I can see you. What's happened? Where am I?"

"Charlie, you're in a hospital. Do you remember the attack by a lion? You were badly bitten and scratched."

"Don't remember lion. Remember safari — safari in Kenya. We still in Kenya?"

Charlie didn't wait for an answer but closed his eye and fell asleep as the morphine kicked in.

Several hours later, Sarai returned. Charlie was awake. Melissa sat beside the bed holding his hand. The Ward Nurse had taken his vital signs and emptied the drainage bags. Sarai injected another dose of morphine.

"You look familiar," Charlie said, his voice stronger but still hoarse, his eye fastened on her. "What's your name?"

"How do you feel now?" Sarai asked.

"How do I feel? I feel wonderful," he said. "I'm deadly hurt and I'm in a jungle hospital. I want a real hospital with real medical staff."

"For God's sake, Charlie," Melissa snapped, "you never would've made it to Nairobi. These people saved your life. Be grateful and apologize."

"Thanks for saving my life," he said. "Next time, don't ask me stupid questions like 'how am I feeling?'"

Melissa exploded in anger and frustration. "Charlie, how dare you talk to Sister Sarai like that? She's part of the reason you're alive." She turned to Sarai. "Please ignore his remarks. He's often pig-headed but now he's too sick to think clearly."

At the mention of her name, Charlie's eye swung past Melissa and focussed on Sarai. Before he could say anything, Dr. Gustav arrived.

"Well, Herr Wingate, you are awake. Good! Allow me a moment, meine damen (ladies). The reports are good but I must confirm them myself."

He prodded Charlie's chest with a stethoscope, took his blood pressure, studied the bandages, and frowned at the drainage bags. He prescribed an antibiotic for the drip line and Sarai left to fill it.

"It will be a slow recovery, Herr Wingate. You are a patient who must be very patient," said Dr. Gustav, chuckling at his joke. "If all goes well, it will be a while before you can travel to Nairobi or any other city. Nature must take its course and we will do everything we can to help nature."

"If you're a good doctor, what're you doing here?" Charlie demanded. "It can't be well-paying. Are you Catholic?"

Dr. Gustav looked at him in surprise. "You should be very happy that I'm here, otherwise you would be dead. I am Lutheran, and you are correct — a doctor is not well paid here. As for your case, I have assigned Sister Sarai to give you special attention until the crisis is past. Of course, I will come by regularly but I have many other patients. Frau Wingate, you appear exhausted. I recommend that Mother Superior find you a bed in the convent and you get some rest."

Gustav bowed and left. Melissa kissed Charlie and went to find Mother Superior.

"Where is Sister Sarai?" Charlie called out.

"I'm right here," Sarai said, returning from the dispensary. "I'm adding the antibiotic bag Dr. Gustav prescribed to your intravenous." She busied herself with the task, dragging it out so she could put off facing him as long as possible. Charlie couldn't turn his head to see her.

"I used to know a Sarai," he said. "You remind me of her. Same skinny face, pointy nose. It wasn't only her face was skinny. All of her was skinny. This was in university. We called her 'Broomstick.' Her last name was Stone. Our favourite song for her was 'Broomstick Stone/No meat, just bone.' Can't remember the rest. I don't know what happened to her. Someone told me she became a nun."

He yawned, closed his eye, and fell asleep.

He did not see Sarai's face flushed with anger, the sneer of contempt curling her lips, the narrowed hate-squinting eyes. It would be so easy, she thought, to fix this bastard once and for all, he's at death's door anyway, a tiny injection here, a lapse of attention there, bit by bit, even Gustav wouldn't know. There must be nuns who committed evil for the sake of humanity. This man must have damaged other women. Surely, getting rid of him would benefit others.

Her lust for revenge shook her. What am I thinking? she demanded of herself. I'm a healer, not a killer. She summoned to her support the memory of the vows she had taken and the principles and commitments she had promised to fulfill. These did not include murder, no matter how justified.

She breathed deeply and said to the Ward Nurse: "I'll be in the clinic for awhile. Call me when you need to."

She would try to limit her exposure to Charlie as much as Dr. Gustav would tolerate. He had a high regard for her and insisted she participate in all the difficult cases, particularly when a patient teetered on the edge of life.

She returned to the ward two hours later to find Charlie awake and Melissa already beside his bed. Sarai fed him juice through a bent straw.

"That's better," he said. "I was goddamn thirsty. I'm not getting the care I need. I want a real hospital."

His face was flushed and his brow feverish. His temperature had risen.

"You're not well enough to travel, Mr. Wingate," Sarai told him. "You'll have to put up with us a little longer."

She tried to keep her voice cheerful but could not control its cold undertone.

Melissa reached over and touched her arm. "Don't let him irritate you, Sister Sarai. I know you and the hospital are doing all you can."

"Melissa, she isn't doing all she can," Charlie protested. "I woke up a few times and only the Ward Nurse was here."

"Mr. Wingate," Sarai said, trying to stay cool and professional, "we have too many patients and not enough staff to provide one-on-one nursing. I return as often as I can from my other duties and the Ward Nurse is always close by. As for our qualifications, Dr. Gustav was a top surgeon in Dusseldorf but has chosen to be with us for a few years. Most of the nursing Sisters, me included, have worked in Missions all over the world and are well-trained and experienced. I graduated from McMaster University and interned at Toronto General. Therefore, consider yourself in good hands."

"Bravo, Sister Sarai, that's telling him," Melissa said, clapping softly. "Charlie, just do what they tell you and stop complaining. Charlie, "she explained, "is CEO of his company and controls everyone and everything. Now he's completely helpless."

"It's a difficult position for anyone to be in," Sarai said diplomatically.

She pitied the people who worked for him. How oppressed their work lives must be. And this was the man she had given herself to with complete trust and devotion, convinced he loved her as dearly as she loved him. He had controlled her too, manipulated her with his declarations of undying love and the temptations of sexual fulfillment. She had succumbed, the victim of a so-called harmless prank. She remembered her humiliation and profound devastation and her conclusion that she could no longer reside in the world of everyday people. Yet, was Charlie really to blame? Was this perhaps God's way of demonstrating that service to Him was the only true path for her? Was Charlie's plot really God's plot to convince her beyond doubt that true happiness for her was through the Church? Did that let Charlie off — that he was merely a cog in a Divine Plan? Did that let Judas off? Charlie, Judas — all they had to say was, "No! I will not do it."

As Sarai thought this through, she tidied the bed, adjusted the drip line, checked the drainage bags, and fed Charlie more juice. Melissa left for supper and a few hours sleep.

"There's no doubt in my mind anymore," Charlie said after Melissa had gone. "You are Sarai Stone. You look like her, you sound like her, you have the same first name, and you're a nun. So you're her. Why don't you admit it? What's past is past. Water under the bridge."

Sarai glared at him. "Mr. Wingate, I am your nurse. The only conversation we need engage in will concern your health and recovery."

Her voice was biting and loud enough for the Ward Nurse to turn from the patient she was assisting.

"OK! OK!" Charlie said, shrugging the one shoulder he could shrug. "Don't get mad. You had a good time. It was just a game. Let me tell you something, it was a fantastic screw. Better than my first with Melissa. If you'd only had some meat on you and bigger tits, we'd be an item now."

Sarai, bottled up with outrage, was unable to speak. She walked to the foot of the bed and pretended to mark something on his chart. When she had control, she smiled sweetly and said very softly, "Mr. Wingate, does it not worry you that if I were indeed Sarai Stone listening to your despicable remarks and aware of the incident to which you refer, that I might be very angry and allow this anger to influence my care of you?"

She noted with pleasure his eye widen, his mouth open and puckered worry lines form on the part of his brow not covered by bandages.

Before he could answer, she said, airily waving her hand as she walked away from the bed, "Now Mr. Wingate, relax and rest. I'll be back later."

She ate quickly in the refectory, went to her cell for a few hours sleep, and joined the other nuns off duty at Compline. After the service, Mother Superior took her aside and they walked back and forth in the square outside the church.

"Mrs. Wingate came to see me before Compline while you were asleep. She was quite upset. Her husband does not want you treating him. He claims you've threatened to kill him. The Ward Nurse says there seemed to be an argument between you and Wingate. What's going on, Sister Sarai?"

Sarai cursed herself for allowing her anger to give way to him. "Mother, he thinks I'm someone he met once whom he despoiled as some kind of schoolboy prank. He believes I'm out to get him. I've tried to reassure him we are doing the best we can. His speech is so detestable that I would be happy not to care for him. All he talks about is sex."

"Sex with you?"

"Sex with the person he believes I am. Mother, please relieve me from treating him. Find someone more hardboiled than I am."

Mother Superior sighed. Despite the darkness, the night air was still warm and muggy; their habits clung to them. "Sister Constanze absolutely refuses. She claims Wingate purposely thrust his elbow between her thighs when she leaned against the bed to adjust his oxygen mask. We can tag him a sinner, but he's still a human and needs our care. I'll ask Dr. Gustav for his advice. Let's go into the hospital. It's a little cooler there."

Based on her experience with Charlie and her judgement of his character, Sarai wasn't surprised by his brazen behaviour. Constanze had been a fashion model before joining the Order and even in a nun's habit, her beauty was evident. Poor Melissa, she thought, putting up with such a man.

Sarai relieved the Ward Nurse for her twenty minute supper break. She examined the other patients slowly and carefully. When she approached Charlie, his eye was closed and he appeared asleep. Relieved she would not have to talk to him, she proceeded with the injection prescribed by Gustav. Charlie awoke and saw her as she withdrew the hypodermic needle and slipped it into the sharps container hanging on the wall.

"What did you give me now?" Charlie asked querulously.

"Just something to reduce your fever and relieve your pain," she replied evenly.

She inserted a thermometer into his ear but Charlie, with his good hand, tried to push her away.

"Get away from me, you bitch. You're out to kill me — I know you want to kill me. Help someone! Help!"

The Ward Nurse returned at that moment and Dr. Gustav came running.

"What's wrong, Herr Wingate?" Gustav asked, his voice calm and low. "You must not get excited."

"Doctor, get her away from me," Charlie shouted shrilly. "She's planning to kill me."

Sarai did not move. "Doctor, he's delirious and hallucinating. Since my presence seems to bother him, it is best that I not treat him."

Mother Superior came up behind Sarai and took her by an arm. "Dr. Gustav, if you agree, I will assign another nurse to look after Mr. Wingate."

"A moment, Mother Superior," Gustav said holding up a hand like a Stop sign. "I must determine whether Sister Sarai has made an error."

"Dr. Gustav, are you implying that there is merit to Mr. Wingate's claim?" Mother Superior retorted. "Sister Sarai is a nurse whose competence has been proven beyond a doubt. She comes here with a sterling reputation."

Gustav shrugged. "Very well, meine damen. Let us not argue here. Shall we go to your office, Mother Superior?"

He walked out of the ward, followed by the two nuns.

"However, let me make myself clear," he said firmly as they walked past the operating rooms and down the corridor that led past the second ward to the head nun's office. "Sister Sarai has shown a change in her attitude to this patient compared to all the others we have treated in the past four weeks. Is that not so, Sister Sarai?"

Sarai nodded. They entered Mother Superior's small office. A desk, a filing cabinet and three chairs took up most of the space. A window looked out on the supplies containers, dimly illuminated by a light on a pole.

"There is something between you, nicht wahr?(is it not true)" Gustav asked.

Sarai could no longer hold back her relationship with Charlie. "I apologize to you, Mother Superior, for not being truthful. In this case the truth brings back painful memories of another time. Charles Wingate and I knew each other in first year university. He was not a nice man and he behaved dreadfully toward me. I have no reason to like him. Over the years, I have been able to push the memory aside and take joy in my work. I was shocked — paralyzed — when I recognized him. All those terrible memories came flooding back." She stifled a sob. "Excuse me. He knows who I am and believes I will repay him for the hurt he caused me. For his sake and mine, it would be best if I didn't go near him."

"May I also note, Dr. Gustav," said Mother Superior, "Sister Constanze, too, does not wish to care for him because of his insulting behaviour toward her. He is a problem quite apart from his injuries."

Gustav, deep in thought, pursed his lips and slowly bobbed his head up and down.

"Well, Mother Superior, since we have no male nurses, we must use the ones we have. It is now nearly midnight. Let's put our decisions off until the morning. With the Ward Nurse, I will ensure he is settled for the night. Then I must get some sleep."

"A good idea for us too," Mother Superior agreed.

Sarai awoke at daybreak, washed and dressed quickly, and took her post at the triage station. Who would be assigned to Charlie was not her decision. After a couple of hours, hunger and the need for a cup of coffee overtook her. The refectory was partly filled with staff and patients but she found a seat alone away from the others. Famished, she ate quickly and then settled back, sipping her coffee. She saw Melissa enter the room, looking wildly about her, tears staining her face. Sarai waved.

"The Triage Nurse said you were here," Melissa gasped, choking back sobs.

Sarai hugged her. "What's happening, Mrs. Wingate? Have you seen your husband this morning?"

Melissa nodded and buried her face in Sarai's shoulder.

"Mrs. Wingate, has he...?" Sarai hesitated.

Melissa lifted her head and shook it. "No, he's not dead but, God forgive me, I wish he were."

"Mrs. Wingate, what a terrible thing to say," Sarai admonished her gently. Although, she thought ruefully, don't I wish it too?

"I know it's not very Christian," Melissa said through her tears. "I don't have a nun's forgiveness and compassion. When I saw him now, he told me things that I find heartbreaking — things about you but also about me."

"Mrs. Wingate, would it help you if you told me what he said?" Sarai asked, her breakfast already curdling in her stomach.

Melissa wiped away her tears, embraced Sarai and kissed her on both cheeks. "I'm almost too ashamed to talk about it." She paused, choking back sobs until she could speak clearly. "My husband has always been difficult but this morning he became impossible."

"Perhaps," Sarai suggested, "it was the fever and pain talking. Delirious people often say things they would not say if they were rational."

"You are too kind, Sister Sarai. He was feverish but in complete command. He laughed when he told me about that terrible joke he played on you. I was aghast that he could be so callous. I said to him, 'It's horrible what you did. How can you think it's funny?' 'It's time you lighten up, Melissa,' was his comment.

"Then he hit me with a bombshell. If he survived, our marriage was over and he planned to marry his Executive Assistant with whom he'd had a lengthy affair. 'She's pregnant,' he says, 'and it's time I bit the bullet.' He wanted a child and I hadn't been able to give him one. He never told me he wanted children — the subject never came up. Then he laughed and said, 'You remember all those nights I worked late? I did work late — screwing is fun but it's hard work. And those business trips? I often had to take my Executive Assistant along but we had to be careful. The Board doesn't like scandal. Now we won't have to hide anymore. Just play ball, Melissa — I might be generous in the settlement.'"

She buried her face in Sarai's shoulder again, coughing and choking on her sobs. Abruptly, she leaned over Sarai's empty breakfast plate and retched. Sarai held her, waited until the spasm ended, and settled her back on the chair.

"I'm so sorry," Melissa apologized. "I need some tea and something to eat."

"Wait here. I'll get it for you."

Refreshed, Melissa took Sarai's hands in hers. "When he told me all those things, I felt like you must have felt, Sister Sarai — devastated, humiliated. But now I feel utterly cold toward him. What a fool I've been. Even before we married, I had concerns, but he was so loving then. In our early years together, he was often grumpy and short tempered, but I put up with it. He was rising in his company and I felt he needed an understanding wife who would provide him with the solace of a quiet home to offset the stress of his work. He sometimes slapped me when we argued or if I didn't respond quickly enough to something he wanted. I suspected he strayed at times but I closed my mind to it and never confronted him. A few years ago, he got worse in his treatment of me and now I know why. Sister Sarai, it's been ten years of my life wasted. I hate him. This final outrage has destroyed any love I had for him. I want him dead. Then I won't have to face a lengthy, messy divorce proceeding as he tries to grind away every cent he can out of a settlement and alimony."

She dissolved into tears again and buried her face in Sarai's shoulder. Sarai held her tightly and gently stroked her back.

"Mrs. Wingate, I'm terribly sorry for you and I do feel your anguish. In my case, devotion to God and good works got me through my awful moment and gave me a sense of peace. You, too, must find your way through this ugly time. You are still young and beautiful and will have no trouble finding a more suitable husband. Apart from talk and sympathy, there's not much more I can do to lessen your pain. If prayer can offer you some comfort, I will be happy to assist you."

Melissa kissed her on the cheek and whispered, "I wouldn't want you to pray beside me, Sister Sarai. I will pray for a quick death for Charlie. But you're a nun. You pray that sick people will live. I want Charlie to die — do you hear me — I hate him, I want him to die. I don't want your prayers offsetting mine. I don't want God to be confused. If God is truly just, He will end the life of this horrible man. Do I disgust you, Sister Sarai?"

Melissa was no longer crying. The whisper had become a low-pitched venomous tirade, each word precise, clipped, and clad in hatred.

'Hell hath no fury like a woman scorned,' thought Sarai. She was not surprised by the change in Melissa from a tearful wife concerned about her husband to a vengeful woman thirsting for his death. She remembered her own hatred of Charlie after his betrayal of her.

Still holding her, Sarai said, "I may not be as altruistic as you believe, Mrs. Wingate. Even nuns hate. As you know, I have no love for Charlie. I helped keep him from immediate death because it was my duty and I always carry out my duties well. But I can tell you — he was the first patient in many years of nursing where I didn't care if my duty was successful or not. Right now, both Dr. Gustav and Mother Superior have tentatively agreed to my request to not care for Charlie. Frankly, I believe they don't trust me. I don't know how I would pray. Would I ask God for his life or his death? So you see, Mrs. Wingate, even as a nun, I am torn between the two."

Melissa stood up and said evenly and firmly: "I am no longer torn, Sister Sarai. I shall not pray for him nor see him anymore. I'll stay a few more days to see whether he lives or dies, then I'll return to Toronto and find a good lawyer. Whatever happens, his company will get him home. Of course, if he dies, I shall be the grieving widow proclaiming loudly that the world has lost a great man."

She looked long and hard into Sarai's eyes. "It would be for the best if he dies, Sister Sarai."

Melissa started to walk away but Sarai held her back.

"Are you asking me to kill him?" she demanded.

Melissa sat down. "How can you believe I would ask such a thing?" Melissa replied, raising her eyebrows in mock wonder. "All I meant was his death would relieve both of us of a burden."

"It would get you out of a mess but what would it do for me?" Sarai retorted. "Whether he lives or dies, I retain the memory of his outrage. If I kill him, it's revenge and nothing more." Although my lust for revenge is what embitters my soul, she thought.

"My dear Sister Sarai, by now you know what a rat my sweet husband is. He likes to crow about his exploits to all his buddies on Facebook. I do not doubt he will announce to all and sundry that his safari nurse was the very girl he'd played his fabulous trick on at university. He will embellish the details and describe how eager you were for his body. The news will get around and you will become a laughing stock but quite famous. You may count on it that even your fellow nuns will hear of it as well as your people back in Toronto. Of course, you can sue Charlie but that will make you all the more ridiculous. However, you have your vows and your duty."

"But, Mrs. Wingate, what you ask is impossible without detection," Sarai protested. "As much as I hate him, why would I want to spend the rest of my life in a Kenya prison?"

Melissa laughed. "Sister Sarai, I know it's possible. You never asked me what my profession was before I met Charlie. I was a nurse for eight or nine years. So I know and you know how to do it."

Sarai stood up. "I must return to the triage station. Let's talk no more of this."

Late afternoon, Sarai was summoned to Mother Superior's office.

"Wingate's condition has deteriorated," the head nun explained. "Dr. Gustav and Sister Constanze are setting up the OR. Dr. Gustav has decided the damaged hand must come off. It has become gangrenous and is threatening Wingate's life. Dr. Gustav wants you to assist. Are you comfortable about doing so?"

Sarai sat down and gazed out the window to the darkening sky and the stars that had already appeared. Not a cloud disturbed the serene expanse of the heavens. No, all the clouds hovered over the bed where Charlie lay. Sweet Jesus, she pleaded, guide me.

"Wingate will not allow me to assist, Mother, whether I'm comfortable or not."

"Wingate is delirious, barely conscious, and has difficulty breathing. I doubt he'll even recognize you. Once on the table and anaesthetized, he never need know you're there. His wife is by his bedside and insists you can make a difference and has complete confidence in both you and Dr. Gustav. She urges us to do whatever is necessary and has signed the authorization."

Melissa at his bedside? Sarai thought. She's playing the anguished loving wife. I can guess why she wants me there.

"Am I allowed to refuse to assist?"

Mother Superior looked at her sternly. "You are a member of the Order of Nursing Sisters, sworn to duty and service. I expect nothing less. However, if you absolutely refuse and he dies, there may be a liability issue — we didn't use our best resources. I believe this unlikely but Dr. Gustav would take it as a blow to him and may not stay. Therefore, I urge you to remember your vows and to do your duty."

Gustav smiled in satisfaction as Sarai entered the OR dressed in scrubs.

"Hurry, Sister Sarai, there is no time to lose."

Sarai quickly washed her arms and hands and pulled on gloves, gown and mask. Sister Constanze nodded her approval and continued to monitor the anaesthetic.

Melissa had met Sarai as she walked to the OR.

"I hope everything goes well," Melissa said. "It would be terrible if he died on the operating table." Her voice was flat and cold.

"Your husband will survive the operation," Sarai said matter-of-factly. "I've severed limbs before without the aid of a doctor and the patient survived."

Melissa mouthed the words "Too bad" and said aloud, "I'll wait in the refectory."

After the surgery was completed and they were cleaning up, Sarai lingered, focussed on the severed hand lying in the tissue tray. It was purplish and laced with green, but Sarai remembered when it was sunshine brown with strong supple fingers. The hand had cupped a buttock, caressed her small breasts until the nipples grew, and slid down her body below her waist.

"Ugly, isn't it?" Sister Constanze said as she put away the anaesthetic equipment.

It was beautiful once, Sarai thought, a magical preamble to the unrivalled pleasure that was soon to follow.

"Time it came off," Sarai said. "We may have waited too long."

They followed the orderlies pushing the gurney to Charlie's bed and helped with the transfer. Constanze affixed an oxygen mask to his face and set the valve on the large cylinder beside the top corner of his bed.

Dr. Gustav was frowning. "His heart races and he suffers hypokalemia. We must replenish his electrolytes. Therefore, I prescribe a moderate dose of Potassium Chloride of 10 mEq per hour. If that doesn't help, I may have to increase the dose, but we shall see. Ward Nurse, inject him intravenously each hour and take the vital signs every 15 minutes. Also, continue the antibiotic. We will watch him carefully over the next two hours."

He looked at his watch. "It is now a few minutes before eight o'clock. Start the injections sharp on the hour and every hour thereafter until midnight."

Sarai took the scrip to the dispensary and brought the doses back to the Ward Nurse. They watched as she made the first injection.

Gustav left to look after other patients. Constanze and Sarai went to the refectory for coffee and a quick snack. They joined Melissa, languidly reading through a long email.

"Your Admin Office printed this out for me. It's a reply from the Company to an email I sent earlier telling them about the accident. They're asking for a report from the doctor. They want to know when Charlie can travel and they're arranging a private jet. There's no mention of me. It must have been written by his Executive Assistant." The last was said bitterly.

Constanze looked at Sarai quizzically. Sarai simply nodded and said, "Mrs. Wingate, your husband survived the operation but is in very fragile condition. The next few hours are crucial. We're doing all we can."

"Ladies, I'm sure you're doing all you can. What are you doing?" Melissa asked, straightening up and showing interest.

Sarai explained the several measures they had undertaken to improve Charlie's situation. "We'll let you know when he regains consciousness."

"Don't bother. I'll drop in from time to time." Again her voice was flat and cold.

The two nurses returned to the ward.

"What was that all about?" Constanze asked.

"Mrs. Wingate told me their marriage is on the rocks. I think she doesn't care whether he survives or not."

Over the next two hours, Charlie's vital signs improved, his heart slowed somewhat, and the electrolyte count was rising. At midnight, Charlie awoke and although not quite lucid smiled as he recognized Gustav.

"You are making good progress, Herr Wingate," Gustav was quick to reassure him. Charlie smiled again and fell asleep.

"I think we can leave him for the night. Ward Nurse, you may reduce taking vital signs to every half-hour. Continue with the hourly injections for two more hours. Do not hesitate to call me in my room should you have any concerns or questions."

Melissa was present when Charlie awoke, made no effort to talk to him, watched with interest, and then left by the door beside Charlie's bed and went down the steps to the refectory. Constanze and Sarai went to their cells.

The Ward Nurse turned off the lights plunging the ward into darkness. She sat at her desk just outside the far end of the ward writing reports, her work lit by a tiny light bulb on the tip of a flexible wire.

In the Ward Nurse's final report on patient Charles Wingate, she noted that he had died between 4:00 am and 4:30 am. Vital signs taken just before the hour showed slight improvement in blood pressure and heart rate but no change in a persistent low fever. When she returned at the half-hour, she discovered the patient was not breathing and she could not detect a pulse. She immediately applied resuscitation techniques and called for help. Dr. Gustav was summoned and employed the defibrillator machine. After 30 minutes of strenuous and unremitting effort, Dr. Gustav declared the patient dead.

Melissa, lying on a hard refectory bench, heard the commotion and ran up the stairs to the ward. She watched as nurses and doctor tried in vain to revive Charlie. When Gustav reported that he could do no more, Melissa appeared dazed and would have fallen had Gustav not caught her. She muttered incoherently, tears sprang to her eyes, and she held on to Gustav. He gently sat her on a chair.

"I am terribly sorry, Frau Wingate," he said. "We tried everything. He was emerging from the crisis but still very weak. I had every reason to believe he would succeed."

Melissa held Gustav's hand tightly and thanked him. "Perhaps God decided it was for the best. Charlie would not have been happy with an eye and hand missing."

She buried her head in her arms and appeared to be weeping uncontrollably. After awhile, she dabbed her eyes with a handkerchief and blew her nose.

Dr. Gustav had remained standing beside her, occasionally patting her shoulder. She took his hand. "Dr. Gustav, may I ask you to email my husband's company, announcing his death, and explaining what happened. They will inform you of the arrangements. I can't bring myself to do it."

"Of course, Frau Wingate, I will attend to it immediately. In the meantime, take this sedative and get some sleep."

At nine o'clock that morning, Sarai was summoned to Dr. Gustav's house. The news had already spread about the compound that Charlie had died. In his living room, she found Gustav at a window, his back to the room, Mother Superior sitting in an armchair, a solemn expression on her face, and Sister Constanze and Sister Agatha, the Ward Nurse from the night shift, standing, looking around uneasily. Gustav turned when Sarai entered. He was haggard and grim.

"My Daughters," Mother Superior began, speaking softly, "this will be a difficult meeting. Let us pray that Jesus will fill our hearts with the truth of his love and remind us of the vows we made when we joined the Order." The nuns bowed their heads and held their crosses and rosary beads. After a few moments, Mother Superior nodded to Gustav.

Gustav stared directly into the eyes of each nun as he spoke. "I wish to also remind you that you are nurses, committed to the care of the sick and hurt, to do everything you can to restore them to health. I am disturbed by the sudden death of Charles Wingate. My investigation leads me to the strong suspicion that his death was not a natural outcome of his condition."

He paused. The nuns looked apprehensive, turning to Mother Superior who looked back at them gloomily.

"I repeat the word 'suspicion.' I cannot be certain but I believe an unauthorized intervention took place earlier this morning which precipitated the patient's demise. I ..."

Constanze interjected: "Are you blaming us?"

"How can you say that?" Sarai snapped.

"Sir, I did everything you told me to," Agatha pleaded.

"At this point, I'm not blaming anyone," the doctor responded, raising his voice. "Please sit down."

The nuns settled on a sofa.

"These are grounds for my suspicion, "Gustav continued. "At 4:00 am the patient is alive and responding to treatment. Sometime during the next half-hour he dies suddenly. When I investigated, I found two indications that aroused my doubts regarding his death. First, there appeared to be a reduction in the flow of oxygen from the rate set at midnight. This in itself was unlikely to cause the patient's death and may have come about inadvertently during our efforts to resuscitate him.

"A more serious indication was the presence of burn marks at the intravenous entry site. As you all know, this is caused by Potassium Chloride when it is introduced through a peripheral vein rather than a centre line. The dose I prescribed should not have showed such indications although I admit, over a number of hours may have a cumulative effect. On the other hand, a larger dose of the chemical would definitely have such an effect and could also result in stopping the patient's heart."

Gustav paused, allowing his observations to sink in. He turned to the Ward Nurse.

"Sister Agatha, could you have mistaken the amount of dose or the number given?"

Agatha clutched her cross and nervously slipped the rosary beads through her fingers. "Oh no, sir, it is impossible. Every medicine, the dose and time are logged in my shift book and tick marked as soon as delivered."

"Yes, I've seen the shift book and it appears in order. Did you see anyone other than the patients in the ward during the half-hour in question?"

"Sir, I swear to you I saw no one."

"Were you at your desk or in the ward the whole time?"

Sister Agatha was sweating profusely. "Sir, all but ten minutes when I helped patient Ngoro — the old man, sir — to the lavatory. The poor man has difficulty walking, isn't that so, Mother Superior?"

The head nun smiled reassuringly. "Do not be alarmed, Sister Agatha. The doctor knows it is all part of your duty."

Gustav nodded. "It means there was a ten minute opportunity for someone to enter undetected."

"But Doctor," Mother Superior said, "even if Sister Agatha had not been away, the ward was dark, Wingate was at the other end away from the desk light, someone could have waited until the vitals were taken and then slipped in from the door at that end."

"True, Mother Superior, besides, no one could count on the Ward Nurse being away at exactly that time."

Gustav was silent, biting his lower lip. He appeared to come to a decision and turned to the seated nuns. "Sisters Constanze and Sarai, when you left at midnight, where did you go?"

Constanze emitted a gasp, and angry, slipped into her native German: "Mutter, muss Ich diese frage beantworten?" (Mother, must I answer these questions?)

"Sister Constanze," Mother Superior said reassuringly, "You don't have to answer the doctor's question but I would like you to. I'm sure all the doctor is trying to determine is whether you saw anything untoward, different from our usual routine. Isn't that so, Doctor?"

Gustav shook his head. "If indeed there was an action of ill intent — and I repeat I have no real proof — then I believe the perpetrator is in this room."

Constanze and Agatha jumped to their feet and protested loudly. Sarai remained seated.

"Calm down, Sisters, I'm the suspect," she said, her voice calm and even.

The two nuns looked at her in surprise and glanced at Mother Superior. The head nun was silent, her face expressionless.

"Sister Constanze," Gustav continued doggedly, "please tell me where you went after you left the ward."

Clearly troubled, Constanze took her seat beside Sarai. "Both Sister Sarai and I left together and went to our cells. We bid each other goodnight and entered our cells which are beside each other. I slept soundly until I was awakened to come to this meeting."

"I echo my Sister's account," Sarai said and then added sarcastically, "or do you believe we are conspirators?"

"Sister Sarai, you will treat this matter seriously," admonished Mother Superior.

"Mother, how can I treat it seriously?" Sarai retorted. "Dr. Gustav admits he has no proof yet he subjects us to an interrogation. Charles Wingate was near death from the moment he arrived. Despite every medical procedure we attempted, he remained near death. Why should it surprise anyone that he died? I understand the doctor takes great pride in his work and the patient's death is a blow to him. But that's no reason to cast doubt on our integrity."

His face flushed, Gustav glared at Sarai. "I beg to differ," the doctor said, stamping a fist into his other hand for emphasis. "Wingate was not near death at 4:00 am this morning. Yet he died suddenly a few minutes later. Therefore, as his physician, I have a right, indeed a duty, to explore how this could happen. We know there was severe anger between you and the patient. Wingate openly expressed his fear that you would harm, even kill, him. Taking everything into account, including the indications that I found, why then should I not be suspicious in general and of you particularly? Let me ask you — did you kill Charles Wingate?"

On her feet, Sarai spoke without emotion, "Doctor, let me tell you how I killed him. Once in my cell, I threw myself on my knees, grasped my bible to my bosom, raised my eyes to Heaven and begged God to put an end to this evil and worthless man. Rather than strike me dead for indulging in the sin of hatred, God answered my prayers. You see, Doctor, the power of prayer sometimes trumps the science of medicine."

Rage and frustration struck Gustav mute. Mother Superior rose, her face stern.

"My Daughter, you are insubordinate and your statement blasphemous. I must confer with the Bishop as to appropriate discipline."

"What will you tell the Bishop, Mother? That a nun, 20 years in the Order, with over a decade in nursing all over the world, whose reputation is unblemished, whose performance is judged outstanding, defended her innocence vigorously in the face of an unsubstantiated allegation."

Sarai clenched her fists and began pacing the room. Agatha was weeping, Constanze was slowly shaking her head in disbelief, and Mother Superior stood with head bowed.

"You are putting me in an impossible situation," Gustav thundered. "I no longer can work with you."

"Nor I with you," Sarai shot back.

The tension in the room was palpable as Sarai continued to pace up and down. Finally, she stopped in front of the head nun.

"Mother, it is clear there is no room for both Dr. Gustav and me in this Mission. The doctor is less dispensable. I hereby humbly request reassignment elsewhere. I ask, as well, unless Dr. Gustav can prove his allegation, that this taint to my reputation not be transferred with me."

Mother Superior had tears in her eyes. "It shall be so, my Daughter. May Our Lord bless you and guide you."

In the darkened ward, the only sounds were the snores of the old man Ngoro, an occasional sigh from the women and the hoarse breathing of Charles Wingate. His bed was in total darkness, engulfed in the blackness far from the tiny pool of light at the other end of the ward. A shadow appeared to disengage from the door at Wingate's end of the ward and move slowly along the wall closer to the sleeping patient. Ngoro called out and the Ward Nurse, wielding a flashlight, came into the ward. The shadow slid down below the level of the bed and rose again as the nurse and Ngoro left. The shadow hovered over the bed and then retreated soundlessly out the door and rejoined the deeper shadows. After a few moments, the sound of Charles Wingate's breathing ceased.

CHAPTER 9
- Dulcigno, 1673-1674 -
Death of Sarah Zvi

Shabtai reported the next morning that his wife was too ill to attend the Governor in his audience room. Much to the Governor's regret, he had to send the mid-wife nurse to Sarah. With the help of a bribe from Tepel, the nurse declared Sarah unfit to leave the apartment and prescribed a period of bed rest. Poultices of cooked bulgur, as hot as bearable, were to be applied to Sarah's chest and she was to inhale the fumes of boiling chamomile tea. In response to Shabtai, the nurse agreed that his special infusion would also be helpful in ridding Sarah of the congestion that plagued her breathing.

Tepel allowed himself the salacious thought that his warm hand massaging her chest would be more effective than poultices. He called on her every day or, rather, he called on her husband every day, trying to appear nonchalant as he inquired of her health. Occasionally, he was rewarded with her appearance. Relieved, he could tell that the congestion was eased for she breathed without hindrance. He noted, too, that her eyes, bright as ever, sparkled with pleasure when she gazed at him.

After the second week of his visits, Sarah greeted him without Shabtai in the antechamber receiving room. Sarah dismissed the servant after she had brought them tea. Tepel bowed and turned to leave.

"Madam, it is impossible for me to stay without your husband or at least the servant present."

"Please do not go, my sweet Captain," Sarah whispered. "My husband sits solemnly in his writing room, indifferent to the world around him. The Lord has turned His face away and my husband despairs and prays that He will soon return to him. The servant is provided by our family and is loyal to us and is discreet. Therefore, we may speak without fear."

Still uneasy, Tepel resumed his seat on the stuffed pillows. "What is there to speak of, madam? You well know of my love for you. I am not a poet. I cannot embellish it further. As a soldier, I conclude you are behind a fortress wall that is impregnable and all my efforts to assail it are in vain."

"Then why do you come every day?" Sarah asked softly, pulling her face veil off. "I have not thanked you for your spirited defence of my husband at the gates of Dulcigno. I am also grateful that you arranged matters to keep the Governor away." She chuckled, "He is not as concerned about my health as you are."

Tepel was absorbed by the admiration of her face: the large brown eyes, the unblemished white cheeks, the aquiline nose, the parted lips. She pulled off her headdress and allowed her dark curls to fall around her face.

"Madam, you provoke me beyond control."

He leapt the space between them, clasped her to him, and rained kisses on her lips, face and hair. They held each other for a while and then slowly pushed apart.

Sarah held his hands. "We can go no further, my sweet Captain, not here, not now. But there is something I must do before you leave. I have wanted to do this since I began to love you."

She reached up, grasped the ends of his moustache and tweaked and twirled it. They laughed soundlessly as she stepped back and replaced her headdress and veil.

"Madam, I puzzle over your evident willingness to accept my love now but not on the way to Adrianople. What has changed?"

She moved into his arms again. "Nothing has changed. I have loved you since the days of the Smyrna celebrations — or riots, as you call them. When, after many years, we met again on the journey to Adrianople, my love was rekindled. Now, on this long sea voyage, my love has become a longing. On the way to Adrianople, I felt if we consummated our love,

I could no longer support my husband and his mission was precious to me. In Dulcigno, unless my husband's prayers come true and God decrees the final Redemption, we shall live out our days here. I continue to believe in my husband's goals but I become less important to him in this backwater of the Empire. We are exiled. No doubt we will have visitors — you shake your head but you do not know the resourcefulness of my people — but these visitors will be few. Thus, I no longer need to put off the satisfaction of my own longing."

Tepel, still holding her, said sadly, "Madam, there is no opportunity here without endangering you. Remember, you are now a Muslim. An adulterous wife is stoned to death. Rest assured, the Qadi will enforce the measure and the Governor will have no choice but to agree. No, I must leave the city as soon as possible and remove temptation from both of us."

Sarah stepped angrily away from him, pouted, and crossed her arms akimbo. "So! My life in Dulcigno is to be one of utter tedium. My husband neglects me as he pursues his dreams. The man to whom I have declared my love rewards me with his immediate departure. Perhaps I shall have to submit to the Governor after all."

Tepel flushed and spat out angrily, "If he touches you, I will kill him."

"Will you, Captain Tepel?" she said, bitingly sarcastic. "How will you do that? Do you have a musket that reaches its target from Constantinople or Adrianople, or Crete or wherever you may be? I am blessed with such a protector."

Tepel stared gloomily at the floor. "According to my orders, I may put off my departure until after you are ensconced in your dwelling and I am satisfied the populace is not hostile and will not harm you. Longer than that, I may not stay."

"Excellent, my sweet Captain," Sarah said, beguilingly. "I shall see to it that the populace remains hostile. Be not so sad. I ..."Abruptly, she clutched her neck, and coughed violently, uncontrollably.

The servant swept into the room, grasped Sarah by the arm, and helped her into the inner apartment. Tepel sat there helplessly, listening to Sarah gasping for breath. Soon the coughing stopped and there was silence. He continued to wait. After awhile, the servant returned and reported that Sarah was asleep and breathing easily.

For three days, neither Shabtai nor Sarah appeared when he called. He directed his worried inquiries to the mid-wife nurse who reported that the patient was resting and would soon be on her feet. Her husband was locked in his writing room and hadn't eaten in two days. She could hear him wailing and singing when she visited the patient.

"The Jew is possessed of devils," she said knowingly.

"Mind your tongue," Tepel admonished her sharply. "He is no longer Jew but Muslim. His mind is sick at times."

On the fourth day, to his great relief, Sarah came into the antechamber assisted by the nurse and the servant. They seated Sarah on a chair, instead of the stuffed pillows. Tepel stood and bowed.

"How are you today, Madam?' he asked, trying to stay formal but solicitous.

"Much better, Captain Tepel," she replied. "I grow stronger each day. I believe these damp rooms are to blame. If we could be moved to our prescribed dwelling which I am told has large fireplaces and an oven, then my illness would be gone."

Sarah's health did improve when she, Shabtai, and the servant took up residence in their new home several days later. With the help of the nurse, Tepel had persuaded the Governor to authorize the move quickly. The Governor was repelled by sick women, no matter how beautiful, and had quickly lost interest in Sarah.

A single storey stone building with a peaked slate roof, the house lay just outside the rear gates of the city wall on the main road leading along the coast. The house, set close to the road with a large enclosed garden at the back, was commodious enough to accommodate Shabtai, Sarah and the servant as well as the three children who were soon to join them. At the rear of the garden, nestled in a copse of trees, was a small mud brick building meant for servants or visitors.

Sarah liked the new home immediately. Although not as fine or as large as the family home in Smyrna or the mansion they occupied in Adrianople, its small rooms were easy to keep warm and gave Sarah the protection she needed against the winter cold.

For the first week, Tepel assigned his Janissaries to patrol the area to ensure the neighbours were, if not friendly, at least indifferent. Not to be outdone, the Governor sent the Qadi and several of the Civic Guard to monitor the area.

The two rooms in the mud brick building had a stove in one and a large fireplace in the other. Sarah ordered a fire to be set in each. She told the maid that while her husband was in the doldrums, she could not sleep because of his incessant wailing and singing throughout the night. She would therefore sleep in the mud brick house until he recovered.

That became their clandestine meeting place. Tepel slipped in after dark through the woods behind the house and left before dawn. They made love passionately and frequently as though making up for the many years since their first meeting in Smyrna. The arrangement worked satisfactorily for several days.

"Madam, I am extremely happy," Tepel declared after their first encounter as they lay in each other's arms.

Sarah giggled: "My sweet Captain, in bed you may call me Sarah and I will call you Mahmud."

"But Sarah is your Jewish name," Tepel protested.

She tweaked his moustache. "Sarah is my bed name and unlocks the secret gate to my desire for you. No other name will do."

"Then Sarah it shall be," he said laughing. They were silent for a few minutes, and then Tepel whispered, "Sarah."

"The gate is unlocked," she murmured.

On the fourth day after their love making had begun, Tepel was patrolling with two of his Janissaries the stretch of road that led past the Zvi house. It was a raw February morning. Dark clouds scudded across a leaden sky accompanied by squalls of rain mixed with flakes of snow. A cold wind blew the Adriatic crashing against the strand below the road and whipped its salt spray into the faces of the patrol.

"Good morning, Captain Tepel," a voice shouted from the beach and Tepel knew that his idyll with Sarah was over for the time being.

"A bracing morning, is it not, Captain Tepel?" Shabtai said, his black wool embroidered mantle billowing out behind him, his cheeks red with exertion and frost. "I find such days invigorating. They blow away the devils and demons that beset us."

The two men bowed while the soldiers stood back respectfully.

"You are well again, Effendi?" Tepel asked.

"Yes," Shabtai replied. "Allah has turned his face to me. I was particularly grateful to Him in my morning prayers and thanked Him for restoring me to my normal state."

"Are you satisfied with your dwelling, Effendi?"

Shabtai wrapped his mantle tightly around him and motioned to the captain to step aside with him.

"Very satisfied, Captain Tepel. The house is of good size and comfortable and my wife has made it a real home. However, there is a request I must make of you. My life here would be greatly improved if I could send and receive correspondence and, in time, enjoy the company of visitors. Otherwise, I am condemned to the sole company of my wife."

Would that I were so condemned, thought Tepel. "Mehmed Aziz Effendi, you are aware the Grand Vizier has prohibited any contact outside Dulcigno. Therefore, I do not know how I may help you."

A blast of cold wind caused both men to lower their heads. Tepel shouted an order for the soldiers to continue their patrol. Shabtai invited Tepel into the house and they seated themselves in the small receiving room warmed by a brightly burning fire in the grate. The servant brought them tea but Sarah did not appear.

"Captain Tepel," Shabtai said, "I have many friends and family who are wealthy and some who have influence at Court. Surely, it may be relied upon that any inconvenience or cost occasioned by satisfying my request will be compensated."

Tepel was silent, staring stonily at Shabtai.

Shabtai continued: "Captain, please do not consider my request outlandish. What harm can I do to the Empire from this remote perch? My children will come soon. Would it not be in order for my brother Elijah, their uncle, to accompany them here? All that is required is a message to him and he will make all the arrangements. This cannot be construed as violating the Grand Vizier's orders. Knowing that the children are in the company of a trusted relative will greatly ease my wife's concern for them and help in her recovery."

He is a great general, thought Tepel. He knows exactly where to attack. Yet he has learned nothing. Twice the Sultan has repulsed his sallies and spared his life and still Aziz perseveres in his manoeuvres.

"I will speak with the Governor," Tepel said. "Only he can decide whether your request is permissible."

The Governor did not reject the request out of hand. The scent of bribe money is in his nostrils, Tepel concluded.

"The orders from the Grand Vizier are quite clear," he reminded the Governor.

"Of course they are," the Governor agreed. "And they shall be upheld. However, to ask an uncle to accompany the children here is a normal course of events. After all, the Grand Vizier has not forbidden the family from coming together."

The Governor was deep in thought for a moment. "As for getting a message to his brother, perhaps the Qadi can help. A young mullah, Ali Hussein, who is visiting the Qadi, leaves on the first barque to Constantinople. He can either break his journey in Smyrna or find someone travelling there when he reaches his destination."

At first, Mullah Ali was reluctant to participate, despite the Governor's insistence. The Qadi had warned the Mullah that Shabtai was not to be trusted, that his theology was suspect, and it was not clear which side of the line between Islam and Judaism he actually trod. Mullah Ali asked to meet with Shabtai to satisfy himself he was not engaging in a transaction that would sully his reputation. In his mid 20's, tall, slim and lithe, a thin black beard clothing his sun browned cheeks, dressed in white caftan and mantle, the Mullah was an image of youthful vitality and energy.

He was no match for Shabtai and Sarah. Shabtai in his normal state, robust, richly dressed, self-confident, and charismatic charmed the Mullah immediately.

"Aziz Mehmed Effendi, I am warned that you are a heretic and not truly a Muslim. Sometimes you observe the Jewish ritual. It is rumoured that while you have converted Jews to Islam, you have also converted Muslims to Judaism. The Qadi has reports that you claim to be the messiah of the Jews," the Mullah began, almost apologetically.

Shabtai chuckled. "I have never claimed to be the Messiah. These are monstrous accusations by my enemies. As you are a mullah, I was once a rabbi. Because I developed a profound knowledge of the Kabbalah, I became known as a mystic. Mystical understanding and teaching is seen by some as heretical, as undermining the Jewish faith. Yet our great

Kabbalists are esteemed and are deemed sages, and not only by the Jewish community. As a Muslim, I remember that Allah is the God of all the children of Abraham and have preached that Redemption is for both Jew and Muslim. Is this heresy? At the end of days, will not the People of the Book — Jews and Christians — be admitted as well to Jannah, the Garden of Paradise, if they have behaved righteously?"

The Mullah nodded. "Yes, it is true. The Prophet recognizes that the People of the Book have a place in Jannah. However, the Qadi has warned me that you can make black appear white and white, black — that you may be ad-Dajjal, the tempter who comes just before the end of days to persuade people that he is the true messiah and in so doing blocks the resurrection and Day of Judgement."

Shabtai slapped his knee and laughed loudly. "Come, come, Mullah Ali, let me put that notion out of your mind. Ad-Dajjal is blind in his right eye. Let me cover my left eye, and you point me to move around the room."

The test was completed quickly. "You agree that I can see. As for my skills of persuasion, they cannot be strong since I find myself fixed in Dulcigno, unable to leave. Ad-Dajjal can roam the entire world and conquer the good judgement of everyone. Yet I must beg to even send a message to my brother. Surely we must conclude that the Qadi is grossly mistaken."

Mullah Ali was still not convinced. "As I have said, the Qadi judges you are not truly a Muslim. In Adrianople, you sometimes preached in synagogues and were observed participating in Jewish ritual. How do you respond to such charges?"

Shabtai rose and walked solemnly about the room, his hands clasped behind him. "These charges are very troubling to me. I am accused of being a Jew and yet it was the Jewish community that conspired against me with accusations that caused the Sultan to banish me. Even my friends at Court could not help. When I put on the turban, the Sultan himself asked that I make every effort to convert my former community to the true faith. With zeal, I set out to achieve his wish. What is the best strategy to attain this goal? Preach in a mosque to Jews who are not there? Obviously, one must preach in a synagogue in order to convince rabbi and laity that our holy Torah is considered sacred by Mohammed, that the Qur'an is a further and final revelation by the one God, and to demonstrate that the rites of Islam are not that different from Jewish ritual. After all, Jews, too, pray at least five times daily, proclaim the one true God, and have fasting as well as feast days, and are enjoined to give alms. However, my very strategy and my efforts to convert their congregations caused rabbis to oppose and to conspire against me. Even Muslims, like the Qadi, see only the surface and do not understand the underlying nature of my actions. Thus, Mullah Ali, in zealous pursuit of my Sultan's holy command, I was misunderstood and my reward was banishment."

At that moment Sarah appeared, and whatever lingering doubts the Mullah had were assuaged entirely. She entered the room with her headdress in her hand, the veil trailing on the floor. All the mullah saw was a vision of paradise.

"Oh!" she shrieked. "I had no idea anyone was here."

She quickly retreated while Shabtai looked stern. "I apologize for my wife's immodesty and beg your forgiveness. I will remind her once again to be more careful."

The Mullah merely nodded, still entranced by the beautiful face surrounded by dark curls.

"I beseech you," Shabtai said cutting in to his reverie. "Please take this letter to my brother Elijah Zvi in Smyrna. It is in Hebrew but I will translate it for you so that you will be satisfied that it contains nothing suspicious. The first part tells my brother that we are safely in Dulcigno and happy in our new home and that we are well treated. The second part asks him to bring our children here."

The Mullah accepted the letter after Shabtai had read it out to him and sealed it.

"I will be ever grateful," Shabtai said. "Not only will my brother reward you, but, should you come this way again, I will tender you the hospitality of my home. I have enjoyed our conversation and, until you leave Dulcigno, please call on me again."

As the Mullah walked back through the gates of the city, he assured himself it was the attraction of more contact with this interesting man that made him want to return and not just the thought of being under the same roof as his bewitching wife.

Much to the Qadi's disgust, Mullah Ali called at the Zvi's home in the few days before his ship departed.

"The man is dangerous," the Qadi warned. "You are young and not yet fully grounded in all the elements of Islam. He will lead you into heresy."

"I wish to learn his Kabbalah," the Mullah asserted. "It will help me develop arguments against it."

It was only on the last day when he came to bid farewell that Sarah appeared instead of Shabtai.

"My husband is ill today," she said. "Allah has turned his face away from him. When that happens, he fasts and prays until Allah returns to him."

Deep within the house, the Mullah could hear a high-pitched wail from time to time.

"I am grateful that you have agreed to deliver the message," Sarah continued. "A mother is nothing without her children close by. It is a great deed that you do for me."

As she bowed to him, he caught a glimpse of her face as her loose veil fell away slightly. Once again, he envisioned himself in Jannah with this woman in eternal love making.

He bowed in turn, asked to be remembered to her husband, and hurriedly left for the harbour. Not until Dulcigno was an indistinct speck against the backdrop of the rugged coastal mountains did he tear himself away from the gunwale of the barque and proceed below.

With Shabtai in a depressive state, Sarah and Tepel were free to continue their nightly meetings, but felt a growing sense of despair.

"Must you leave soon?" Sarah asked, knowing and dreading the answer.

"Yes, my sweet. The Governor raises the issue daily, declares my orders are fulfilled, and he can no longer support our keep. He is not comfortable with a Janissary officer around. I should have left with the Mullah but made some excuse. I fear he suspects I have a reason to prolong my stay. His spies will ferret out our secret which would be deadly to you. I cannot let that happen. The next sail is expected tomorrow and I must board it."

They were lying side by side. Sarah rolled against him and grasped him tightly.

"I will not let you go, ever," she said, tears flowing. "This has been the happiest time of my life and of yours too. This cannot be our last night together. I pray to Allah to keep you here."

Whether it was the will of Allah or the vagaries of chance, Sarah's prayer came true.

The next morning, and for three days, a dense fog enveloped Dulcigno and the sea around it and no ship appeared in port. Sarah and Tepel rejoiced in their extra time together. That too came to a halt as Shabtai recovered and resumed his normal state.

On the fourth day, the fog, warmed by a brilliant sun in an azure cloudless sky, lifted and slowly dissipated. In a short time, a galleon pushed through the lingering wraiths and anchored off the city. Lighters quickly surrounded it and unloaded cargo bound for Dulcigno and loaded supplies of food and water for the ship's continuing voyage. The ship's captain came ashore and was escorted by the Governor to the castle. By early afternoon, it was announced that the galleon would leave very shortly.

Shabtai and Sarah joined other citizens and the Governor at the departure point to bid farewell to the Janissaries. The mehter and drummer played an impromptu concert as Captain Tepel called his soldiers to order and inspected them. A platoon of Civic Guards stood at attention close by.

At first, a deeply grieving Sarah was further disheartened when Tepel appeared to be totally focussed on getting his men and equipment prepared and did not look in her direction. Then she realized their parting was too painful and even one moment of fleeting contact would have rendered them unable to contain themselves.

Tepel saluted the Governor, gave a command and the Janissary soldiers shouldered their bivouac bags and carrying their muskets moved slowly toward the steps leading down to the lighter waiting below. Tepel and the ship's captain followed them.

Suddenly, the festive air was shattered as the Qadi, screaming for the Governor, propelled by his short legs, came running madly through the city gate. The Janissaries paused as all turned to see what the problem was. The Qadi pulled the Governor aside and spoke rapidly to him. The Governor motioned for Tepel and the ship's captain to join them. The four men conversed earnestly and seemed to come to a decision.

Tepel ordered his soldiers to follow closely behind him. Then the Governor, the Qadi, Tepel and the ship's captain walked quickly to the main square, followed by the crowd and the Civic Guard. Sarah, flushed with relief that, for whatever reason, Tepel was to stay, light heartedly skipped along and kept up with Shabtai's long strides.

A stench of death and blood assailed Sarah's nostrils as she came out of a narrow laneway into the open square. A horrific scene greeted the crowd. A wagon pulled by two oxen was filled with bodies of men and women, some of them headless. Two small children sat amongst the dead clutching the body of a woman and screaming. The wagon driver was slumped on the ground leaning against a wheel, blood welling from head wounds and seeping out of gashes in his caftan. A mounted Civic Guardsman led three horses with dead soldiers draped over the saddles. Other men and women lay on the ground, some moaning or crying out in pain, blood staining the stones of the square. The mid-wife nurse and other women attended to them.

The crowd looked on in stunned silence. A cacophony of screams and cries filled the air. More people flooded into the square, attracted by the noise and by the tocsin belling out its alarum.

Tepel and the Governor helped the soldier to dismount and began questioning him.

"Why do we stand gawking?" Sarah called out and ran to the screaming children, pulled them off the wagon, and led them aside and comforted them. Shabtai and several other men brought buckets of water from the well at the bottom of the square to a cauldron set over a raging fire.

"The water must boil," shouted the nurse. "Bring towelling."

They did what they could. The wagon driver died of his wounds. Some of the bodies were identified by relatives or friends and were carried away for burial. The rest were laid out on the square. The least wounded, bandaged, but able to walk were led away to the town hostel, but were first questioned by Tepel or the Governor. The badly wounded were carried into the castle and bedded down in the large entrance hall. A relative claimed the two children Sarah was caring for.

The Governor mounted a horse and raised his arms for silence. The tocsin still tolled in the background.

"Citizens of Dulcigno, the village of Donja Klezna was attacked during the night by brigands led by that infamous bandit Bulka Khan. The attack was ruthless and spared no one. The village was sacked and those who did not escape were killed. The four soldiers stationed there were hopelessly out numbered but fought bravely. The soldier who survived was knocked senseless by the attackers and left for dead. It is not known where the bandits will attack next. As a precaution, I have ordered our city gates closed and those living outside the gates to move into the city until the danger is over.

"Citizens, one of the bandits displayed the flag of Venice. Therefore, this is not merely a case of banditry but an attack on the Empire — a rebellion that must be stopped. I will lead a force of Civic Guards and armed citizens, aided by Captain Tepel and the Janissaries. We take to the field just before dawn tomorrow morning. The Qadi will be responsible to guard Dulcigno until we return. Prepare yourselves."

An intense bustle of activity ensued. The crowd quickly dispersed. A long line of men formed in front of the armoury to be armed and outfitted for battle. Platoons of Civic Guardsmen mustered in the square with muskets and cutlasses. Bags of bulgur and flat breads were brought out of storage and heaped in the square. During the night, the food supplies along with musket balls and gunpowder would be loaded onto horses to follow the troops. The Governor and Tepel were everywhere, inspecting the armed citizens, the Civic Guardsmen, the supplies and the five Janissaries. The mehter and drummer marched around the square playing martial music, adding to the general air of excitement pervading the military preparations.

The ship's captain departed with a message for the Sultan informing him of the threat and the actions planned. Shabtai, along with the older men and those unable to fight, were conscripted by the Qadi to mount guard on the walls. Sarah watched her husband from the edge of the square where she and the nurse were still patching up some of the wounded. A Civic Guardsman, supervised by the Qadi, was trying to teach Shabtai the intricacies of loading a musket.

"I am a man of peace. I do not kill," Shabtai declared.

"You are now a Muslim warrior, charged with the defence of the Empire against a horde of infidels," replied the Qadi.

Tepel intervened. "Esteemed Qadi, Aziz Mehmed Effendi armed may be more dangerous to us than to the enemy. He clearly has never held a gun or a cutlass. I suggest we post him as a lookout over the main gate."

The Qadi, annoyed by the Captain but unwilling to contradict a Janissary officer, reluctantly agreed and dispatched Shabtai to the main gate.

In the late afternoon, the attack party assembled for prayers. The Qadi reminded them that Allah was on their side and if some did not return, they died as martyrs and would be rewarded in Paradise. The Governor exhorted them to fight bravely. "The enemy has killed friends and family and if not stopped will kill us. They must be exterminated. Show no mercy. Allah bless us all and our arms with victory."

Tepel organized the fighters into groups of ten, each led by a Civic Guardsman or a citizen with military experience. In total, they were a little over a hundred men. Tepel had in the meantime sent his five Janissaries to patrol the area outside the gates to ensure no bandits waited in ambush.

The Governor, Tepel and the ten platoon commanders assembled in the castle's audience chamber to lay out strategy and logistics.

"The bandits' likely next target is Gornja Klezna," Tepel told them. "It is only a half-day march from Dornja Klezna and is larger and richer. The only other town in the region is Shkoder on Lake Skadar which they will not attempt. Its fortifications are strong and have repelled previous attackers. We will move up the inland road with patrols ahead and on either flank. If we can advance fast enough, we may put the enemy between us and the defenders at Gornja Klezna."

Shabtai remained on duty during the night which allowed Tepel and Sarah a frenzied moment of love and leave taking.

"Stay in the castle apartments until the enemy is vanquished," he urged her.

"I will do as you say," Sarah said tearfully. "But you must promise me to return safely. Allah protect you and bring you back to me."

The sky was just lightening, when the attack party assembled on the square. Tepel's Janissaries had scoured ahead and reported no observers or scouts. Led by the Governor and Tepel walking side by side, the platoons marched out of the square and threaded their way through the narrow streets out the rear gates and onto the strand road, followed by a line of twelve packhorses burdened with supplies for the battle ahead.

Dulcigno citizens and residents, including the women, lined the square and the route out of the city, waving, cheering, and wishing the soldiers well. Sarah joined in the general air of exhilaration but felt a growing sense of guilt. Allah had answered her prayers and kept Tepel here but would the cost be too high? She pushed the fear out of her mind and replaced it with the image of the two men in her life acting to protect her — her lover advancing into battle, her husband on the ramparts of Dulcigno.

She joined the women climbing the steps to the top of the wall to catch a last glimpse of the war party as it turned onto the cart track leading inland. Soon the small army disappeared as the track twisted into thick forest. Occasionally, Sarah caught a brief sight of a red cloak in the deep woods.

The days passed slowly. Sarah and the servant brought food to Shabtai who refused to leave his post.

"Redemption is close, my Sarah," Shabtai declared. "The final battle has begun. I will soon be called to lead the ten Tribes into the Promised Land.

She recognized that Shabtai was in his Illumination state where God smiled on him and gave him direction. Could it be that the End of Days was to begin here in a battle with brigands in this remote corner and would spread and engulf the Empire and indeed the whole world? While she continued to have faith in Shabtai and his messianic mission, she doubted that this battle was anything but a suppression of a gang of cutthroats. So she continued to feed him at his rampart station and fidgeted impatiently for news of Tepel.

After two weeks, the first inkling of what was happening arrived in the form of a wagon with some dead and wounded and three horses to be reloaded with supplies.

The wagon driver reported that Tepel's patrols had flushed out the rear guard of the bandit force and had inflicted heavy casualties. As Tepel had planned, the main body of the enemy was surrounded by the defenders of Gornja Klezna and the Dulcigno platoons. Tepel was slowly closing in on the rebels. Dulcigno casualties were light.

While the news was encouraging, the screams and wails of the families receiving their dead saddened the atmosphere of elation that victory was near.

Two more weeks went by before the wagon returned. As it came into the square, Sarah spotted a red cloak covering one of the bodies. Too fearful to go close, almost faint with apprehension, she waited until the names were called out. Relief swept over her in a profuse sweat. Tepel's name was not amongst the dead.

The Civic Guardsman manning the wagon and the wounded reported in glowing terms that the siege of Gornja Klezna had been broken. The bandits were attempting to flee in disparate groups but were under constant pursuit and attack by the victorious fighters of Gornja Klezna and Dulcigno. The Governor had ceded full control to Tepel whose military experience and skill had proven superior to that of Bulka Khan. Tepel and a small party were chasing after the bandit leader.

Each day now, news trickled in, sometimes by a few of the walking wounded, or a Civic Guardsman driving the wagon with some wounded and the occasional body. The main body of Dulcigno fighters were still mopping up the fleeing. Tepel was far to the east as the bandit leader had fled into the Albanian mountains.

A wounded Janissary had made his way to Gornja Klezna and was transported to Dulcigno. Sarah joined the crowd around him and helped the mid-wife nurse to treat him.

"The terrain is very rough," the soldier told them. "The bandits try to hide in ravines and behind boulders in order to ambush us but our Captain is too clever for them. He finds ways to outflank them and it's the bandits who get ambushed. Now, it's even worse for them. Snow has fallen on the upper levels and bandit tracks are visible. It's only a matter of time."

Sarah beamed with pride as she heard the soldier praise Tepel but worried that her lover was still not out of danger.

A week later, the Governor returned, walking proudly at the head of his small army, followed by the wagon with some wounded and dead and the pack horses.

At the square, he dismissed the fighters and addressed the cheering crowd that had gathered.

"Citizens of Dulcigno, Allah has blessed our arms and given us victory. The enemy is vanquished, utterly destroyed. There will be no more attacks on defenceless citizens in our region. All we await now is the imminent death or capture of Bulka Khan and Captain Tepel will soon see to that. Citizens, we have been through a trying time. We thank all our fighters and congratulate them on their bravery and determination. Those who have died are martyrs. We pray that all those who were wounded will recover fully. We thank as well those who have seen to the defence of Dulcigno while we were away."

April drifted into May without any further news. Sarah began to fear the worst. The residents outside the walls had returned to their homes although there were still frequent precautionary patrols in the hills and woods.

"Until Bulka Khan is finished, we cannot be certain the danger is over," a Civic Guardsman pointed out to the questioning residents. "Therefore, we continue to be watchful."

Shabtai had fallen back into depression and stayed in his writing room, praying and fasting. With the bandits eliminated and the fighting largely over, he realized that the End of Days had not yet come and his mission was once again in abeyance. His wails and singing penetrated the house and Sarah fled back to the mud brick hut at the back of the garden.

Come to me soon, my Mahmud, Sarah thought. Opportunity and my bed are nigh.

Late one afternoon, near the end of the month, a Janissary soldier, red cloak flying behind him, galloped past them on the strand road and clattered through the gate and the narrow streets to the square. The soldier leapt from his horse and ran into the castle. Sarah joined the gathering crowd attracted by the event.

The news spread quickly. Tepel had captured Bulka Khan and would reach Dulcigno in several days. The crowd cheered. Sarah was silent, tears of happiness flowing down her cheeks, wetting her veil. Her lover was returning and the threat to his life was over.

She rushed home to tell Shabtai and burst in on him as he prayed in silence. She waited impatiently until he became aware of her presence.

"What means this intrusion?" he asked crossly.

"Husband, the bandit leader is captured, the fighting is over, and our friend, Captain Tepel, is safe."

Shabtai looked at her sorrowfully. "And this makes you happy, my Sarah? Truly I believed the End of Days had begun but it was nothing but a mere skirmish. Once again our Lord puts off the Redemption because we are not yet ready. Once more I must waste away in this prison, my work in danger of unravelling. My followers will flounder in my absence and like Aaron at Mt. Sinai will embrace the temptations of the Golden Calf. No, Sarah, this is not an event to celebrate but further proof the Lord has forgotten me."

His depression dampened her mood but only momentarily. She reminded herself that in a day or two she would be locked in the arms of her lover. But even in the glow of her erotic reverie, she realized that with his work done, Tepel would be gone.

I call upon the One, she prayed; please keep him here a little longer, alive and well.

Dulcigno was festooned with flags and pennants to welcome the small group of fighters when they arrived at noon two days later. The three surviving Janissaries came first, muskets at the ready. After them, a single pack horse pulled a wagon with the caged prisoner, flanked by six Guardsmen on either side. Bulka Khan completely filled the small cage and appeared naked. Tepel marched behind them.

Sarah stood at the roadside. Tepel bowed to her and the other people watching the procession go by. He looks awful, Sarah thought and her eyes filled with tears. His clothing was torn and filthy, a ragged beard covered his cheeks, and his moustache had lost its points and drooped. But more painfully to her, he seemed totally exhausted. His usual straight proud stature was bent slightly and he walked with the aid of a staff. Her presence appeared to give him added strength for he straightened up and threw away the staff.

The crowd grew as she followed the returning soldiers and their prisoner to the main square. The cheers of the welcoming populace drowned out the drummer and mehter leading the parade.

In the centre of the square stood the Governor dressed in his formal ceremonial attire. His white turban was decorated with peacock feathers.

A white silk mantle covered his shoulders and framed his indigo striped caftan and pantaloons. Calf leather slippers with turned up toes graced his feet. The sash of office was fastened diagonally from his right shoulder and held a gold handled cutlass at his left side.

On either side was a Civic Guardsman with spear and pennant, and a few paces behind were the Qadi and a heavy set Guardsman, face veiled in black, carrying a large cutlass, its edges gleaming. Troops of Civic Guardsmen formed a wide circle around the Governor, and provided a barrier against the public eagerly pressing forward.

The wagon bearing Bulka Khan stopped a good distance from the Governor. Tepel halted his troops, ordered them to attention, and bowed to the Governor.

"Nay, esteemed Captain, it is I who must bow to you," the Governor said loudly so all could hear. "It was your sagacious counsel, your courage, and persistence despite the rigours of the field that has won us a complete victory. Now, let your prisoner be removed from the cage so all can see how we deal with those who would rebel against the Sultan."

The stocky Guardsman lifted his cutlass and moved forward. The drummer played a rapid series of beats as the cage was opened. A rope around his neck and bayonets from behind forced the prisoner to emerge from the cage and fall to the ground. He was bare-footed, hatless, stripped to the waist, clad only in ragged pantaloons. He rose unsteadily to his feet and stretched.

Bulka Khan was a giant in stature. He had massive shoulders and powerful arms. Long shaggy hair and an unkempt beard hid most of his face except for his eyes which glared hatred as he swivelled his head from side to side. His legs were tightly shackled so that he could walk only inches at a time. A heavy chain, passed through the centre of a millstone, clasped his wrists.

Directed by Tepel, two of the Janissary soldiers held their bayoneted muskets at the ready as Bulka Khan, his arms held down by the heavy stone, shuffled toward the Governor and stopped several yards in front of him. The executioner moved behind the prisoner.

Before the Governor could speak, the prisoner spat. The gob of spittle sailed through the air and splattered the dust at the Governor's feet. The Governor whipped out his cutlass and angrily strode forward. "We shall behead you ourselves," he shouted.

Bulka Khan roared, flexed his shoulders and swung the millstone toward the advancing Governor, hitting and smashing his head. Khan's triumph was short lived. The muskets fired and he crumpled to the ground.

There was stunned silence on the square. Tepel ran to the Governor and summoned the mid-wife nurse but, after a hasty examination, both realized the Governor was no more. Clearly shaken, Tepel pulled the shocked Qadi forward. "Pray for him." Apart from the wails and shrieks of the Governor's family, the crowd was silent, completely overwhelmed by the tragic outcome of what was to be a victory celebration.

The Governor was buried later that day. The Qadi judged he had died a martyr and therefore he was carried to his grave in the clothes he was wearing. A white cotton cloth shrouded his crushed head and face. All Dulcigno mourned for three days.

Shabtai shrank more deeply into depression. Sarah attempted to comfort him but he ordered her away.

"Do not come near," he warned her. "I am possessed of devils. Samael predicted the Governor would die, the exact hour, the exact method. It is the time of demons. The world is awash in them. Flee! Save yourself!"

He could not be consoled and continued in constant prayer and fasting. Although concerned for him, she relished the opportunity it afforded for her dalliance with Tepel. She moved to the house at the back of the garden.

The first night Tepel did not appear. Although terribly disappointed, Sarah reasoned that he was wrapped up with the problems resulting from the Governor's death. On the second night, he arrived looking like the man she knew: washed, shaved, moustache restored, resplendent in a new uniform. They embraced for a long time, swaying slightly, whispering their longing for each other over the preceding months.

On the third night, after the first passionate love making, Tepel pushed himself up on an elbow and looked at her sadly.

"This is the end of the mourning period. The Qadi has asked for a meeting of the Council and wants me in attendance. No doubt I will be told my services are no longer required and that I must depart with the first sail."

She clutched him hard against her. "I will not let you go. I have prayed to Allah to keep you here."

He ran his fingers through her hair and said tenderly, "If Allah wishes it, I will stay. Otherwise, my sweet, we must prepare ourselves to bid farewell."

At noon the next day, Sarah discovered that Allah did wish her lover to stay. The Town Crier came by announcing that Captain Mahmud Tepel was appointed Governor until the Sultan decided otherwise. An ecstatic Sarah reckoned that it would be months before the Sultan received and reacted to the information and more months to send a replacement. She would have Tepel well into the next year.

That summer was a period of extended pleasure for Sarah. Shabtai was frequently depressed and provided sufficient opportunity for the lovers. Their idyll was marred by a recurrence of Sarah's coughing spell which seemed more intense and lasted longer than the previous attack. Since the days were warm, the illness could not be blamed on the cold and damp winter. Tepel, very worried, insisted she be cared for by the mid-wife nurse. He ordered Sarah moved to the castle for closer attention by the nurse and, with the latter's connivance, was able to sit by her bedside when his day's business was done.

I am like a husband to her, he thought. I do my duty during the day and then return to her at night. Just to be close to her gave him a sense of heady satisfaction, a feeling that was quickly sobered by the realization that this would come to an end shortly. The Sultan would most likely appoint someone else. Then, Tepel reminded himself, I will have to leave her in the clutches of that madman she still reveres.

There was no doubt in Tepel's mind that Shabtai was an impostor who varied from a state of lunacy to that of a scheming troublemaker. Tepel was frequently importuned by Shabtai to allow him to send and receive letters and to allow visitors. He agreed to the letters but refused the visits.

When Sarah's illness was sufficiently relieved, she returned home. Their clandestine meetings began again. On one of his nocturnal visits to the house in the garden, Tepel greeted Sarah and both sat on the edge of the bed, fully dressed, discussing the day's events. Sarah giggled appreciatively at some of the requests made to Tepel as Governor at his weekly audience.

"One man brought his two wives with him and complained bitterly that their constant bickering with each other was burdensome and was destroying the serenity of his household."

"What did you advise?" Sarah asked.

"I admonished the two women to respect their husband's need for peace and suggested that if the situation persisted, he should take a third wife, one who was young and very beautiful. At this, the two women interrupted and promised to settle their differences peacefully."

"You are so wise, my Mahmud," Sarah said admiringly and kissed him on the cheek.

"I don't know. The man said it sounded like a good idea regardless."

Their conversation was interrupted by a light knock at the door. Tepel moved swiftly into the other room and exited through the back window by which he had entered. Sarah replaced her headdress and veil and opened the door.

A man in a hooded cloak carrying a lit candle inclined his head.

"Wife of the Messiah, I greet you."

He pulled the hood off his head. Despite the turban, she immediately recognized Samuel Primo, Shabtai's scribe and secretary.

"Reb Primo, how come you here?"

He removed his cloak. "I came overland from Adrianople. I wish to see the Messiah but he is locked in his writing room. The house vibrates with his prayers. The servant said you were here. Can you talk to him?"

"Reb Primo, it is dangerous to visit him. Are you not aware?"

He nodded. "I am here secretly, disguised as a Muslim. It is imperative that I speak with him. Also, I must prevail upon your hospitality."

Peering around the corner of the building, Tepel watched them go, the pinpoint of candle light seemingly floating through the air. He was troubled. He should stop the man but to do so would compromise Sarah. He crawled back through the window and waited patiently. After a long while, Sarah returned and fell into his arms.

"My husband refuses to see him. I have put him up in a room overlooking the road. I beg you, do not arrest him. When he and my husband meet, they will discuss only the fine points of my husband's mystical thoughts. The visitor is not a danger to the Empire."

"But my sweet, he defies the conditions of your husband's exile. My orders are clear, both as a Janissary officer and the Governor of Dulcigno. I must at least send him away."

"Wait a few days," she pleaded. "He will leave quietly. If we were not together tonight, you would not know that a stranger was here."

True enough, he thought, and slowly removed her clothing.

As Sarah had predicted, Primo left after a few days. There were other visitors after that, each bearing gifts which Tepel distributed to the family of the dead Governor and the Qadi.

"You do not keep any for yourself?" Sarah asked, admiring his honesty but concerned for his modest means. "What will you live on when you are no longer a soldier?"

"The Sultan does not forget his Janissaries," he replied. "Besides, I have a gift worth more than pieces of gold, a treasure beyond my wildest imaginings."

In early autumn, the three children arrived along with Elijah, Shabtai's brother. The excitement pulled Shabtai out of his funk and added to the joyous family reunion. Much was made of Ishmael, now six years old, tall for his age and growing in stature like his father. Shabtai declared him his successor and the person who would redeem the Other Nations. Both Elijah and Sarah bowed to him, leaving the youngster pleased with the attention but quite bewildered.

The meetings between Tepel and Sarah became sporadic. Sarah insisted that the house at the back of the garden was her bath house. Once each week after dark, the servant would fill the bronze bathtub and then leave. The lovers had to be careful since Shabtai, as husband, could walk in at any moment unannounced.

The beginning of winter coincided with Sarah collapsing with a severe coughing fit. Shabtai sent for the nurse who ordered Sarah brought immediately to the castle. Both Shabtai and Elijah looked on gloomily as she was carried away in a litter. Tepel's concern now bordered on panic.

Sarah coughed frequently, had trouble breathing, spat up blood occasionally, and slept most of the time. Shabtai and Elijah visited her frequently during the day, but at night, Tepel was at her bedside. He kissed her hand and prayed vehemently for Allah to make her well again. When she awoke, he held her in a sitting position and spooned the broth carefully into her mouth. After the broth, she refused to lie down and leaned against him. She touched his face and stroked his moustache.

The days went by and she improved to the point where, with his help at night, she could leave the bed, take a few hesitant steps around the room and, in front of the grate, toast in the heat of the blazing log.

"My husband says I am no longer pretty and Allah has abandoned me," she said mournfully to Tepel one night.

Your husband is a fool, he thought. "You have been ill but you will recover and your beauty will return," he said encouragingly.

"What if it does not? What then? Will I still have your love?"

He kissed her on her cheek. "My love is for you. It is steadfast."

She became well enough to return home but never regained her normal health and well being. She left the caring of the children entirely to the servant. She rested often and showed no interest when Shabtai and Elijah tried to explain the next steps in the messianic mission.

She managed one bath night during this period, marshalling her strength and pretending she was capable of bathing alone. Tepel realized at that meeting that the bloom had indeed left her. Instead of its luscious roundness, her body had become angular and bony. Her breasts had lost their fullness and now hung listless. Her face was sallow and gaunt.

Their lovemaking had always been robust and passionate. Now, Tepel was cautious and gentle as he possessed her. She responded weakly but insisted she had enjoyed it.

"You must give me up," she said as they parted. "I can no longer satisfy you."

"Nonsense," he said, kissing her. "I shall never give you up. Just holding you is satisfaction enough."

It was not a hard winter that year. There were many days of sunshine warm enough to allow Sarah to sit on a pillowed bench in the garden and watch the children play.

Despite the clement weather, it was clear that Sarah's illness was progressing and her body was slowly wasting away. The coughing fits came daily, with much blood in the sputum. Shabtai judged the end was near and dispatched Elijah on a special mission to find a wife for him. "The work of the Messiah must go on," he told Elijah who nodded in agreement.

In March, the nurse informed Tepel that Sarah's condition had worsened and she should move back to the castle.

"Her last days have come, Governor Effendi."

Shabtai brought the children to see their mother for the last time. Shortly afterwards, he fell into a deep depression and did not return. Tepel sat every evening with her and sometimes during the day. She awoke infrequently, smiled at him, and sipped the broth he offered her.

"You are a loyal lover," she said to him one night. "We can no longer love but still you are here. I am indeed fortunate."

Tears streamed down his face. He kissed her hand. "I too am fortunate. To have your love is a boon. But where is your husband. Does he not attend you?"

She reached out and wiped away his tears with her hand.

"My husband is in the state where he is possessed by Samael and other demons."

"I should have been your husband," Tepel said, grasping her hand.

Sarah shook her head. "No, my sweet Governor. As much as we love each other, you would have been a poor husband. You are a soldier. You were away five years in Crete. That would have been five long lonely years for me — waiting, longing, hoping, fearing. No, Allah has allowed us some splendid moments and has kept you here. I thank Allah for that."

A paroxysm of coughing engulfed her. The fit passed but left her exhausted and she dozed off. Hours later she awoke to find him still there.

"I will leave you very soon." She paused, gasping for breath. "... in my reticule... a silk handkerchief framed in lace...keep in memory of me... bring it when you join me in the Garden of Paradise."

He sobbed uncontrollably as he retrieved the handkerchief. A further fit of coughing racked her and after the spell, she fell asleep. He kneeled on the floor and held her hand. After awhile, he realized the hand was cold and the fingers stiffening. His cry of anguish echoed throughout the castle.

CHAPTER 10

- SIOUX LOOKOUT, ONTARIO -
2008 - SARAI AND DONALD

Sarai leaned into the biting winter wind and felt the sleeting snow needling the unprotected parts of her face. Despite the parka and the furred hood pulled tightly around her, the cold seemed to slice right through her.

It must be my many years in tropical missions, she thought, that makes me so vulnerable to the cold. Her two paramedic companions, Daniel with the unpronounceable Eastern European family name and Mike Urban seemed impervious to the weather. Parkas open, hoods off, they bent only slightly to the worst of the wind.

"When you been here as long as us," Mike had assured her, "you won't notice the cold as much." Daniel, not given much to talk, nodded.

There might be another reason, Sarai thought. Both her companions were well fleshed men.

They walked the short distance from the Sioux Lookout Airport Terminal to the twin engine turbo prop air ambulance already warming up on the tarmac. The interior wasn't large: room for one gurney, four passenger seats and space to stow their medical bags and supplies. One of the two pilots called out "Prepare for takeoff," and Mike answered "All secure." The plane turned onto the runway and lumbered into the sky, buffeted by side winds and tossing wildly as it climbed above the storm.

Their destination was Sandy Lake, the home of the First Nations Nitam-Anishinaabe people, about 340 kilometres north, a one hour flight if the weather allowed. Apart from ice roads in winter, the town was accessible by air only. The medical emergency calling Sarai and her fellow paramedics there was a very pregnant young woman, ready to give birth but whose baby had not turned. Their job was to pick her up, stabilize her, and fly her to Winnipeg for surgery and post natal care.

The ride was bumpy. The pilots managed to get the plane above the worst of the storm but still under the clouds. The paramedics settled into a relaxed state of alertness, marred only by the occasional burst of exceptional turbulence. After a half-hour they left the storm behind and flew out into the brilliance of a rising sun over snow covered forest and the rugged terrain of the Canadian Shield decorated with diamond studded iced lakes.

In a way, Sarai thought, I'm back to mission work, at least that part of the job I always loved, bringing medical help to vulnerable people. She had been six months with the air ambulance service flying to medical emergencies in aboriginal communities that dotted the west and north of Ontario. Sometimes the work was routine — transporting a patient to hospital in Winnipeg; often it was gripping — stabilizing a patient slipping in and out of cardiac arrest in the nursing station at the reserve or in the air. Twice she'd flown in with a doctor to provide emergency surgery. For the current mission, she'd packed her surgery kit, just in case the patient waiting for them in Sandy Lake could not tolerate the three hour trip to Winnipeg. In her previous missionary work, she had sometimes performed a caesarean.

The demands on her time and the intensity of the work allowed her to put Donald out of her mind although she thought of him now. She still felt the glow of their love but reminded herself that she was the one to bring their relationship to an end.

Donald had been deeply troubled by the Kenya incident. He made it clear to her that he suspected there was more to the death of Charles Wingate than purely natural causes. She insisted there was nothing more but perhaps he detected a subtle subconscious blip of insincerity on her part. For her own sake and Melissa's, she did not tell him the entire truth.

The warm openness between them began to erode and their love slowly cooled. They argued more about Donald's dedication to the Kabbalah and his support of the Sabbatean version of it. Whereas before, he seemed to accept her gnawing doubt that a divine being even existed, now, he claimed, it left him feeling dissatisfied and uneasy about their relationship. Sarai did not wait until the growing tension between them became acrimonious. She preferred to remember him as a loving, caring man, pursuing a vision — perhaps illusionary, but who knows anyway — a vision inspired by his idol Shabtai Zvi of making the Godhead whole again and launching the process of Redemption.

She had applied to become a flying paramedic and took her acceptance as the right moment to inform him she would be leaving Toronto and him. Although he protested vigorously, she sensed relief. They saw each other a while longer as her new position required training at a hospital in Toronto. In late 2007, she moved to Sioux Lookout.

She telephoned him to say goodbye. "Donald, for your own sake, don't fall into the clutches of Lily Thegn. She is not there to help you."

She could hear the smile in his voice. "I could tell you it's no longer your business but I know you mean well for me. Sarai, thanks to you I learned something about love. You were the first woman I fell madly in love with who didn't have the Lily Thegn look. It got me thinking. Since we broke up, I've had long talks with my wife, Roberta, and we've agreed to start again. So you see, even though you don't believe in my Kabbalah, you have retrieved the Holy Sparks within me."

"Prepare for landing," the pilot called out and the plane began its quick descent toward the gravel landing strip in Sandy Lake. Sarai pushed aside all thoughts of Donald and the past and prepared her mind for the patient that awaited her.

CHAPTER 11

- DULCIGNO, 1674 -

MULLAH ALI

For the first time in his twenty-five years, Mullah Ali Hussein saw himself at the edge of a precipice and felt cold prickles of sweat trickle down his back as he stared into the remorseless eyes of the Qadi. They were seated at a table in the Qadi's study, one of the two rooms he occupied in the castle. The room was lit by a couple of candles on the table.

"You are a fool. You allow a dabbler in heresy to outwit you," snarled the Qadi, his hand a gnarled fist striking the table. "The man is a false messiah, a false Muslim, an infidel. He was exiled here to keep him away from Jewish communities, so as not to cause dissension. Yet, with your help, he succeeds in disrupting these communities."

The Qadi held out several scrolls. "Here is correspondence we have received. Read them carefully."

Apprehensively, the Mullah unwrapped each scroll and scanned through them. Each scroll was a letter of complaint — one from the Chief Rabbi of Constantinople, one from the rabbinate of Adrianople, another from the Chief Rabbi of Smyrna — all concerning the spreading of the false messiah's teachings to their communities through letters and visits of his followers.

"I have not yet presented these letters to the Governor," the Qadi said. "Remember, the Governor is no longer Captain Tepel. Ibrahim Abdul Pasha is a devout Muslim who will not hesitate to take extreme measures against Aziz Mehmed and all who help him. Do you not know what happens to heretics and apostates?"

Instinctively, the Mullah reached for his throat.

"Exactly," the Qadi said coldly. "I have prepared a juridical opinion regarding you. Read it."

With trembling fingers, the Mullah unwrapped the scroll and read through it. The Qadi had listed the Mullah's failings and recommended to the Governor of Dulcigno that Mullah Ali Hussein be publicly flogged and executed.

"I plead for mercy, esteemed Qadi," the Mullah said, his voice shaking. "I do not serve Aziz Mehmed Effendi. I was told by the Grand Vizier to ensure Ishmael is raised as a Muslim and to keep close contact with the family. As part of this, occasionally, I have arranged for travellers to carry his letters but I was told these letters were simply family news and greetings. I cannot read the Hebrew. As for visitors, they seemed harmless scholars."

"Why carry his letters?" the Qadi asked contemptuously. "The terms of his exile are clear — no correspondence or contact outside Dulcigno."

The Mullah was about to protest that Aziz Mehmed's family paid generously for the privilege of correspondence and contact, but thought better of it. This was not the moment to accuse the Qadi and the Governor of taking bribes.

"Esteemed Qadi, I beg of you," the Mullah said, leaning forward, stretching his arms appealingly. "What can be wrong with carrying letters for Aziz Mehmed? He is a Muslim, therefore I am not assisting an infidel. True, many of his friends and family have not converted, but many have and others will."

The Qadi snorted, slid off the bench he was sitting on, walked around to the Mullah and shook him by the shoulders. Still sitting, the Mullah was taller than the enraged Qadi but was pulled off the bench and fell to his knees.

"Fool! You are about to die and yet you defend this madman. Yes, madman! He continues to pursue his messianic pretensions. The messages bring his associates here, not just his family. His associates are as mad as he is. And you are prepared to sacrifice your life for them! Why? It cannot be for the harlot, his wife. She is dead two years. It cannot be his new wife. Even robed and veiled, she is tall and shapeless. What attracts you? It cannot be his Kabbalah. It is a monstrous heresy. Even the rabbis of Constantinople, Adrianople, and Smyrna condemn him and his teachings. These Jews wanted him dead, not just exiled. But Mullah Ali Hussein, a man learned in the Qur'an, a man I have taught myself, a man sent here by the Grand Vizier himself, not merely dips his toe into the cesspool created by this madman from Smyrna but swims in it."

The Qadi shuffled up and down his study room, his short stocky form enveloped in a dirty, frayed white mantle and caftan. The Mullah returned to his bench and sat there with lowered head, his mind casting about for an argument, any argument, a way of escape.

Why did he help Aziz Mehmed Effendi? he asked himself. He need never have returned to Dulcigno, he thought now with regret. The Qadi's guess was in the right direction. It was Aziz's wife — the harlot, the Qadi called her — that had pulled him back. He had to be near her, to walk the streets where she walked, perhaps to spy her in the main square or market place, or when visiting Aziz Mehmed as part of his duties, to be under the same roof, hopefully to even see her.

What am I thinking, he would berate himself. She is a Muslim wife and I am contemplating adultery, and if not adultery, then worship, worship of a goddess made manifest on Earth. I must get over this madness.

Like the wind in the sails of the barque that bore him away from Dulcigno, his passion drove him to be part of her life. He delivered Shabtai's letter personally to Elijah, his brother, and resided for a short time as a guest in his house. He made it seem like coincidence that he arrived in Adrianople at the same time as Elijah and accompanied him to meet with Vani Effendi, the army chaplain and a close confidant of the Sultan. Vani Effendi considered Aziz Mehmed a good friend and easily granted Elijah's request to accompany the children to Dulcigno.

The Mullah joined the staff of Vani Effendi and tried to forget Sarah as he immersed himself in his Islamic duties. At that time, there were large numbers of infidels who wished to convert and the Mullah was kept busy guiding and teaching the new entrants to the Faith.

It was late in the year of 1673, when Vani Effendi asked for a volunteer to move to Dulcigno to become the tutor and mentor of Ishmael, the son of Aziz Mehmed Effendi. Mullah Ali Hussein readily assented.

"Kuprulu Fazil Ahmed Pasha, the Grand Vizier, is disturbed by some reports from Dulcigno that there are activities related to Aziz Mehmed that are worrisome," Vani Effendi told him. "It is most important that we ensure Ishmael grows up and remains a loyal, observant Muslim and does not become another false messiah. We have heard rumours to this effect. Despite his conversion and banishment, many Jews still believe Aziz Mehmed Effendi is their messiah. I have recommended that we obliterate them all, but the Grand Vizier insists the Jews make important contributions to the Treasury. Therefore, we must satisfy ourselves with watching Aziz Mehmed, reminding him of his vows, and eliminating any influence he has over Ishmael."

Mullah Ali travelled from Adrianople overland to Dulcigno arriving late at night several weeks before Sarah died. The next morning, he met first with the Qadi who brought him up to date on all that had happened since his departure. He presented his orders to Captain Tepel, the interim Governor, and then called upon Shabtai.

He had to stifle his excitement as the door opened but it was only the servant. She informed him that Aziz Mehmed Effendi was in his writing room but could not be disturbed. He asked for Ishmael, hoping Sarah would accompany him, but the boy came into the receiving room alone. The six year old, was comely, tall for his age, and wore only a floor length caftan and no headdress.

"Why are you not dressed properly?" the Mullah asked sternly.

"I am the next messiah and I answer only to my father and the One above."

The Mullah restrained an impulse to slap him across the face. Instead, he saw an opportunity to involve Sarah.

"Then I must address your mother since your father is not available. Your behaviour is intolerable."

The boy struck a belligerent pose, his hands on his hips, his head thrust forward.

"My mother is ill. She lies in the castle hospice attended by the midwife. My father says she will soon die."

Deep within Mullah Ali a black well of dread flooded into his consciousness and threatened to wash away the pillars of discipline and composure that anchored him to the Earth. It had never occurred to him that the star which shone brightly in his firmament could possibly be extinguished. She was young, a little older than he. How could she be at death's door and her much older husband live on? How could Allah allow this? Was He punishing the husband for his messianic visions and turning a naive Ishmael into an apostate?

"You are wrong. She cannot be dying," he said to the boy, grasping him roughly by a shoulder.

The boy pulled away and tried to escape but the Mullah caught him and held him back forcefully.

"We will go see for ourselves and pray for her recovery."

"I will not," Ishmael said defiantly. "She has brought on the demons that possess my father. I hate her."

The Mullah gave way to grief and frustration and hit the boy hard across the mouth, knocking him to the floor.

"I will hear no more talk like this. I am your teacher and your lessons start now." He yanked Ishmael to his feet. "You will prepare yourself in proper dress and then we will visit your mother."

He pulled the reluctant, whimpering boy along as he strode quickly to the castle. He was appalled at the sight of Sarah. The round even features that had so entranced him were now emaciated, lined, and bloodless pale. Only the large brown eyes retained their brilliance but here too there were signs of fading.

She looked at them quizzically. "Who is my visitor, Ishmael, and why have you come?"

The boy stubbornly refused to answer, turned away, and was stopped by the Mullah from leaving. The Mullah was unable to talk as he struggled to hold back his tears.

"Is this to be a silent visit then?" Sarah said, smiling, the thin lips drawing away from the still white teeth. "Sir, I have seen you before. Are you not the generous man who carried the message that brought my children here?"

He nodded and found his voice. "I am Mullah Ali Hussein assigned by the Grand Vizier to be Ishmael's teacher and tutor. Aziz Mehmed Effendi was not available to receive my orders, therefore I have come to the boy's mother."

Sarah laughed, a dry rasping chuckle that sounded more like a cough. "I am hardly a mother anymore. The boy insists I am evil and obeys me grudgingly because his father tells him to. It is out of my hands now. I can only lie here and wither away if that is the one God's wish. But I beg you, do kindly with my Ishmael. I see the mark of your knuckles beside his mouth."

The Mullah bent his head guiltily. How could he bring anguish to this dying woman?

"Madam, his speech and behaviour are intolerable. If he is heard by the Qadi or others, he will surely be punished, perhaps lashed, and he will bring consequences to your husband as well."

A line of concern joined the other lines on Sarah's forehead. "Ishmael, listen carefully to Mullah Ali. He will tell you what things you may say and do in public to avoid trouble for you and for your father. Become a scholar like your father and others will respect and want to be with you. Sir, I beseech you. I feel you are a friend. Do kindly with my husband as well."

A sudden fit of coughing seized her. The nurse appeared, raised Sarah into a sitting position, and wiped away the sputum from her mouth. After settling back in her bed, Sarah reached out, motioned Ishmael to come closer, and gently stroked his arm.

"Goodbye, my sweet. Be strong. Remember a mother who loves you."

After a moment, she fell asleep.

Tears rolling down his cheeks, the Mullah said, "We will pray to Allah for her."

Ishmael, crying, his truculence gone, readily assented. Both stood beside the bed, praying softly, voices choked with emotion, and then, hand in hand, took one last look and left.

The Mullah never went back to visit Sarah. Shattered by her appearance, he preferred to remember her as she had looked the day she walked into the reception room without headdress or veil. Truly a jinn in female form, he had thought. Now the jinn had vacated her body and allowed it to decay.

Sarah died two weeks later. Mullah Ali went to Shabtai to inform him. Despite the servant girl's insistence her master could not be disturbed, the Mullah knocked politely on the door to the writing room and stepped inside.

He was assailed by the stench of stale body odour and flatulence, and urine overflowing a large chamber pot near the door. He stood in the doorway adjusting his eyes to the semi-darkness. The window was shuttered and the only light came from a three branch candlestick with one candle. In the gloom, he made out Shabtai, angrily shaking his fist at him, dressed in a knee length shirt and a close fitting leather bonnet covering his head.

"We will not be disturbed," Shabtai shouted.

"Aziz Mehmed Effendi, I bring sad tidings. I must speak with you."

Shabtai threw himself flat and pummelled the floor with his fists. "Leave me! I want no more of you. Lord, take them away."

The Mullah realized Shabtai was not talking to him. He tried to penetrate the darkness but could see no one else.

"Effendi, there is no one here but you and me."

Shabtai stood up, swaying dizzily, barely looking in Ali's direction. "What is it?"

By this time, the Mullah was eager to quit the room and said simply. "Your wife has died. She will be buried in the morning."

Shabtai said nothing but waved a dismissive hand and the Mullah quickly departed, not certain that his message had registered.

"Leave me too!" Shabtai commanded the apparently empty room.

The one quivering candle flame flared and illuminated Samael, naked, leaning against the window wall, his arms akimbo.

"Now is not the time to dismiss us, learned Rabbi. Now is the time to join us. You are free. The One you worship has turned his face from you. He has taken away your most faithful supporter. Your followers turn against you. Why prolong your life? Lillith desires you. Behold the Serpent of Paradise!"

The candle flame increased in brilliance and shed a soft lambent light into the dark recesses of a corner. A large serpent lay curled. It raised its head, tested the air with its forked tongue, and unwinding, slowly moved toward Shabtai. He shrank back, nearly knocking over the candle. The serpent reared up and began to metamorphose. Its crusted outer skin softened and fell away, revealing a beguilingly beautiful woman with long flowing hair and a curvaceous body wrapped in a silken diaphanous shawl that hung on the nipples of her prominent breasts. She held out graceful arms.

"Embrace her," Samael urged. "Lillith wants to be pleasured by you."

Lust mounded Shabtai's shirt at the junction of his legs. He reached toward Lillith, then hesitated.

"Why do you stop, sweet Shabtai?" said the woman. "Your Lillith awaits you with such pleasures even your Sarah could not bestow. All men yearn for me, dream of me. I am yours to command. You can lie with me as often and as long as you wish. I can prolong the eruption of your seed until you beg for release. My sisters and daughters are equally beautiful and clamour for you. Sweet Shabtai, I beg of you. Be one with us. Be one with me."

Samael leaped from the wall and landed beside Shabtai. "Heed her, Shabtai. She is yours for eternity. Heed not your God — He is powerless in our realm. Will you live out your days in this prison devoid of delights, spied upon and hounded by your jailers? Your God has deserted you — desert Him and come with us."

Shabtai tore off his bonnet and slapped it hard against Samael, sending him sprawling. He grasped his hair, trying to tear it from his head, and shrieked, "No! No! You offer nothing but the desecration of the flesh. We are the anointed of Israel and we will prevail. We want no more of your filth, your lies and temptations."

He threw open the writing room door, shouting, "Away! Away with all of you!" and staggered down the short corridor to the reception room.

The servant girl, who had returned to the children's bedroom, was startled by the commotion and felt her way down the dark steps to the reception room.

"Master, are you well?" she asked Shabtai, a shadow against the dim light emanating from the writing room.

He grasped her to him. "Save me, Amilah. The demons taunt me. They would take me to their dens in the lower worlds."

"There are no demons here, Master," she said soothingly. "There are only you and me and the children sleeping upstairs."

She felt the pressure between his legs. "Do you have a need, master?"

"A need? Yes, a need."

She led him to his bedroom, helped him take off his shirt, removed her own nightclothes, and crawled in beside him. This was not the first time she had sated his lust. Before, she had always trembled, fearful of discovery and the punishment that comes with adultery. But now, her mistress was dead. Perhaps her master would marry her for he did seem to like her.

In the early morning, just before sunrise, he awoke her. "Come, Amilah, prepare the children. This morning we must bury my Sarah."

He was no longer in agony and had returned to his normal state.

The Qadi asked the Mullah to perform the funeral rite for Sarah.

"The woman was not of sufficient honour and integrity to warrant my presence," the Qadi explained. "However, she is a Muslim and shall be buried properly."

The Mullah found the Qadi's remarks offensive but controlled his anger and merely nodded.

The Qadi saw the flash of feeling in the Mullah's eyes and said, sneering, "You, too, have been bewitched by her, just like our Governor and the other men who fawned over her. Because of them and the generous considerations they have received from her husband's followers, we must continue to bear the burden of this monstrous heretic."

The funeral was held in the square in front of the castle. The body, shrouded in clean white sheets, was placed on a blanket on a stone step. To everyone's surprise, Shabtai appeared, tall, strong, resolute, his face emotionless. He held Ishmael by the hand, followed by the servant girl Amilah leading the older son, Abraham, and carrying the two-year old daughter. Shabtai accepted the condolences of the mourners with a brief nod. They were joined by two other women — the mid-wife nurse and the widow of the previous Governor.

Captain Tepel, as interim-Governor, stood just behind the Mullah with Shabtai at his side. The Governor's face was drawn, the points of his moustache sagged, and the occasional tear welled out of his eyes. Looking at the two men, it dawned on the Mullah that Tepel appeared more grief stricken than the husband.

Ishmael pointed to the shrouded body. "What is that?" he asked.

"Your mother lies there, Ishmael. She has left this world."

The boy began to cry and moved toward the body but was held back by Shabtai.

"Do not grieve, my son. It is not death but merely an occultation as a cloud sometimes drifts across the moon and blocks out its light. She will return to us at the Redemption which will come soon."

Shabtai spoke in Hebrew so that he would not be understood by the mourners. "You must be brave," he went on. "If Redemption comes not in my time, then it will be up to you as the next messiah to lead our people. Remember, you must speak naught of this to anyone."

Facing the corpse, Mullah Ali led them through the service. Afterwards, two Janissaries carefully lifted the blanket with the corpse, and accompanied by the male mourners, carried it along the coastal road, past Shabtai's house, past the livery stables, to the cemetery and the waiting grave site. The corpse was placed on its right side facing Mecca and the grave filled.

The clouded sky which had darkened now displayed its grief, releasing a mixture of rain and snow on the mourners as they took their leave of the grave and solemnly left the cemetery.

Shabtai invited Captain Tepel and Mullah Ali to share tea with him. The two guests sat on mounded cushions in front of a roaring fire sipping on steaming bowls of a fragrant infusion. Shabtai had removed his boots and sat on a low hard bench.

Mullah Ali looked at him suspiciously. "Do you mourn the Hebrew way, Aziz Mehmed Effendi, bare foot and on a hard seat?"

"Not at all, esteemed Mullah. I have not torn my clothes as I would in the Hebrew way, and I will mourn for only three days and not seven as is customary among Jews. Fear not, I am solid in the Faith. However, I have lost a dear wife and my grief causes me to seek discomfort."

Tepel squinted at him through eyes bloodshot by weeping. He noted the shawl wrapped around Shabtai's neck, its ends tucked into his mantle. One end had pulled loose and was nearly cut in half. Sarah had once explained to Tepel that many Jews, rather than tear their clothing, substituted a shawl which they then cut as symbolic of their grief.

We are fools, thought Tepel. This man deceives us at every turn, yet we accept his excuses and blandishments.

" Effendi," Tepel observed, "your shawl is torn at one end."

Shabtai pushed the end back into his mantle and sighed. "You are right, Captain Tepel. The servant is always busy with the children and my wife put it in her work basket to mend. Now, I will have to discard it. A pity since it is made of silk from a country far to the east. Yes, when the wife ceases to function, the husband drifts helplessly."

He says this to two unmarried men, Tepel marvelled, and despite his grief had to suppress a smile. Oh well, he thought, the Mullah nods in agreement and Aziz Mehmed is no longer my responsibility. He reached absentmindedly into his mantle pocket and fingered Sarah's handkerchief.

"Aziz Mehmed Effendi," Tepel said, "I offer my condolences on the death of your wife and I also bid you farewell. Mullah Ali brought messages from the Grand Vizier. The new Governor arrives shortly and I am to join the Grand Vizier in Adrianople to embark on the Polish campaign. May Allah bestow upon you and your children a return to happiness, and good health."

Shabtai was visibly disappointed. The Captain had made things easier for him, had allowed correspondence and some visits, and had not accepted bribes and gifts. Would the new Governor be as accommodating?

"Esteemed Governor, I thank you for your many services and kindness to us. My wife often talked about how good a friend you are. You have been of immense help to us. May Allah protect you in battle and war."

The Mullah looked quizzically at Tepel. He suddenly realized that the facial pallor, the drooping moustache, the bloodshot eyes, the stubble on the cheeks was the face of real grief. Tepel, too, had been trapped by the beauty and charm of the peerless wife of Aziz Mehmed.

"Esteemed Governor," Shabtai continued, "may I ask one further favour? Can you see that a letter reaches Rabbi Joseph Filosoff of Salonika. The letter asks his approval for the betrothal of his daughter to me."

Both guests stood up in astonishment.

"Aziz Mehmed Effendi," Mullah Ali protested, "your wife is barely cold."

Shabtai stood up as well and bowed to the two men. "Yes, it is quite true, this may seem a callous act by me. However, I am mindful of the need for my children to have a mother and it will be many months before everything can be arranged and my new wife can reach Dulcigno. I beseech you Captain Tepel. If you have the letter translated from the Hebrew, you will confirm it is simply a request for a betrothal and marriage of Filosoff's daughter. It also informs him that his daughter will convert to Islam as a condition of the marriage."

Tepel heaved an internal sigh. Even an exile should have a wife and Sarah's children deserve a mother. Therefore, for Sarah's sake alone... "Very well, Aziz Mehmed Effendi, I will take the letter."

Shabtai embraced Tepel. "I cannot thank you enough, Captain Tepel. May the one God... may Allah watch over you and keep you safe. Farewell."

Shabtai readily welcomed Ali into his household, partly because he had no choice, partly because he recognized in the Mullah an empathy toward him and his family entirely lacking in the current Dulcigno authorities. He had no illusions about the role the Grand Vizier had given the Mullah. He would try to render Ishmael useless as a successor to Shabtai and would report on the latter's activities where these contained suspicions of heresy and apostasy. But the Mullah had already proven useful in getting Shabtai's message to Elijah and accompanying him to Vani Effendi. Elijah had spoken highly about the Mullah and his helpfulness.

The Mullah enrolled Ishmael in the small madrassah attached to the main mosque. After a few months the boy showed an aptitude for the Arabic and the study of the Qur'an. The Mullah reported confidently to his superiors that Ishmael was making good progress as a true Muslim and his father's influence was diminishing.

The Mullah's tendency to balance reward and punishment exerted an appropriate discipline to which the boy responded. The two came to like each other to the point where the boy felt he had a real friend and like true friends, secrets can be shared. After Ishmael divulged one important confidence, the Mullah deemed it necessary to talk to the boy's father.

Shabtai was still in his normal state when Mullah Ali called upon him one Saturday morning. As he waited in the reception room sipping a bowl of tea, he heard the sound of song emanating from the writing room. The mellifluous voice penetrated the house and brought even the servant into the reception room to listen in rapt attention. The song ended on a long drawn out note at the top of the singer's register. There was silence and then Shabtai emerged from the writing room.

He bowed and greeted the Mullah and, turning to the servant, said, "Amilah, you must not stand about. Return to your duties."

The Mullah noted that his command was gentle and the devoted look on the girl's face did not fade as she spun about and disappeared into the interior of the house.

"How goes it with Ishmael?" Shabtai asked, seating himself on a cushion.

"The boy is very quick," the Mullah assured him. "He learns his lessons well and shows enthusiasm and eagerness in the pursuit of his studies."

Shabtai nodded appreciatively. "It is to your credit, esteemed Mullah. Ishmael enjoys your friendship and help." Anticipating what was coming next, Shabtai added, "He is a clever boy but needs guidance for which I am grateful to you."

"There is a problem," the Mullah said after a short pause. "He continues to insist he is the next messiah and when I admonish him, he insists his father tells him so, and I must take it up with you."

Shabtai slapped his thigh and doubled up with laughter. "I am guilty," he exclaimed.

"Aziz Mehmed Effendi, this is no laughing matter. The boy will bring punishment on himself and you."

"Mullah Ali Hussein," Shabtai said still chuckling, "Ishmael is a boy — a child with a lively imagination. When he first came to Dulcigno, he announced he would be the next Governor, then he would join the Janissaries and become a captain like the Governor and do brave deeds, then he declared he would become the Sultan, and when he heard the malicious rumours bandied about that I was the messiah, he naturally believed as my son, he would be the next messiah. Now, I say to him, if you want to be the messiah, you must learn your lessons well. In that regard, I am guilty but I believe I am supporting you and giving him added motivation to learn. Soon, you will see, he will want to be an Imam, then a Mullah, then a Qadi, and perhaps even the top jurist, the Sheik-hul-islam."

"Then you do not believe you are the messiah?" the Mullah asked.

Shabtai laughed again. "Mullah Ali Hussein, I am a Muslim. Even as a Jew, I never claimed to be the messiah. There were fools that started this rumour and credulous people who believed it and continue to believe it. Take no note of them. As for Ishmael, I will impress upon him that although he is the next messiah" — Shabtai chuckled — "he is not to tell anyone but you and me."

The Mullah shook his head. "No, no, Aziz Mehmed Effendi, it cannot be so. You must disabuse him of the notion. His classmates ridicule him. The other Imams and Mullahs are suspicious of him and want to exclude him. I will fail in my duty as his teacher and the Grand Vizier will justly reprimand me."

"But surely, Mullah Ali, if the boy stops talking about his role as the next messiah and if you insist he will not be excluded from the madrassah, then you may continue to teach him. Will that not satisfy everyone?"

"No," Mullah Ali said emphatically. "It may be too late. Ishmael must find some other goal and state he is not to become the messiah. If not, it will affect you. You are seen as persisting in your messianic visions, that it is your influence that causes the boy to make his outrageous claims. Ibrahim Ahmed Pasha, the new Governor, is staunch in his faith and does not tolerate behaviour he believes is heretical in nature or direction. He is eager to rid Dulcigno of you. His spies watch you and report back to him."

Shabtai regarded the Mullah uneasily. He was certain the Mullah was one of the spies. Why was he warning him? Was he a friend as Tepel had been a friend? Shabtai had no wish to endanger his life or the well-being of his children. He remembered the ordeal he had gone through at the time of his conversion to Islam and involuntarily shuddered.

"What do they report?" Shabtai asked, trying to keep his voice steady, and affected a nonchalance he little felt.

"That you sometimes pray in Hebrew and wear Jewish prayer articles. That the occasional stranger enters your house and stays for a period, sometimes a few days, sometimes longer."

"I suppose this is what you report too," a disconsolate Shabtai said, looking anxiously at the Mullah.

"I report I have not seen any strangers and that you revert to Hebrew only when you are in your state of sadness or talking to your children. I lie to protect you."

"Why?" an astounded Shabtai asked.

"Because your wife on her deathbed begged me to."

Shabtai lowered his head and struggled to keep his lips from twitching. He wiped away a tear. Even from the grave, Sarah worked her magic. He thought back in shame to that time more than three years ago when, in a demonic state, he had divorced her. Fortunately, God had once again turned His face to him and they remarried several months later. It had been a difficult time for her yet she never complained but simply took up as his wife again as though nothing had happened. During that interim period, he had betrothed another woman who died before the marriage could be consummated. Clearly, God had intervened and had designated Sarah as his true wife. She had supported him in his mission even when he at times lost confidence.

"I am grateful to you," Shabtai said. "However, let me assure you that my visitors are innocent of any attempt to cause trouble to the Governor or to the Empire. They bring me information regarding my request to marry the daughter of Rabbi Filosoff of Salonika. Since I converted to Islam, many Jews revile me. As a result, Rabbi Filosoff, if he accepts, puts himself in jeopardy and censure in the Jewish community. With the help of my visitors, we are trying to find a way to mitigate these problems."

"Once the betrothal is agreed, will these visits stop?" the Mullah asked in a tone of resignation, fully anticipating the answer.

"Mullah Ali, I sincerely hope not. Remember, I am considered a scholar in the study of the Kabbalah. Some come to me now for understanding and learning of the Kabbalah. I perform this duty for them as a way to persuade them into the Faith. After all, was it not the Kabbalah that provided me with the insight to accept Islam with enthusiastic wholeheartedness?"

The Mullah had heard it was the threat of torture and death that provided the needed insight. Nevertheless, whatever his reasons for converting, Aziz Mehmed had brought many Jewish families into the Faith.

"Aziz Mehmed Effendi, you are a Muslim now. Why is the Kabbalah still important to you?"

Shabtai stood up, raised his arms, his face glowing. "Mullah Ali Hussein, the Kabbalah does not challenge Islam. It is the result of centuries of speculation by learned sages, rabbis and scholars to better comprehend the nature of God. To get closer to this understanding,

Kabbalists focus on the Creation. How did it come about? How is it that a perfect God created an imperfect world with evil men in it, pestilences, droughts, floods, upheavals of the land, and death. We are called mystics but Islam has them too in Dervish and Sufi adherents. It is the need to better understand God that draws people to Kabbalah and to me. But like all good Muslims, I believe that Allah is the one true God, great, all powerful, all knowing. Nothing in Kabbalah takes me away from this belief."

Shabtai paused, and resumed his seat on the pillows. "Mullah Ali, consider my situation. I am banished far from Smyrna, my city of birth and where my brothers live, far from the cities in which I have resided with my many friends. There is nothing here. Does the Empire begrudge me if I indulge in the study of the Kabbalah and enjoy the occasional letter or visit from family and friends? How can this be construed as a danger to the Empire?"

The Mullah frowned, stood, and paced the floor, his hands behind his back.

"Aziz Mehmed Effendi, the Grand Vizier clearly believes your activities can be harmful. You have many enemies among the Jews who continue to persuade him that you are dangerous. They would have you executed. You also have many friends, including at the Court. They have convinced the Grand Vizier that executing you would cause great unrest among the Jews. Right now, the Grand Vizier wants only to concentrate on and to prepare for the campaign into Poland. He does not want to be distracted by troublous factions among the Jews. Therefore, you must conduct yourself with great discretion and not allow those who spy on you to send damaging reports. I can protect you only so far."

Shabtai embraced Ali who looked uncomfortable as the taller man swept his arms around him and hugged him.

"Mullah Ali Hussein, I shall do as you say."

Even as the Mullah took his leave, he had the uneasy feeling that Shabtai's idea of discretion would not be adequate.

Shabtai did have a talk with Ishmael that night.

"Understand, my son, that the messiah cannot make himself known until the time is ripe. Until then, secrecy is imperative. You must reveal to no one that you are the next messiah, not even to Mullah Ali and definitely not to your classmates who laugh at you and blabber. Remember, you will only become the messiah should I leave this world prior to the Redemption. Even then, you must keep your mission secret until the Almighty informs you to declare yourself. In the meantime, tell everyone you wish to become a Mullah. Learn your lessons well not only at the madrassah but from me too. The messiah must be learned in the Torah, the Qur'an and the Kabbalah in order to come close to an understanding of the Almighty, and to attract the respect of men."

Ishmael looked dismayed. "But, father, if we are the messiah, why must we hide?"

Shabtai pulled the boy onto his lap and hugged him. "Because many do not believe us and will do us harm. Just as Mohammed had to flee from his oppressors, we too must stand apart from those who would hurt us. Until the Almighty deems the time is ripe for the Messiah, we must be still and pretend we are not. Many of my loyal and trusted followers claim they deny me but are ready to rise to my support at the Redemption. Therefore, if anyone asks you whether you are the next messiah, you must laugh and answer, 'Of course not.'"

Ishmael promised to do as his father cautioned.

Shortly after, Shabtai slipped into his depressive state, sequestered himself in the writing room, and filled the house with moaning and wailing. The demons badgered and harassed him. Lillith appeared, the silken diaphanous shawl slowly slipping down her body leaving her naked. Each time this happened and lust threatened to overtake him, he sought out Amilah who was all too ready to satisfy him. Even when he returned to normalcy or in his state of illumination, she frequented his bed.

"What will become of me once your new wife arrives?" Amilah asked one night.

"You will remain in my household," he told her grandly. "You are needed here. Our mission must continue and must not be hindered by children and the issues of the home. Together, you and Esther, will grant us the peace we require."

"Shall I not become your second wife then?" She suggested pleadingly.

"Amilah, we cannot have a second wife. Although Esther will become Muslim, as a condition of her betrothal, her father insists she be the only wife."

Even in the darkness of the bedroom, he sensed her disappointment. "However, do not despair. We have affection for you and from time to time we will offer you our body."

A seed of anger and resentment planted itself deep within Amilah and, as time passed, grew into a tumour. She was to remain a house slave after all, denied even the status of wife to this strange, erratic man, himself an exile, banished by the Sultan. Her role would be to assist his wife to manage the house, to care for him and his children, and occasionally to provide a convenient outlet for his erotic fancies. Her dream of breaking the bond of slavery through marriage collapsed and joined her long dead other dream of someday returning to her native Iran. Somehow she must find a way.

Esther arrived in early February, 1675, accompanied by Shabtai's brother Elijah. Shabtai was closeted in his writing room. It was several days before normalcy restored itself and he could meet his bride.

A widow in her mid-thirties, Esther was tall, almost Shabtai's height, and gangling with long arms and legs. She had a plain but pleasant face and a direct warm manner. The children, after a bout of shyness, took to her and eagerly showed her around the house, the garden, and the hut at the back. Perceptively, she recognized Amilah's sullen but civil reserve, embraced her, treated her with respect and soon felt some of the coldness easing.

Esther's presence precipitated Shabtai into a long period of normalcy, occasionally enlivened by a state of illumination. She knew these were moments when the Almighty turned His face to the Messiah and whispered revelations that only Shabtai could hear. And so, like Sarah before her, she not only tolerated but condoned his extreme behaviour, even when she saw Amilah disappearing into the writing room. Esther's accepting, relaxed and pleasing personality permeated the household and lifted the gloom that had descended on the family after Sarah's death.

Despite his stated desire to concentrate on his work, Shabtai became more involved with the children. Under Esther's direction, and with the boys helping, he chopped and collected firewood for the fireplaces and the ever demanding oven. The smell of baking loaves of bread and roasts of chicken, meat and vegetables filled the house. Esther and Amilah were both excellent cooks and the Mullah was always eager to receive an invitation to join Shabtai at the midday meal.

In addition to the delectable food, the Mullah enjoyed the conversation with his urbane host. They debated interpretations of passages in the Qur'an or in the Jewish and Christian testaments. It was during these dinners that Shabtai slowly introduced his guest to the mysteries of the Kabbalah.

"Is it not sufficient," the Mullah asked at one of their first discussions of the Kabbalah, "to accept what our holy scriptures tell us —in the beginning Allah created all? Is Allah not powerful enough to create by a simple exercise of His will?"

Shabtai nodded, "Your statement is correct and is sufficient for the vast majority of believers. Kabbalah does not diverge from this view. Not at all, esteemed Mullah."

Shabtai ran his fingers through his beard and, although gazing at the Mullah, appeared to be looking well beyond the dining room in which they sat. The remnants of the meal were being cleared away by the two women.

"But the Kabbalist is curious. How did Allah actually create this world? What steps did He take to bring such a complexity into being? We do not profane the one true God by asking these questions. It is our intense and profound love of the Almighty that compels us to investigate and to better understand His process of Creation."

Shabtai stood up, hands held high, touching the ceiling. Esther and Amilah backed away and scuttled out of the room. Shabtai spoke at first slowly then more rapidly, excitedly, his words tumbling out, his eyes flashing with exultation.

"Consider, Mullah Ali Hussein. When Ibrahim Ahmed Pasha arrived, he decreed a new mosque to be built. Immediately, a dozen architects spent many days and nights drawing up plans which were finally approved by our new Governor. Then, hundreds of stone cutters and workers were dispatched to the quarries north of Gornja Klezna where they saw, chip, and hammer away. Dozens of baggage wagons with their burdens of stone clog the road from the quarries to Dulcigno. The kilns of scores of potters from Dornja Klezna, Gornja Klezna, Krule, Sas and as far away as Shkoder fill the sky with smoke as they fire the tiles that will clad and adorn the walls of the mosque. Masons, carpenters, joiners, glaziers, weavers, seamstresses, rug makers add their skills to the building of the mosque. All this enterprise, all these people are necessary to create — what? — one mosque in one city. Is it any wonder then that many of us gaze in awe at this world in which we live, its vast size, its ability to nourish us, a world which appears flat, yet is round with life on all its sides, attended by a sun and moon that give it light and warmth, and fixed in an ocean of stars that float around it. Is it sacrilege to so admire Allah that one wishes to come closer to understanding how He accomplished such a miracle?"

Shabtai paused, breathing heavily, his face still alight with the ecstasy of worship. Despite his suspicions regarding his host, the Mullah was swept away by Shabtai's evocation of the deity and his obvious devotion to the one true God. How could this be heretical? He had always accepted that Allah had created the world and never thought more about it. Aziz Mehmed was not questioning this, he was simply advocating a more profound study of Creation. What could be the harm in learning his Kabbalah? At any time, if he felt Aziz Mehmed questioned traditional Islamic tenets, he could simply withdraw from contact with him and concentrate solely on Ishmael.

There was also a practical reason to stay in touch with Aziz Mehmed and his ideas. If he was corrupting the boy with his Kabbalah teachings, the Mullah would be in a position of knowledge and could take action to forestall the father's influence.

The Mullah met frequently with Shabtai as the latter taught him the basics of Kabbalah and imbued him with the spirit of the mystical process. On some occasions, Shabtai was in a depressed state and refused to see anyone. Amilah or Esther would announce that Aziz Mehmed Effendi was struggling with his demons.

On one visit, the Mullah entered the reception room and found a stranger, a travel bag beside him, sipping a bowl of tea. The man wore a white turban and was dressed in a flowing black robe, edged in fur, that completely engulfed him. He was disturbed by the Mullah's entrance for he jumped up, slopping tea onto the rug.

They bowed in greeting. The Mullah introduced himself but the stranger merely nodded. There was a long interval of tense silence. The Mullah was convinced the man was not Muslim despite the turban.

Esther came into the room followed by Amilah carrying a tray with more tea and a plate of a delicious smelling stew of lamb, onion and carrots. Esther greeted the Mullah and then said to the stranger: "Reb Primo, Amilah will show you to the guest house where you may wait in comfort for my husband."

Primo thanked her, nodded to Mullah Ali, and followed Amilah.

"Esteemed Mullah, as you can hear, my husband is still not ready. If you wish, I will see that you are called as soon as the situation allows."

The wailing in the writing room had increased in intensity, punctuated by screams, cries of anguish, and drumming on the floor and walls.

"Your visitor is a stranger to our city," the Mullah said, trying to sound mildly interested but nonchalant.

"You are right, esteemed Mullah," Esther readily agreed. "Reb Samuel Primo is a close friend of my husband and is well known in Kabbalah circles. It is important for his well-being that my husband has such contacts from time to time and the Governor allows this."

Yes, thought the Mullah with cynical bitterness, the Qadi and the Governor are generous with their permissions when their money wallets are stuffed.

"Is there not a danger that the authorities may come to view these contacts between your husband and his friends as troublesome?" It was more a warning than a question.

Esther chuckled. "Esteemed Mullah, neither my husband nor his friends has the power or the desire to pose any threat to the authorities. These are scholarly meetings for study and prayer."

At that moment, the wailing stopped, followed by silence. Then the writing room door opened and Shabtai emerged, clad only in his knee length shirt, hatless, greying hair surrounding his head like the corona of the sun, a wide smile on his face, his eyes ablaze with visions only he could see.

"Esteemed Mullah Ali Hussein, the anointed of Israel welcomes you. Allah has once again turned his face to us and banished the demons that have plagued us. We must strive together, our brother in Islam. We must rid the world of the evil that lurks even in our Dulcigno."

The Mullah had risen and Shabtai hugged and kissed him. The unwashed scent of Shabtai's body and the sour smell of his breath caused the Mullah to turn away and to relinquish the hug quickly. Besides, he was disturbed by his messianic allusions and wondered how he could explain them to the Qadi.

Esther quickly intervened. "Husband, you are not dressed properly to greet visitors. You must repair to the bath immediately. Your great friend, Reb Primo, awaits you as well as Mullah Ali."

"Samuel is here? We sent him a message awhile ago to Sofia to come. Why has he taken so long?"

Esther took Shabtai gently by an arm and tried to move him into the interior of the house but he did not move.

"Husband, he became ill in Skopje and only now has had the strength to obey your wish."

Shabtai turned to the Mullah. "You see, Mullah Ali, these demons not only afflict us but harass those who would visit us. But, our dear wife, it is you who are not proper. In the presence of the Mullah, you are not veiled and your shawl seeks to leave your head. Your unmasked charm threatens to entangle his senses."

The Mullah couldn't help smiling and quickly lowered his head and covered his mouth. Esther's face was large and square with wide mouth, large nose and narrow brown eyes. While he felt favourably inclined toward her, his senses remained unentangled.

"Forgive me, Mullah Ali, but I will not be veiled in my own house. Besides, you are not a stranger here but more like a member of the family. Even our Ishmael calls you his uncle Ali."

"I take no offence, madam," the Mullah said. "I am gratified that you consider me a member of the family."

It was not the first time Esther had appeared unveiled. Her pleasant but homely face and obviously angular body had no erotic impact on him. However, Amilah unveiled caused him a certain excitement. Shorter than Esther, she had an agreeable olive skinned face, almond shaped brown eyes, a thin upturned nose and pert mouth. She often wore a housekeeping apron instead of a mantle which while still full suggested a slimmer, rounder body than Esther's.

Esther managed to pull Shabtai into the interior of the house. Ali was about to leave when Amilah entered bringing him tea and sweetmeats.

He noted her face was covered. "You veil in my presence but not in the presence of the stranger. Why is that?"

"The stranger is a Jew. My mistress says we need not veil for Jews," Amilah replied, her tone sullen.

"The stranger wears a turban," the Mullah persisted.

"But he is a Jew nevertheless. And so are other strangers who visit. There is one they wait for now who seems very important. I am to watch out for him and greet him as though he were the Grand Vizier."

The Mullah sipped his tea and munched on one of the candied fruits. He was intrigued. "Why is it that I never see the visitors in Dulcigno? Primo is the first that I encounter here."

Amilah shrugged. "They arrive, they never leave the house until they depart."

"What do they here?" The Mullah was now more than just interested.

Amilah shook her head. "I do not know. They jabber away in their Jew's language. When I bring them refreshments, either in the writing room or in the guest lodging at the back of the garden, they may be looking through books or talking quietly. Sometimes my master is speaking and the visitor is writing on a scroll. Once when I came into the room with tea, my master was whispering into the visitor's ear. The visitor's eyes were shut tightly and his mouth wide open like a man when he is about to..." She broke off, slapped her hand against her veiled mouth, and turned as though to flee the room.

"Wait, Amilah, do not go yet."

"I speak too much," she said, her back to the Mullah.

"Are you happy here?" he asked.

"I am a slave. How can I be happy?" she said, turning to face him.

"After I returned to Dulcigno and until Aziz Mehmed's new wife came, you seemed quite content. I often heard you humming or singing and you seemed to enjoy the children. Ishmael often spoke well of you. What has changed? It cannot be the new wife — she seems an easy mistress."

Amilah nodded, resignedly. "Yes, she is a friend in that sense. We never have disputes and we work together agreeably. She is also very kind to the children although they are not her own and the children like and obey her. I have anger but not for her."

"For your master then?" the Mullah suggested.

Amilah looked at him appealingly. Would this man betray her and divulge her confidences? His face remained concerned and sympathetic.

"I hoped he would make me his second wife. I would no longer be a slave although, as his wife, I could never leave Dulcigno unless he died or the Sultan pardoned him. Yet, as a wife, I could go to the market with my head held high and mingle with the other wives. Nothing else would change but I would have a higher state. Instead of Amilah the slave servant I would be called Madam Aziz Mehmed. But he refuses to grant me this simple wish and claims it is his father-in-law's condition that his daughter be my master's only wife."

"I see," said Mullah Ali, although in fact he was surprised, even confused. He knew that the Sultan's mother and mothers of previous Sultans at the Court had exerted great power and influence. He was aware that mothers of the princes not selected to be Sultan actively pressed forward their sons' claims even to the point of engaging in plots and conspiracies. However, it had never occurred to him that women in the lower classes had ambitions to move up in their constrained society circle. The change in status that Amilah sought — to rise from slave servant to the second wife of a man banished for life to an outpost of the Empire — seemed too imperceptibly small for him to comprehend.

He understood without thinking about it that he, as a man, had sought preferment at the Court. If he performed his duties successfully, he could envision himself rising in real status and responsibility at the Court. However, a woman was meant to serve her husband, raise the children, see to the household needs, and grace his bed. This last thought caused him to consider Amilah in a new light.

"Are you innocent?" he asked.

Amilah laughed contemptuously. "I am a slave. I was captured six years ago at the age of twelve by your Ottoman Empire soldiers. I have had several masters since then. Need I say more."

The Mullah was silent, troubled by the grimness of the girl's plight. The Empire had every right to invade and conquer infidel states, particularly where it felt threatened. Sometimes the invading Ottoman soldiers saw rapine and plunder as the just rewards of war and victory. But Amilah was a Muslim and should not have suffered such atrocities at the hands of other Muslims. His sympathy merged with pity and elevated his feelings for her to a warmth he hadn't experienced since Sarah.

"I am sorry that you suffer so," he said. "Shall I talk to Aziz Mehmed to see whether the situation can be remedied?"

She shook her head vigorously, "No, it will not help and he will no longer trust me for talking to you and they will turn against me. I thank you for listening to a mere slave, but I expect no escape. I will live out my life as a slave and serve this master and perhaps other masters until my time comes. I pray to Allah every day that when I leave this world, He will allow me into the Garden of Paradise."

"Yet I hear anger and scorn in your voice. You are not happy in this household and with Aziz Mehmed. The Sultan and his officers are also not happy with Aziz Mehmed. They are suspicious of him. They fear even from this edge of the Empire he can cause unrest among the Jewish communities. It would help if I knew more about his visitors, who they are, where are they from, how often do they come and go, and is scholarly study all they are interested in. I can then assess how much of a threat his activities are to the Empire and so report to my superiors."

Amilah laughed, "Mullah Ali Hussein, are you asking me to betray my master for the sake of the Empire. Why should I?"

The Mullah rose and stepped closer. Amilah moved back, ready to bolt out the door.

"Do not be afraid. I mean you no harm. I want to help you. If you cooperate, I will petition the Governor to ease your situation, even to free you."

Amilah was scornful, "Am I to believe the Governor will agree?"

He reached out and grasped her hand and held it as she tried to pull free. "He will agree because I will marry you. You will be my first wife."

She stared at him in astonishment, "How can I...?"

He interrupted her, "Because I make the promise as a Mullah."

In the very far distance where only the mind's eye can travel, Amilah saw the leaded clouds that blanketed her life part and a beam of sunlight poke through. Marriage to this man meant not only an end to slavery but also a chance to leave Dulcigno should he move elsewhere. In addition, he was a handsome man, slim, a thin face with strong brows and a sparse beard. It was easy to imagine rapturous moments in bed with him. No doubt he would have more than one wife, but as his first, she would enjoy a dominant position.

"Will my master be hurt if I help you?"

It was the Mullah's turn to be amazed. He was offering Amilah a way out, and in her eyes he saw ready acceptance, yet she expressed concern regarding Aziz Mehmed. The man seemed to attract loyalty, however undeserved.

He took both her hands now and she made no attempt to pull away.

"Amilah, the Sultan and his officials worry that Aziz Mehmed continues to proclaim himself the messiah. This causes division among the Jews since he still has many followers. As a result, unrest and fractious violence has erupted in many of the places where Jews live. The Empire wants peace within its borders so as not to distract from its efforts outside. If I know what Aziz Mehmed is up to, I can stop him before he goes too far. If all he does with his visitors is engage in study and prayer, then I can report that the meetings are harmless and my superiors will leave him alone. More than that, I cannot promise. I hear your mistress calling you. I must go. Remember our discussion."

In the guest lodging, Primo waited patiently for Shabtai to appear. He washed the meal down with copious cups of wine. The food was excellent and instilled in him peaceful thoughts and contentment that counteracted the long days of travel across the rugged Balkans from Adrianople to Dulcigno. He removed his boots and mantle, replaced his turban with a linen head cloth, stretched out on the bed, cupped his hands over his full belly and allowed himself to doze.

He awoke and leapt to his feet as the door was flung open. Resplendent in white from mantle to caftan to pantaloons, his arms wide, Shabtai strode into the room.

"Reb Primo, the anointed of Israel and Judah welcomes you."

The two men embraced. Primo was lifted off the floor then fell back on his bare feet as Shabtai released him. Primo's tears flowed freely as he contemplated his master.

"Anointed one, Messiah of Israel," Primo gasped, his voice breaking, "I, who am unworthy to be in your presence, thank the Almighty that I may once again feast upon the rays of divine light that stream from your blessed eyes. In you I see the presence of the God of Israel and the promise of the Redemption soon to come. I beg to know when it will be."

Shabtai put an affectionate arm around him. "It will be soon, Reb Primo, but exactly when the Almighty has not yet revealed to us. We must continue in prayer and penitence, avoid despair and resignation, and exercise great patience. Consider the consequences that befell the Israelites who could not abide the absence on Sinai of our great leader Moses and turned to false gods. No, we must remain steadfast in our faith. How fares it with our Faithful?"

Shabtai sat down on one of the mounds of pillows while Primo quickly pulled on his boots and sat on the other.

"Blessed Messiah, Anointed of Israel, I have corresponded or met with many of the Faithful. The circle in Livorno in Italy is very strong. It meets daily in the home of Moses Pinheiro and is attended by Meir Rofe of Hebron whom you have met on a visit here, by Moses Harari, a young but brilliant scholar who has also visited here, by my teacher Judah Sharif, as well as several others and by the occasional traveller. Their prayers and piety and the privacy of their meetings do not excite the community and, therefore, the rabbinate do not interfere. However, they must keep their faith secret and even pretend, when asked, that you are a false messiah. The same is true of Modena, Kastoria, Sofia, Adrianople, Constantinople and Smyrna. All the Faithful must keep secret their knowledge that the messiah is among us or else they are excommunicated and often forced to leave their homes. All wait in expectation of the great moment when Redemption is at hand."

Shabtai nodded. "Yes, we are aware. Letters brought to us inform us of the travail of the Faithful. Have you word of our father-in-law? We have received no letters from him."

Primo was hesitant for a moment. "The tidings are not felicitous, blessed Messiah. Rabbi Josef Filosoff is no longer a rabbi. He was deposed and his salary stopped as soon as the rabbinate learned of Esther's betrothal to you. He lives in straitened circumstances but the Faithful of Salonika secretly provide for him."

There was a knock at the door. "Sir," Amilah called through the closed door, "my mistress informs you that she welcomes in the reception room the visitor you await."

Shabtai opened the door. "Amilah, bring him to us."

Amilah returned moments later followed by a slim man of average height, sumptuously dressed in a full length dark blue mantle, a white caftan garnished with pearl buttons that formed a line from under his chin to his waist, and white pantaloons stuffed into soft leather boots. His head was covered by a large blue shawl that fell loosely to his shoulders. His face was clean shaven except for a moustache that separated his thin lips from a prominent ridge of a nose. His eyes under dense eyebrows looked solemnly out at the world. Amilah guessed from his clothing and bearing that he was a man of substance and serious purpose. Yet, there was a grimness behind his fine appearance that made her apprehensive.

Primo rose and bowed. Shabtai held out his arms, "We bless the Almighty for allowing us once again to gaze upon our brother, Nathan, the Prophet of Gaza."

Nathan bowed and fell into Shabtai's embrace. "Anointed of Israel, it is I who bless the Almighty for guiding me safely to your presence. And Reb Samuel, I greet you as well. I hoped all through the journey we would be here at the same time."

As Shabtai made to close the door, Amilah asked, "Sir, will your guest require food and drink?"

Nathan turned to her and said in Turkish, "I require nothing. The divine aura surrounding the Anointed of Israel has filled my famished soul and slaked its thirst."

Primo felt a pang of guilt and surreptitiously touched his stomach but then remembered he had eaten and drunk before Shabtai had appeared.

Shabtai sat on the bed, his two visitors on the plumped up stuffed cushions before him.

"Revered Prophet, we are discussing the state of those who believe in us, the Messiah of Israel and Judah. From letters sent to us and from the tidings that Reb Samuel brings, it is clear the Faithful suffer and must keep their loyalty to us secret. Our Prophet of Gaza, is this your understanding?"

Nathan stared fixedly at Shabtai as though trying to absorb the godliness that he felt emanating from him. "Blessed Messiah, it is as you say. Those of the believers who speak out or follow not the traditional ritual are vilified by the rabbinate and ill-treated by the community. Therefore, as you have commanded, most keep their faith and their practices secret and pretend to deny you. Even in Morocco, in Meknes, where my father was exalted in the community and lies buried there these two years, the forces against you are dominant and the Faithful cower in fear of discovery. All anxiously await a sign."

The three men fell silent, deep in thought. Finally, Primo spoke up, "Beloved Anointed One, who, hand in hand with the Almighty, will lead us through the agonies of the Redemption, I must express one anxiety that troubles me. If Redemption does not occur soon and if you do not appear among the faithful, they may dwindle in number and passion of belief."

Nathan nodded. "Beloved Messiah, Reb Samuel speaks wisely. In the cities where Jews live, the Faithful adjust to the persecution of the rabbinate by maintaining their prayers and meetings in secret. They are still loyal and vital in their devotion to you as the Messiah and in your teachings and interpretation of the Torah and the Kabbalah. However, in time, they may forget or lose direction if, in their view, there is no forward progress."

Despite his state of illumination, Shabtai briefly lost his smile and air of ebullience. He stood up and paced the room, his hands behind his back, his head bent down. His two visitors feared he was about to fall back into his demonic state.

"Reb Nathan and Reb Samuel, truly we say this to you. It pains us to sit here in safe but ignominious isolation while our followers suffer the evils and hate of ignorant minds. But the Almighty offers us no direction at this time, merely hints that the Redemption is close. We are the true Messiah but even we need a message from the Almighty. You are our two closest friends and advisors. What do you recommend?"

Nathan jumped to his feet excitedly. "Blessed Messiah, the message may not come to you directly but may come through your Prophet.

Did I not prophesy that you are the true Messiah long before you were anointed in Smyrna?"

Shabtai turned to him. "And have you a prophesy now?"

Nathan was virtually dancing, his face suffused with an ecstatic glow. "Blessed Messiah, on my way here from Berat, early on the third day, I had just passed Leshe. The road was empty of other travellers and the sun was still low in the sky. I tell you this so you will understand the enormity of the event that followed. At this point in the journey, the Adriatic comes into full view. I slowed my horse to a walk to observe the sight of the blue sea, now as still as glass, stretching away to Italy. A spell of dizziness beset me and I quickly dismounted and sat upon a boulder at the side of the road."

Nathan paused, barely breathing, his eyes unfocussed, oblivious to the two men gaping in wonder at him.

"Suddenly there was a flash of light, so brilliant as to momentarily blind me. When I could see again, I stood upon the boulder, the orb of the sun completely filled the sky, so close I could reach up and touch it, and the road was crowded with a multitude of divine beings, truly a heavenly host of angels. Terrified, I leapt off the boulder and threw myself prostrate upon the ground.

" 'Hear, O Israel, the Lord is our God, the Lord is One,' I shouted, prepared so I thought to join the host and leave this life. 'Nathan of Gaza,' a familiar voice called out. There before me you stood, Blessed Messiah, arrayed in a gold embroidered caftan, a gold helmet covering your head.

"Utterly confused, I shrank back in fear and huddled against the boulder. 'Blessed Messiah,' I cried, 'is it you? You are here? You are no longer in Dulcigno?'

" 'Fear not, Prophet of the Anointed One, it is the soul of the Messiah that stands before you. Our body continues to reside in Dulcigno. Know you this, it is time for our body to rejoin our soul. We must be at large to complete our task to capture all the Holy Sparks of the Divine Light and to restore them to the Godhead. Remember, we must be at large.'

"There followed a sustained crash of thunder and flashes of lightning and the vision disappeared. The sun was once again where it should be, the road was empty and my knees shook so uncontrollably that I had to hang on to my horse to stay upright. When I calmed sufficiently, I mounted and rode as hard as I could the rest of the way."

Shabtai beamed and lifted his arms heavenward. Primo hugged Nathan and kissed him on both cheeks.

Primo was not a visionary and considered himself a practical man, a man who could think clearly when faced with challenges and could ferret out solutions to the difficult problems confronting the progress of their messianic mission. Long before he had arrived at Dulcigno, he knew what had to be done and was determined to persuade Shabtai. Now Nathan had supplied the key. His vision on the road as a divine manifestation could not be doubted. Much of Nathan's prophesies came through visions and had formed the basis for the proclamation of Shabtai Zvi as the Messiah.

"Blessed Messiah," Primo said, "the message of the vision is clear. It is time to leave Dulcigno, to reappear among your followers, to refresh their loyalty before it decays, to assert your mission in the face of an obdurate rabbinate too blind to accept you as the Messiah despite all the portents discovered in the Kabbalah and the prophecies of Reb Nathan and too cowardly to stand up against the Ottoman authorities. We must immediately begin to devise a plan of escape."

At the mention of 'escape,' Shabtai's mood changed. The broad smile on his face faded, his exhilaration evaporated and he sat down heavily on the bed, clearly troubled.

"The vision experienced by Reb Nathan disconcerts us," he said sombrely to his guests. "We have felt for some time that our soul has left us and we have wrestled with the problem of reintegrating with it. We have devoted prayer and penitence to this enterprise but to no avail. The Governor of Dulcigno spies on us in order to find evidence to execute us. If we disappear from Dulcigno, we will be pursued and tracked down. The only solution we can envision is that at the moment of Redemption, our mission will become clear and even our enemies will fall in behind us."

"Beloved Messiah," Primo persisted, "the time of Redemption is entirely in the will and discretion of the Almighty. In spite of many predictions made by our most learned scholars, we cannot know when the Almighty will decide the time is nigh. My fear is if the Redemption is long in coming, there will be no Faithful left to follow you or Ishmael. The agonies of the Redemptive world will be aggravated if you are not recognized as the true Messiah. It is imperative to find you a way out of here."

"That is clearly the message of my vision," Nathan agreed. "But our beloved Messiah is right. How does he escape without bringing down on his head the wrath of the Turks?"

There was dead silence as the three men pondered the conundrum. It was obvious to Nathan and Primo that if Shabtai lived out his life in Dulcigno, he would slowly disappear from memory and become merely a scribal footnote on the scroll of Ottoman and Jewish history. Shabtai and Nathan cast their minds into the Torah and the Kabbalah seeking the answer the Almighty must have surely inserted into the sacred writings at the dawn of time. Primo pursued another course, deep in thought, his brow creased, a hand stroking his beard.

"If I may interrupt," Primo said finally, "I offer three actions that may help resolve our problem. All three should be carried out simultaneously for they all lead to our blessed Messiah keeping his sacred presence alive in our communities throughout the Empire and Europe."

"Speak then, Reb Samuel," Shabtai said. "We listen with care and expectation."

"The first action," Primo began, "is to increase your correspondence to all prominent believers in each community. Instruct them to copy and pass on your letters to others. Your letters should include observations on your mission, your Kabbalah teachings and interpretations, and instructions regarding prayer, penitence, and ritual. In this way, your thought will circulate throughout and demonstrate that you are alive and determined to lead your people at the time of Redemption."

"Excellent, an excellent suggestion," Shabtai exclaimed enthusiastically, but then after a moment's reflection said somewhat morosely, "However, apart from the Mullah who teaches Ishmael and the occasional visitor, it is difficult to find safe emissaries."

"That is where my second action comes in," Primo continued. "Blessed Messiah, invite more visitors. Many scholars are eager to be in your presence. Not only will they provide a willing source of messengers but the scholars themselves, imbued with your spirit, will spread the word."

"Excellent, excellent, our dear friend," Shabtai said, almost beside himself with delight. "These are two actions easily capable of carrying out and keeping our mission vital." Then his face clouded: "However, over time will these two actions be sufficient? Will not the Faithful despair that, in reality, we do not walk among them?"

"That is why the third action is necessary," Primo said.

Both men looked at him questioningly.

"We must appeal to the Sultan and the Grand Vizier for your release."

An incredulous Shabtai exploded: "Reb Samuel, these are the two that decreed our banishment. On what grounds would they agree to revoke it?"

"I, too, cannot understand your third action," Nathan said. "The Sultan and the Grand Vizier are our enemies."

Primo held up his hands as a gesture of peace. "Blessed Messiah, Nathan of Gaza, you are quite right to consider my last action likely to fail. For success, we must practice guile. Certainly we cannot plead that our blessed Messiah should be released from exile because he is the Messiah or because he wants to be among his followers to ensure their loyalty. Such an appeal will have the opposite effect."

"How then?" asked Shabtai and fell heavily back on the bed, completely deflated.

"The appeal to the Sultan and the Grand Vizier must be on the importance of family ties. Aziz Mehmed Effendi is reaching his fiftieth year. His father-in-law is much older, too ill to travel, and desires desperately to see his son-in-law, daughter and grandchildren before he dies. Further, Aziz Mehmed Effendi pleads to join his brothers in Smyrna or Adrianople as a family matter."

Shabtai's good spirits were restored. "Yes, yes, Reb Samuel, your counsel is excellent and will succeed. The Sultan is very devout — he will respond to an appeal based on reuniting our family. The Sultan has affection for us and will override any objections from the Grand Vizier. But, Reb Nathan, you seem perturbed."

Nathan nodded, frowning. "Perhaps Reb Samuel can explain how a letter or a representation may be delivered to the Sultan. Which messenger will be allowed?"

"It will be difficult," Primo agreed. "However, we have contacts at Court and the Messiah's brother Elijah has been received there. In addition, I believe generous testimonials of our sincerity will help open the iron gates of the Imperial Palace. Vani Effendi will respond on our behalf as he is convinced Aziz Mehmed Effendi will bring more converts to Islam. Without a doubt, the path to the Sultan must be strewn with petals and it may take some time to find the right blossoms."

Shabtai leapt off the bed. "Reb Samuel is right, Reb Nathan. There are many who will help us. Even Ishmael's Mullah is willing to protect us and is directly linked to Vani Effendi. Our plan is a good one, my dear friends and advisors. We embark upon all three actions immediately."

Shabtai's face was a portrait of ecstasy as he considered his mission was about to be re-launched. Nathan smiled happily, pleased that his vision on the road near Leshe would soon be realized. Shabtai looking heavenward, slowly raised his arms and danced, stamping his slippered feet rhythmically, and slowly turning. Then he strutted up and down the room singing at full throat his favourite song 'Meliselda.' The other two animated by his infectious ecstatic frenzy followed behind, joining in at the chorus, as loudly as they could and not always on key.

The sound drifted out across the garden and into the open windows of the house and brought Esther and Amilah to the guest hut. At first made anxious by the uproar, they quickly realized a celebration was in full swing and watched, laughing at the antics of the three.

Nathan was the first to drop exhausted onto the cushions. Shabtai and Primo continued but soon slowed and stopped, gasping for breath, sweat beading their foreheads.

In the silence that followed, Esther said, "Husband, why do you sing and carry on so? May I remind you, Nathan of Gaza has had nothing to eat or drink since he arrived."

Shabtai laughed heartily." Why do we sing? You must sing too. We celebrate our coming departure from Dulcigno. We will visit your father and our brothers. As for Reb Nathan, bring him food and bring us wine, much wine."

As the two women went to do Shabtai's bidding, Esther, shaking her head dubiously, explained to Amilah what her husband had said.

"Perhaps my husband has already had some wine. I cannot believe our departure is imminent or even possible."

Later that afternoon, Ishmael returned home and was led by Esther to meet the visitors. They found the three men asleep. Nathan lay sideways on the floor, his head propped against a pillow. One arm was stretched out holding a tipped goblet, the wine pooling beside it. The two jugs of wine, bowls of soup and chicken lay empty, scattered around him. Primo sat slumped in a corner, his head resting on his knees. Shabtai, stretched out on the bed, snored loudly, deep rumbles ending in a prolonged whistle.

Esther laughed uproariously and had to hold onto her bonnet. "The Almighty forgive them," she said between gasps. "Here lie the Messiah and his two apostles meditating on the coming Redemption. Come, Ishmael, let us leave them in peace. They must sleep off the wine."

"But father is a Muslim," Ishmael objected. "He would not drink wine. He is ill."

He stepped over Nathan and gently shook his father. Shabtai snorted and turned sharply on his side, sending a half-filled goblet of wine resting precariously on his chest flying across the bed, spilling its contents. Surprised, Ishmael stepped back, tripped over Nathan and was caught by Esther.

"A Messiah has his own rules," she explained to Ishmael, carrying him in her arms. "Do not mention this to Mullah Ali. He will think ill of your father."

But Mullah Ali's thoughts were far more complex than a simple concern for Aziz Mehmed's drunkenness when Amilah informed him the next day of the events in the hut. While he shunned the drinking of wine as contrary to Islam, he knew of many officials who imbibed regularly, including the Grand Vizier. What the three men were celebrating caused him great uneasiness and presented him with a difficult choice: should he act immediately, have the two visitors expelled from Dulcigno and Aziz Mehmed sanctioned; or should he watch and wait until there was clear evidence of a plot to escape. If he acted now, Aziz Mehmed would suspect either Ishmael or Amilah had provided him with information.

"You are certain Aziz Mehmed Effendi plans to leave Dulcigno?" he asked Amilah again.

She had brought him tea to the reception room when he arrived in the early morning to conduct Ishmael to the Madrassah. She had let her veil slip sufficiently so that most of her face was visible as she bent over to serve him. She enjoyed the admiring look in his eyes and recognized a tinge of lust as he contemplated her.

"Yes, it is what my mistress explained to me. My master wishes to visit his family, his brothers and particularly his father-in-law who is too old and too ill to travel. He will appeal to the Sultan and the Grand Vizier to be released from exile."

The Mullah shook his head. "It is a foolish idea. The Sultan is too wary to let him loose. Once he is among his people, he will cause dissension. There will be repercussions. I must dissuade Aziz Mehmed. You must trust me that I will do it in such a way that you will not be implicated."

"You have not forgotten your promise?" she asked.

In answer, he took her hand and kissed it.

Shabtai embarked vigorously on the first two actions. He wrote a letter to Filosoff informing him that he would soon have the pleasure of a visit from his son-in-law and his family. He wrote similar letters to his brothers. He sent invitations to his Faithful to join him in Dulcigno for Kabbalah studies and discussions and to learn the Mystery of the Godhead.

The Mullah was aware of the sudden increase in correspondence because he was often called upon to find travellers who could be trusted to deliver the letters.

"Aziz Mehmed Effendi," the Mullah asked one day, "you must tell me what is in these letters." Several weeks had passed, Primo and Nathan had departed, and the Mullah and Shabtai sat in the quiet hut.

"Esteemed Mullah, the muscles of my body are stimulated regularly because I must chop wood to keep my Esther happy. However, the strength of my mind diminishes rapidly because it lacks the exercise of debate and discovery. For that I need people, visitors, those with a scholarly bent. If enough come, and if Allah wills, Dulcigno could become a centre of Kabbalah to rival Safed in Galilee."

"But Aziz Mehmed Effendi, you are a Muslim now and the Kabbalah is for Jews."

" You wear a worry frown, Mullah Ali, but mistake me not. As I have said before, the study of Kabbalah is not heretical for Islam or Judaism. Therefore, you may reassure your superiors that I have no intention of advancing views that will cause unrest among Jewish communities. Furthermore, I may convince more Jews to join me in Islam. Of course, any expenses to Dulcigno as a result of my visitors will be well compensated as in the past."

The Mullah reported to the Qadi and the Governor that Aziz Mehmed's desire to have scholars visit him seemed innocent and might result in more conversions. He did not mention the exile's hope to establish an important Kabbalah centre nor his intention to leave Dulcigno. He would wait with this information until he had a chance to confirm its likelihood. If he revealed all now, Aziz Mehmed would be arrested, clapped in prison, and perhaps executed. All for what? Empty intentions that would go nowhere? If he saw the plans developing, he would have enough time to report.

Why did he care? he wondered. Was he so entranced by the memory of a face and cascading curls that he felt compelled to fulfill the promise he had made to Sarah? Yet there was something special about her. Although, on her deathbed, her beauty and charm had been completely vitiated, it was replaced by a dignity and calm acceptance of her imminent death that enhanced his image of her. He was entrapped in the coils of her memory, unable to wriggle free, a slave to a vision of femininity.

Despite this memory of Sarah, he became more and more enamoured of Amilah and looked forward to their brief moments of contact when he called upon Aziz Mehmed or came to help Ishmael with his studies. He perceived that Amilah welcomed his interest but he was uncertain whether she was responding to him as a man or to his promise of marriage.

"My master faces his demons," she said to him one day when he was let in to the reception room. He could hear the wailing and screams through the thick door of the writing room but he could also hear other voices from within the house. He turned to go but she scoffed: "Are you so eager to escape the one you promised to marry? Do you not want to hear about the visitors?"

He faced her angrily. "I have not forgotten my promise. There are others in the house and I do not wish to compromise you."

His anger dissipated rapidly when he saw the dark brown eyes glaring at him fiercely then softening as a smile spread across her face. He grasped her arm, pulled her to him and held her tightly. After awhile, she pushed him gently away.

"On our marriage night, you will have all you desire but not before. I will be a good wife. I cook well, I will keep your house clean and tidy, and I will mend and launder your clothing. You will not wear a soiled caftan and a torn mantle as you do now. If Allah allows, I will bear your children and happily be their mother. All I ask in return is that you treat me well and take me away from here."

Mullah Ali wanted to embrace her again but, chuckling, she held him off. "Let me tell you about the visitors. There are three and all arrived last night. They are in the dining room. My mistress is with them at the moment so we have a few minutes to talk. Two are from Livorno. One is called Rofe, another is a young man whose name is Harari. Both have been here before. The third man is from Morocco. My mistress says he is Abraham Cardozo, a very learned and famous scholar."

The Mullah regarded her with admiration. "What language do they converse in? How do you know their names?"

Amilah shrugged. "I guess they speak in the language of the Jews. They all wear turbans but they are Jews. It is my mistress who proudly tells me their names as their visit is a mark of esteem for my master. Yes, my mistress keeps me well informed."

She tilted her head provocatively. "Perhaps you offered to marry her too."

He smiled. "Can you tell me anything more?"

"I helped them unpack their travel bags. Apart from clothing, they also brought books. I cannot read but I guess the books are written in the script of the Jews for they resemble books my master has."

In the midst of calling to the Almighty for Divine rescue from the assaults of Samael and Lillith, Shabtai, exhausted, breathless, paused and fell to the floor. In the silence that ensued, disturbed only by his ragged breathing, he heard the muted sound of voices through the writing room door. He raised his head. Lillith had resumed her serpent form and lay curled up a short distance away. Samael was dozing in a corner. Shabtai listened carefully but all he could make out was the voices were those of a man and a woman.

"Go, blind one," he said to Samael. "Tell us who is there."

Samael yawned, drifted up off the floor and poked his head through the door.

"It is Meliselda," Samael said chuckling. "Your favourite."

Shabtai leapt to his feet. "Meliselda," he exclaimed. "Our Meliselda, the daughter of the King. To possess her is to possess the Shechina, To possess the Shechina is to restore her to the Holy Ancient One. Redemption is here. The Almighty has ended our captivity."

He flung open the door, ran down the short hallway, pushed a startled Mullah Ali out of the way, and threw himself upon Amilah knocking her shrieking to the floor. He tore wildly at her clothing, oblivious to the Mullah's presence.

"Desist, Sir, desist," the Mullah shouted. He grabbed Shabtai by the shoulders and dragged him off Amilah. Shabtai struggled loose, screamed, "You cannot stop us, Samael!" and hit Ali hard across his face, sending him backwards over a mound of bunched pillows to sprawl dazed on the floor. Amilah struggled to her feet and attempting to escape collided with Esther.

"What is happening here?" Esther asked, her voice calm and controlled, an arm around a weeping, trembling Amilah. "Husband, you are not dressed for company. Retire immediately to our bedchamber and prepare yourself appropriately." The three visitors stood in the doorway.

Shabtai did not move, staring uncomprehendingly around the reception room. Mullah Ali rose slowly to his feet, replaced his turban, and ruefully felt his cheek which was already swelling.

"I hope, Mullah Ali," Esther said, "that whatever happened here will stay here."

"Madam, I ignore the violence done to me. However, I cannot remain silent concerning the egregious attack on a servant of this household. I must be assured of Amilah's safety, and security from further such outrages."

"And why should this be in doubt?" Esther asked.

"Aziz Mehmed Effendi assaulted and attempted to rape her. If I had not been here he would have succeeded."

"Is this true, husband?"

Shabtai, still looking helplessly around, suddenly spied the three visitors. Smiling broadly, he held up his arms in greeting, "Our brethren, welcome and blessings from the Messiah of Israel and Judah. May the Almighty shine His countenance upon you."

The three men flowed around Esther and Amilah, nodded curtly to the Mullah, and embraced and kissed Shabtai. He led them down the hallway to the writing room and closed the door.

"I am sorry, Amilah," Esther said. "It disturbs me that you should be harmed. I will be more attentive on your behalf. You see, Mullah Ali, my husband has promised not to take a second wife. Neither do I want him to have a concubine and I have told him so. Sometimes men just do what they purpose to do. But, Mullah Ali," she said, regarding him suspiciously, " even your authorities would not pay much attention to the plight of a house slave. Why do you express concern? I would think that being hit by my husband would be ample reason to register a complaint."

The Mullah did not reply. Amilah realized he was debating whether to reveal his promise to her. The family had to agree to the marriage and the family had not been approached. Would a premature disclosure ruin the arrangement?

"Mullah Ali is of a noble mind, mistress," Amilah said. "I see this when I hear him discussing Ishmael's lessons with him. He teaches 'mercy' and 'love' and 'generosity of spirit' in dealing with others, particularly family and those close to the family. It does not surprise me that he ignores his own hurt and worries about mine."

"It is true, Amilah," Esther said, "I have noticed that Ishmael behaves more lovingly to me now than when we first met. Mullah Ali, I thank you for your wise guidance of him."

"Mistress," Amilah continued, "as long as you will support me should I need to repulse any further assaults by the master, I will feel quite safe and Mullah Ali need have no fears."

Esther hugged Amilah. "Have confidence in me. We two women will stand together."

Mullah Ali walked back through the city gate to his quarters behind the madrassah. A smile lit his normally serious face, agreeably surprising the people he encountered on his route. I am a lucky man, he thought. Not only is my betrothed pretty and competent in the home, she is clever as well.

Amilah continued to report the activities of the three visitors and their host.

"My mistress says her husband is in his state of illumination where he is in direct communion with Allah. His visitors are clearly in awe of him for they follow his every move and listen carefully to his every word. I see this when I bring food and refreshments to the guest hut. Sometimes they argue loudly, each pointing to something in a book, all talking at the same time. Then the master holds up his arms. They are immediately silent and the master says something. Their eyes and mouths open wide, they drop to their knees before him, and nod so strongly that I fear their heads will fall off."

The Mullah chuckled, "You describe typical scholarly behaviour, Amilah. When we Mullahs and Imams get together, we argue the same way. But you did say he was in communion with Allah."

"It is what my mistress said. She used the words 'the God of Israel' but I am sure she meant Allah."

The Mullah was not so sure. Could this be evidence of heresy or simply the ravings of a madman. Should he denounce Aziz Mehmed to the Governor of Dulcigno, and to his superiors in Adrianople? Yet what harm could Aziz Mehmed do if all he did was entertain scholars and remained confined to Dulcigno? Surely, what was required was evidence of a real plot that would cause dissension within Jewish communities or a plot to escape Dulcigno. If such evidence emerged he would act immediately.

In his meeting with the Qadi later on that day, the Mullah noted that Aziz Mehmed's encounters with his visitors seemed to be totally related to scholarly issues. "Aziz Mehmed begs that these visits be allowed to continue as they assist him to properly adjust to life in Dulcigno. He appears content to live out his days here. At times his behaviour is odd. He suffers from spells which he believes are caused by demons who plague him. At such times he hides in his writing room, wailing and screaming, fasting and praying. I have heard him so. When the spells end, he becomes excessively ebullient, singing and dancing. It is at these times that he makes statements that appear at odds with what we believe. In between, he is quite normal, refreshing, affable, eloquent, and pleasant to be with. I believe the mind of this man is sick but he is harmless confined to Dulcigno."

"You seem to know a great deal about what goes on in that household," the Qadi said, quizzically. "How so?"

"I am there often to make sure Ishmael is learning his lessons. I speak with Aziz Mehmed occasionally and sometimes I am invited to the mid-day meal. Ishmael very proudly tells me who the visitors are and where they come from because they are people of note. I also have an informant in the household."

The Qadi raised his eyebrows. "It cannot be his wife. It must be the slave girl."

The Mullah nodded. "It is. Amilah recounts as much as she witnesses and understands. Her mistress tells her quite a lot."

"Be careful," the Qadi cautioned. "Can you trust the information? Why does she inform against her master. Do you pay her?"

The Mullah felt his cheeks reddening. "I have promised to marry her — if she cooperates."

The Qadi snickered, "To fulfill your duty, you will wed a slave girl? You are either very conscientious or mad, perhaps both. Well, so be it. When the time comes, your union will be authorized. We will not ask Aziz Mehmed Effendi for his permission. Meanwhile, continue to keep him under close supervision."

In his lucid moments, Shabtai recognized that Mullah Ali had become a more frequent visitor to his home. He noticed, too, a growing familiarity between Amilah and the Mullah. She would greet the Mullah, often without an obeisance or unveiled. He had no illusions about the role of the Mullah but felt that favourable contacts between the Mullah and the members of the household could subvert or lessen his loyalty to his superiors. As Sarah's influence waned, perhaps another woman could take her place.

Mullah Ali had expressed curiosity about the Kabbalah. Shabtai undertook to give him formal teaching sessions. Twice each week they met for several hours, either in the writing room or the guest hut. The Mullah's motive was to engage more often with Aziz Mehmed in an unsuspicious manner but he soon found himself more deeply involved in the study of Kabbalah than he cared to admit to the Qadi. Shabtai described the speculations of the sages as they pondered the nature of the Creation and the existence of evil, through the hundreds of years leading to the Zohar, the first written compendium of Kabbalistic thought.

"There are many interpretations of Kabbalah and many disputes among scholars still to this day," he said to Mullah Ali after many weeks of teaching. "Most are inscribed in books and letters. I have come to understand the true nature of the Godhead and teach it to my many visitors. However, only if you swear to keep my revelations secret, can I relate them to you. I ask the same of all my scholars and disciples."

The Mullah was reluctant to take the oath and asked for time to consider. He felt instinctively that the Mystery of the Godhead would be considered heretical and he would be forced to break his oath. He returned a few days later to regretfully inform Shabtai he could not accept the revelation. He heard the screams and wails from the writing room and breathed a sigh of relief. It was a week before Shabtai returned to normalcy and by then, more visitors had arrived and Shabtai was occupied with them.

"One of the visitors is Samuel Primo," Amilah informed him after they had briefly embraced. "There is something happening. Esther is very excited and told me that a letter is being prepared for delivery to my master's brother in Adrianople who would give it into the hands of a special person. 'Perhaps,' Esther said to me, "I may see my father before he dies.'"

It was clear to the Mullah what was taking place. The letter would be given to an influential contact at the Court who would then try to get a release for Aziz Mehmed from exile. Was it not time to act? Why did he hesitate? Torture would reveal the Mystery of the Godhead, Aziz Mehmed would be declared an apostate and executed. He had to admit that he had grown fond of Aziz Mehmed. Despite the man's frequent bouts with madness, Mullah Ali respected his knowledge and learning and enjoyed the teaching sessions with him. As he delved into the study of Kabbalah, he found it deeply stimulating, accompanied by feelings of ecstasy. Could he allow this to undermine his better judgement?

"The letter must not leave Dulcigno," he said.

"It will be in your hands," Amilah said. "According to my mistress, Primo was stopped and searched as he entered Dulcigno. He will likely be stopped when he leaves. My master will ask you to find a traveller."

Two days later, when the Mullah made his regular visit, he was greeted by Esther and brought into the writing room. Primo and Shabtai both bowed. On the writing table was a package, carefully wrapped in parchment, tied with hemp string, and sealed.

"We need this letter delivered and call upon you once again to find a traveller who can be relied upon." Anticipating the Mullah's question, Shabtai continued, "Reb Primo would carry the letter but he travels to Italy and the letter is destined for my brother who resides in Adrianople."

"What is in the letter?" Mullah Ali asked. "I must explain this to any traveller who agrees to take it."

"It is nothing you or any traveller need be concerned about. It relates to my brother that we are all well — praise be to Allah — that the children grow, that my wife is an excellent mother, and that a visit from him would be most gratifying."

Mullah Ali waited a few days until a ship left Dulcigno for Constantinople. He then informed Shabtai that the letter was on board and the traveller would ensure its safe arrival in Adrianople.

It was that night the Qadi confronted him.

Chapter 12

- Dulcigno -1676 - Death of Shabtai Zvi

"Esteemed Qadi," the Mullah said at last, breaking the protracted silence, a slight quaver in his voice, "I realize I have made a mistake. I put too much trust in what Aziz Mehmed told me about the letters and the visitors. I deemed he could not excite his followers to any great extent locked away here in Dulcigno. I believed, too, in time, even his most ardent followers would see that he was simply mad and turn away from him. But there is one mistake I did not make."

He paused and the Qadi stopped pacing and returned to his bench.

"Really? And what is that?" he asked sceptically.

"For some time, I feared Aziz Mehmed would use his contacts at Court to appeal for release from exile. I have the proof now. A letter was given to me to arrange for delivery to Adrianople. Aziz Mehmed believes the letter is on board the ship that sailed for Constantinople today. The letter is in my possession. I have not opened it yet but I know its contents. It asks someone at Court, possibly Vani Effendi or the Sultan's mother, to intercede on Aziz Mehmed's behalf to allow him to visit his father-in-law in Salonika and his family in Smyrna. He appeals on grounds of family love. I was about to reveal this letter to you."

"Bring it to me," the Qadi ordered, disbelief showing in the pugnacious thrusting forward of his chin.

The Mullah raced breathlessly to his quarters behind the madrassah and quickly retrieved the package. The Qadi unwrapped it. The address in Turkish was to Joseph or Elijah in Adrianople.

"They are his brothers," the Mullah explained.

The first letter was in Hebrew. They both guessed it gave instructions to the brothers. The second letter in Turkish left a space for a name to be inscribed.

"You are right," the Qadi said after reading it out loud. He fell silent, deep in thought, his brow puckered with lines of concern.

"You have done right, Mullah Ali, by withholding and revealing the letter. It is one thing for the rabbis to be upset by Aziz Mehmed. But if the Grand Vizier becomes irritated by an appeal that he does not expect or wish to consider, it will rebound on us. We will be accused of lax supervision and suffer for it. Your action has saved us."

The Mullah expelled a sigh of relief. "Shall I confront him?"

The Qadi shook his head. "No, the man can simply not be trusted. He must die."

The Mullah was not surprised. "He will be arrested and executed?"

"No. Such an action will make the rabbis happy but cause uproar among his followers. This is not a time for riots. He must sicken and die as though naturally."

"Poison?"

"Poison."

Dread tightened the muscles of the Mullah's neck and shoulders and reached down into the knot that constricted his stomach. He knew that poison was often used and frequently suspected in cases of sudden unexplained death.

"Esteemed Qadi, Aziz Mehmed has a sick mind but a strong and vigorous body. Should he die suddenly, no one will believe it was natural. There will still be unrest among his followers."

The Qadi chuckled, a dry rasping sound, almost a cackle. "He will not die suddenly. He will become ill, suffer for a period, then expire."

The Qadi lowered his voice so that the Mullah had to lean forward to hear him. "There is a poisonous plant called Belladonna in the Italian language that comes to us from just across the water. All parts of the plant are lethal but the berries if taken in very small doses cause no immediate symptoms. However, if consumed over a period of time, the poison accumulates and the victim eventually dies. The berries can be crushed and dried into a powder. We will introduce into the diet of Aziz Mehmed the powder of three berries each day until death seems near. Then we will stop and let natural processes take over. He will become nauseous, lethargic, and suffer great gastric pains and upheavals as the poison takes effect. Soon thereafter, we will be rid of him."

The knot in Mullah Ali's stomach tightened as he contemplated the protracted suffering of Aziz Mehmed leading to his death. No doubt, Aziz Mehmed was a difficult husband and father, yet there was love and respect for each other among the members of the household. The family would suffer, if not the pangs of poison, certainly the pain that comes with grief and the finality of death. The Mullah was not concerned about Esther's and the children's well being. Aziz Mehmed's brothers were rich and would look after them. Despite the man's erratic behaviour and frustrating adherence to his messianic convictions, Mullah Ali had come to admire and respect him and felt some attachment to him. He was impressed with his knowledge and understanding of the Jewish scripture and Kabbalah as well as his increasing command of the Qur'an. They had spent many enjoyable hours together in discourse and debate on intricate points of religion. For a brief moment, he considered warning Aziz Mehmed and pleading with him to abandon his disruptive activities. But he knew full well that Aziz Mehmed would pretend to agree and clandestinely carry on. The Qadi was right. There was only one solution.

"How will you administer the poison?" the Mullah asked.

The Qadi smirked. "How will I? How will you?"

Shocked, the Mullah sprang to his feet, knocking over the bench. "I? I do not murder. You have people who carry out these sorts of acts. I have been an accepted part of that household for two years. You cannot expect me to personally kill its head. He is a Muslim after all."

The Qadi was unperturbed. "Sit down and speak softly," he admonished the Mullah. "Even these thick walls may have ears."

He waited until the Mullah had picked up his bench and seated himself. "Now hear me. Do you truly believe that Aziz Mehmed is a Muslim without blemish of heresy?"

The Mullah lowered his eyes and shook his head.

"In killing him you kill an infidel, an apostate, a man who continues to cause unrest among the Sultan's Jewish subjects. He violates continually the terms and conditions of his exile. Therefore, it is your duty to carry out this order. Besides, let us be practical. Who has unchallenged access to the home besides you —" here the Qadi paused and squinted hard narrowed eyes at the Mullah — "and your betrothed?"

The Mullah looked up sharply. "Amilah is just an informant. She cannot be involved."

"How can she not be involved?" the Qadi asked. "Who feeds him every day? Who knows what foodstuffs only he eats? Who can direct the poison to him and him alone so we do not poison the entire family?"

"I cannot ask Amilah to participate," Mullah Ali asserted.

The Qadi shrugged. "You do not have to ask her. It is your mission to find a way to poison Aziz Mehmed so that his death seems natural to his followers. How you do it is up to you. I have merely suggested that your betrothed can help. However, understand one thing." The Qadi leaned over the table until his face was inches from the Mullah. "If you fail, I will have no recourse but to recommend that you and your betrothed be executed for treason."

A horrified Mullah grabbed the Qadi by his lapels. "How dare you? How dare you? You would harm an innocent girl to punish me? This cannot be. I will not respond to such threats. I will petition the Governor."

The door to the Qadi's study opened and a cloaked figure slipped into the room.

"The Qadi speaks for me," a male voice said and pulled the hood down to reveal the round bearded face of the Governor.

Both the Qadi and the Mullah bowed deeply.

"Mullah Ali, it is my judgement that Aziz Mehmed has become a threat to the peace and tranquillity of the Empire's Jewish subjects and therefore an unwarranted disturbance to the Empire. It is my decision that he be removed quietly and carefully. I had tentatively reached this decision based on the petitions received from the rabbis. However, given the letter you withheld from delivery, my decision is firm and imperative. I will not risk a loss in confidence of the Grand Vizier in my ability to govern Dulcigno. I cannot simply arrest Aziz Mehmed and throw him into the dungeon. His family has influence at the Court and there will be an outcry on his behalf. No, Aziz Mehmed Effendi must be eliminated.

"However, I will not be as harsh as our esteemed Qadi. Even if you fail, as long as I am convinced that you made a credible and sincere attempt to carry out your mission, you and your betrothed will be united and allowed to leave Dulcigno peacefully."

The Governor spoke calmly and evenly but it was clear he would brook no argument. The Mullah's anger dissipated and was replaced by an anxiety ridden acceptance of his role.

"I shall do as you say, esteemed Governor," he said bowing low. The Governor inclined his head and left.

Mullah Ali did not sleep well that night. It was not his conscience that kept him tossing and turning. It was not his decision to eliminate Aziz Mehmed. Besides, the administration of poison was a remote and non-interactive killing method. He adjusted his thinking to simply ignore the fact that it culminated in the death of its victim. What kept him awake was dread of Amilah's reaction when he revealed the plot and asked for her assistance. She might adamantly refuse or sound the alarm thus precipitating their own fates. But the Qadi was right. The poison had to be inculcated into the normal habits of the family to avoid suspicion and rumour and only Amilah was in a position to do this.

He called at the house in the morning. He could hear screaming and shouting as he approached the door. To his knock, the door opened slightly and Esther stuck her head out. "Come back later," she said and made to shut the door. He shoved a foot into the gap and winced as the heavy door slammed against his soft leather boot.

"Help me!" he heard Amilah call.

He shouldered open the door, forcing Esther back, and stepped into the reception room. Amilah lay sprawled on the floor, her pantaloons stripped off, her apron, shirt and caftan pulled up revealing a tantalizing view of leg and thigh.

"This is no time to call," Esther shrieked. "We will settle this."

"How dare you intrude, Sir?" blustered Shabtai, clad in his knee length shirt, head uncovered, feet bare.

Mullah Ali pushed past them, helped Amilah up, and stood in front of her.

"How dare you use this woman so?" he demanded of Shabtai. "Even for men, adultery is against our laws."

"Laws, Sir," Shabtai spat out contemptuously. "You speak of the laws of man. We are the Messiah of Israel. We answer only to the Almighty. A shard of Divine Light lurks in her body. It must be rescued and restored to the Godhead."

The Mullah realized Aziz Mehmed was in his state of illumination and while his person was there before him, his mind was somewhere else. It was useless to reason with him. He ignored him and turned to Amilah. A bruise grew on her cheek and a thin stream of blood coagulated below her nostrils. Anger gripped him so profoundly that for a moment he hesitated to move, fearing he would lash out. Had he been armed, he would have killed Aziz Mehmed then and there.

Controlling his rage, he faced the two. Esther was weeping and wringing her hands. Aziz Mehmed stood impassively, his head raised imperiously.

"This woman is hurt. Madam, you and I will take her to the nurse mid-wife to treat her injuries. As for you, Sir, your utterances are completely heretical and blasphemous and evidence of apostasy. One word from me to the Governor and you will be immediately arrested and publicly executed."

The threat penetrated even the thick psychic walls erected by the Messiah of Israel when the Lord smiled upon him. He remembered the misery of his trial before the Divan ten years before and the terror it had caused him. He seemed to deflate, hunched over, head lowered, eyes downcast. Esther took his arm, led him to the writing room, closed the door, and returned.

"Mullah Ali, I beg you," Esther pleaded. "Say nothing of this. I am sorry to see Amilah hurt. I will go with you to the nurse. I apologize for my husband. He was in a frenzied state and lost account of himself. We were able to stop him but not before he hit her. It will not happen again."

Amilah shook her head resignedly. "Mullah Ali, alas, this will happen again and again. It occurs during his melancholic state. He believes I am someone called Meliselda, the daughter of a king. There is no persuading him otherwise. He insists he must possess me. I resist and he hits me. He will kill me someday."

"He will not," Esther insisted. "I will not let him."

"Like you stopped him now," the Mullah said. "Come. Let us go."

On the walk to the castle where the nurse resided, a plan began to form in Mullah Ali's mind — a plan that would garner Amilah's fulsome cooperation.

He asked the two women to wait in the large entrance hall while he went in search of the nurse. He stopped first at the Qadi's office, pacing impatiently while the Qadi dispensed justice to several petitioners. When they were gone, he pushed into the office before other petitioners could be called and closed the door. The Qadi regarded him warily.

He explained his idea to the Qadi who swiftly agreed. From a hidden recess in the wall, the Qadi removed a small leather bag tied with a strip of hide.

"There is enough berry powder in this bag for several months if dispensed a spoonful at a time," the Qadi whispered. "There is no alchemist in Dulcigno — at least none we would confide in — therefore, the nurse has prepared this, knows what we are about, and can be trusted."

He sought out the nurse and told her of his plan.

"The plan is very clever and should work," she said.

The nurse insisted Esther return home as her ministrations would require much time and led Amilah to the treatment room. She examined the welts and bruises on Amilah's face and body, applied cold water compresses to reduce swelling and smeared on salves and ointments.

"These will soon restore your skin and body to its original smoothness and suppleness. The Mullah is very concerned about you," the nurse said smiling slyly. "Very concerned."

Amilah blushed and dressed quickly, veiling herself.

Mullah Ali joined them. Despite the nurse's assurances, the Mullah pulled aside Amilah's veil and examined her face. The bruise had turned purplish but the swelling had receded. He reattached the veil.

"Amilah, you are quite right," he said after staring thoughtfully into the almond eyes, worry and sympathy puckering his brow. "Aziz Mehmed will continue to have irrational moments and may harm you grievously, even more than today. No doubt, your mistress will do everything she can to stop him but she was not successful in this instance. To better control him, with the help of the nurse, I have devised a scheme whereby he will be generally quietened and less likely to have mad periods, or if he does, he will be gentler in his behaviour. We must introduce a medicine into his daily diet."

He took the leather bag from his inside mantle pocket and showed Amilah the grey-black powder it contained.

The nurse explained: "This medicine is a tincture of opium from the bulb of the poppy plant. In large doses, it is a sleeping potion but can also cause hallucinations. In small doses, it will make Aziz Mehmed Effendi more agreeable, particularly when in his state of illumination. He will become more sluggish, less prone to outbreaks of lust."

Amilah looked doubtful. "Am I to give it to him? Why would he accept it? Will the mistress not object?"

"They must not know," Mullah Ali said. "When you serve him his food or drink, you must surreptitiously add a spoonful of this powder. Is there something only he eats?"

Amilah thought for a moment. "Yes, there is — a special infusion which is sent to him from Smyrna. At one time, he shared it with others but now there remains only a meagre supply and he alone drinks it. I prepare it for him according to his instruction — three spoonfuls of the infusion are placed in a drinking bowl, boiling water is poured into the bowl, and the mixture steeps for many minutes. After he drinks the tea, he usually asks for the bowl to be refilled with boiling water. He repeats this until the tea is too weak. This way, he stretches out his stock until the next supply arrives."

"Then the special infusion is the way to go, although you may add the opium to other food if the opportunity presents itself. Remember, we are doing this in order to protect you."

Amilah stuffed the bag into her apron. "There is another way to protect me from him," she said.

Despite the presence of the nurse, he embraced her and held her tightly. "I have not forgotten. The Governor has agreed to our union. As soon as my orders arrive from Adrianople, we will be married and away. It will not be long, but we must still watch what happens in that household."

She sighed wistfully and pushed gently away. "I shall wait patiently and continue as your spy. Right now, there is only one visitor, a young man, a scholar. I know not his name. He and the master are all day in the writing room. The master sits or lolls on pillows while the scholar writes at the table everything the master says. I bring the steaming infusion for the master and wine for the scholar. If the master becomes upset by demons, he locks himself in the writing room and the scholar retires to the guest hut."

"Do you know what the scholar writes?"

"The mistress says the master dictates the full summary of his thoughts about scripture and Kabbalah and something called the Mystery of the Godhead."

"Did your mistress say anything about the Mystery?" he asked.

" 'It is not something for women to understand,' my mistress said."

The Mullah smiled for Amilah had mimicked perfectly Esther's deep voice and throaty speech. He knew the Mystery would be heresy but chided himself for not taking the oath and learning Aziz Mehmed's interpretation of the Godhead. There was much intelligence in the man accompanied by a profound intellectual curiosity and desire to explore the limitations bounding the Unknowable God. But what was the point. The Prophet, in direct communication with Allah had recorded all there was to know or possibly to know. And yet...

After Amilah had gone, he reported to the Qadi who pronounced himself pleased with the course of action the Mullah had put in place. "We must carefully observe him. The poison must do its work slowly to allay any suspicions."

After three weeks, Amilah reported that the medicine must be having an effect because her master was more benign to her even after a melancholic episode. He had made one attempt but she was easily able to fend him off. She had had to reduce the dose after the first application because the infusion had became weak after several boilings, and he had detected a strange taste. He ascribed it to not letting the tea steep long enough.

The weeks became months as the hot, hazy summer dragged on. From time to time, Amilah noted that her master had lost much of his appetite and occasionally complained of nausea and dyspeptic bowels.

Sometimes in the chamber pot she found traces of blood. True, he no longer harassed her, but he was easily irritated and occasionally twitched even at rest.

"Can it be the medicine is causing this?" she asked the Mullah.

"According to the nurse, it cannot be the medicine since it has a calming effect. For your safety you must continue it," the Mullah said reassuringly.

It was at the end of August that the Mullah became convinced that the poison was working. The nurse, summoned in the afternoon by Amilah to attend her master who was very ill, immediately sought out the Mullah to accompany them.

"The master stopped in mid-sentence, crawled to the chamber pot and vomited," the Scholar related. "He complains of severe belly pains."

The nurse offered Shabtai a vial of a yellowish liquid that she claimed would settle his stomach but he refused it. "I shall eat or drink nothing the remainder of this day nor on the morrow. That will starve my belly into submission," he declared. "Come, Reb Zalman, we must return to our enterprise."

"Blessed Messiah, should you not rest?" the scholar suggested solicitously.

"Reb Zalman, we will rest when the Almighty allows us to. In the meantime, we will proceed. We have examined and described the role of the Ein Sof in Creation and have addressed the emergence of the Holy Ancient One. Now we will turn our attention to the creation of the Creator, the God of Israel, that is, the Almighty, the Final Cause, the God we serve and answer to."

The others left but Esther waited awhile outside the slightly open door to the writing room and listened to the whispered dictation of her husband and the scratching of the quill as Reb Zalman captured his every word. Now and then, she heard Shabtai pause, utter tortured sighs or groans as spasms of pain shot through him, and then continue. She shook her head in the hopeless gesture of those who realize they cannot help or won't be allowed to and returned to her domestic duties.

Master and scholar continued throughout the day and late into the night. When Amilah brought in the morning infusion for her master and tea for the scholar, she found both asleep. The scholar sat slumped forward at the writing desk, his forehead almost in the inkstand, a hand still clutching the quill. Shabtai had rolled off the pillows and was lying on a side, an arm cradling his head.

The slight rustle of her apron and pantaloons as she turned to leave roused them both. Reb Zalman sat up straight, yawned, scratched the thick beard that clothed an otherwise sallow, pinched face, then remembering where he was, cast a guilty look about him. Shabtai opened an eye and slowly rolled over on his back. Amilah helped him to sit up. He refused the infusion. "Today I will fast as well," he said, still groggy, his voice hoarse. The scholar drank the tea thirstily.

"Reb Zalman, you must fortify yourself with nourishment," Shabtai ordered.

The scholar did not protest and followed Amilah to the kitchen where she prepared him a breakfast of eggs and flatbread. When he returned to the writing room, Shabtai was stretched out on pillows, fast asleep, his breathing shallow but rhythmic.

As he fell into the welcome oblivion of sleep, Shabtai felt his ear pulled and opened his eyes. Samael kneeled beside him, a grin suffusing his face so that even his blanked out eyes seemed to smile. He clicked his tongue sympathetically.

"Shabtai, why suffer so? End it. A time of pleasure awaits you — a time without pain, without illness, without the constraints of a body — a time of endless twining with Lillith and her many sisters and daughters. Come with us, join us, be one with us."

With the stroke of an arm, Shabtai flung Samael across the room and watched him disappear through the wall. Out of the corner of an eye, too late to stop it, he saw the serpent thrust toward him and felt her fangs clamp around his waist. Convulsed with hot searing pain, he screamed, contorted his body wildly, and threw the serpent off.

Esther and Amilah rushed into the room, pushed away the scholar who was vainly standing there panic stricken, grasped Shabtai by his flailing arms and gradually calmed him.

"The demons are here," he whispered. "The Serpent of Eden attacked us. There..." he said pointing to a corner, "there she lies, curled up. Do not go near. Bring more light. Candles. Many candles. Throw open the shutters."

The women leapt to his bidding while the scholar intoned prayers, his arms raised, beseeching the Almighty to rid the Messiah of the demons. The candles and the unshuttered window lit up the room.

Shabtai looked carefully around the room. "The evil ones are gone," he declared. "Reb Zalman, we must continue."

Once again, the scholar took up his quill, sharpened the point with a small blade, dipped it into the ink and scratched away as his master dictated the Mystery of the Godhead.

Later that day, Shabtai stopped dictating and stood up. Most of the candles had burned out but the few that remained and the open shutters still allowed much light. To the scholar, as he insisted ever afterwards, the face of his master glowed with a beatific light, signalling that the Almighty had turned His face to His Messiah.

"We are without pain," Shabtai announced and strode out of the room, beckoning the scholar to follow. Mullah Ali had just returned with Ishmael from the madrassah and was talking with Esther while Amilah stayed respectfully in the background.

"Our Lord, the God of Israel, has cured us of our ailments. His Messiah must offer his gratitude. Wife, bring the other two children and all wait for us here."

Shabtai returned quickly, clad in spotlessly white pantaloons, shirt, caftan, mantle and turban. "We will thank our Lord at His temple of worship."

In accordance with Shabtai's instructions, they formed a line of procession and set out from the house. Shabtai led, directly behind him came the scholar and Ishmael, then Esther dragging along a reluctant Abraham, then Amilah and the four year old daughter and finally the Mullah who walked beside the procession rather than be part of it. It was already darkening, the Mullah thought, maybe no one will notice.

Shabtai had no intention of going unnoticed. From his inside mantle pocket, he pulled out a shofar and blew loudly on it. The guards on the wall overlooking the gate jumped to attention and readied arms, believing an attack was imminent. They saw a small line of men, women and children and the Mullah waving his arms and calling out a message of reassurance. The guards relaxed but one of them left his post and musket at the ready followed behind the Mullah.

The procession meandered through the narrow city streets until it reached the square in front of the mosque. The mansions of the Turkish authorities and other elites of Dulcigno lined the square. Shabtai announced his arrival with further long blasts and trills on the shofar. The Mullah could see curious onlookers standing at the windows and on the rooftop patios. The Mullah pressed back into the shadows at the bottom of the square. A tug on his sleeve and a whispered greeting told him the Qadi was there too.

Shabtai faced the mosque, blew once more on the shofar, a long rising note that arched high at the climax. He tucked the instrument back in his mantle pocket. He held his arms up, and in Hebrew sang three times the traditional call to Jewry: "Hear, O Israel, the Lord is our King, the Lord is One."

His arms still upraised, his head held high, he walked slowly and deliberately to the minaret and climbed to the gallery where the muezzin summoned worshippers to prayer. Again he blew a long trilling blast and then a prolonged note.

"In praise of the Lord, and grateful for our release from the bondage of pain, we sing of Meliselda, the daughter of the king," Shabtai announced.

His strong baritone voice easily carried the melody to the square below and to the curious in the houses adjoining the square. When he finished the song, he proclaimed in Turkish so all would understand, "We were ill and we recovered. We give thanks and express our gratitude to..." he paused and despite the messianic enthralled mists of his brain suddenly realized where he was "...to Allah the Great, the omniscient, the omnipotent, the One and only One, blessed be His name."

He blew one last long note and then clambered down from his perch. The procession left the square and returned quietly to the house.

"He has desecrated our mosque," the Qadi snarled, fisting his hands in anger and frustration. "We must throw him into the dungeon."

"It would not be politic, esteemed Qadi," the Mullah whispered. "Leave him be. He will soon die. If he dies in prison, it will be rumoured that we executed him."

The soldier with the musket had stood beside the Qadi and Mullah Ali during the incident and now turned to them for orders as Shabtai passed by.

"Shall I shoot him?" the soldier asked, as the Qadi walked off muttering to himself.

"No," the Mullah replied. "He is quiet now. You may return to your duties."

For several more days, Shabtai experienced some discomfort but little or no pain. He fasted for long periods and only occasionally drank his special infusion. He still dictated to Reb Zalman but now he paced up and down the writing room, an arm held up grandly, his eyes raised to the ceiling. Reb Zalman in later years swore that light beams emanated from the Messiah's eyes, that an aura of divine light clothed him, and that Reb Zalman's quill seemed to race across the parchment. Shabtai's state of illumination and positive mood uplifted the entire household. He hugged and kissed the children, played games with them, cut firewood for the coming winter, and pronounced himself confident that the document he dictated would soon be complete.

His mood was further enhanced when two visitors arrived from Sofia near the end of the first week in September. Joseph Karillo and Isaac Haber were strong supporters of Shabtai and critical to his messianic movement. Both men, learned in Judaic scripture and interpretation as well as the Kabbalah, had earlier converted to Islam at Shabtai's urging. He had expressly invited them as part of his campaign to bolster his presence among his followers.

Karillo was heavy set, shorter and a few years younger than Shabtai. His puffy face was awash in tears as he greeted Shabtai. Haber, a much younger man, slim of build, a thin face encircled by a thick black beard, was equally emotional as he hugged and kissed Shabtai. Both men were startled by Shabtai's appearance. His face was pale and somewhat emaciated. His tall form was slightly stooped and his clothes hung loosely on his once brawny body. Yet his voice betrayed nothing of the pain that still coursed through him as he sang a hymn praising God for the safe deliverance of his two friends. They listened intently as though mesmerized as Shabtai spelled out the Mystery of the Godhead, the necessity to retrieve the shards of Divine Light, the Holy Sparks that litter the world of substance, the exigent need to restore the Shechina to the God of Israel so as to make Him whole once again and start the process of

Redemption. Exalted, they clung to him, begging for his pearls of mystic lore, and beseeching him to come once more amongst them.

They welcomed and blessed the Jewish New Year and not even the scholar remembered that the other three were apostate Jews and Muslim converts. Esther and the children joined in the festive dinner, while Amilah served and was allowed to sit with the children.

"Blessed Messiah," Karillo said, standing up and raising his flagon of wine high, "may this New Year bring with it the sign we all await and pray for that the Lord directs our Messiah to lead us to the Redemption."

All shouted 'amen' in unison and Shabtai danced, twisting and turning around the family and guests, and sang 'Meliselda,' not boisterously but longingly, his voice soft and seductive. Amilah had little idea what the Jewish New Year signified but recognized the word 'Meliselda' and uneasily looked for an escape route. In his dance, Shabtai came close to her and put a hand on her head but at a wagging finger from Esther moved quickly away.

His good spirits continued all the next day. He recited the prayers joyously and led the men in procession throughout the house in rapturous delight as the sunlit September day waned into darkness. Again, Esther had prepared a feast of roasted chickens, succulent greens and puddings of fruit in which the men indulged, toasting each other and their 'Beloved Messiah' with drinking bowls of wine. It was only during the 'Grace After Meals' conducted by Reb Zalman that Shabtai's internal pains returned.

He went pale, cried out and slumped over on his mound of pillows. Karillo and Haber helped him up, and led by Esther, assisted him into his bed. They stood about the bed praying for his quick recovery.

"No wonder he becomes ill," Esther wailed. "First, he fasts for days, then eats huge amounts of food. Just let him rest."

He was restless throughout the night but then fell into a deep sleep at dawn and slept throughout the day. In the late afternoon, he rose, pronounced himself better and went to the guest hut to join his friends. They were overjoyed to see him and once more the sound of laughter and song and prayer drifted across the garden and into the house.

The guests spent two more days with their master but noted that Shabtai's ebullient manner had changed and he had become despondent and anxious. On the morning of their departure, Shabtai took them for a short walk to the beach. His pains had abated but he was weak and had to lean on Haber.

The day was warm despite the advancing autumn, the sea a glassy blue reflecting the cloudless sky, ripples of water lapped softly and sedately the pebbles of sand bordering the beach. The only sound was the crunch of the men's boots.

"Blessed Messiah," Karillo exclaimed, "is not a day like this a sign by the Almighty that our Messiah will soon be triumphant?"

Shabtai shook his head gloomily. "We feel no such direction, my friends. The day is indeed sublime and evidence of the masterly work of the God of Israel. However, we are not yet absolved of our difficulties. Nay, we say unto you. Return to your homes. Tell every man to return to his home and there take shelter. The evil times are yet to come."

He paused to catch his breath. "How long will you hold fast to me?"

His two friends looked at him, affected by the solemnity of his tone.

"Master, how can you ask..." Haber started to say but Shabtai held up a hand.

"How long will you hold fast to me?" he repeated. "Perhaps until you can see the sand that lies beside the bottom of that boulder perched at the strand there. Observe. Now the boulder is half immersed, yet in six hours the tide will have left it high and dry and the sand beside it visible. Would that you would remain loyal at least that long."

Karillo and Haber protested vigorously, proclaimed their eternal loyalty but were shocked by Shabtai's mood of dejection and despair. They insisted they would prolong their stay.

Shabtai refused and bid them farewell. They walked back to the house where the two visitors collected their belongings and climbed onto the cart that would carry them back to Sofia. He watched them depart and was still standing by the roadside long after the cart had disappeared around a bend.

At Reb Zalman's urging, he returned to the writing room and their work continued. For several more days Shabtai persevered but his flow of thought and dictating was now laboured as he experienced recurring cycles of pain and nausea. He no longer walked about the room but sat or lay on the stuffed linen pillows, sometimes dozing off in mid-sentence.

"Beloved Messiah," Reb Zalman implored, "shall we not stop until you feel more at ease? Yom Kippur, the Day of Atonement, is here in two days time. Shall we not wait until afterwards?"

"No, our dear Reb Zalman. By the start of Yom Kippur, our work will be completed and the manuscript ready for dissemination. Thus has our God of Israel directed."

On the morning of Yom Kippur eve, Shabtai pronounced his treatise on the Mystery of the Godhead completed. He rose stiffly, hunched over slightly with abdominal pain, embraced and kissed Reb Zalman who wept shamelessly in joy. Shabtai staggered off to trumpet his triumph throughout the house, singing his prayers of gratitude to the God of Israel as loud as his weakened voice would allow. He found Esther and Amilah in the kitchen with the three children having breakfast. Much to the delight of the children and the anxious looks of the two women, he tried to dance but could only stumble about. He left the kitchen still singing and dancing.

They heard him move along the corridor to the reception room. Suddenly, his singing was interrupted by a loud sustained scream and cry of anguish. The two women ran to him where he lay thrashing his arms and legs about, clearly in terrible pain. "The nurse!" Esther shouted and Amilah leapt over Shabtai and ran out to collide with Mullah Ali who was just approaching the house.

"The Master is terribly ill. I must get the nurse," she said.

"I am faster than you. Go back," the Mullah said and ran quickly to the castle. He returned soon after with the nurse.

With Reb Zalman's help, the Mullah was able to control Shabtai's flailing limbs and carry him to his bed. Despite his still contorting body, the two men pulled off his mantle. Under the nurse's direction, they also removed his caftan which was stained with sputum and spots of blood. With Esther in attendance, the nurse pulled up his shirt to reveal his torso and pushed down his pantaloons slightly. Shabtai still twitched and groaned with pain but was relatively quiet. The nurse leaned her ear against his chest and then poked about his abdomen and found an area which elicited pain and caused Shabtai to cry out.

"It is a blockage of the gut," the nurse pronounced solemnly. "It will cause Aziz Mehmed Effendi much dolour but should slowly improve.

The body must cure the blockage. There are herbs which can help. I can make a tincture of these herbs."

"I want none of your tinctures," Shabtai said. "I will eat and drink nothing until I am better. I trust in Allah alone."

"Very well," the nurse said shrugging. "At least allow me or your wife to apply cold water compresses to your forehead to reduce the fever."

"I have no time for compresses. I must prepare for Yom Kippur which arrives at sunset."

The Mullah standing just outside the bedroom rolled his eyes. Yom Kippur was a Jewish fast day, not something Aziz Mehmed, supposedly a Muslim, should prepare for. When he left with the nurse, he cautioned her to say nothing about this conversation to anyone.

Shabtai tried to rise but needed the help of Reb Zalman and Esther to stand on his feet. He took some faltering steps and would have fallen but for the scholar. He was eased back into the bed and fell into a deep sleep. During the course of the day, he intermittently awoke, acknowledged Esther who was sitting beside the bed, and after a few moments, slept again.

Just before sunset, he roused himself from the bed, and, leaning on Esther, staggered to the reception room where he collapsed on a mound of pillows with barely enough strength to sit upright.

"It is time to begin the evening service," he said, his voice a high-pitched sibilant whisper. "Assemble all."

Esther stood beside him, Reb Zalman before him, Ishmael and Abraham a pace behind, while Amilah and the daughter peeked in from the hallway. Despite his weakened voice, Shabtai sang the prayer opening the solemn fast of the Jewish Day of Atonement. He cried out for dispensation from any and all vows he had entered into or would enter into with the Almighty, pleaded for His mercy and understanding and begged for His forgiveness. As is the custom he repeated this two more times. The utter grief he expressed, his sincerity and the poignancy of his plea brought everyone to tears, including Amilah who had not understood a word.

Shabtai continued with the service, reciting the prayers from memory and aided by Reb Zalman who read from the High Holidays special prayer book. About half way through, Shabtai floundered, out of breath, unable to continue. He listened while the scholar carried on reciting the service until its end. By this time, Shabtai could not hold up his head and slumped forward on his seat. Reb Zalman, Esther, and Abraham helped him to his bed.

Shabtai was restless throughout the night, frequently groaning and twisting as cycles of pain mounted within him and then subsided. Shortly after daybreak, his restlessness diminished and soon abated entirely as he lapsed into a state of profound oblivion. Esther, intermittently dozing and waking in the long night vigil beside his bed, watched the steady rise and fall of his chest which, although feeble, gave her reason for optimism.

Reb Zalman was not so certain and was terrified that his master was departing the material world. Robed in his prayer shawl, he concentrated on reading out the long Yom Kippur morning service, hoping his master would hear the prayers even in his sleep and that the Almighty would be drawn to the plight of His Messiah.

Despite thick layers of blackness that blanketed his consciousness, Shabtai was dimly aware of a mumble of sound. He was suffused with a pervasive sense of relief from the constant pain that had assailed him. He smiled to himself, relaxing in the effluvia of bliss that he now experienced.

"Smile not." The sardonic voice of Samael cut through. "Where is your God that He allows you to wallow in such dolorous condition?"

"Begone Samael," Shabtai said chuckling. "My deliverance from illness is assured. Even now the pain is gone."

"Is it gone?" Samael said, standing on the bed beside Shabtai. "Perhaps it is but the calm before the storm. Avoid the storm. With us in the demon world, limitless pleasure awaits you. Your Lillith barely controls her impatience."

"I want neither you nor Lillith nor your domain of evil and sin. If I must leave this life, I will beg the Almighty to allow me to join His circle."

Laughing, Samael leapt into the air, somersaulted and planted his feet on the ceiling, his head hanging down close to Shabtai. "Your Almighty will have none of you. You have failed Him. You forsook your faith. Your followers dwindle and hide. The people rise against you, they spit on you, the false messiah who first raised their hopes and then dashed them. Abide with us. We love, we favour, the fallen."

Shabtai vigorously shook his head. "I will not forsake my God for your empty banalities. I am not a false messiah. I am the Messiah of Israel and Judah."

Samael doubled up with laughter and fell off the ceiling, narrowly missing Shabtai who recoiled. Reb Zalman saw the sudden twitch, stopped praying and waited until he heard his master's rhythmic breathing before resuming his reciting of the Yom Kippur morning service.

"It is true," Samael said still laughing, mocking him. "You are not a false messiah. But neither are you the Messiah of Israel and Judah. No, you are nothing but the Messiah of Smyrna, for that is where the great Shabtai Zvi proclaimed himself messiah. Perhaps Smyrna will become the new Jerusalem. Perhaps your God will bring His Heaven there."

Samael rolled over and over in the space between the bed and the ceiling, laughing uproariously. "Lillith," he called, "come see the Messiah of Smyrna."

Shabtai reached up angrily and swatted Samael as he rolled past, knocking him into a corner of the room. A woman appeared in the open bedroom doorway, and unlike Lillith, was fully dressed in traditional clothing. In the split second he saw her, a blaze of light enveloped her blinding him. It is the Shechina, he thought, but he had to be sure. He staggered out of bed, dizzy, eagerly grasped the woman both to steady himself and to identify her. There was a shriek, a hand pushed him away, and he fell back on the bed, his feet splayed on the floor.

Esther had come running when Amilah screamed and shooed her away to the kitchen. Reb Zalman helped her put Shabtai properly into the bed. She picked up the coldwater herbal poultices that Amilah had dropped and applied them to Shabtai's forehead.

"He burns with fever," she said, disconsolately. Reb Zalman continued the service.

"Brazen demon," Shabtai admonished Samael. "You will not fool me again. You have no power over me. Your bewitching Lillith is like the drinking bowls that come from the East — beautifully crafted empty vessels."

Samael was not so easily dismissed. "Yet you fill those empty vessels with your drink and enjoy them nonetheless. Lillith's empty vessel yearns for the infusion of your seed. Behold all the empty vessels that await you."

The walls of the bedroom flew back leaving Shabtai in the centre of a large open hall. In the far distance he could just make out the fuzzy outline of Reb Zalman who seemed to be crying and tearing his mantle lapel. He heard Esther scream, disappear into the haze near the door and heard her shout, "Amilah, fetch the nurse." He sprang from the bed, his pain gone, vital with energy once again, the duress of his illness and the illness itself a fading memory.

"The Lord has healed me," he shouted to Samael who hovered in the air close by.

"Fool," laughed Samael. "It is I who have healed you. Drink the medicine only I can provide."

The scent of woman in desire assailed Shabtai's nostrils. All around him, dozens of young women danced in a circle, weaving their bodies provocatively as they passed. Most were naked, others dressed in alluring diaphanous gowns or shawls that hid little. Astounded, he felt his lust rise uncontrollably and he waded into the dancing lines, touching, holding, embracing. As Lillith swept by, he arched an arm around a thigh stopping her and buried his face in her breasts while she let her head fall back and moaned seductively. He dragged her to the bed and was about to mount her.

"Messiah!" a woman's voice hailed him from somewhere high above.

Irritated at the interruption, he looked up. The ceiling to the room was gone and a brilliant sun shone on him. "Pay no attention to her," Lillith urged. "She but interrupts our pleasure."

"Begone," screamed Samael. "He belongs to us now."

Although unable to see the woman because of the impenetrable light, Shabtai knew who she was. He looked down in shame, aware, if not for her intrusion, he had almost given way to the temptations posed by the demons.

"Shechina, forgive us," he shouted to her. "The Messiah of Israel and Judah rejects the demon world, its filth and sin. We yearn to possess you and only you."

Samael lunged at Shabtai, grabbed him around the chest, propelling him back onto the bed and into the arms of Lillith. "Fool. You are not the Messiah. You are not the Messiah of God. You are a fool. You are nothing — a false messiah, the messiah of Smyrna. Cleave to us." The dancing women picked up the refrain and sang over and over: "A false messiah, the messiah of Smyrna, cleave to us." Exerting all his strength, Shabtai freed his right arm and smashed Samael in the jaw sending him headlong to the floor. He wrench himself free of Lillith.

A change came over him. A huge white prayer shawl crept over his head and body. His filthy night shirt was replaced by an indigo caftan and pantaloons, and a splendid white mantle. He could feel his face was no longer emaciated, his straggly unkempt beard returned to its fullness, his whole body clean and fresh. He rose slowly into the air toward the bright sunlight while his prayer shawl bloomed out in a wide triangle covering Samael and the demon women and trapping them in its folds. As he rose closer to the excruciatingly bright light, he saw all around him hosts of angels floating in the air like feathery clouds in a blue sky, their voices raised in harmony as they sang hymns in praise of the one true God.

"Divine Shechina, where are you?" he called.

A blazing star appeared beside him and a slim hand bejewelled with diamonds reached out. He grasped the hand. Intense happiness, ecstatic euphoria engulfed him.

My work is complete, he thought, my life fulfilled. I return the Shechina to the God of Israel.

EPILOGUE

– Loose Threads

Dulcigno, 1676
— Mullah Ali and Amilah

Mullah Ali and Amilah were wed two weeks after the death of Shabtai Zvi. They were granted a private apartment in the castle until the Mullah's orders came from Adrianople. The consummation of their marriage went beyond their expectations and left them erotically besotted for several days.

The Mullah was ordered to move to Constantinople to take up a senior post in one of the city's celebrated mosques. Amilah was elated at the news. She would finally escape Dulcigno but more than that, she could display her new status in a larger and brighter arena.

They boarded a barque bound for Constantinople and stood side by side at the ship's gunwale as it moved away from its anchored station and headed out into the Adriatic. They watched as the walled city of Dulcigno slowly diminished until it was just a break in the coastal bluffs.

The Mullah saw tears in Amilah's eyes, put an arm around her and hugged her close.

"Dulcigno is a chapter in both our lives that we must now close, my sweet Amilah," he said. "It was an eventful time for us. Now, it is over except for the memories we shall preserve of the people we engaged with and came to love and hate. Thanks to Allah, blessed be He, we take away each other."

Amilah, speechless with emotion, could only nod. She pushed up her veil to wipe her eyes and breathed deeply the fresh salty air. They stood there a long time as the Albanian coast slid by. The oarsmen, aided by a mainsail to catch the light breeze, moved them leisurely along.

"There is something I must return to you," Amilah said. "It is the remainder of the tincture of opium I put into my master's infusion."

She pulled the leather bag from her mantle pocket. Curious, he opened it and examined the contents.

"It is yet half-full" he said, surprised.

Amilah looked at him, lines of concern puckering her brow. "I stopped giving it to him in late summer because it seemed to make him sick and he was too weak to hurt me." She paused. "Are you angry with me?"

The Mullah raised his eyes to the sky. Was there enough poison accumulated in Aziz Mehmed's body when she stopped, he wondered, or had Allah stepped in? He would never know and the guilt he continued to feel regarding Aziz Mehmed's death was eased somewhat. He threw the bag and its contents into the sea.

Smiling, he turned to her and tweaked her nose playfully through the veil. "I cannot be angry with you. But next time tell me when you decide to disobey me."

Toronto, 2007
— Donald and Roberta

"Well, Donald, things look good. We've been back together a month and haven't had one bad moment," Roberta said. "Hopefully, the honeymoon period will go on for a long time."

"That's my plan," Donald said. "I know you still worry I'll go after the first shapely body I see but that's all in the past."

"From what you told me about Sarai Stone, I don't think I need worry about shapely bodies," Roberta said, laughing.

It was close to midnight. They had celebrated their first month together with dinner and a movie and were sitting side by side in their living room enjoying a nightcap.

"One thing I don't understand," Roberta said, turning toward him and putting an arm around his neck, "your dedication to Shabtai Zvi. Your knowledge and understanding of Kabbalah goes well beyond his brand which is wildly controversial. In fact all the criticism you get comes from the orthodox community because of him. You would be much more popular if you treated him as just a side show."

Donald reached up and stroked her cheek. "Roberta, he wasn't just a side show. He was the most prominent Kabbalist of the 17th century. He had an enormous impact not only on the Jews but also on Christians and Moslems. Even today, there are groups, some secret, some open, who consider him the Messiah and try to follow his dictates. Why should I not feel the same pull, the same tug."

Roberta eased onto his lap. "Donald May, Shabtai Zvi was a madman. Today we would say he suffered from Bi-polar Syndrome. Not only that. You clean him up for your lectures but the man was also sex crazy. When he was high, he did things that would land him in jail today or in a prison mental hospital. I'm talking about sex orgies and relationships with underage girls. Surely you don't follow him because you want to do the same things."

Donald pulled her face close and kissed her. "For a while I think I did," he said. "Or at least I felt I had licence. Perhaps I got too close to Shabtai, revelling in the story of his life and his mysticism. I was hooked when I prepared for my lectures on religious studies and did a lot of research on Shabtai."

"Do you really believe he's the messiah or even a messiah?"

"How can anyone really know? It's easy to say he was false, deluded, manic depressive. But who knows whom God chooses? For a few years everyone believed —well, maybe not everyone. The Ottoman authorities saw him as just a problem. But then, the Roman authorities saw Jesus as just a problem. For a long time, followers of Jesus had to be secretive about their belief. Am I a follower of Shabtai? I don't really know. I find him compelling and for that reason I emphasize his teachings in my Kabbalah course. But one thing you can count on. I'm a loyal follower of you."

"Amen," said Rebecca."

Outside the Walls of Vienna, September, 1683 — Tepel and Sarah

After a two month siege of Vienna by the army of the Ottoman Empire, the combined forces of the Hapsburgs and Poles broke the siege in a massive attack down Mount Kahlenberg. The Ottoman army, caught between the attacking troops and the fortifications of the Viennese defenders, fought desperately for two days but was decimated and retreated in disarray.

The slopes of the hills descending to the walls of Vienna were strewn with the bodies of soldiers from the three armies. Twisted, torn, bloodied, friend and foe alike lay intertwined, clasping each other in the final frenzy of death. Now and then a groan or a cry could be heard from those not quite dead. It was two days after the battle and the stench of rotting bodies clogged the breeze blowing toward liberated Vienna.

From a breach in the wall, a unit of a dozen Austrian soldiers led by an officer appeared, followed by dray wagons pulled by horses. Ottoman dead were unceremoniously thrown onto the wagon to be hauled away to a massive gravesite further down the Danube; allied bodies were carefully placed in another wagon for blessing and internment. Now and then the crack of a musket was heard as a badly wounded Ottoman was dispatched.

As the first wagon of Ottoman dead trundled away, a soldier laughed and called out, "There goes a load of Turk meat to feed our worms." The others responded by singing their regimental song. "Shut up, all of you," the officer with them shouted. "Save your strength for getting this job done while we can still breathe."

The work proceeded quietly after that as wagon after wagon was filled and pulled away.

"Captain, here's one who wants to surrender," a soldier called.

The captain and some of the other men came to view the body. The blue uniform and red cloak and the turban with its peacock feather and pointed cap identified the dead man as a Janissary officer. He lay stretched out staring at the sky, a blotch of blood stained his white caftan where the shot had met its target, his right hand was stiffened and curled up, his fingers clutched a white lace handkerchief.

He hadn't been dead long, perhaps a few hours. His face slackened in death still had some colour, a pointy moustache maintained its jaunty pose, the lips appeared to be set in a smile. Overall a picture of calm, the dead officer must have known he was mortally wounded and calmly waited for his end.

Something about him and the tableau he presented erased momentarily the callous triumphalism of the men. They looked at the body with respect.

"I recognize this man," the captain said. "While others ran, he stayed behind to cover their retreat. He fought bravely and skilfully, repelling us several times until we were able to cut him down. That is not the white flag of surrender you see. This man does not surrender. I believe in his death throes, he brought forth a memento, probably a keepsake from someone he loves. Note — he holds a woman's handkerchief with a beautiful lace border. Place him carefully in the wagon for officers. I will see that he gets a proper military burial."

END

ACKNOWLEDGEMENTS

I am grateful to Rachael Preston (Sheridan College} and Richard Scrimger (Humber School Of Writers) for teaching me the essential basics of creative writing. Whatever craft I have, I owe to them.

This is my second book with Friesen Press. I found the help and support provided by the publisher was indispensable and a learning experience in itself.

Further Reading

Kabbalah, Gershom Scholem, Meridian, Penguin Books, 1978

Osman's Dream, The History of the Ottoman Empire, Caroline Finkel, Basic Books, 2007

Sabbatai Sevi, The Mystical Messiah, Gershom Scholem, Princeton University Press, 1975

CPSIA information can be obtained at www.ICGtesting.com
Printed in the USA
LVOW10*1606190815

450173LV00005BA/9/P